BEND,
DON'T BREAK

BEND, DON'T BREAK

JULIE L. BROWN

Bend, Don't Break © 2025 by Julie L. Brown

Printed in the United States of America.

For information, address JAB Press, P.O. Box 9462, Seattle, WA 98109.

Cover Design by Damonza
Library of Congress Control Number: 2024919939

ISBN 978-1-7354750-6-6 (paperback)
ISBN 978-1-7354750-7-3 (Kindle)
ISBN 978-1-7354750-8-0 (EPUB)
ISBN 979-8-9917654-2-8 (audiobook)

First Edition: February 2025

To the women in my life who would not break:

My grandmothers, Lillie and Helen

My mother, Julia

My wife, Audi

My daughter, Jasmine

Me, Julie

My Master had power and law on his side; I had a determined will. There is might in each.

-Harriet Jacobs

Sometimes I feel discriminated against, but it does not make me angry. It merely astonishes me. How can anyone deny themselves the pleasure of my company? It's beyond me.

-Zora Neale Hurston

I am no longer accepting the things I cannot change. I am changing the things I cannot accept.

-Angela Y. Davis

Freedom is never really won. You earn it and win it in every generation. That is what we have not taught young people, or older ones for that matter. You do not finally win a state of freedom that is protected forever. It doesn't work that way.

-Coretta Scott King

By Julie L. Brown

Bend, Don't Break

No One Will Save Us

By J. L. Brown

Books

The Divide

Rule of Law

Don't Speak

Short Story

Few Are Chosen

Aisha's Dynasty

(from a page in Dinah's Bible)

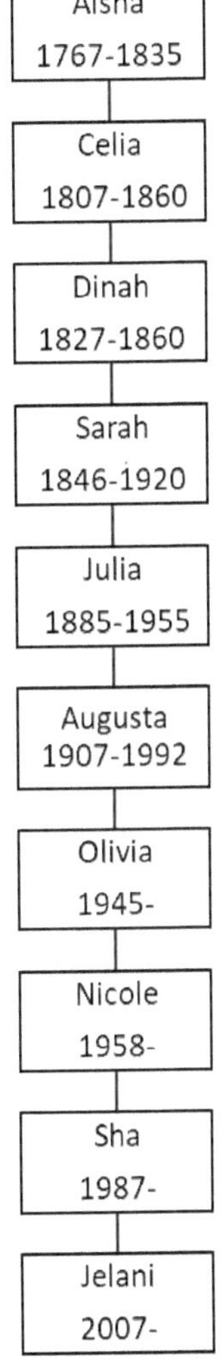

CHAPTER ONE

AISHA

FOUR-YEAR-OLD AMARE CLIMBED the four steps to the top of the wooden platform. Aisha wanted to race up the stairs after her youngest daughter, grab her and the rest of her children, and take them far from here.

Instead, she waited with the hundred other captives crowded behind the platform. Beside her, a woman coughed from the dust. The dry ground was hot beneath Aisha's bare feet. Aisha wrinkled her nose. Nearby, the stench of cattle and horses and manure emanated from a timber-framed building with two tall doors that swung outward. From above one door, a red, white, and blue flag with fifteen stars and fifteen stripes hung limply in its holder. Smaller buildings of plain wood sat a stone's throw away.

White puffs floated across the pastel-blue sky, guided by the wind. The blazing sun beat down on the captives, whose skin sheened with sweat. The heat was not unlike Aisha's homeland's, and was therefore the only comfort Aisha could find in this hostile place.

Aisha had been trying to understand what was happening ever since the big ship had left Africa. Why had her family been brought to this foreign village? From where she stood, she could see the sails of the ship that had brought them docked at the harbor.

Thirty men and women, their skin pale or darkened by the sun, gathered around the platform. A few sat astride their horses. The men were dressed in tight-fitted trousers that fastened at the ankles, linen shirts with high collars, and dark buttoned waistcoats. Some wore hats. The women were attired in white or pale cotton or linen dresses with low necklines, cinches just below the bust, and short puffy sleeves. Muslin shawls with floral patterns were draped over some of their shoulders. Others wore fitted jackets that fastened at the top of their necks, with long sleeves that covered most of their hands. An excessive amount of clothing for the weather. A few women held parasols or fans, offering relief from the heat.

Amare's dark skin shone from the wool grease the white men had rubbed on all the captives after they had doused them with water from buckets in the holding pen on the other side of the barn. The water could not completely wash away the foul smell—the urine, the excrement, the vomit— that had clung to the captives for two full moons.

Amare turned her round eyes up toward the stocky, pale-skinned man on the platform.

A fly buzzed close to Aisha's ear. Her wrist shackles prevented her from swatting it away. She shook her head to force the insect to move, but it didn't obey.

The man spoke quickly to his audience, his voice a visceral drumbeat. The pale men and women in the crowd raised their hands or nodded, which encouraged him to keep talking.

Finally, he yelled one word and pointed at the last man in the audience who moved and banged a mallet on a high pedestal table.

A skinny man with long, greasy hair and musty clothes jogged up the steps. He dug up several coins from his pocket and slapped them in the fast-talking man's hands. Skinny Man grabbed Aisha's daughter by the arm. The child propelled her arms and pumped her legs to liberate herself from him. Unchained, Amare was Aisha's fastest child, even with those thin legs that curved inward at the knees. She had liked to run around their village outside the Benin Empire on Africa's west coast, pretending to be chased by lions, her giggles floating all the way through their hut's open door.

Skinny Man said something to Amare, his tone an order.

Raising her pointy chin, Amare said, in Edo, "Release me!"

Skinny Man squeezed her arm. She yelped.

"Don't hurt her!" Aisha shouted in the same language.

Amare reached for her mother, but, with the shackles cutting into her ankles, Aisha couldn't reach back.

A different pale man stepped up to her, a coiled rope in his hand. He said something to her in their foreign language with a harsh tone. Aisha grabbed his shirt. "Tell him to take his hands off my daughter."

The man pushed her, and she fell back against the woman she used to see in the village market. Since the captives were all enchained together, they all tumbled to the ground. Aisha extricated herself from their arms and legs and stood while the other women helped each other up. The man raised the coiled rope and said something threatening to her.

Meanwhile, her daughter was still fighting the skinny man. "No! No! No! I won't go with you!"

The man lifted Amare by the waist, held her under his arm like a rolled rug, and descended the steps.

Aisha could barely breathe. "Where are you taking her?"

"Iye!" her daughter cried. *Mother.*

"Remember who you are!" Aisha said to her.

The man with the rope punched Aisha in the cheek. Aisha swayed but did not fall.

Cheek throbbing, her face trembled with anger. She stared at the man until his dark eyes flittered away and he returned to where he'd been standing.

From the barn, a horse neighed. Birds chirped in a nearby tree with limbs veering off in different directions.

Amare continued to call to Aisha as she struggled in the man's arms. The man walked away and didn't look back.

Aisha screamed. Her daughter was gone.

A piece of her soul left her body, hovered above her, then floated away. And then another piece, when a different pale man took another daughter soon thereafter. Then another daughter was taken. Aisha felt lightheaded and empty. She tottered, the strength of her legs deserting her. After her eight daughters were taken, despair tore through Aisha's chest. She was responsible for them: to watch them grow up, take husbands, have children, make things. Despite her grief, she felt pride in the children she and her husband, Oba, had made.

Someone roared.

Aisha started like everyone else. The sound came from Oba, who was standing with the men from their village. The man who had whacked her uncoiled the rope. He flicked it with his wrist as if he were casting a fishing line. It slithered through the air like a snake, its tip striking her husband's face. A wound opened on his jaw, and blood trickled onto his bare chest. Two pale men wrenched Oba from the rest of the group and hauled him onto the platform. They held him between them. His thick hair, which formed a point at the frontal hairline, stuck out, uncut since they had left their home. The nostrils of the wide nose Aisha loved flared. Aisha was still unaccustomed to seeing the buzz of hair on Oba's face. His gaze met hers, and she was infused with the same warmth she felt when he embraced her at night. She had never regretted marrying him, and he'd never blamed her for not having a son.

Aisha rubbed her belly.

The fast-talking man on the platform shouted the same word he'd shouted every time someone had been about to make off with one of her daughters.

"I love you!" her husband said.

"I will find you!" Aisha yelled. "Every lifetime!"

Rope Man stomped over to her and punched her again. The pain slammed into her. She cried out and dropped to the dirt. The woman next to her, who was still coughing, tried to come to her aid, but Rope Man whipped the rope toward her and she screamed as it tore through the flesh on her neck.

Aisha's arms shook as she pushed herself up. Her head throbbed. She couldn't breathe normally. A man lassoed her husband's naked torso and led him away, his muscular back her last glimpse of him.

Aisha had never been alone. She'd gone from living at her father's house to living with Oba. An overwhelming shame blanketed her. She had failed to protect her family, and now she'd lost every one of them.

Gods, what did I do to deserve this? *Where are you when I need you?*

A pale, wiry hand gripped her arm just below her small birthmark and led her to the bottom of the steps. Many of the pale people came up to her, their gazes—blue as the ocean or green as tree leaves—roaming over her body. Some held long pieces of paper with writing on them. When residents of her village looked at her, it was with respect. These people appraised her as if she were cattle. The men's gaze lingered on her face.

Her stomach churned in anguish, and she cried soundlessly, as they prodded her buttocks with a hand or a cane, squeezed her free arm, pried open her mouth, and poked her in the stomach.

Aisha prayed they wouldn't harm the baby.

When they finished their inspection, another man— tall, his skin tanned—came forward. He wore tan trousers, a brown knee-length coat with three buttons on each side pocket, a white shirt, and a three-buttoned vest. A silk cravat concealed his neck. The color of his boots matched that of his pants. He removed his winged black top hat and held it against his chest as he circled her. Smoke escaped from between his lips, his teeth clenching a strange-looking pipe. His breath smelled sweet, earthy. Like a forest. She stared straight ahead during his visual examination. When he finished, he stepped back and rejoined the crowd.

He had not touched her.

The man who was holding her pulled her toward the platform. She shook off his hand. With her chin uplifted, she contained her rage as she ascended to the platform unassisted.

As the man's staccato voice drummed on, Aisha thought about how she would search for her family.

The men before her raised their hands, touched their noses, and shouted. Soon, only two of them kept gesturing.

After the man on the platform said the word that meant Aisha would be leaving with someone, the tall man approached her. His short hair was black and curly. His eyes were jungle dark. Three months later, she would understand what he said next.

"Look at me, girl," he whispered. "Look. At. Me."

His voice insisted that she lower her gaze to his.

"My name is Solomon Devereaux, and you belong to me."

CHAPTER TWO

SHA

"DO YOU NEED help with your hair?" Sha shouted through the ceiling.

"I'm good, Mom!" came Jelani's response from the second-floor bathroom.

On the seventy-five inch, flat-panel TV mounted on the wall over the gas fireplace, the Warriors won the tip against the Lakers. Bathed in white and gray, the living room displayed an understated modern décor, reflecting the peaceful home that Sha desired.

The code Sha had reviewed today, created by one of her IT staff, crossed her mind. There was an error in the program, but she hadn't figured out how to resolve it yet. Why was she thinking of work? This was *her* time.

Ten minutes later, her seventeen-year-old daughter entered, holding her smartphone—another appendage. With her expressive eyes and straight, white teeth, Jelani's diamond-shaped face lit up whatever room she entered. Today, Jelani's light-brown hair was dyed auburn and straightened with a flat iron. Sha's hair was naturally curly brown. She sometimes forgot to brush it, unaware that the back was pillow-flattened until someone at the office pointed it out.

Sha paused the game with the remote control and eyed Jelani's short black dress. Sha didn't know the latest brand names and never bothered trying to keep up with teenage fashion trends. The low neckline revealed the swell of her daughter's breasts. "Guys like a mystery, you know," she said.

Jelani's hazel eyes narrowed. Sha wasn't sure where her daughter's eye color came from. Sha's father's eyes were dark brown, and Sha's eyes were light brown, like her mother's and grandmother's. Jelani's eyebrows were full, unlike Sha's thin, straight ones.

"If you had your way, I'd wear a hazmat suit everywhere."

"What's wrong with that? You'd still be the center of attention." Sha asked her next question as lightly as she could. "Where are you going?"

Jelani peeked at her phone, her ten beaded bracelets—each one different from the others—dancing on her thin arm. "To Z21. Downtown." She loved the three Cs—crowds, clubs, and concerts.

Sha masked her displeasure. And worry. "Don't be out too late. You're a junior now. You need to take school more seriously."

Jelani glanced at her phone again. "Why? I'm a B-plus student. Besides, there's no school tomorrow. It's a teacher workday."

"Shouldn't that be every day?"

Jelani pursed her lips. "Funny."

"Okay…You can stay out until midnight."

"Mom! We need time to drive home!"

"Twelve-fifteen. Final answer."

Jelani's cell phone jingled. She read the text. "Gotta go. Don't wait up."

She kissed Sha on the cheek, her hair caressing Sha's face.

"I won't," Sha lied. "Call if you need me."

Jelani flashed her the peace sign and shot her a winning smile before skipping out the front door. A car door slammed in the driveway, and her friend's vehicle backed up and roared away. Sha hoped the girl had not left skid marks on the road. This was a quiet, well-to-do neighborhood.

Sha didn't deny Jelani much. She wanted to give her daughter everything without raising a spoiled brat. It was difficult. Whether it was phones, clothes, or shoes, Jelani's interest in an item waned once a new or trendier version became available. Sha's phone was behind a few generations. Since there wasn't a significant difference between each version, she usually waited until her phone would no longer charge to upgrade. She disdained companies that forced their customers to repeatedly replace obsolete products. She preferred organizations that made products that lasted, like the classic HP calculators.

Sha felt uneasy whenever Jelani went out with her friends. Her daughter was a Black woman in America. That was enough to be concerned about.

A few minutes later, Sha padded to the adjacent dining room, where a two-thousand-piece jigsaw puzzle overlayed the white and gray marble table. She and Jelani rarely ate in this room—both preferring to eat on individual tables in front of the living room TV—so a puzzle was usually in progress. Sha enjoyed the nights when the two of them sat side-by-side working on it, Sade playing at a low volume on the speakers throughout the house, until Jelani went to bed. Sha surveyed the orphan pieces now and stayed until she fit three of them.

In the kitchen, she crossed the travertine floor and grabbed a Hefeweizen from the stainless-steel Viking refrigerator. Two bottles left. She grabbed a pen, added "beer" to the running grocery list she kept on the side of the fridge with a magnet, then returned to the living room and settled into her comfortable leather recliner. She placed the bottle next to the game controller. The Legend of Zelda series, which first came out a year before she was born, was her favorite game. She loved how it kept evolving and pushing the medium forward. Sometimes, she and Jelani played against each other from their separate bedrooms.

Sha loved this daily ritual. After being surrounded by people all day, it was nice to be alone. Just her and this humongous television. She'd laugh, cheer, yell, and cry in the privacy of her own home. She wished Jelani enjoyed watching sports so they could watch games together. But televised games bored her daughter. Jelani didn't mind attending men's sporting events, though she concentrated on the cute players with the nice bodies rather than on the game itself.

Sha resumed the basketball game and took a long pull of the cold, fruity craft beer. She sped through the commercials to catch up to live play. The shooting guard swished a three.

Fans in the stands lifted their arms and flashed their middle, ring, and pinky fingers as Sha made the same gesture in her living room. Sha finished her second beer and set the bottle beside the other one.

Although she was tired from a long day at the office, she would force herself to stay awake until she heard Jelani's key turn in the doorknob and saw her face. God had had the last laugh in giving her a daughter—payback for how Sha had tormented her own hardworking parents. She'd been a closeted rebel. They didn't know half the mischief she had gotten into as a teenager. Though she suspected her daughter drank, Jelani was a good kid and Sha trusted her. It was other kids that worried Sha.

It had been just the two of them for a long time. Sometimes Sha wished she could find someone to share her life with, but she'd learned from her mother's stories about the women in their family that the right person would come along at the right time.

Her ring tone awakened her. With her eyes half-closed, she reached out to the end table until she found her phone laying on top of it.

"Hello," she croaked.

No response.

"Hello," Sha repeated, sitting up.

Silence, then a sob. "Mom...come get me."

Sha's eyes flew open. She looked at the display. Normally, Jelani FaceTimed her, but this was a regular call. She couldn't see her daughter's face. "What's wrong, baby?"

"It hurts."

Sha's heart stopped. Her hand shook. "Where are you?"

CHAPTER THREE

OLIVIA

OLIVIA HADN'T COME to this party to meet anyone or to find love.

She should be back at her apartment at the square kitchen table she used for a desk, piled high with textbooks and binders, preparing for tomorrow morning's eight o'clock class, American Constitutional Law II. A member of the first integrated class at LaSalle College, Olivia was determined to graduate in three years.

Instead of studying, however, she was leaning against a yellow-painted concrete wall in a dorm room in St. Basil Hall, watching students dance. Two narrow beds were pushed onto their sides against one wall. All these dorm parties were the same. Olivia's friend, Sandra, had begged her to come because she didn't want to give James, the guy she was interested in, the impression that she was desperate. Olivia had needed a break from her studies, so she'd agreed to go along.

She'd thrown on a gray knit turtleneck with aqua stripes to complement her black tapered pants. Mrs. Parks, the old lady who lived on the first floor of her building, was looking after Nicole.

As soon as they'd arrived, Sandra had spotted James dancing and entered the fray. Olivia hadn't talked to her in the hour since.

The Capitols' "Cool Jerk" blasted out of the small plastic speakers connected to the turntable. The song was meaningless; its title was repeated a hundred times. Other students in the room disagreed with Olivia. Their arms flailed as if they were attached to puppet strings, and their gigantic afros swayed to the music. Part of Olivia wished she were dancing with them, but she wasn't a great dancer and wouldn't want to make a fool of herself. Others stood against the wall or sat on the two small desks talking, laughing, and drinking Pabst Blue Ribbon, while watching the dancers. Still other students dawdled in the hallway. The room reeked of cologne, perfume, and hairspray. For the umpteenth time, Olivia wondered why she was there and not in her apartment. Her homework awaited her.

"I need to leave," she said.

She didn't realize she'd uttered it aloud until the guy next to her looked at her shyly with soft, dark-brown eyes.

"Excuse me?" he said.

"I should be studying."

"What's your name?"

"Olivia. What's yours?"

"Davis." He sipped his Coca Cola. "What're you studying?"

"Pre-law."

"You want to be a lawyer?"

"Sure do. And don't tell me that women can't be lawyers."

"I wasn't going to. I think it's amazing."

She peered more closely at Davis to see whether he was joking. He was the same height as her, with dark skin and a flat nose. His afro was neatly trimmed.

"You do?" she asked.

"Sure. Women are intelligent and great debaters. Trust me, I know. I grew up in a house full of them. I lost every argument. What kind of lawyer will you be?"

Olivia hadn't decided on her specialization. "A great one."

Davis grinned. "I don't doubt that."

"What's your major?"

"Accounting."

Boring, Olivia thought. "That's nice."

"You must like to read."

Olivia nodded.

"I read an excellent crime novel recently. A classic. It's about a boy whose father gets lynched in the South—"

"*A Southern Lynching*."

Davis's mouth gaped in surprise. "How did you know?"

"I just do."

"Richmond St. Clair is one of my favorite authors."

"Mine, too."

"I'm surprised you've heard of him. He's not as popular as other Harlem Renaissance writers."

If Olivia told him the truth, he'd want to know more. They always do. Though she missed her mama and daddy, she'd come to LaSalle to get away from home. To be her own person.

"Both my parents are writers."

Even in the dorm room's darkness, his eyes sparkled with admiration. "Lucky you."

"I'd sit on the floor reading books I brought home from the library while my parents wrote at matching desks." She'd observed their dedication to their craft. They wrote every day; they'd be writing when she woke up in the morning and when she arrived home from school. Two hours before dinner, they'd stop working and make time for her.

Davis's shoulders lowered as she spoke.

Why am I telling this boy my business?

"My grandma encouraged me to be a lawyer." Now that Olivia had started talking, she couldn't stop. "She'd never met a child who argued with adults so much."

Davis laughed. He seemed smart. Sort of handsome. He wore a black pullover sweater, with a red V inside a white one on the front, over a white button-down shirt and above gray tapered slacks and black loafers. His arm touched hers. It felt nice.

Leaving her family had been hard, but Olivia had had different goals. Her parents were content with their quiet writing life. Her grandma was right. Olivia liked to argue and win arguments. She wasn't close to her older sisters, who'd moved away from home by the time she was born. Since she'd grown up as the only remaining child in the household, her parents had spoiled her and treated her like a miniature adult.

She and Davis returned to watching the dancers for a while. Two female students almost knocked each other out with their waving arms.

"That was close," Davis said. "Do you want to dance?"

"I can't. It's getting late. I'm leaving."

He furrowed his brow. "Was it something I said?"

"No. I've just gotta to go."

"I'll walk you."

"You don't have to."

Davis shrugged. "I know."

Olivia waved at Sandra; she was unsure if her friend waved back or whether it was part of a dance move. Olivia and Davis walked near the kids standing by the wall to avoid being struck by the dancers and left the room unscathed.

After the stale air of the dorm room, the crisp April air was refreshing. Olivia should have brought a jacket but hadn't because of her last-minute decision to attend the party. Cars lined the quiet street, which was lit intermittently by streetlamps. No ambulances rushed by with sirens blazing. It felt as if they were the only two people awake in the entire world.

Olivia liked Philly. Its rhythm was different from Harlem's, although her old neighborhood had changed since she'd lived there—and not for the better. Philly was home now. She couldn't imagine ever leaving.

As they walked, Olivia told Davis that she'd been captain of the debate team and valedictorian of her high school class. Davis had been the president of the math club and received an academic scholarship to LaSalle.

A few blocks from campus, she stopped in front of a three-story brick apartment building. "This is me."

"Um…you want to see a movie sometime?"

"I'm a mother." This sentence alone usually had a guy

giving her an excuse and hurrying away. Davis's expression didn't change. She gestured toward the building. "I have a five-year-old daughter. It's school and her."

"She can come, too."

"I'll be at the library tomorrow studying. If I finish my work, maybe we can go."

CHAPTER FOUR

Augusta

AS AUGUSTA GIBSON walked down Seventh Avenue, she read Alain Locke's *The New Negro: Voices of the Harlem Renaissance.* The drumbeat of Harlem boomed around her. Cars honked. Policemen blew whistles and directed traffic. Shop owners greeted her as she passed by, calling to her either through their open doors or as they swept their entryways. Under the awning of Livingston Flowers, a man in a gray double-breasted suit was bent over smelling pink and yellow cabbage roses in a white bucket. He looked up at her. "Wow." He straightened. "Hello."

"Hello." Augusta kept walking, her eyes focused on the page.

"You look lovely."

"Thank you," she said over her shoulder. She was used to receiving compliments on her looks, especially from men. She didn't pay it any mind.

She entered Rose's. New, pressed dresses hung on a rack along one wall.

"They're so colorful!" Augusta said.

The proprietor of the shop was a solid white woman with massive breasts who could not fit into any of the dresses she sold.

"You people do good work," said Rose.

Augusta frowned at the backhanded compliment but refrained from responding. She needed this job. As did her mother.

At the back of the store, she opened the door between two dress racks. Singer sewing machines hummed, operated by five middle-aged Negro women, the noise like a swarm of bees confined in a jar. The women engaged in conversation, raising their voices to be heard over the machines. None of them wore the dresses they made.

At the nearest machine, Augusta kissed the cheek of a woman with high cheekbones and the same unblemished complexion as her own. The woman's short brown hair tapered to the base of her neck. "Hey, Mama."

Julia Betty Cabot Gibson smiled. "Hey, Baby Girl."

"I'm not a baby anymore. I just turned eighteen."

"You'll always be my baby." Her mama's deft, slender hands guided a dress sleeve under the needle. "How was school today?"

"Fascinating! In English, we started reading"—she showed her the book cover—"an anthology that contains the work of my favorite authors. Zora Neale Hurston, Langston Hughes, and Claude McKay."

"Slow down, child, and take a breath."

"In class today, we discussed how we should not only champion but demand civil rights." The bell over the shop's front door dinged. "Gotta go!" Augusta said. It was her job to greet the customers in the showroom and guide them to the higher-priced clothes.

Before she made it out of the sewing room, Rose opened the door. "Augusta, there's a customer asking for you."

Augusta's head jerked. "Me?"

"Who is it?" her mama asked.

Rose said, "Hurry. You mustn't keep him waiting."

Augusta glanced at her mama, smoothed her ash-grey pleat skirt, and followed the proprietor into the showroom.

The man was standing with his back to her. He was slim and an inch taller than Augusta's five feet and seven inches. He tapped his foot to a silent tune.

Augusta said, "May I help—"

The man turned to face her.

It was the man she'd passed earlier, who had been smelling flowers. He was in his early twenties, with light skin and conked hair parted on one side. A thin mustache framed his upper lip. His suit had faint black stripes. Her friends would say he was fancy. He held a fedora in one hand and a bouquet of cabbage roses in the other. He proffered the roses to her. "Yes. You can take these. They're for you."

Augusta's hands flew to her face. "For me?"

"For you." After a few seconds, he gently peeled one of her hands away with long, elegant fingers, the tips of which were hardened. Augusta's cheeks warmed with embarrassment. He handed her the flowers.

She brought them to her nose and inhaled their lovely

scent. "These are beautiful. No one has ever bought me flowers."

"Then I'm happy to be the first."

Hangers clanked together. Rose glared at her as she placed them on the back wall rack.

"Uh…will there be anything else?" Augusta asked him.

"I'm also looking for a dress," he said. "For my sister. It's her birthday."

"What size does she wear?"

"The same size as you."

Augusta led him to a rack. On the way, he stopped in front of a full-length mirror and turned his head from side to side, eyeing his hair. It didn't move.

He joined her. "Which dress do you like?" he asked.

"There are so many! This afternoon dress." Augusta handed him a blue-gray dress with three hem layers at the bottom and then shifted two hangers aside. "Or this party dress." She pushed the indigo dress at him. "Or this one." She extended a tunic day dress to him, then paused at a red French Crepe dress. "This is my favorite, though." She held the dress against the front of her body, its neckline under her chin.

He clutched the three dresses against his chest. "I'll take it. Trade?"

She handed him the French Crepe and returned the others to their rightful place.

"My name is Jean, by the way. Jean Wells. What's yours?"

She hesitated. "Augusta."

They gazed at one another. His eyes were copper.

Finally, Jean held up the dress. "I guess I should pay for this."

"Oh, right."

Augusta rang up the sale at the cash register. Rose pretended not to watch her every move. The drawer cha-chinged opened. "That'll be $11.79."

Jean handed her fifteen dollars. She placed the bills in the proper slot, fished out his change, and held it out.

"Keep it," he said.

"I can't. We don't accept tips."

"It's not a tip. It's so you can buy a pretty dress. Or a book."

She shook her head and pushed the money toward him. "I'm not allowed to accept it."

He placed the bills in his gold clip and put it and the coins in his front pocket. "How about your phone number instead?"

Augusta blushed.

"Ahem." Her mama leaned against the back door jamb, her arms crossed.

"You need something, Mama?"

"No."

Augusta pleaded with her eyes for Julia to leave. Julia hesitated then retreated to the back room, leaving the door ajar.

"I can't give my number out to a stranger," Augusta said.

"Is that right?" Jean donned his hat and grinned. "Okay, then."

When he reached the front door, Augusta said, "Excuse me, sir!"

"Yes?"

She held up the hanger. "You forgot the dress."

"Oh, yes." His fingers brushed her hand as he took the dress from her. Her skin tingled. "Thanks."

After Jean left the store, which was empty except for Rose, Augusta went to the back room.

Her mama slipped a hem under the sewing machine's needles. "Who was he?"

Augusta sat on the nearest chair and picked up her book. "Jean Wells. I passed him on the way to work today."

"Who's the dress for?"

"His sister."

"He must have a lot of them; he's in here all the time."

"Rose didn't mention she'd seen him before."

Julia pursed her lips. "'Cause we all look the same to her."

✑

The next day, Augusta was sitting at the cash register reading *The New Negro* when the front doorbell clanged and Jean Wells entered. From the street, the sounds of honking cars and talking people grew louder, then diminished as the door closed. Jean scanned the room until he saw Augusta at the cash register. Today, he wore a brown suit and matching fedora. Augusta's hands became clammy, and she almost dropped the book. She set it on the counter.

Jean removed his hat, set it next to the book, and placed his forearms on the counter. "I see you're still reading Alain's book."

Her mouth gaped. "Alain? You *know* Mr. Locke?"

"Sure. I know everyone who's anyone in Harlem."

Augusta mirrored his position. Their faces were only a foot apart. Freckles dotted the bridge of Jean's nose and cheeks. "What's he like?"

Jean shrugged. "Like all writers, I suppose."

She wasn't sure what that meant. She didn't know any. "Have you read the book?"

He shook his head. "Not yet."

A regular customer entered. Jean drifted over to a rack of dresses. After Augusta helped the woman find a dress for an evening party, she rang up the purchase and guided the customer out of the store.

"Do you work every day?" Jean asked her.

Augusta shook her head. "Only three days a week after school. I'm a senior in high school. Are you in college?"

"No," he scoffed. "I'm in a jazz band. I play the piano. Stride."

"Fats Waller plays stride. Do you know him? He's the best."

Jean tsked. "I'm better than that cat."

He told her his band practiced in a row house near the shop every day, except on Sundays, or when they performed a gig.

Rose came in from the back room. "If you're not planning to buy something, mister, you'll have to leave."

Jean bought Augusta's second favorite dress and stayed.

They talked between the times she waited on customers.

Jean visited the store every day Augusta worked.

One morning, over breakfast, her mama remarked, "He's bought enough dresses to open his own store."

After three weeks of visiting, Jean entered the store, removed a pen and a piece of paper from a pocket inside his suit jacket, and handed them to Augusta. "I'm not a stranger anymore. How about that phone number?"

CHAPTER FIVE

DINAH

"ARE YOU LISTENING to me?"

The North Carolinian summer heat had finally abated, though the tree leaves had yet to turn. Dinah had been counting the veins on a dark tobacco leaf. Two rows over, a slave sang a song with surprising richness, even though he was making it up as he went along. Dinah shifted her gaze to Betty, crouching in the same row, three yards away from her. They both wore thin, wheat-colored cotton dresses that fell just past their knees. Their skin and clothes were overlaid with an ever-present layer of dust.

"Sorry, what did you say?" Dinah asked.

Her friend's heart-shaped face and round cheeks beamed with excitement. "You don't listen. I was talking about the new man brought in from town yesterday. Master Devereaux bought him to help with the horses. His name is Ellis."

Dinah smiled. "Yesterday, you say? And you know so much about him already?"

Betty giggled. "Someone needs to know these things, since you don't seem interested."

Men were the last thing on Dinah's mind, although the boys she and Betty had grown up with were now taller than them and displayed sinewy muscles from hours spent working in the fields.

A shadow crossed Betty's face, and her sweet smile dimmed. She removed the tobacco leaves from the base of the plant in front of her at a more feverish pace than she had a moment ago. The slave two rows over stopped singing.

Nelson, the overseer, loomed over them. Tight, curly hairs the same wool-like texture as the hair on his head covered the deep-brown skin on his barrel chest. A six-inch scar ran along his shoulder blade. His previous master at another plantation had hung him from a meat hook for insubordination. Nelson had changed his ways after that.

Dinah folded inward, trying her best not to attract attention.

"Dinah," he said.

"Yes, Nelson."

"Master Beaux is asking for you."

The master's eldest son sat astride his black mare at the end of the row she squatted in. Next to him, a brown dog chased its tail.

With calloused, tobacco-stained hands, Dinah piled a handful of leaves onto the mule sled. "What does he want?"

"Doesn't matter. Go on."

As she rose, her heart plummeted from her chest to her

stomach. Her back and legs were stiff from kneeling all morning, a position she normally would remain in until dark, with only a brief break for supper. Tomorrow, she'd wake up and resume that position, and again the day after that, and the day after that, until she died. All the old slaves—the several still living—were broken from a lifetime of labor. Dinah passed Betty, who was removing leaves faster than she'd ever plucked in her life.

Two. Four. Six. Eight. Ten. As Dinah trudged by the other slaves one by one, none of them looked up at her, their concentration fully on their work. Dinah's toes clenched the dirt as she continued to count the tobacco stalks on each side until she reached Master Beaux. Forty-two. She stared at the ground.

"What took you so long? It's like you were walking through molasses."

Eyes downcast, Dinah clenched her fists to stop the shivering. Her momma had told her to respond when spoken to, but her fear wouldn't allow her mouth to work. The dog stopped his paces and sat still.

"Hey, girl," Beaux said to Dinah.

Dinah opened her mouth. It was dry. No words came out.

"Hey, girl," he said again, his lazy drawl more insistent. "Something wrong with your hearing?"

"Yes, Master. I mean no."

Her hands resumed shaking. She hid them behind her back.

"Look at me."

Dinah inched up her gaze without shading her eyes from

the autumn sun. Beaux sat on his horse with an ease she would never feel. He dismounted and grasped the mare's reins. In his knee-high black boots, he towered over Dinah by eight inches. A whiff of the horse dung he'd stepped in wafted up from the bottoms of his boots. His wrinkled white cotton shirt hung on his lanky frame, untucked in his brown breeches. "Mmm mmm mmm. You sure are pretty."

He stepped closer to her, so that they were only six inches apart. Dinah took a quivering breath. The smell of tobacco and sweat radiated from his tanned skin. He removed his hat, and the bangs of his straight, light brown hair fell over his forehead. Beaux was all angles: sharp cheekbones, straight nose, and pointed chin. A toothpick dangled from his mouth. His hazel-eyed gaze met Dinah's. The white women probably thought he was handsome.

Dinah wanted to turn around and call out to Betty. She needed her friend to put an arm around her and tell her everything was going to be all right. But she didn't want to bring trouble upon her.

"The sunlight brings out the lighter strands in your hair." Beaux rubbed a single strand of Dinah's hair between his thumb and his index finger. "How are you on this fine day?"

Dinah held his gaze and her tongue.

"You can answer me," Beaux said, his tone gentle.

The mare shuffled her hooves in the overturned dirt.

"Good, sir."

Beaux released Dinah's hair and raised her chin. "I do like 'em the color of my tea."

He chuckled, his teeth stained brown by the product his slaves harvested.

Dinah's skin was lighter than most slaves', although several shades darker from toiling outside throughout the summer. After she'd turned eighteen, her looks had begun drawing unwanted attention, especially from men.

Beaux shook his head. "Where have I been? I can't believe how much you've grown up, Dinah." His gaze brushed her face. She tried to move, but his finger held her in place. Her cheeks grew hot from his intense scrutiny. She shifted from foot to foot as his appraisal trailed from her eyes to her lips, to the sweat-soaked valley between her full breasts. She realized with horror that her nipples were visible through her dress. Beaux lingered there before continuing his visual journey to her waist and then to her bare, ashy feet.

He squeezed her chin and let go, shifting the toothpick to the other side of his mouth with his tongue. "Turn around." Humiliated, the heat rose behind Dinah's eyes as she complied. "All the way."

Aside from Beaux's voice, the field was quiet. The slaves had stopped working and were watching her and Beaux in silence. Even the birds in the faraway oak trees had ceased their chirping. The Devereauxs' tobacco fields stretched out as far as the eye could see. Dinah wasn't sure what Beaux's role was on the plantation, except for riding his mare everywhere and teaching her tricks, like jumping fences.

Beaux stared past Dinah at two dark male faces peering at them over the stalks.

He sneered at them. "What are you looking at?"

Their eyes darted away before they lowered their heads and returned to their work.

Beaux donned his hat, re-mounted his horse, and settled

into the saddle. He leaned over and patted the mare's neck, then straightened and pinched the hat's brim. "Be seeing you, Dinah." To the dog, he said, "Come on, Jake." To the horse, "Git!"

The horse's hooves kicked up dirt, which settled on Dinah's skin and crept up her nose. Dinah coughed, spit, and wiped the dust off her face as Beaux departed.

CHAPTER SIX

SHA

SHA'S KNUCKLES FOUGHT to break through their skin as she gripped the leather steering wheel. She screamed into the silence of her electric Audi SUV during her frantic drive through the city. *My baby is hurt! My baby is hurt!* When she'd gotten off the phone with Jelani, she'd read the stream of text messages her daughter had sent while she was asleep. Each one was increasingly desperate, asking where Sha was and why she hadn't responded.

After the initial shock, she had scanned her living room wanting to throw something, to break something—the beer bottles, the throw pillows, the lamp, the TV. What good would that have done? Why hadn't she stayed awake? Why had she let her daughter go out tonight?

She punched the horn as she ran several red lights, southbound on Shattuck Avenue, and roared through STOP signs. She was lucky she didn't get pulled over. She laughed maniacally, tipping into madness. *I'll never let Jelani go out ever again.*

Sha needed to focus. She couldn't help her daughter if she crashed into the parked cars lining the streets. She opened the meditation app on the console connected to her smartphone. *Inhale for four, hold for four, exhale for four, hold for four. Again, inhale for four…* Sha's smartwatch showed her blood pressure was elevated.

She slammed her hand onto the dashboard. "It's not fucking working!"

The club was in the middle of a block of trendy restaurants, coffee shops, pubs, an art gallery, a bookstore, and a cannabis emporium. Sha hadn't only relied on Jelani to tell her of her whereabouts. She had used the FIND ME app on her phone to verify her daughter's location. Sha double-parked on the avenue in front of Z21. She couldn't recall the drive from her house. All she had seen was a mental image of her daughter's face, and now she needed to see the real thing.

A huge, dark-skinned Black man wearing a security headset blocked the entrance to the club. He was wearing black pants and a black T-shirt that stretched tight over his gallon-jug biceps. He was stationed in front of a red velvet rope held up by gold stanchions. People stood flush against the facade, smoking weed and chatting, or staring at their phone screens. The queue stretched past the building and snaked around the corner onto the cross street. Loud music emanated from the club.

Sha rushed toward the bouncer. He raised his hand inches from her flat chest. "I need to see ID, lady."

She glanced at his hand, then at her old gray Berkeley

hoodie, the cuff sleeves frayed, over a white T-shirt, her "home" jeans—which she never wore outside the house—and her white Stan Smith Adidas sneakers. "Listen, Gym Rat, do I look as if I'm going clubbing?"

He smirked and looked at the line of club goers, all in their early twenties. The women were dressed in skirts and tights, though some wore jeans. One was wearing shorts despite the cool night air. "Pretty much."

The heat rose to Sha's face. "I don't have time for this. I need to find my daughter."

"You can wait for her here."

"No. I. Can't." Sha would not cry. "She's hurt. Either you let me in, or I'll go through you."

He crossed his arms. "You can try."

She glowered at him. "Wanna tell me how she got in? She's only seventeen. And I'd bet she's not the only under-aged kid inside."

The bouncer's eyes shifted as if the Berkeley PD were swarming toward him. He unclipped the rope and waved her through. "Don't be long, or I'll come in after you."

"Hey!" a young man shouted, waiting in line. "Why does she get in for free?"

"Yeah…it's unfair!" said another. "She just got here!"

The girl wearing shorts asked, "Is it AARP night?"

I'm only thirty-four, Shortpants.

Sha entered the club.

The thump of the bass heard from outside was deafening within, reverberating through her bones. Her teeth chattered. Strobe lights darted around the dark, cavernous room. Two long bars packed three rows deep with thirsty customers lined the gray brick interior walls. On the stage, the DJ was wearing sunglasses and had headphones over one ear. He pointed upward as he shouted undecipherable words into a microphone.

Sha bumped her way through the dancing crowd. Too many people. She took deep breaths to ease her growing anxiety. She stopped to ask a young woman where the restroom was located. The woman waved vaguely and Sha moved in that direction, stepping over puddles of spilled drinks. As she squeezed by, dancers conversed at screaming volumes to be heard over the music. The smell of alcohol and sweat and weed blanketed the air.

A woman dance-jostled her into a young man who appeared to be in his late teens. He ensnared Sha in both arms, a smile spreading across his face. "Happy birthday to me."

"Let go of me." She pushed him away. "I'm old enough to be your mother."

His grin widened. "But you're not my mother."

She scowled and stormed to the women's restroom, cutting to the front of the line and ignoring the howled protests from the women and girls who were waiting. She stood at the entryway. For such a large establishment, there were only three stalls. At the mirror, several of the girls—Black, white, Hispanic, Asian, and mixed-race—laughed and chatted while reapplying their makeup and fixing their hair.

"Jel," Sha said at the stalls.

No response.

Louder, she said, "Jelani, where are you?"

"Here." Her daughter's voice sounded as if it were floating.

Sha tried to push open the door to the last stall, but it was locked. She leaned against it, her face almost touching the metal. "It's me. Let me in."

At first, nothing happened. Then there was a rustling. The latch clicked and the door opened an inch. Sha's push met resistance. Jelani moved, and the door eased open.

Sha's baby was lying on the sticky concrete bathroom floor, her black dress ripped at the front. Jelani's eyes were teary, unfocused. The makeup that stained her face did not mask the bruise on her cheek. Sha covered her mouth so Jelani couldn't hear her cry out. A powerful feeling of déjà vu washed over her. And shame. Her only real job in life was to protect her daughter, and she'd failed.

She knelt and touched Jelani's hair, face, and shoulder, then held her hand. "Where does it hurt?"

A pause. "Down there."

Sha could barely hear Jelani over the laughter from the girls at the mirror and the blast of the hand dryers. The music blaring from the club rose and fell with the opening and closing of the bathroom door. Sha tried to hug Jelani. To absorb her pain. The tight space made it awkward.

Sha's eyes watered. "Where are your friends?"

"Probably still dancing." Jelani's lips trembled. "I don't want to be like those teen mothers on that reality show."

Sha flexed her jaw. "You won't. Come on. Let's go."

She took off her hoodie and wrapped it around Jelani, gathered her daughter in her arms and lifted her. Sha was not strong and didn't work out as often as she should, aside from taking long walks through the neighborhood. She had read about the wonders of a mother's strength when it came to saving and protecting her children, though. She'd always been skeptical of those stories until now.

Sha inhaled the jasmine fragrance of Jelani's shampoo. "Who did this to you?"

Jelani squeezed her eyes shut, shook her head, and buried her face in Sha's chest. Blood stained her legs as well as the floor. Sha maneuvered Jelani out of the stall. The other girls in the bathroom ignored them, continuing to gossip, apply makeup, and take selfies, as if a woman being carried out was a frequent occurrence.

Maybe it was.

Sha weaved her way across the dance floor the way she'd come. None of the dancers got out of her way or tried to assist her. Outside the club, she passed the bouncer, whose face was inscrutable as he followed her movements with his gaze.

Sha approached the Audi, wondering how she would unlock the door and open it while holding her daughter.

Behind her, the bouncer said to the line of club-goers, "If anyone enters, I will hunt you down and kill you."

Footsteps pounded toward her.

"Give her to me," the bouncer said.

Sha already knew how seriously this man took his job. She hesitated, then handed her daughter to him. She fished the fob out of her front pocket, unlocked the car, and opened the passenger-side door. The bouncer gently placed Jelani in the seat, buckled her seat belt, and closed the door.

A nod was all Sha could give him by way of thanks.

CHAPTER SEVEN

OLIVIA

THE DAY AFTER the party, Olivia and Davis studied together at the Connelly Library. That weekend, they took Nicole to see *That Darn Cat!* Davis bought Nicole Starburst candy and a Dr. Pepper. Prior to the movie, the two of them chatted away, like old friends, as if Olivia weren't there. Had Davis sensed that it would be a deal-breaker if Nicole didn't like him? Nicole fell asleep before the movie ended, and Davis carried her for six blocks, up three flights of stairs, and down the hall into Olivia's apartment. He waited in the living room while Olivia put Nicole to bed.

∽

Olivia had once trusted the wrong boy and paid for it with a broken heart. Since then, she'd often wondered if she'd be doomed in the love department for the rest of her life because of one bad decision.

She'd met Ted in high school. He had a good head on his shoulders and didn't play sports, so they spent time together after her debate class. They talked and had fun together. He wanted to go to college, too. Olivia had dreamed they would be one of those high school sweetheart couples who got married.

She'd told him she was pregnant at a park in Harlem where she used to play. He'd shot up from the bench and said, "What does that have to do with me?" He'd walked away on the path that cut through the locust trees and left her sitting there, without looking back. He'd avoided her in the school hallways and in class. Olivia's friends had shied away from her as if her condition were contagious. As if they weren't doing the same thing with their boyfriends in the back seats of cars or at parties.

One day, she passed Ted as he stood at his locker with a few friends. She was showing. He said something to them, and they snickered. Her face flushed with shame, then anger. She turned and marched up to him.

"What's so funny?" she asked.

His expression sobered. "Nothing." His friends had stopped laughing, except for one who was slow on the uptake.

"I should be the one who's laughing," Olivia said. "I thought you were a real man who could handle his responsibilities. But I was wrong. You're weak. It's your loss. You'll see."

She spun around and walked away.

Ted had tried to talk to her a few times during their final year of high school, but she'd ignored him and never spoken a word to him again. He'd lost his chance.

Because of Ted, Olivia had vowed not to need anyone. She'd dated other boys, but her low expectations had always proven right.

❧

In Philly, she and Nicole led a structured life; they had a routine. They woke up and got ready, then Olivia walked Nicole to her elementary school, after which she attended class. She tried to schedule her classes so that she could accompany Nicole home from school. Mrs. Parks looked after Nicole when an afternoon class was unavoidable. Olivia and Nicole ate dinner together—something out of a box, as Olivia wasn't much of a cook—then Olivia did her homework while Nicole read or drew until her bedtime. Often, Olivia would study for a couple of hours more after her daughter fell asleep.

Olivia planned to date Davis until he got bored and moved on.

❧

After a year of dating, Davis showed up at Olivia's apartment with sunflowers and asked Nicole if she'd go on a date with him while Olivia studied for the LSAT. Olivia had been more determined than ever to pass the test ever since Thurgood Marshall had become the first Negro to ascend to the US Supreme Court.

Davis took Nicole to the 20th Street diner for a cheeseburger, fries, and a chocolate milkshake. Between bites, Nicole chatted away about her day in the first grade. At the end of the meal, Davis knelt on one knee and proposed to be her dad. Nicole said "yes," as long as he kept the burgers and milkshakes coming. They walked hand-in-hand to Leo's jewelry store down the street, where he paid the remaining balance on the ring he'd bought on layaway for Olivia. He bought a toy ring for Nicole at Sunny's drugstore and slipped it on her finger.

When they arrived back at the apartment, Nicole, eyes alight and braids flying wildly, rushed into the kitchen, where Olivia was studying. She showed her mother the toy ring and announced, "We're getting married!"

Olivia looked from the ring to her daughter's grin to Davis's imploring brown eyes.

Olivia would have never let Davis around her daughter if she thought he'd harm her or treat her poorly. After she and Davis had been going steady for a few months, she'd worried that Nicole was too attached to him and would be negatively impacted if the relationship ended. She'd let the situation unfold. If he were destined to be with them, he would.

But Davis had exceeded her expectations. He was gentle with Nicole. Protective. He listened to her. They engaged in actual conversations, like Olivia's parents had with her.

Olivia and Davis were complete opposites. Davis wasn't ambitious or intense. When Olivia got irritated with him, he kissed her on the cheek, grabbed his jacket, and left. When she couldn't stand being away from him anymore, she'd call him at his mother's house—where he still lived—and he'd return to her apartment. When they watched TV together in her cramped living room, she'd glance over at the stacked textbooks on her kitchen table. Davis would say, "Go study. We can watch the re-run."

Marrying Olivia was a risk. Davis had just started a new job with the government, and his salary would have to support them while Olivia attended law school.

Davis fidgeted in the doorway, still waiting for Olivia's response. By his expression, he was bracing himself for her refusal.

Olivia ran to him and jumped into his arms. "Yes!"

CHAPTER EIGHT

JULIA

JULIA PEEKED INTO her daughter's bedroom. The curtains she had made matched the pink-flowered wallpaper. A few dresses hung on hangers in the open closet. On the nightstand rested a pile of loose coins and a stack of books. Augusta's pink bathrobe hung on a hook behind the door. The family shared the apartment's one bathroom.

Augusta lay on her back, propped up by a pillow on the twin bed's cream-colored bedspread. She wore high-waisted plaid pants and a white short-sleeved shirt. Her head was hidden behind James Weldon Johnson's *The Autobiography of an Ex-Colored Man*.

Julia entered the room, stopping on the hook rug at the foot of the bed. "Didn't you hear me calling you?"

Augusta peered over the book with her expressive brown eyes. "No, Mama."

"It's time for dinner."

"I'm not that hungry."

"You must eat. Come on, now."

"I'll be right there." Augusta's attention returned to the page. "Let me finish this chapter."

"I made your favorite: corn pudding. You don't want it to get cold."

"This page, then. I promise."

Julia's face softened. "All right."

This was a daily conversation between them, both prior to dinner and long after Augusta should have fallen asleep. Julia wished she earned a nickel for every time she had to tell Augusta to put a book down, turn out the light, and go to sleep.

Julia joined her nine-year-old son, Hale, at the small round oak table in the kitchen. Hale had a dark complexion and round eyes. Augusta walked him home from school every day before work so that Julia wouldn't have to leave the shop. After completing his homework, Hale played outside with his friends until his mother and his sister arrived home. One of the neighbors kept an eye out for him.

He picked up his fork.

Julia stopped him with a look. "Wait for your sister. You know we're supposed to say grace first."

"But I'm hungry," Hale said, drawing out the "hung."

"Jesus has been waiting for us for almost two thousand years. You can wait a few more minutes."

Hale cocked his head. "But I'm really hungry."

"He will sustain you."

"Then why does my stomach hurt?"

"Don't be smart about Jesus, boy."

Hale opened his mouth to respond, then reconsidered and put the fork down.

Although Julia pretended to be angry, she was proud she'd raised smart children who were unafraid of speaking their minds.

Her daughter entered the room, still reading, and sat on the wooden chair nearest the door. She set the open book next to her plate, her diamond-shaped face in deep concentration.

Julia cleared her throat. Augusta looked at her.

"Prayer is important," said Julia.

"Yes, mama," Augusta and Hale said.

"A family that prays together stays together. Bow your heads."

Julia closed her eyes, then reopened one of them to make sure Hale's were closed. They were. She closed her eye again and recited a prayer:

"O Lord,

Thank you for the food we are about to eat

And for all of our many blessings

In Jesus's name. Amen."

"Amen," her children echoed.

Augusta scooped a spoonful of corn pudding into her mouth. "This is good, Mama." Her eyes darted back to the book.

"Don't think I don't know what you're doing. Close it. How many times do I have to tell you?"

"Jesus doesn't allow it," her son said to his sister.

Julia glared at him. "No jokes about Jesus. Don't let me tell you again, Hale."

He pinched his lips together, swallowing the comment that would have preceded a spanking.

Augusta sighed and closed the novel. "What *can* we do at the table?"

"Eat," Julia said, "and talk"—she pointed her fork at Hale—"but not at the same time."

Her children looked at each other, rolled their eyes, and laughed.

Julia suppressed her own smile.

Besides the corn pudding, they ate baked ham covered in breadcrumbs, collard greens, and a dessert of caramel custard, a recipe Julia had learned from her own mother, Sarah. Hale did most of the talking, reliving the stickball game that he and his friends had played on the street that afternoon. The empty chair was where Julia's husband, Clifford, used to sit. Julia wished for the millionth time he could be here to see his children grow up. He was gone now, taken from her in France near the end of the Great War, a month before the hostilities had ceased. He was only thirty-three years old. He had promised Julia he would come back.

Clifford and the rest of the Harlem Hellfighters had left for Europe proud to fight for their country, proud to be Americans. But when the survivors returned home from the war, instead of being treated like heroes, they'd been greeted by the same old racism. When Julia sat in the living room gazing at pictures of Clifford in the photo album—in uniform, with the children, on their wedding day—she still didn't understand what the Hellfighters had fought for or what her husband had died for while she and the other war widows had stayed behind to raise their children.

Although the meager federal assistance and Augusta's small income helped, maintaining a household and raising children on one salary was difficult. There were many months during which Julia did not think they would make it. Despite the lean times, they made do. Her faith was her salvation and her sustenance. She continued to pray for her family as her momma had prayed for her, and the Lord always provided. Augusta and Hale were healthy and happy and didn't want for anything. Julia had faced the worst that the Devil could throw at her…and survived.

The buzzer sounded.

Hale's fork clattered to his plate as he shot out of his chair midsentence, scraping it against the linoleum floor. He pushed open the swinging kitchen door and sprinted down the short hallway.

"I thought you were hungry!" Julia called after him.

The apartment's front door opened and closed.

"Augusta," Hale sang, "it's your boyfriend!"

Augusta gave Julia a shy glance, then slid out of her seat and hurried out of the room.

"You forgot your book," Julia said to the empty chair.

Julia moved to the kitchen's entrance, held the door open, and looked down the hallway.

Jean Wells stood in the entryway wearing a brown double-breasted suit (of which he seemed to have an endless supply) and holding a brown wool newsboy cap in his hands. Hale gazed up at him with adoration.

Jean rubbed the boy's short, curly hair. "How ya doing, Hale?"

"I scored the winning run in our stickball game!"

"Maybe you'll grow up to play in the Negro National League someday."

"I hope so!"

Augusta reached them. "Bye, Hale."

"We'll talk more later, sport," Jean said.

The boy trudged to the kitchen, looking back over his shoulder. He ducked under Julia's arm and returned to his chair at the table.

"Hey, Jean!" Julia said.

Jean bowed and stared at nothing, just to the left of her. "I hope you're having a good evening, Mrs. Gibson," he said.

"Care to join us for dinner?"

Augusta had been dating him for over two months. Julia knew little about him other than he played the piano, which was unusual for a jazz musician; it was a rich person's instrument. She didn't know his people—they lived in a different section of Harlem—but she knew they must be rich by the way he dressed. She wondered what church his folks attended. Julia attended Mount Zion Baptist Church on West 145th and studied the Bible with other ladies on Wednesday nights. Clifford's grave was in the small, crowded graveyard beside the church. Julia brought fresh flowers and placed them in front of his headstone after every Sunday service.

"I already ate, ma'am. Thank you anyway." He turned back to her oldest child. "You ready?"

"She will be after she finishes her dinner," Julia said.

Her daughter stamped her foot. "Mama!"

"Come on, now."

Jean checked his gold pocket watch. "We have time."

Augusta exhaled. "All right."

Jean extended his hand, allowing her to lead the way.

After they sat, Augusta's appetite returned. She ate quickly.

"Slow down," said Julia. "You're going to make yourself sick."

"My food's cold," Hale said.

Julia paused, her fork halfway to her mouth. "I am not reheating it. It's not my fault you all are finding everything else to do but eat."

"I'm finished," Augusta said.

"We need to go or else we'll be late," Jean said.

"I'll change."

Augusta left the kitchen, her footsteps skipping along the hallway to her bedroom.

Hale finished eating, too, then lay on his stomach on the floor in the narrow space between the stove and the table, where he'd set up the wooden erector set he'd found on the sidewalk outside their apartment building.

Jean slung his arm over the top of Augusta's vacant chair. "What are you building there, champ?"

"A bridge."

"It's looking good."

"Where are you two headed tonight?" Julia asked Jean.

"A literary party. For writers."

"I know what a literary party is."

"Auggie will enjoy it, given how much she likes to read."

"Do you?"

"Nah. I'm not much of a reader."

Julia sipped her iced tea. "How do you read sheet music?"

Jean smoothed his suit coat. "I don't. I listen. I only need to hear something once to play it."

"Where did you learn to play the piano?"

"In church. I played there for eight years until I joined the band."

She relaxed. A God-fearing man. "Which church is that?"

Augusta came back wearing a burgundy drop-waisted dress, a matching cloche hat, and brown reptile-skinned, one-strap shoes. She'd bought the shoes for $2.98 with her recent wages. "I'm ready. Do I look all right?"

Jean gazed at her appreciatively. "More than all right. You look beautiful."

Augusta's coquettish smile lit up the room.

"I agree," Julia said. "Don't stay out too late. You have school tomorrow."

"I won't." Augusta kissed her on the cheek, then glanced at her brother. "See you, Hale."

Hale set another beam over the foundation of his bridge and, without looking up from it, said, "Bye."

Jean followed Augusta out of the kitchen. After the front door closed behind them, Julia washed the dishes and placed them in the dish rack next to the sink. As she picked up a soiled pot, she realized Augusta's boyfriend hadn't answered her last question.

CHAPTER NINE

DINAH

A FEW DAYS after Beaux Devereaux had spoken to her, Dinah awoke to being shaken by the shoulder.

"Wake up!"

It couldn't be time to get up; she'd just laid down her head.

Ceila shook her again. Dinah scowled and opened one eye to an older version of herself looking back at her. Her momma had honey-brown skin, almond-shaped brown eyes, and short, gray hair that framed her high cheekbones. The lines on her face, from suffering more than age, did not detract from her beauty and regal bearing. Celia made her dresses herself, and although they were simple, they were always neat. If it were not for her skin color, she could have been mistaken for the lady of the great house. Dinah's grandmother, Aisha, had told Dinah that their ancestors had been kings and queens.

This queen glared at her only child.

Their log cabin was more of a hut without windows, the gaps between the planks negating a need for them. The gaps allowed sufficient light to illuminate the interior while extending an open invitation to rain, mosquitoes, flies, and rats.

Dinah clung to her thin, coarse blanket, her only protection against the draft. She slept on a narrow board with a pillow made of wood. Although it was uncomfortable, exhaustion enveloped her by the end of each day, and she didn't care where she slept. Sometimes even the dirt floor looked good.

"What do you want?"

Her mother gave her a look that could stop a team of charging horses. "Who do you think you're talking to, child?"

Dinah rubbed her eyes. "Sorry, I'm still with sleep."

"I don't care how sleepy you are. I won't tolerate back talk. You hear?"

"Yes, Momma."

"All right, then. Wake up!"

"I didn't hear the horn."

"You're not going to the fields anymore. Did you forget?"

Then Dinah remembered. Last night, as she, Betty, and the other slaves had begun the long trek from the tobacco fields to the quarters, Nelson had come up behind them.

"Dinah!"

She'd stopped walking; the slave behind her had collided into her and then gone around her. "What?" she'd asked Nelson.

"You're wanted in the great house. Starting tomorrow."

"What for?"

"To drink tea." He'd guffawed at his own joke. "What do you think? You're going to be a house girl. Go see Martha in the kitchen before dawn."

"Get up!" her momma now repeated.

"I'm tired."

"We're all tired. Go wash the fields off you. Scrub your face." Celia glanced at Dinah's womanly parts. "And down there. Hurry!"

As Dinah rose, *The Count of Monte Cristo* fell to the floor. She brushed the dirt off the cover and returned the novel to its hiding place under her bed.

She grabbed a brush and a sliver of soap her momma had "borrowed" from the house—"they won't miss it," she'd said—and closed the cabin's front door.

The dewy grass was soft and yielded beneath her feet. She passed the small patch garden where they grew corn, potatoes, beans, and peas to augment the provisions the master provided twice a week: bread, butter, milk, molasses, cornmeal, and pork. Their meager wardrobes swayed on the clothesline after having been washed in the creek a short distance from the farthest cabin in the quarters.

Tree branches lazed over the creek. A small animal Dinah couldn't see in the darkness rustled in the nearby undergrowth. Water trickled over the rocks as she made her way carefully down the grassy bank. She'd learned her lesson from twisting her ankle once. Despite the swelling and the pain, Nelson had forced her to work that day.

"Nothing wrong with your hands," he'd said.

She steeled herself and waded into the water until it was up to her knees, its coldness almost stopping her heart.

Her feet found purchase in the mud as it oozed between her toes. She made sure no one was watching, then splashed her face and under her skirt. She used as little soap as possible, not knowing when her momma could borrow some more. During those winters, when the creek froze, the slaves either went without bathing or brought water back from the river a mile away and warmed it over a fire.

Dinah inhaled the river smells: salt, plants, and fish. An unseen frog croaked. Minnows and small fish swam just below the surface. A twig or a snake—she didn't want to guess which—brushed against her leg before moving on downstream.

She finished washing, slipped on the dress she'd taken from the clothesline, and returned to the cabin.

Dinah and Celia cut through the cluster of cabins and crossed the expanse of the verdant lawn, its scent fresh. A breeze rustled the tree leaves, which had just turned. Besides the crickets, it was quiet. Mother and daughter walked past a hammock strung up between two magnolia trees, the shade of which the master's youngest son, William—whom everyone called Billy—liked to sleep in on warm afternoons. What would it be like to sleep when you wanted, where you wanted, and not have to work every second of your waking life?

Dinah had never been in the great house. She had been in the yard, of course, when she and Beaux and Nicholas had played together as kids. They'd run around outside for hours, but she'd never been allowed inside.

The white house had two floors above ground and a roof steep enough to slide off. Dinah and her momma entered the house through a rear door that opened onto a narrow hallway. To the right was an area with a wooden bench where one could sit to take off shoes soiled by dirt and mud. The family's riding and walking boots and shoes lined the chestnut-wood floor beneath the bench. To the left was the kitchen, already warm thanks to the efforts of the stout woman standing in front of the cast-iron stove in a white cotton dress covered by a white apron. Her round, dark-brown face lit up at the sight of Celia.

"Mornin', Celia!"

"Good mornin', Ms. Martha."

The cook stopped stirring, clacking the long-handled spoon against the top of the pot to allow the excess grits to fall back within. "I see you brought me some help."

"Yes, I did, and she's a hard worker, too."

"She'd better be." She cocked her head toward the rest of the house. "They might own this house, but this kitchen is the heart of the home—and I make it beat."

Celia removed her shawl and hung it on a brass hook near the hallway door. Dinah did the same.

"Hurry, and no mistakes," her momma said to her. Celia entered the kitchen, and grabbed porcelain plates and cups out of the oak cupboards, and pointed at a drawer. Dinah opened it and stared at the shiny objects inside.

After a moment, her momma set down the cups and plates and came to stand beside her. "These are forks and knives," Celia said, lifting one of each object as she spoke, "and you know what spoons are. Bring six of each and come on."

Dinah grabbed the utensils and rushed after her through

the swinging door. She stubbed her toe on the wooden strip between the two rooms and almost fell.

"Be careful."

"Sorry, Momma."

"This is the dining room."

"Dining room," Dinah repeated.

An oval red maple table dominated the space. Eight chairs surrounded it. A matching side table flanked a wall.

Dinah and her momma ate their meals on their cabin's dirt floor.

White wainscoting divided the floral-papered walls at hip height and encircled the ceiling. Velvet maroon drapery framed the large window. The room was bigger than their cabin, and there were no holes in the walls.

As her momma placed the plates and cups on the table in front of each chair, Dinah tiptoed to the table and met her reflection in the polished surface. Her hair was long and wavy. Her nose, straight. Her eyes were wide with nervousness.

"You can admire yourself later," said her momma. "The table ain't going to set itself."

Dinah gulped, embarrassed.

Her momma showed her where to place the silverware and drew an imaginary line with her finger across the top of the plate. "Line everything up straight. The mistress doesn't like crooked."

After they set the table, they returned to the kitchen. Dinah lingered by the swinging door, peering into the dining room.

"What are you doing, child?" her momma asked exasperatedly, cutting potatoes on the square oak table in the center of the room. "Your head is always in the clouds, thinking fantastic thoughts. You need to *do*." She tilted her head toward a bowl on the table. "Stir something."

As Dinah stirred the gravy, she kept glancing with anticipation through the gap between the door and its frame. Finally, Master Sam Devereaux entered the dining room through the other door, his boots clopping against the floor. He was tall and heavyset, with bushy eyebrows and hair grayed at the temples. He wore pressed dark blue trousers and a high-collared white shirt under a tailcoat and a waistcoat. Master Sam sat at the head of the table at the far end of the room. His wife, Elizabeth, followed and sat at the opposite end, closest to the doors. The mistress's red hair was swept up atop her head, above pale skin and thin lips. Over her petticoat, she wore a burgundy dress with leg-of-mutton sleeves and a white-lace shawl across her shoulders. A matching belt with a gold buckle fit tightly around her waist. Her hem hovered six inches off the floor. Dinah contemplated her own simple dress and wondered what it would feel like to wear something so fine against her skin.

Nicholas, the middle son, sat to the left of Master Sam. His sandy hair was neatly brushed, his brown eyes set in a chiseled face. His boots were as polished as the table. Dressed like his father, though in brown trousers, he sported a neck-cloth, which Dinah later learned was the latest London fashion. The youngest child, Mary, with long, braided, light-brown hair, sat beside her mother. She wore a pink, pointed, long-waisted bodice with tight sleeves over a long-pleated skirt. The youngest boy, Billy, was seated across from his sister, leaving a vacant seat between himself and his father.

Billy's face was square, and he was the only member of the family with black hair. In the front, a tuft of hair grew in a different direction than the rest. He wore plaid trousers and a black frock coat over a white shirt.

Several minutes later, Beaux sauntered in, coatless, his hair tousled, his white shirt and brown trousers wrinkled. He plopped into the chair to the right of his father, who admonished him for being late.

"Where they sit is important," her momma whispered beside her. Dinah hadn't heard her approach. "Shows their power. They sit in the same chairs every day."

Dinah turned to pick up the serving bowl filled with gravy. Her momma clasped her wrist as though in a vise.

"Ow!" Dinah said.

"Ssh!" Her momma shook her head. "Wait."

After Dinah counted to sixty, Mistress Devereaux rang the handbell. Celia nodded, released Dinah's arm, and picked up a bowl of grits. Dinah followed her into the room and placed the gravy bowl next to it on the side table. They made several trips until the side table was full.

Dinah had never seen so much food for one meal in her life, except on special occasions—like Christmas—when the slaves gathered in the clearing at the center of the quarters for a big to-do. But they didn't eat food like this. Besides the grits and gravy there were buttermilk pancakes, eggs, and biscuits. Her stomach rumbled, unsatisfied with the small bowl of cornmeal she'd eaten in the cabin that morning. She glanced around to see if anyone had heard the noises emanating from her stomach. None of the family acknowledged either Dinah or her momma as the two women filled their plates. Returning to the kitchen, they retrieved the silver coffee pitcher, the silver tea kettle, and a glass bottle of fresh milk. Prior to reentering the dining room, Celia whispered, "Don't spill."

Although Dinah's hand trembled as she poured the liquids into glasses and cups, not a drop splashed onto the table.

During the meal, she and her momma stood at attention against the wall near the door to the kitchen, staring at the opposite wall, ready to serve more food and drink or take something away at the family's demand. Her momma had told her the previous night how important it was to stand still in white folks' presence, so they would forget you were there. You didn't want to draw attention to yourself. Dinah's mouth watered as she tried not to dive headfirst onto the table and gorge on the delicious-smelling food. It would be worth Nelson's whipping. The beating from her momma would be a different story.

Cutlery clashed against the plates as the family ate and talked. On the wall, sconces held candles that would illuminate the room at dusk. They would be able to see what they were eating. Dinah and her momma ate with their hands. In the winter, they ate in the dark.

Dinah never wanted to leave this room.

Billy Devereaux mopped up the last of his grits with a biscuit. Celia nodded.

Dinah stepped forward. "Would you like some more, Master William?"

"You can call me 'Billy.' And, yes."

"She will not call you 'Billy,'" Mistress Elizabeth snapped. "She said your name right the first time."

"But I don't want—"

Master Sam rested his forearms on the table's edge, his fork and knife paused in the air. "Listen to your mother, son."

Billy shut his mouth.

Mary cast Dinah a malevolent look. "You should have asked Beaux first, girl. He's the oldest."

Dinah tensed at the iciness in the girl's voice. She must have been around fourteen years old. Dinah's momma continued to stare at an unseen spot on the opposite wall. "I'm s-s-s-orry." Dinah turned to Beaux. "Do you want more to eat?"

"Sir," added Mary.

"Sir," Dinah said to her.

"Not to me, you ninny. Say it to Beauxregard."

"Master Beaux," added Mistress Elizabeth.

Dinah's face felt as hot as the flame from Martha's stove. She wanted to melt into the floor. "Do you want more to eat, *sir?*"

"Leave her be, Mama," Beaux said. "You, too, Mary. She's doing just fine." To Dinah, he said, "Yes, I'll have more."

The family took their time eating, then drank multiple cups of coffee, tea, and milk. After they finished their meal, they left the room. Dinah and her momma cleared away the breakfast dishes.

As Dinah moved to one of the chairs to rest, her momma said, "No, ma'am. We're just beginning."

For the remainder of the morning, Dinah helped Martha prepare supper, which was served at noon. In the afternoon, her momma showed her how to clean each room in the house—each Devereaux child slept in their own bedroom!—make the beds, refill the basins from the outside well, shake the dust from the drapes and tie them on either side of the windows, open the windows to allow in the fresh, pleasant afternoon air, wash the family's clothing, dust and polish every piece of furniture, empty and clean out the chamber pots, and perform other chores.

When Celia entered a room, she could tell if something was out of place, and she returned it to its rightful spot. She tsked when they came to Beaux's room. The sheets on his bed were askew and damp. Prints from the boots he should have taken off in the mudroom tracked the floor. Water sloshed over the rim from his basin and pooled on the floor. Neither of the other boys kept his room that way. Their rooms were neat, as if waiting to be inspected by Nelson.

Celia was exacting in her instructions and expected everything to be perfect. She double checked what Dinah did. If a dresser wasn't shining enough, Dinah had to polish it again. "Perfection staves off criticism," she said.

Dinah couldn't believe only one family lived in this house.

The walnut grandfather clock in the first-floor hallway struck ten o'clock. Satisfied, Celia declared their workday done. The house was immaculate. Celia told Dinah that she kept the finest house in North Carolina. They passed the darkened kitchen, which Martha had left hours ago, and grabbed their shawls from the hooks they had hung them on sixteen hours earlier.

"You did fine today," Celia said.

Dinah struggled to keep her eyes open. They felt heavy. "Thank you, Momma."

Inside the cabin, her momma kissed her forehead. "Get some rest."

As the night wind whistled through the cabin's planks, Dinah laid her head on the hard pillow and stared up at the low ceiling. She thought about the day. Although the hours were long, it was much better working in the house than in the fields. She wasn't stuck in the same position all day, and the house protected her from the weather.

She'd also been too busy to wonder why Beaux Devereaux, after bowing his head but before closing his eyes to say grace at supper, had grinned and winked at her.

CHAPTER TEN

SHA

SHA DROVE STRAIGHT to the only hospital in Berkeley.

She marched through the automatic sliding glass doors carrying Jelani and eased her into an empty wheelchair against the wall.

At the reception desk, she said, "I need a doctor to see my daughter now."

With her head propped in one hand, the nurse handed Sha a clipboard with the admissions paperwork. "I'll need your driver's license and insurance card."

"Look," Sha said, squinting at the nurse's white name badge, "Brittney, when I say 'now,' I mean now."

"Can't you see we're busy?"

Patients sat in blue plastic chairs in the waiting room. A woman cradled a broken arm; blood oozed down a man's face from a cut on the top of his head; another woman sneezed so much that Sha prayed she wasn't contagious; and a man sat alone in a corner, staring off into space. Everyone ignored the *Friends* rerun on the 32-inch flat-screen TV bolted to the wall. A magazine bomb seemed to have gone off on a table. Sha recalled the last time she was in an emergency room, alone, her mother and father still in Georgia. She hated the antiseptic smell of hospitals and avoided them at all costs. She shook her head. She needed to focus on Jelani. Nothing else mattered.

"Brittney, you have one minute to call someone out here to evaluate my daughter before I act the fool."

Brittney stared into Sha's eyes and hurriedly reached for the phone. "I'm calling Security."

"Wait!" Sha said. This wasn't helping Jelani. "I'm sorry. I'm normally not…Do you have a daughter?"

Brittney glanced at a dazed Jelani, still sitting in the wheelchair by the wall, then nodded. "Three of them." Brittney picked up the phone. "What's your daughter's name?"

❧

Behind a dividing curtain, Sha squeezed her daughter's hand as a technician combed Jelani's pubic hair looking for evidence. A nurse provided an emergency contraceptive pill and administered other drugs to avert sexually transmitted infections. She tested to determine whether Jelani had ingested a date-rape drug. Sha suffered the indignities her daughter was subjected to in silence. Although Jelani had consented to a complete physical examination, she refused to tell the police officer what had happened or to disclose her rapist's identity. Sha's raised voice couldn't penetrate her child's blank stare or convince her to file a police report.

Afterward, Jelani sat on the hospital bed's thin sheet, wearing Sha's hoodie over her black dress. Her long, toned legs dangled over the side. A nurse pushed a list of sexual assault counselors and support groups on Jelani, who ignored her. She handed the document to Sha and left. Sha glanced at the paper without reading it, folded it, and slid it into the back pocket of her jeans.

On the drive home, Jelani ignored Sha's questions about how she was faring. When they arrived, Sha led her upstairs and drew a warm bath in her daughter's bathroom. Jelani's numerous shampoos and conditioners—for dry hair, straight hair, curly hair, shea moisture, anti-breakage, sugar cane extract, cleansing (wasn't all shampoo cleansing?)—lined the tub's rim next to the wall. Jelani sat in the tub, staring straight ahead, unmoving, as Sha—holding back tears—knelt on the plush floor rug and bathed her with body wash on a loofah, something she hadn't done for her daughter in over a decade.

Is this really happening? Please wake me up from this nightmare.

Back then, Jelani couldn't sit still in the bathtub. Sha missed the times when the two of them would do everything together, before Jelani's friends had become paramount in her life. Jelani didn't shun Sha as some teenagers did their parents, but the times they went out together, just the two of them, were less frequent.

As the water drained from the tub, Sha wrapped Jelani in an oversize gray towel and led her to her bedroom, leaving only for a moment to prepare a mug of hot chocolate with marshmallows.

She placed the drink on the nightstand next to an empty

can. Why her daughter consumed energy drinks was beyond Sha. Between cheerleading practice and going out with her friends, she barely found time to study. The mug rested untouched for two minutes.

Sha pointed. "I'm not leaving until you drink it."

Jelani hesitated, grasped the mug in both hands, and took a tentative sip.

Sha pried it out of her hands. "I didn't mean now. It's still hot."

Jelani did not react.

"Is there anything else you need?"

No response.

Sha blew on the hot cocoa and handed the cup back. When Jelani finished its contents, she crawled under the covers. Sha tucked her in—something else she hadn't done since her daughter was a child—and perched on the edge of the bed.

Jelani's breathing slowed, then she sat up, her eyes bulging. "Mom, are the doors locked?"

"Of course, sweetie."

"Are all the windows closed?"

"Yes."

"Are you sure?"

"I'm sure."

"Did you set the alarm?"

"Not yet, but I'll do it now." Sha dug her phone out of her jeans and entered the code into her home security app. She returned the phone to her pocket and stroked her daughter's hair. "There, it's all set. Go to sleep. No one can harm you here; I won't let him."

Jelani lay down again. Sha lay next to her and wrapped an arm around her, remaining in that position until Jelani's breathing slowed.

At the door, Sha turned off the light and looked back at her sleeping daughter. She left the door open a crack in case Jelani cried out during the night.

Sha returned to her own bedroom down the hall. Without turning on the light, she crossed the dark gray hardwood floors toward her king-size bed, but she didn't make it to her destination. As her feet touched the area rug underneath the bed, her legs gave way, no longer able to support her. She fell to the rug in tears, covering her face with her hands to muffle her moans.

She'd allowed what had happened to her to happen to Jelani. This was her fault. She was a bad mother. Was this her punishment for past sins?

No. This wasn't her fault. It was his fault. Whoever he was. Sha cried for her daughter's lost innocence. She wished her mother or grandmother were here to guide her.

After what might have been minutes or hours, she crawled to the side of the bed and knelt. She slammed her fist on the top of the bedspread, then slammed it again and again and again until she had no energy left. Until there was only one thing left to do. She placed her elbows on the bedspread, clasped her hands together, and closed her eyes. Sha couldn't remember the last time she'd prayed or set foot in a church, but now she prayed to God to heal Jelani—to heal *her*—and to forgive her for failing to protect her child. Though she was grateful that Jelani was alive, she felt helpless. Her daughter's life would never be the same.

History had repeated itself. She and her daughter were connected by a shared experience as well as by blood. Sha had put that long-ago night in a box and left it unopened. She would rather experience that pain a thousand times again than allow Jelani to experience it once.

Sha climbed onto her bed fully clothed. She lay awake for hours, replaying the night in her mind. While she had been watching a meaningless basketball game, someone had hurt her daughter.

When Sha woke up the following morning, Jelani was curled up beside her.

CHAPTER ELEVEN

OLIVIA

"MRS. BRADLEY!"

Olivia paused before she inserted the key into the brownstone's front door. "Good evening, Mr. Brown."

The old man leaned against the broom he had been using to sweep his stoop. He pointed to his flower beds. "My phlox will be blooming soon."

Olivia didn't bother looking. "I'm sure they'll be beautiful. Have a nice evening."

She entered the house, shut the door, and shrugged off the strap of her brown leather briefcase, followed by her purse and her red coat with the black velour collar. She hung the coat in the closet next to her husband's Members Only jacket, slipped off her black pumps, and leaned against the antique-white-painted wall to rub each aching arch. Her fourteen-carat gold earrings and matching necklace came off next. She placed them with her keys in a bowl on the foyer's slim table, then checked her appearance in the mirror above it. Her swept-back, straightened brown hair looked the same as when she'd left the house twelve hours ago. Hairspray was a wonderful thing. Her eyebrows were waxed to perfection from her weekly visit to the salon. The make-up she'd applied to her oval face that morning was still flawless.

Olivia padded along the hallway floor's large mahogany planks, passing the family room on her right and her home office on the left, then the living room opposite the staircase that led to the second floor.

She pushed the kitchen door open. "Something smells good."

Her husband, Davis, stood at the stove with his broad back to her. He turned, revealing a cooking apron with an Eagles logo. "There you are!"

His face lit up as it had every time Olivia had arrived home over the thirteen years they'd been living together. Olivia wondered if he ever had a stressful day at work. She wrapped her arms around his thickening waist and leaned her head against his back. The smell of the TCB product he used on his short afro and of his perspiration after a full day's work intermingled with the aroma of garlic, onions, and seasoned meatballs wafting up from the saucepan.

Davis wouldn't have stood out in a crowd. His hair, parted on the side, showed flecks of gray. He was still wearing the tan polyester suit pants and brown-striped, white-collared shirt he'd worn to work. One button of the shirt was unbuttoned, and the top of a white T-shirt was visible underneath. His pale-blue- and brown-striped tie hung from the back of his chair. He no longer sported long sideburns as he had a few years ago, but he'd kept the mustache.

Olivia squeezed Davis once more and kissed him perfunctorily on the cheek. Davis returned his gaze to the saucepan. On the adjacent burner, steam rose from a large pot of pasta. Davis never used a cookbook or measuring cups or spoons; he cooked by feel. Olivia stepped around the open dishwasher—Davis liked to clean as he cooked so he wouldn't face most of the mess after dinner—crossed the tile floor, removed her black suit jacket, and took a seat at the round oak kitchen table. There were three chairs and two place settings.

When their daughter, Nicole, had left for college, their quiet home had become quieter.

After Olivia had accepted Davis's marriage proposal, she'd called her mother, who'd worried that they were too young to wed. Olivia had said, "He is good to me. Good to Nicole. Just like Daddy was to you." Kind, gentle, and thoughtful, Davis encouraged and built Olivia up. He considered her needs and listened to her vent about work, since, in her position, she had no one else. The boss must keep workplace woes to herself. Olivia could be herself with Davis, not have to be so strong.

Davis was the father Nicole never had; it had never mattered to him that she wasn't his biological child. He'd say, "My blood doesn't make her my daughter. She's my daughter, because she is a part of my soul." And it hadn't mattered to Nicole either. She'd never met her biological father and, over the years, she'd stopped mentioning him. Earlier in their marriage, Olivia and Davis had discussed having a child together, although it would have derailed her legal career—possibly forever. Davis had refused, wanting Olivia to concentrate on her career. Nicole was enough for him; raising her fulfilled him.

As Davis stirred the pasta, Olivia said, "I'm the luckiest woman alive. A handsome man who cooks and cleans?"

Davis shook his head. "I'm the lucky one."

"No, I am. Most men would wait for their wives to come home from work and cook. If their wives even work, in the first place."

"I'm not most men. I love working women."

Olivia cocked her head. "Women?"

"Woman."

She smiled. "That's better."

As a budget analyst for the city of Philadelphia, Davis worked a predictable nine-to-five workday. He left home after Olivia did and returned long before her, which was why he made dinner—not to mention that he was the much better cook. He'd walked Nicole to the school bus stop, leaving work early to meet her there after both elementary and secondary school, and driven her to her high school debate tournaments.

Olivia sighed, unable to remember the last time she'd only worked an eight-hour day.

"What's the sigh for?" Davis asked.

Olivia rubbed the instep of her foot through the nylon pantyhose, a second skin. "The plaintiffs aren't budging despite our client's significant settlement offer. Looks as if we're going to trial."

Davis opened a bottle of red wine and poured her a glass. "Meaning more late nights and weekends."

"That's me," Olivia said lightly, trying to avoid a recurring discussion topic, "always prepared."

Ever since she'd started her career as a public defender, Olivia had loved the strategic challenge of the courtroom: knowing when to press her advantage, retreat and regroup, or live with the loss of a battle if it meant winning the war. Success wasn't achieved in a straight line, and it could be taken away at any moment…though that wasn't really true unless she committed a crime or an act of gross negligence. But for Olivia, it was not only about being right in a legal argument. It was the approach. The analytical rigor. The philosophical journey. Devising an elegant solution. The billable hours, the client satisfaction, and the closing of the deal were important, but it was how she performed her work that brought her the most satisfaction.

Her year as a public defender had been hard. She'd made little money, and the stress of witnessing the worst ills that people could inflict on one another had been difficult. But Davis was amazing. He'd chosen a nine-to-five job so he could take Nicole to school and pick her up from the babysitter's apartment afterward. Five years ago, Olivia had become a partner at Penn, Franklin, & Ross, one of the country's largest law firms. Few Black attorneys worked for the firm. As the only Black female lawyer and partner, she'd reached the pinnacle. She'd made it. Now her only aspiration was to work on interesting and challenging cases.

Davis crossed the kitchen carrying two plates and kissed

her on the forehead. "That's you. But you should take some time off first."

"I can't, or I'll never catch up."

"I guess that means more late dinners, but I'm proud of you."

Olivia flushed with pleasure. Davis's pride in her achievements never grew old. She didn't need his validation, but she welcomed it.

Davis placed a dark blue plate piled with linguine and gigantic meatballs on the placemat before her, and another on his setting. His gold watch showed it was 8:00 p.m. Olivia loved to eat. She recalled her grandmother's backyard feasts, especially her fried chicken and mustard greens. The aroma of these foods always took Olivia back to Harlem. Davis grabbed a plate of garlic bread from the microwave oven, proclaiming this new appliance was the greatest invention ever.

Sprinkling parmesan cheese onto their pasta, he asked Olivia why she was smiling.

"I'm thinking of the night we met."

"It took me a while to gather up the courage to speak to you."

Olivia sipped her wine. "Why?"

"You were so…haughty."

She set down her glass. "Haughty?"

"I didn't think you'd give me the time of day. I scared most girls away."

"What did you do?"

"I was too nice."

Olivia shook her head at their idiocy. "Lucky me."

"You had it all together. You didn't need anyone."

"Meanwhile, my haughty self was wondering what took you so long to ask me out." She paused. "I thought you were into guys."

Davis almost spat out a meatball. "You thought I was gay?"

"The way you stared at those boys dancing…"

"I was looking at the women!"

She frowned. "That's even worse."

"I was watching them dance. That's all. You know I'm not much of a dancer. I was going to copy their moves if I ever got up the nerve to ask you to dance. I only had eyes for you. Then and now."

"Good save."

Davis leaned forward and kissed her passionately. A tingle started in Olivia's chest and trailed down to her stomach.

"Still think I'm gay?" he asked.

"Ooh, child…no."

He leaned in to kiss her again.

"I need to finish a brief tonight," Olivia said quietly.

Davis sat back. "Delaying tactics might be successful in the courtroom, but they sure do kill the mood."

"It should only take an hour. I promise."

"Okay." Davis twirled his pasta with his fork. "How long will the trial last?"

A casual question that was anything but.

"It could be months." Olivia slid the noodles into her mouth.

"Nicole's graduation is in three weeks. Will you be able to attend?"

Olivia finished chewing. "Nothing can keep me away."

CHAPTER TWELVE

AUGUSTA

JEAN HELD THE door for Augusta as they entered a four-story brick apartment building on West 136th Street. Augusta's heart beat against her rib cage with every step as they walked up three flights of stairs squeezing by the people sitting on them. She was attending her first literary party!

In the darkened hallway on the fourth floor, they navigated between guests in deep conversations, sitting on the floor or leaning against the plastered, peeling walls and made their way to an open door at the end of the hall. Tapestries covered two of the black and red walls. The smell of cigarettes and liquor greeted them at the entrance to the apartment. Inside, people crowded together on couches. A Louis Armstrong record was playing on a Victrola gramophone, but no one was dancing. Most of the guests were holding cocktail glasses or cigarettes, sometimes both.

Jean spotted his musician friends and led Augusta over to

them. After introducing her, he joined the discussion about how some artists were recording their music. He argued that a purist performed live; it left no room for the artist to make mistakes and didn't allow for a producer to gloss over the musicians' incompetence.

Augusta wished she'd invited her best friends, having seen little of Florence and Marian since she started dating Jean. She used to go over to either of their houses after work to do "homework." In actuality, her two friends gossiped about their classmates and fantasized about their futures: who they were going to marry, the type of house they would live in, and how many children they would have. Augusta had kept her dreams to herself; her friends wouldn't have understood them. Florence and Marian didn't care for school or books, and only the presence of all these handsome men could have convinced them to attend this party. Augusta's own handsome man was engrossed in his animated conversation. Augusta wasn't here to discuss music; she wanted to talk about books.

"I'm going to fetch something to drink," she told Jean.

"You want me to get it for you?"

"I can manage."

He kissed her on the cheek. "I'll miss you every moment you're gone."

Augusta meandered over to where a group gathered around a slender man sitting in a wingback chair, holding court. He appeared to be forty, her mother's age. His retinue sat on chairs and ottomans; others lounged on the thin beige carpet.

"Ironic, isn't it?" the man said, in a high-pitched voice, in response to a question. He waved his arm, encompassing the room. "We are all struggling Negro writers. Artists. But even though we are in a mecca for Negros, our white benefactors bestow on us mere coins for our efforts, like plantation owners doling out an extra serving of slop to a deserving slave. Instead of picking cotton, we write books, plays, and poetry."

"But we have to accept the money," said a young, round-faced man. "Royalties alone don't cut it."

Another man with a mustache exhaled smoke from his pipe. "Writing's much better than picking cotton. Our work isn't as hard, and we work inside, where it's not hot."

"Speak for yourself," another man objected. "My apartment is like an oven in the summer."

"And we're not whipped," said a woman perched on an ottoman.

"Not literally," said the man with the pipe. "Though the reviews for my latest book make it feel that way."

"We might have the same reviewers," said the man with the round face.

Several people nodded as the group laughed. One guy said, "You've got that right."

The man in the chair laughed, then grew serious. He sipped a clear liquid from a glass, which he then set back on the small table next to him. "The white man controls the stories we tell and resists promoting our work. The quality of what we pen doesn't matter because we wrote it with a colored hand. How can we change—"

Augusta felt a presence beside her.

"Do you know who that is?" a man asked her.

"Nuh-uh."

"Alain Locke."

Augusta's breath caught in her chest.

She turned back to face the famous writer, who was changing how Negroes viewed themselves and encouraging them to embrace their African heritage while integrating with white Americans.

She should have brought his book with her so he could sign it.

Augusta's new literary guide was several shades darker than Jean. His hair was pressed, and his brown eyes were framed by round-rimmed glasses. Like most of the men in the apartment, he wore a three-piece Oxford suit.

He pointed. "Over there is Langston Hughes. Dapper fellow, isn't he? And over there talking to Claude McKay is Jessie Fauset. You'll want to meet her. She makes things go in this town. Over my right shoulder are Richard Wright and W. E. B. Du Bois. And don't look, but Zora Neale Hurston just walked by us."

Augusta gasped. She almost pulled a muscle, craning her neck to see the woman. "I love her work."

"It is original, like the author." He grinned. "And I told you not to look."

Augusta blushed. "Sorry. How do you know these authors?"

"I'm a writer; I attend a lot of these parties."

"I've never seen so many writers in one place."

"You are in the presence of the intellectual elite. The Niggerati. Isn't it wonderful?" He extended his hand. "I'm Richmond St. Clair. I just signed with Harper Brothers."

He leaned in and whispered, "I am one of their few Negro authors."

Augusta hesitated, then shook his hand. "Augusta Gibson."

"Augusta, what a pretty name. It means reverence. Grandeur. Dignity."

Warmth spread through Augusta. Desperate to change the subject, she pointed at a tall, handsome, confident man with wavy hair, his hands jammed into the pockets of his brown tweed trousers. "Is he a writer, too?"

Richmond shook his head. "That's Hubert T. Delany. He's at NYU law school and teaches at an elementary school here in Harlem. Like me, when I'm not writing."

Across the room, Jean was still in deep conversation with his musician friends.

"What's it like?" Augusta asked.

"Being a teacher?"

"No, a writer."

"Like breathing."

"You can't live without it?"

"Sounds about right. Do you write?"

"I'm a reader."

"Then you could be a writer."

Augusta had never thought of becoming a writer herself. Sure, she had written essays for school and even won a first-place prize for a story she wrote. But to have a reader devour her words, as she did with the books she read, or to change the public's consciousness, like Mr. Locke or Ms. Hurston or Mr. Hughes…

"How long have you lived in Harlem?" Richmond asked.

"All of my life."

"Me, too. They lynched my granddaddy in Mississippi. The day after they buried him, my grandma packed up our belongings and moved our family here."

"You say it so casually."

Richmond shrugged. "My anger is all used up."

"What did your granddaddy do? To get lynched?"

Richmond looked at her, puzzled. "When you're a Negro, you don't have to do anything." He paused. "I'll have my revenge, though."

"How?"

"The book I'm writing is a fictionalized account of what happened to my grandfather." There was a gleam in his eyes. "But with a different ending."

"Sounds fascinating. I can't wait to read it."

"I'd like that," Richmond said, smiling. His smile soon faded. "My grandmother's gone. I miss her. She was the backbone of our family. She taught me how to read."

When she was young, Augusta's mama had told her that there was a time when colored people weren't allowed to read. Augusta couldn't imagine a world without books. She did not take the right for granted.

"Mine, too." Augusta's voice became quiet. "She died five years ago." Brightening, she said, "Maybe someday I could write a story about how she escaped from slavery and started a new life for herself."

"You should," Richmond said eagerly. "I believe art and literature elevate our race."

"Especially the literature created by the people in this room."

"What are you reading now?"

"*The Autobiography of*—"

"Auggie?" came Jean's voice from behind her.

Augusta started.

Jean looped his arm around her waist and nuzzled her neck with his nose. To Richmond, he said, "I'm Jean. Auggie's boyfriend. And you are?"

Richmond held out his hand. "Richmond St. Clair."

Jean never shook men's hands. In fact, Augusta had never seen him touch a man, even his friends.

He turned to her. "We're leaving."

"So soon?" she asked.

"It's a school night; I promised your mother I'd get you home early. And I don't break my promises."

"I was going to introduce her to Mr. Locke," said Richmond.

"No need, good fellow. I can introduce her. Let's go, dear."

"It was nice talking to you," Richmond said to Augusta.

"You, too," Augusta replied.

Jean pressed his hand against Augusta's lower back as he guided her toward the door.

"What about Mr. Locke?" she asked.

He glanced over to where Alain Locke was still pontificating to his eager acolytes.

"The cat looks busy. There will be many parties. I'll introduce you to him next time."

"Really?"

"I promise."

CHAPTER THIRTEEN

DINAH

A FEW MORNINGS after being assigned to the great house, in a small room off the kitchen, Dinah heated the bottom of a sadiron on the Dutch oven in the brick fireplace. She gripped the smooth wooden handle and bore the iron down onto the smooth fabric of Nicholas's trousers. A pile of his clothes brought to her by a house girl rested on the thin rectangular table. She was glad Martha had suggested keeping another sadiron heating on the stove; she could just switch out the handle without waiting for the one she was using to reheat.

After she completed the ironing, she helped Martha prepare supper. While the cook was placing a pan of tarts in the oven and Dinah was cutting up another red apple, Beaux nudged open the kitchen's swinging door with the toe of his boot and leaned in. Dinah and Martha stopped what they were doing and stood at attention more swiftly than any man serving in the militia. The bowl Dinah had been filling tipped over, and apples bounced across the table and onto the maple floor. Dinah's stomach rumbled from the apple tarts' aroma.

Beaux entered, ambling over to where one wayward apple stopped rolling. He picked it up, inspected it, and rubbed it against his shirt before spitting out his toothpick, taking a bite, and grinning. "What's a little dirt?"

When neither woman answered, his gaze skipped the older woman and landed on Dinah.

"Boy, it's hot out there. Fetch me some water, girl."

"Yes, sir."

Summer was experiencing its last gasp before fall. Although the windows were open throughout the house, only hot air blew in. A water pitcher sat on the table, replenished from the backyard well by one of the slave children over the course of the day. Dinah hustled to retrieve a glass from the cupboard and filled it to the brim. As she crossed the room, the liquid crested over the top and spilled onto the floor. With downcast eyes, she raised the glass to Beaux, whose fingertips brushed her hand as he accepted it. He placed the half-eaten apple in her empty hand. Unsure what to do, she held it. Its juice seeped between her fingers. Revulsion rippled through her, but she didn't dare react.

Beaux stared at her as he drank the water, wiped his lips with the back of his hand, and handed her the glass, a smug look on his face. "More."

She set the apple core on the table and wiped her hands on her dress. She refilled the glass, leaving room at the top this time, and handed it to him without spillage. Beaux gulped this one down, too. He held her hand and placed the glass within it. His hands were soft.

"See you at supper," he said.

The smirk on his face froze when he saw Martha's expression. He backed out of the room, leaving behind the scent of tobacco.

Martha, her hair wrapped in a white scarf, shook her head as soon as the door swung closed. "That one," she said. She turned back to the oven and lifted a long wooden spoon to taste her potato soup. The faded scars on her hands exhibited the number of times she'd missed her mark chopping vegetables and slicing meats. "His charm don't work on me. Don't let it work on you."

Dinah glanced at the door, hoping Beaux wasn't listening. "What do you mean?"

"You're not fooling me, acting like you don't know what he's doing. All you have to do is look into his demon eyes to know what he's up to."

Dinah picked the remaining apples off the floor and rinsed them with water from the pitcher. She sat at the table and returned them to the bowl. She began cutting carrots for the soup.

Martha's round, dark-brown cheeks shone from the oven's heat. "I see the way he looks at you." She sized Dinah up. "Like he wants to eat you for breakfast." She shook her head vigorously and turned back to the pot. "It ain't right. Them needs to stick to their own kind."

Dinah chopped up a carrot and tossed it into a bowl. "He's being friendly, is all."

Martha whirled around to face her. "That kind don't

know friendly. They're always wanting something; taking what isn't theirs. And don't you forget it. It happened to your…"

"Who?"

"Never mind." The cook stirred the soup. "I reckon he's the reason you're here," she said softly.

Dinah believed her working in the house had been her momma's doing. Inside, she felt warm. Maybe Beaux cared about her and didn't want her working in the fields.

Martha tasted the soup again. "Enough talk. We need to get ready."

"For what?"

"His wedding."

Dinah's mouth gaped. "Wedding?"

"Your momma didn't tell you? He's marrying the Lawrences' oldest daughter. Anna. Their family is well-to-do. They grow tobacco, too. The ceremony will be here in a few weeks, and—"

Martha continued regaling her with details of the food they would prepare.

Dinah stopped listening. What would it be like to get married in a house like this? To a handsome man? To marry for money or for love, rather than for breeding more slaves?

Dangerous thoughts, she knew, but she contemplated them anyway.

CHAPTER FOURTEEN

SHA

THE MORNING AFTER Jelani's rape, Sha called in sick to work. Her staff would be surprised. As Chief Information Officer of GirlsCode Ventures, a start-up company that helped young girls of color learn how to code, a day off was rare for her. She cared deeply about helping the next generation of female technologists.

Unlike Jelani, Sha hadn't been popular in high school. She'd blended in with the crowd, not wanting to attract attention. She'd become interested in coding when she'd accidentally signed up for a programming class, and she'd been the only Black girl in the class. A fast learner and an eager student, she'd possessed a talent for noticing flaws in code patterns that no one else saw, as well as a keen ability to find the root of a problem. Losing herself in the code, she could program for hours with no thought of eating or sleeping. She'd received a scholarship to the University of California at Berkeley after developing a program that could hack into corporate websites. Her parents could have afforded to send her to any college in the country, but entering this field had required that she move west. She ended up loving Berkley, both the college and the city. It had been the right choice. She'd gained the freedom to be herself. To speak her mind. Until that day…

GirlsCode was her third successful startup—she'd learned a lot from the one that had failed. It was also the most rewarding: discovering the next generation of Black female tech talent and making their journeys easier than her own had been. Sha's job provided her with a sense of purpose and got her out of bed every morning. And the company was making an impact. So far, fifty-seven girls had landed jobs or internships at a slew of tech companies in the Valley. GirlsCode was preparing to expand to Seattle.

Sha no longer worked crazy hours—twelve-, sometimes eighteen-hour days—as she had earlier in her career. Having never been a competitive person, she did not miss the scratching and the clawing required to move ahead at a company. The only person she'd needed to prove anything to was herself, and she'd gotten to where she wanted to be: a challenging job that didn't stress her out. Sometimes, after Jelani went to bed, she coded at night for fun, as her teams did most of the coding at work now.

Sha held the tray in one arm and knocked on Jelani's bedroom door with the other. After a long moment, she heard a faint "come in."

Jelani's backpack, stuffed with books, leaned against her reclaimed wooden sit-stand desk, atop which sat her laptop.

Mounted on the wall were two monitors, her game console resting on a shelf. A silver lamp curled from the desk's corner to illuminate her sleeping laptop. Jelani's dirty clothes were piled in a corner of the room. If she wanted clean ones, she had to wash them herself. Unlike the rest of the house, decorated in gray and white, Jelani's bedroom was pink: pink-painted walls, pink bedspread, pink TV.

Jelani was lying in bed in the fetal position.

Sha set the tray on the nightstand and deftly picked up the pink-case-protected cell phone beside it, without Jelani noticing. She sat beside Jelani and caressed her daughter's cheek. Jelani recoiled. Sha retracted her hand and clasped it in the other, resting both on her lap.

"How are you feeling?" she asked.

"Okay."

"Do you want to discuss what happened?"

"Not really."

"Are you sure?"

"I'm not ready yet."

Sha needed to remain calm. Nothing she could say would make her child feel better. She'd tried to teach Jelani to be strong, just as her own mother had taught her. But she was still trying to understand how to be resilient, herself. A part of Sha wanted to grill her daughter until she told her what had happened and who had done this to her, but it would be counterproductive and only upset Jelani further.

"Are you hungry? I made my special chicken noodle soup."

Jelani rolled over and offered her a weak smile. "Campbell's?"

An old joke between them. Sha wasn't much of a cook. When Jelani was little, Sha used to tell her that the soup was homemade, until, one day, five-year-old Jelani fished the red-and-white can out of the kitchen's trash receptacle and confronted her mother with the evidence.

Sha forced out a laugh. "Sit up."

Jelani moved as if she were ninety years old. Sha arranged the pillows behind her back and placed the tray on her lap. It held a large white bowl of soup, half a sleeve of saltine crackers, and a heavy steel spoon that looked like something from the Middle Ages.

"Eat," Sha said.

Jelani took a tentative spoonful. She didn't love this soup anymore, but Sha loved her for eating it. She probably couldn't stomach much else anyway.

Inwardly, Sha was fuming. While her child was slurping soup she didn't like, her attacker was probably out with his friends eating a pizza or a burger or sushi.

Sha rose and kissed Jelani's forehead. "I'll check on you later. I'll be in my office if you need me."

Sha closed the white French doors to her home office and moved to the ergonomic executive chair behind the glass desk.

Sha pulled the phone she'd swipe off Jelani's nightstand out of her pocket. Leaning back in the chair, Sha stared at the phone's screensaver: a picture of her and Jelani, their heads touching, their hair commingled, their smiles wide, taken last summer while they hiked Big Sur. She hesitated. Not because Jelani's phone was password-protected; Sha decoded tougher passwords at work. Besides, she knew the password. Jelani had told her. Unlike Sha, who changed her passwords every thirty days, her daughter kept the same one.

Sha hesitated because she'd always allowed Jelani her privacy. She believed that their relationship should be based on trust. Her daughter had never given her a reason to inspect her room or her belongings. Today, Sha needed to make an exception. To protect her child, she had to violate that trust.

She pressed the text icon and scanned the messages. There hadn't been any incoming or outgoing texts since she'd found Jelani. Her friends had not checked on her at the club or afterward.

Next, Sha perused the photos. Toward the end of the camera roll were photos of Jelani and her three besties, whom she'd known since kindergarten. The four girls had taken many photos that night, inside and outside of Z21. Their poses were silly or serious, dazzling or provocative. In the background, the bouncer directed an unwelcoming stare at the camera. In the last photograph, Jelani had taken a selfie with a guy unfamiliar to Sha. Sha texted this photo to her own phone and cropped it to display only the young man's face. She navigated to a facial recognition app and uploaded the photo. Within seconds, a name appeared on her screen: ERIK STEVENS.

"Got you," she said.

She perused Jelani's text messages again. Jelani had received texts from guys, including many from Erik, the day and evening of the rape. And before. So, they knew each other. Their texts were typical of teenagers, with many acronyms and emojis.

She deleted the text of Stevens's photo to herself from Jelani's cell. Curious, she pressed Settings and Screen Time. Sha's mouth gaped, although she shouldn't have been surprised. Her daughter spent an average of seven hours a day on social media. Almost a full-time job. Sha locked the phone and made her way to Jelani's room, astonished that Jelani hadn't declared a national emergency that her phone was missing. She poked her head in and found her daughter asleep, clutching a raggedy teddy bear Sha hadn't seen in at least eight years. She stood in the doorway, brushing away her tears, then crossed the bedroom and replaced the phone on its charger on the nightstand. She tugged the comforter up to cover Jelani and the bear, kissed her baby, grabbed the tray of half-eaten soup, and left the room, closing the door quietly behind her.

CHAPTER FIFTEEN

OLIVIA

OLIVIA CRIED WHEN Spelman College President Donald M. Stewart said "Nicole Dinah Bradley" into the microphone and her daughter strode to the front of the cavernous hall. In a black cap and gown with a blue and white sash, complemented with high heels, Nicole walked up the steps and crossed the stage to shake the president's hand. Olivia wasn't only crying with the pride she felt for Nicole's accomplishment, but also at the sight of the other young Black women's smiling faces, their heads held high, diplomas in hand. The rain outside did not drown out the joy within the auditorium.

Olivia recalled the stories of how slave owners had not permitted her ancestors to read, driving them to read in secret. But these women had gained their education publicly and could be proud of it. For most of them, this was the first step toward their future careers. An unexpected sadness suddenly came over Olivia. A feeling of loss. Her baby would never live at home again.

Olivia had taken the day off work. The Burlington case was going to trial, and she had three weeks to prepare: finalize the strategy, conduct depositions, assemble the exhibits, and prepare questions for witnesses. So much to do. Despite herself, she thought of time in billable hours. She always felt as if she were missing something: a meeting, a client introduction. Would the partners realize they didn't need her when she wasn't there? The male partners didn't think this way. They always felt wanted. Assured of their place. The firm couldn't survive without them. They all competed for Robert Penn's favor, while she fought to continue to be one of them.

She needed to focus. Today was her daughter's day.

All smiles, Nicole returned to her seat among her classmates.

In the plastic chair to Olivia's right, Davis reached into his back pocket, brought out a white handkerchief, dabbed his eyes, then handed it to her. She wiped her tears, then took his hand. He pursed his lips, reading her thoughts.

"Our daughter looks beautiful," he said, anchoring Olivia to the moment.

An overwhelming love for Nicole flowed through Olivia. As a single mother, she'd worried about whether she had done enough for her child. She'd had to figure a lot out for herself. But she had tried her best.

"She's so happy," Olivia said, crying again. She clasped the light-skinned hand of the older woman seated to her left, the veins too large for such a small hand. She smiled through her tears. "She did it, Mama."

Augusta was crying, too. "Yes, she did."

CHAPTER SIXTEEN

AUGUSTA

"YOU SHOULD HAVE seen the men!"

Florence and Marian listened to Augusta with rapt expressions as she told them about the literary party. The three friends cradled their schoolbooks as they stood in the main hallway between classes at Wadleigh High School for Girls. Saddle or patent-leather shoes squeaked on the scuffed tile floor as other students walked or ran by, talking, laughing, and shouting to each other.

"Tell me more," Marian said in her sultry voice.

Augusta disclosed just enough details to titillate their curiosity. She didn't bother discussing the authors who'd attended and their literary works; her friends would be unfamiliar with and uninterested in them. She told them about Richmond but did not divulge his name or how smart he was. Or that he was good-looking.

Florence's eyes widened. "Was Jean jealous?"

Augusta shrugged. "Why would he be? He's Jean."

"He's serious about you," Marian said.

"Who's serious about her?"

Augusta whirled around. "How long have you been standing there, Ray Ray Walker?"

Ray Ray lived on Augusta's street. She'd known him forever. He had the annoying habit of sneaking up on her.

"You're not talking about that high yella fella I've seen you with in the neighborhood, are you?"

Augusta glared at him. "That's none of your business."

"Something's off with him."

"Well, then it's a good thing you're not dating him."

Florence and Marian giggled.

The bell clanged, signaling it was time for the next class.

"What are you doing here?" Augusta asked.

"Walking my sister home. She's not feeling well. Hey, what are you doing later? Want to go to Pop's with me and have a soda?"

Augusta liked Ray Ray, but he was like a brother to her. He was her age, but shorter and chubby. His brown eyes and dark-complexioned face looked mournful.

"I can't. I have to watch Hale."

"He can come, too."

"I can't, Ray Ray."

Ray Ray hung his head the way he used to when they were twelve years old and Augusta had preferred going to her girl-friends' houses to playing stickball with him. "Next time, then."

"Sure."

Ray Ray ambled away.

"He'll get over it," said Florence.

"Jean's the bee's knees," added Marian. "How could Ray Ray think he could ever compete with him?"

The three friends burst out laughing as a moping Ray Ray shuffled down the hall toward the main office.

❧

The next six weeks were a whirlwind for Augusta.

She and Jean attended performances at the Lincoln Theater, saw the Lafayette Players, and partied at the Renaissance ballroom and the Rockland Palace. Every Saturday night, after Jean's band finished playing their gig, they dropped by one of the rent parties happening in Harlem. The twenty-five-cents admission helped the party's host pay for the apartment's monthly rent payment. Augusta got in for free, along with the rest of the band members' girlfriends. The band would play until dawn. In addition to the music and the dancing, mouth-watering food was served: fried chicken, collard greens, black-eyed peas, and rice.

Many of the luminaries who had been at the first literary party Augusta had attended frequented the same rent parties. Augusta hadn't befriended them, but she'd become acquainted enough to say hello. Once, she'd bumped into Zora Neale Hurston and hoped the floor would open and swallow her. She'd offered a breathless apology, wanting to add "I love your work." Or "I'm a deep admirer of your work." Or "I'm your biggest fan." She'd ended up not saying anything more. The author had joked that Augusta had created a new dance before moving on to talk to someone more interesting. Zora was the life of any party she attended; she could tell a story, written and oral.

Sometimes Augusta saw Richmond at these parties from a distance. He'd nod or wave to her from across the room, but he never spoke to her. He seemed to sense that Jean wouldn't want them to be friends.

The who's who of Harlem attended these parties. Before Jean had come along, Augusta had lived a sheltered life between her family, at home, and her friends at and after school. But now she hung out with the "It" people. The "In" crowd. And she loved every minute of it.

Jean and Augusta would walk down The Stroll, the street for seeing and being seen, stopping at Seventh Avenue and 135th Street to watch people walk by, or hanging out on The Corner at Seventh and 131st, where Jean would scope out other jazz musicians, who came from all over Harlem, jamming on their instruments. Nearby, the Tree of Hope, an elm tree with far-reaching branches, welcomed everyone and provided shade from the sun. The rustling leaves told stories of strength and resilience. The tree purportedly possessed magical powers; people believed that if they rubbed its bark and divulged their dreams, their dreams would come true. Jean had touched the tree to conjure up success for the band, and Augusta had touched it for Jean's success.

During this time, Jean bought Augusta many gifts. At first, they were inexpensive ones like trinkets, chocolates, or a flower. Then they became more expensive: hats, dresses with mesh bags to match (which he bought from Rose's), and a diamond bracelet for her high school graduation.

After she graduated, she and Jean were together every night. She no longer had to study and didn't have time to read.

One Saturday, after a late lunch, they strolled arm-in-arm along Lenox Avenue's ample sidewalk. Lattice-like clouds offered little relief from the July sun. Streetcars and automobiles navigated the expansive street, while traders hawked their wares on pushcarts parked alongside the curbs in between cars.

Augusta glanced at Jean. "Lunch was delightful."

"Thank you, my dear."

Jean was wearing a cream-colored, three-piece wool summer suit. Despite the material, he never sweat. Augusta was wearing an eggshell-white dress and a straw hat.

As they passed by storefronts, Augusta spotted a bookstore and stepped to the window, shading her eyes from the glare of the sun's reflection. Books filled the display. On a small stand next to each book was a photograph of the author and a card summarizing the book's contents. All the authors were Negroes. A small sign in the window's corner bore the words Negro- Owned.

Something Augusta hadn't felt in months stirred inside her. She spun around, bouncing on the balls of her feet. "Can we go in?"

"We don't have time, Auggie. My set starts at six."

"Please?"

"When you look at me that way, how can I ever deny you? We'll come back tomorrow. I promise."

Augusta was disappointed, but at least tomorrow she would have more time to browse.

They resumed walking.

A pregnant woman walked in their direction holding a man's arm, presumably her husband's. Her long hair was pulled back into a tight bun. Jean tipped his cap to the couple and smiled. He was friendly with everyone. The woman averted her eyes.

"Who was that?" Augusta asked.

"Beats me," he said.

"She acted as if she knew you."

"Maybe she's heard me play." Jean tucked Augusta's arm in his. "We should get married."

Augusta's heart leaped. "I'm only eighteen."

He shrugged. "You're old enough. We can start a family. Have beautiful babies together."

"How many children do you want?"

"Six."

"Six! Who's going to have all those babies?"

Jean stopped in the middle of the sidewalk. Passersby veered around them. Jean grabbed Augusta's hands and brought them to his heart. He kissed her nose.

"You are, my dear."

CHAPTER SEVENTEEN

DINAH

DINAH CARRIED AN enormous bouquet into the ball-room, where the wedding was to take place. The scent of the roses, bougainvillea, and lilies filled her nostrils. Was this what heaven smelled like? She couldn't see in front of her, so she had to rely on her momma's directions to guide her to the table at the far end of the room.

When Dinah had first started working in the house, she'd polish the furniture, then misplace the items that sat on top of them. Her momma would follow behind her and set the items in the right place before the mistress could discover Dinah's mistakes.

After several weeks, her momma no longer had to cover up for her or tell her what to do.

Although Mrs. Devereaux was the mistress of the house, it was Celia who commanded the other slaves as, in synchronized movements, they prepared the house for the festivities.

Most of them had not yet been born when Master Sam Devereaux married Elizabeth Alston thirty years ago. Dinah's grandmother, Aisha, had been the house conductor then.

Over the past week, the slaves had swept the vast balcony, washed the antebellum house's exterior, cleaned every interior surface, polished the wood and brass, snapped white tablecloths over the tables, and set out the porcelain cups and silverware. Earlier, Dinah had helped Celia convert Beaux's second-floor bedroom to a marital one by picking his discarded shirts and breeches off the floor, airing out the mattress and placing new sheets on the feather bed, replacing the bedspread with a colorful quilt, organizing perfumes on the vanity table, and hanging fresh, floral-printed towels on the washstand's side rail.

Dinah finished arranging the flowers and candlesticks on the table and returned to the kitchen, where Martha was cooking a feast: hens, hams, turkeys, ducks, potatoes, and beans. For dessert, she was baking sweet potato pies, Sally White fruit cakes, and apple turnovers. Dinah's mouth watered as she helped the cook. Iron pots, skillets, and baking pans occupied every surface of the spacious room.

Martha used a white towel to wipe the flour from her hands. "I need you to stay late tonight."

"Yes, Ms. Martha."

They worked through the afternoon and evening.

Later, the cook removed the towel from her shoulder—the daily signal her workday had ended—then folded it and placed it on the table.

"We ain't doing any more tonight. Be back here at dawn tomorrow. Get on home. The mistress will be here soon."

Every night prior to retiring to her bedroom, Elizabeth Devereaux locked the kitchen doors to prevent any slaves from reentering the house and taking food back with them to the quarters.

Dinah removed her apron, her eyelids heavy. The slaves had been working every day from dawn to midnight readying the house for Beaux's nuptials. She hadn't seen Beaux. He'd been traveling to and from Raleigh to get fitted for his suit and attend to other preparations. The boy who took care of the horses said Beaux came home drunk most nights, barely sitting upright on his mare. Sometimes, he didn't return until the following day.

"He smells good," the boy had told his father, who'd repeated it to other slaves. "Sweet. Like a flower, tho' each night it's a different smell."

Dinah lingered in the kitchen after Martha left. The house was quiet. She tiptoed back along the hallway's wide wooden planks, entered the ballroom, and didn't stop until she reached the middle of the floor. Crown molding surrounded the high ceiling. In its center, the chandelier held fifty candles. Dinah lifted her arms and twirled, then twirled again, the bottom of her simple dress floating in the air.

A chair scraped against the floor upstairs. Then a floorboard creaked from a footstep. Dinah didn't wait to find out who it was. She rushed to the back of the house, grabbed her shawl from the hook, and stepped outside, closing the door noiselessly behind her.

She breathed in the cool night air and wrapped the shawl tightly around her. Bright stars blanketed the sky. Several years ago, a boy who was sweet on her had told her that if she made a wish when a star fell, her dreams would come true. She didn't believe him and hadn't bothered to make a wish. Instead, she'd gazed at the stars because they were pretty, as if they were twinkling only for her. How far away were they?

The hair on her arms prickled as if she were being watched. She needed to get home. Her momma had left the house hours ago and would be worried. She'd scold Dinah for wasting time looking at the sky.

"I've been waiting for you."

Dinah jumped and yelped. She spun around, her heart thumping so hard she thought it might pop out of her chest. Beaux slouched against the house's back wall. His face was masked by the shadows, but she knew his voice. He pushed off the wall and stepped toward her until he was no longer in darkness. Dinah stepped back.

Beaux pointed upward. "I saw you looking." His Adam's apple stuck out. "Beautiful, huh?"

Dinah looked up but said nothing.

"That one is Polaris, the North Star." He moved his arm, pointing out the brightest ones. "There's Sirius. Vega. Pleiades."

The stars have names? "How do you…know all that?"

He chuckled. "Must've been paying attention in school that day. You don't talk much. Not like you used to when we were kids. Back then, you couldn't stop talking about things." He paused. "I know why you don't now, but still… I want to hear your voice. Say my name."

Dinah wrung her hands. "Master…Master Beaux."

He drank from a brown bottle.

"Nuh-uh." He stepped closer. His breath stank of liquor, tobacco, and smoked meat. "Just my given name."

"The mistress said we should call you Master Beaux."

"I don't care what my mama said." Another step. "Say my name."

"Buh…Beaux."

"That's better." He raised the bottle to her. "Want some?"

"No."

"More for me, then." He took another swig and stared at the bottle. "The fellows had a party for me tonight at the broth…a tavern in town. It was my last night of freedom. Ah…but you wouldn't know anything about that."

Dinah shivered. Whether from the coolness of the nighttime air or her proximity to Beaux or the length of this conversation, she wasn't sure.

"Cold?" he asked.

"Master…sir…I need to get home to rest for your big day tomorrow."

"Big day. Right."

He guzzled the bottle's remaining contents and threw it away from the house. It didn't make a sound when it landed on the grass. He removed his frock and slipped it around her shoulders, his hands holding the lapels on either side.

"I could have bedded any girl tonight, but I only wanted one."

"And…and…you'll see her tomorrow."

He guffawed. "Silly girl, I'm not talking about her." Beaux's eyes were shiny from the liquor or excitement. "I can't stop thinking about you." He kissed her hard. His breath was foul, the skin around his lips rough with stubble.

Dinah had never kissed a man.

Beaux pulled back. "That wasn't so bad…was it?" He leaned in to kiss her again. Dinah averted her face.

"Master, I need to get—"

In the quiet night, the slap sounded like a rifle shot. It stung. Beaux stifled Dinah's howl with his hand, then with his mouth. Lifting her, he carried her, lurching, into the shadows. His tongue forced her lips apart. She couldn't move. Her arms were pinned to the sides of her body, still trapped within his coat.

A magnolia tree branch scraped against the outer wall of the house.

As Beaux continued to explore Dinah's mouth, he pressed her against the back wall of the house. He reached inside his frock, then her shawl. When he cupped her breasts on the outside of her dress, her nipples hardened. Dinah didn't understand why. She didn't want them to. Beaux grinned. Dinah tried to move her arms, free herself from the frock. Beaux slapped her again. This time, she expected the blow, but the pain hurt no less. A metallic flavor filled her mouth. Beaux kissed her, his tongue probing as if seeking her blood, seeking to possess her—all of her. He ripped the front of the dress and rubbed and pinched her breasts. It hurt. His manhood swelled between them. Dinah struggled against it, which only made him breathe harder, then scratched his face.

"God damn it!" he yelled. He reared back and punched her. Stars swam around her head, much closer than the ones she'd been gazing at earlier.

Beaux unbuttoned his trousers, hoisted her skirt, covered her mouth again, grabbed her hips, and entered her.

A searing pain split her in two, as if he'd stabbed her with Martha's largest kitchen knife. She screamed into his mouth. He grunted and pumped hard into her, and as he did, she stared at the stars, the real stars in the inky night, willing herself to be up there twirling with them instead of down here with him.

One, two, three, four, five…

Finally, a guttural groan escaped from somewhere deep within Beaux. He sighed, then lay still. After a while, he pulled out his member, and Dinah fell to her knees, her legs unable to support her. He buttoned his trousers and crouched beside her.

"Next time," he said, "don't be so difficult."

Dinah whimpered.

Beaux stroked her hair. "What did you say, dear?"

Dinah bit her tongue. If she were silent, maybe he would leave. His hand dropped to her cheek, which he rubbed with his knuckles, oblivious to the pain shooting through her from the bruises he'd imprinted there.

"You will always belong to me," he said.

Dinah later reckoned she must have passed out. Her momma found her lying there, alone, still wearing Beaux's frock.

CHAPTER EIGHTEEN

OLIVIA

TWO MONTHS AFTER Nicole graduated from Spelman, Olivia heard Prince's "Why You Wanna Treat Me So Bad" coming from her daughter's bedroom.

Olivia tightened the belt on her lavender terrycloth robe and leaned against the door frame. "What are you doing?"

Nicole was still dressed in her going-out clothes: high-waisted, acid-washed jeans, an off-the-shoulder gray sweatshirt, and, under it, a white A-frame T-shirt. Her arm sported a pink Swatch and more jelly bracelets than Olivia could count. Although it was seventy degrees outside, there was a jean jacket with Nicole's name embroidered in purple cursive over the left breast slung over her desk chair. Her white high-tops were stacked in front of her closet. Nicole, whose narrow face—the same shade as Davis's—was beautiful without makeup, wore blue eye shadow, red blush, and clear lip gloss. The scent of her Poison Girl perfume reached Olivia's nostrils in the doorway.

Nicole pressed the STOP button on her Sony radio cassette player. "Making a tape for Tara. She's moving to New York soon."

A small birthmark dotted her forearm. Olivia was marked in the same place.

"That's nice. What's in New York?"

"A job. She'll be a systems analyst at IBM," Nicole gushed. She did everything fast: talk, eat, and walk.

She had yet to tell Olivia her own career plans. Olivia hadn't wanted to push.

"Did you have fun tonight?"

"Yes and no."

Olivia frowned. "Why is that? Where did you go?"

"Tower Records. We didn't buy anything. Just hung out."

Nicole had been popular in high school, part of the cool crowd. Olivia could afford to send her to a private school, but she had wanted to stay with her friends, whom she'd known since junior high. Olivia hadn't wanted to be one of those over-doting mothers. She'd given Nicole a lot of freedom, trusting she would do the right thing.

Alice Walker's *The Color Purple* rested on Nicole's nightstand next to a white phone and a solved Rubik's Cube. A thirteen-inch TV and Nicole's high school cross-country running and cheerleading trophies sat on a white dresser. More paperbacks lined a shelf attached to the wall, along with the complete Encyclopedia Britannica. Eight years ago, Davis had bought the collection from a door-to-door salesman. Nicole had read every volume. A Commodore 64 rested on her white desk. Even the shag carpet was white—Nicole's favorite color.

"And what part of it wasn't fun?"

Nicole snorted. "You should see your face. You hate not knowing the answer to something!"

"Knowing the answers is my job, as a lawyer and a mother. Now, out with it!"

"Because I was saying goodbye."

"Goodbye?"

"I got it! I got the job!"

Olivia didn't ask why Nicole hadn't told her before telling her friends. Instead, she let out a "whoop," hustled over to the bed, and threw her arms around her daughter. They bounced up and down. Nicole's Jheri curls brushed against Olivia's face. When Nicole was a girl and it was just the two of them, Olivia would relax her daughter's long brown hair in the bathtub of the first apartment's cramped bathroom. Kneeling, she'd lean over the rim, the pile bath rug inadequate protection for her knees against the tile floor.

"My baby has landed her first grown-up job." Olivia leaned back. "Who's the lucky employer?"

Nicole's smile faltered. "National & World News Network."

Olivia's smile evaporated. A pang stabbed her stomach, and she relaxed her embrace. "But that's in Atlanta."

Nicole had never wanted to be an attorney, despite her debating skills and Olivia's entreaties. When she'd selected mass communications as her major at Spelman, Olivia had clung to a sliver of hope that she'd still go to law school.

"I know you and Dad wanted me to stay close to home… that's why I was hesitant to tell you."

"Every national TV network has an affiliate in Philadelphia. I can cite many reasons you should stay here."

"Mother, we're not in court! Besides, it's not the same. You don't understand. NWNN's going to be huge. Global. And I want to be a part of it."

"What did your dad say?"

"He's all for it. He wants me to be happy and to follow my dreams."

Olivia sighed. "He would say that. Are you sure this is what you want?"

Nicole's gaze intensified. "I'm called to do this. Don't you remember what that feels like? You didn't choose the law; it chose you." She was right. Olivia would have chosen the profession even if her grandmother hadn't encouraged her. The courtroom was her second home. Davis would say it was her first home. "You should be happy for me! NWNN is amazing! After graduation, I took Dad on a tour and he was impressed with the complex."

Davis had shown Olivia the Polaroids he'd taken of the network's facilities. She had left for Philly right after Nicole's graduation to prepare for a deposition. She'd also missed the celebratory dinner at Atlanta's best restaurant, The Abbey. Her mother and Davis had said the food was delicious, and that Nicole hadn't been able to stop talking throughout the meal.

"I'm sorry I missed it," Olivia said. "What will you do at the network?"

Nicole gave her a broad grin. "I'll be an assistant producer. Same duties as when I interned there last summer, except that it's full time and I'll get paid."

Olivia hid her disappointment behind a smile. "It sounds like a wonderful opportunity. When do you start?"

"In two weeks."

"Two weeks!"

"I already found an apartment. On my own."

"You did?"

"Don't look so surprised. I found it through the Atlanta paper. Dad offered to help me move. Will you be able to go with us? He thinks we can fit all of my stuff in the wagon."

Although they could afford a newer, more stylish car, Davis adored his light blue 1975 Buick station wagon and wouldn't part with it. Olivia would have much preferred a brand new, red Cadillac Seville.

Not for the first time, Olivia proclaimed to herself that she was determined to have it all: a career and a family. And she would be there for her daughter.

"I wouldn't miss it," she said.

CHAPTER NINETEEN

AUGUSTA

"AUGUSTA CELIA GIBSON, get in here!"

Augusta jumped, her stomach filling with dread. Whenever her mother called her by her full name, she was in trouble. It was quiet in the apartment. The silent radio should have been Augusta's first clue that something was wrong. Her mama liked to listen to the news before she went to bed.

Augusta closed the apartment's front door and hung her coat on one of the iron hooks by the doorway. She trudged down the hall and swung open the kitchen door. "Yes, Mama?"

Her mama sat at the round table in her thin housecoat, a steamless cup of tea on the tabletop. Julia did not drink alcohol. Not because of Prohibition; she didn't like the taste. "Want to keep my wits about me," she'd also say. Next to the cup was her Bible; Augusta was standing too far—and it was too dark—to see what passage her mama had been reading.

The only light came from the open window over the sink. The shade was raised. A cool breeze offered respite from the day's heat.

"Why are you sitting in the dark?" Augusta asked.

"Sit down, child," her mama said. Augusta obeyed. "What time is it?"

"I don't know, but I can find out for you."

"I don't need to know the time. My point is, it's late. You've been coming home late every night. I worry."

"I'm eighteen and a woman now."

"I lost my husband. I will not lose you, too. And you live under my roof. I could ground you."

Augusta laughed. "I'm too old for that."

Her mama gave her a stern look. "Maybe so, but nothing good happens after midnight."

The small room was still filled with the smell of the fried chicken and baked beans her mother and Hale had had for dinner. Jean had taken Augusta out to dinner, but that was five hours ago. Her stomach rumbled.

"But that's not true, Mama. I'm having the time of my life."

"How well do you know this boy?"

"He comes from a well-to-do family. His daddy's a doctor. Jean is smart and ambitious, and he takes good care of me."

"He seems more important to you than your own family."

"That's not true, Mama. I love my family."

"This is your first serious boyfriend. I want to make sure you're making the right choices."

Augusta crossed her arms. "I'm not doing anything crazy, Mama."

Well, not that crazy.

On one hand, Augusta didn't want to discuss Jean with her mama, who didn't approve of him. But she wouldn't have approved of anyone Augusta dated. On the other hand, she was bursting to talk about nothing but him. She wanted to shout his name from the rooftop of every building in Harlem, shout how he made her feel special, how he'd opened a new world to her. He was the best thing to happen to her. How had she gotten so lucky? Being with him was like getting lost in a good book all the time.

Augusta had been a good girl her entire life. She deserved a man like Jean.

Julia sipped her tea. "You were a straight-A student. The smartest at your school. You used to talk about college and becoming a teacher."

Augusta glanced out of the window at the fire escape of the apartment building next door. "Jean says I don't need to. That I'm already smart enough. But I'm still going to college; I'm just not in a rush. I have plenty of time."

Julia set the cup down. "That's good. I was worried you were headed to the altar."

Augusta recalled Jean's statement that afternoon about getting married and having six children. She didn't want to lie to her mama or keep things from her, knowing how much Julia had sacrificed for her and Hale.

"Trust me," Augusta said, "marriage is the last thing on my mind. I'm having too much fun."

Members of the Palmer Parks Band and their girlfriends sat around a table covered with a white linen tablecloth at the front of Bill's Place, a speakeasy on 133rd Street. The blocks between Seventh and Lenox Avenue, known as "Swing Street" because of their many jazz clubs, were also called "Jungle Alley" because Negroes and whites mingled there.

Inside the club, the dim lights and flowing bootlegged liquor blended with the patrons' loud conversation and laughter. A cloud of cigarette smoke hovered over their heads. The room reeked of perfume, cologne, and reefer, strong enough that one could get high simply being there.

Palmer was light-skinned, with a high forehead and slicked back hair. His arm lay draped atop the back of the chair around his girlfriend, Mae, and his saxophone rested in its case, as always, beside him. Mae had an oval face, eyelashes lengthened by mascara, and big white teeth. In a crimson-red dress with a string of pearls and a black cloche hat, she looked like Josephine Baker. Her gloves, which she wore no matter the weather, reached her elbows. She idolized the dancer, singer, and actress and emulated her style, like many women around the world did, both Negro and white. Some girls believed Mae put on airs, but Augusta thought she was all right. If she was happier wanting to be someone else, who was anyone to judge?

The Palmer Parks Band performed anywhere they were offered a gig—speakeasies, dance halls, cellars, lounges, supper clubs—but they loved playing here and at the Smalls Paradise nightclub over on Seventh Avenue, because both places were Negro-owned.

Sometimes, the band and its entourage headed over to

Smalls after a gig because, in addition to performances by famous musical acts, the waiters performed the Charleston, sang, or roller-skated orders to their customers. The 6:00 a.m. floor show and breakfast dances were not to be missed. Or they would head over to the Nest Club, an after-hours cabaret on West 133rd Street. All of them would stumble out of these establishments blinking in the daylight as kids made their way to school.

"I played with the Duke," Jean said to Jessie's new girlfriend, who sat next to him. Jessie was the band's drummer.

Augusta, sitting on the other side of Jean, refrained from rolling her eyes. He'd only jammed with the Duke once, as a stand-in when the regular piano player fell ill prior to a performance. Jean told the story as if Duke Ellington had asked him to fill in. The famous musician didn't know Jean's name and wouldn't recognize him if he saw him again.

Augusta took another sip of her Gin Rickey. When she'd first started drinking them after she'd met Jean, she hadn't cared for their sour flavor. But over the last few months, she'd grown accustomed to them.

Jessie's big-breasted girlfriend leaned forward, her eyes huge. "Are you that good?"

Jean smirked. "The best."

"Watch yourself, Jean." Jessie smoothed his thin mustache. His tone was light, but there was a hint of warning underneath.

"Have you ever played at the Cotton Club?" the girlfriend asked Jean.

Jean scowled, tapping cigarette ash into an ashtray. "You couldn't pay me to play for all those white folks."

She blinked at the vehemence in his voice and turned to resume her conversation with Jessie.

Across the table, Francis asked, "You all right over there, Augusta?"

After Jean, Francis was Augusta's favorite guy in the band. He had soft brown eyes and a crooked nose, from a childhood fight. He played the trumpet and had been friendly with Augusta from the start of her relationship with Jean. And he never hit on her.

Augusta held up her Collins glass and smiled. "I'm fine."

Palmer clapped his hands. "Time to go!"

"I'm the only one for you, right?" Jean whispered into Augusta's ear.

"Of course."

He kissed her on the cheek. "Miss me."

He gave her his patented grin and left with the band, hustling toward the dressing room.

As the other girlfriends gossiped and giggled, Augusta stirred her drink with a straw and scanned the speakeasy. Waiters and waitresses wended around the tables serving drinks. Posted advertisements announcing upcoming shows plastered the walls. Colored patrons packed the place, but there were plenty of white folks, too, who came to enjoy the illegal liquor and to immerse themselves in the Negro culture. It was unlike the Cotton Club, where colored people served and entertained but were refused as guests.

Twenty minutes later, the bar's middle-aged owner took to the stage.

"Ladies and Gentlemen, we have another great show for you tonight! Give it up for the Palmer Parks Band!"

The band members, in matching black suits with white shirts, white ties, and two-tone shoes, jogged through a nearby door and up the three steps where their instruments awaited them on stage. Standing at his piano, Jean played a scale, then winked at Augusta. Other customers—especially the women—looked at her with envy as the band began its first song. She did not enjoy the attention. Heat rose to her face from embarrassment, but she didn't take her eyes off Jean. The music infused her. Soon, like everyone else, she was bobbing her head and swaying in her seat. Some folks migrated to the dance floor. Augusta never danced while Jean played. He wouldn't appreciate her dancing with another man, even a harmless one.

She clapped at the end of the first set, along with everyone else. The band returned to the table, and a waiter refreshed everyone's drinks. Jean sat next to Augusta, sweat dripping down his narrow face. Unlike some musicians, he didn't need chemical substances; performing was the only high he needed.

His eyes danced. "How did we sound?"

"Wonderful!"

Augusta, herself, was giddy. From the alcohol or the energy in the club, she didn't know. The heat outside couldn't compare to the temperature within the room. The band and the crowd fed off each other. It made her feel—made all of them feel—invincible. There was no place in the world she would rather be.

"You're beautiful," Jean said with a boyish grin. "You know that?"

Augusta's cheeks flushed.

Jean glanced away and his smile faded. Augusta followed his gaze. A woman across the room averted her head and blocked her face with her hand. Strange. She looked familiar, but Augusta couldn't place her. Jean drank his Hanky Panky, put the glass down, leaned over, and kissed Augusta, his lips soft. He returned to the stage with the rest of the band for the second set. Instead of taking his seat behind the piano, Jean moved to the microphone. Augusta stirred her drink, although there was barely any liquid in the glass. What was he doing? He wouldn't sing; the group only played instrumentals. And he could not sing as well as he thought.

"Everybody, can I have your attention?"

Jean waited for the noise to die down, then held his hand out to Augusta. "I'd like to introduce you all to my girlfriend, Auggie Gibson."

A rising dread spread through her. She shifted in her chair and waved to the crowd.

"Auggie," he said, "stand up!"

What now?

"She and I have been together for a while," he continued, "and I wanted to ask her a question in front of the band—my brothers—and all of you." He released the standing microphone and bent to one knee. He dug into his pocket, pulled out a small box, and opened it. Inside was a ring with a tiny diamond.

He grinned at her. "Auggie, will you marry me?"

A few women gasped. Others said, "Awwwwww."

Augusta's hands flew to her face. "Oh, my Lord!"

"You can just call me Jean, darling."

Customers chuckled.

Except for that day on Lenox Avenue, she and Jean had never discussed marriage. Before she met him, she'd wanted more out of life than being a wife and a mother. She could still follow her dreams, but it would be difficult to do so while supporting her husband's burgeoning career.

Jean's smile faltered.

A white man in the back yelled, "Say, 'yes,' honey!"

Patrons chanted: "Say 'yes!' Say 'yes!' Say 'yes!'"

She scanned the faces in the audience. The wide smiles. The bright eyes.

Her heart thumped to the beat of the customers' chants. She recalled the conversation about marriage she had with her mama a month ago. Her mama would be disappointed if she married Jean. Her grandmother had extolled the importance of getting an education. Everything was happening too fast. Augusta needed more time to think.

She stared at Jean's adoring face. Her man loved her.

"Yes!" she screamed.

He whooped, closed the box, hopped off the stage, and ran to her. He knelt again on one knee, slipped the ring on her shaking finger, then stood and swept her up into his wiry arms. He swung her around once, then kissed her hard on the mouth.

"I love you, Auggie."

He'd never told her that. She counted the freckles on his face before looking into his copper eyes.

Breathless, she said, "I love you, too."

She feared her heart would burst with happiness and spurt blood all over Jean's suit.

Jean hugged her. She wrapped her arms around his

shoulders and buried her face into his sweaty neck. She peeked at the stage.

The band members smiled and clapped along with the audience—except for Francis, who held his trumpet against his chest, an inscrutable expression on his face.

CHAPTER TWENTY

DINAH

WHEN DINAH WAS a girl, her grandmother, Aisha, used to comb her hair with hands gnarled with age. She always wore a twine-woven ring on the third finger of her right hand. It was the only item she had left from her mother. The only item she'd brought with her from her country. The only thing that was hers. Dinah's momma wore the ring now.

Every night, Aisha had told Dinah stories about the motherland and what it was like to be free. Only when Aisha discussed her homeland had she smiled or laughed. At all other times, she'd worn a stoic expression and executed her tasks efficiently. Even in the quarters, it had been hard to solicit a smile from her. Often, when they were alone, Aisha, Celia, and Dinah had conversed in Edo. Dinah loved the sound of the words and wished they could speak it freely. But if Nelson or a Devereaux family member caught them, they'd endure severe whippings. The only time Dinah spoke it now was in the privacy of the cabin she shared with her mother. Although her grandmother had learned to speak English, she'd never lost her Edo accent.

Aisha had spoken of the rainy forests, the wonder of the Benin wall, their homes, their industry, their art, the taste of their succulent fruit, their conversations, the gorgeous dresses, and their dancing. And oh, how she'd loved to dance. That was how Aisha had met her future husband, Oba.

CHAPTER TWENTY-ONE

AISHA

A DELEGATION FROM Oba's village, of which Oba's father was the well-respected leader, came to Aisha's village to negotiate a trade agreement. Aisha's father was the ruler of their village. After they reached an accord, the palm wine flowed and the villagers danced. The more they drank, the more frenzied their dancing became. Aisha and Oba stood across the clearing from each other. Named after a queen who'd sacrificed everything for her husband and her kingdom, Aisha Iden had never been shy. She met Oba's gaze. Oba didn't speak a word to her. Eight years later, when he turned sixteen, he returned to ask Aisha's father for his blessing. After their union ceremony, Aisha returned with him to his village.

One night, many years later, a man showed up in silhouette in the entryway to their hut, the moonlight lengthening his shadow across their dirt floor, more men standing behind him. Aisha had never been so frightened. She spotted the ring, given to her by her mother, on the small table next to their sleeping mat, and hurriedly braided the jewelry into her own hair.

The man entered their home and started shouting commands. Oba rose and asked the man what he wanted. Aisha and Oba's knowledge of the Portuguese language was limited to what was required for trade. After Oba said he didn't understand, the man struck his face with a rifle, and Oba dropped to the dirt floor. Aisha rushed over to his prone body and touched the blood oozing from the gash over his eyebrow. The soldier pointed the gun at her children, motioning for them to stop crying. Aisha rose, her chin held high. She wouldn't let these men harm her children. They would have to go through her first.

The leader broke off their standoff gaze, then ordered the men to seize Aisha's family. Aisha was placed in shackles pulled tight past the point of pain. She didn't cry out for fear of upsetting the children, but fought tears as the men shackled her offspring and her unconscious husband. They slapped Oba's face until he revived. Aisha told her family not to resist. By going with these men, they'd survive to fight another day.

The Portuguese men kidnapped everyone in their village, killing the villagers who resisted.

For three days, the villagers marched over seventy miles through the jungle to the sand, where their captors herded them onto a ship with three massive white canvases and forced them to lie in rows in the ship's hold.

After days at sea, the human cargo stunk of urine, excrement, vomit, and sweat. The crew threw those who'd died overboard. Others played dead to join their brethren. Although they could hardly walk because of inactivity, dehydration, and lack of food, some villagers were brought up on deck to dance for the captain and his crew.

Only three-quarters of the villagers survived the journey.

Aisha stood whenever possible to look through the gap in the ship's planks. She counted twenty-one sunrises.

She bore witness. And held on.

She got sick like the others, but for a different reason. She was with child. At those times of her greatest despair, Aisha prayed to her gods to give her the strength to survive for her children and her unborn baby.

When they arrived in the harbor at Portsmouth, Virginia, and after Aisha's family had been sold, Master Solomon bought her and brought her back to the Devereaux plantation in North Carolina.

Celia was born six months later.

Aisha never joined the slaves at gatherings where they danced or drank. For a woman who used to love to dance, it not only reminded her of home, but of what should have been. Whenever she spotted a child who resembled one of her children or a man who resembled her husband, she became agitated and enveloped in an overwhelming despondency. Many slaves grew tired of her telling them of what she'd lost. All of them had lost someone. They also thought she was uppity because the master favored her. Never fitting in anywhere—neither the quarters nor the house—she kept to herself. Although surrounded by the Devereaux family all day, she'd felt a deep loneliness in her soul from having been separated from her husband, Oba, and their eight children.

Nothing, not even her gods, could dispel that loneliness. Her saving grace had been her daughter, Celia, the only part of Oba that had remained with her.

She begged to be sent away so that she could search for her family, but Solomon told her that would never happen. He'd never let her go.

CHAPTER TWENTY-TWO

DINAH

AFTER TELLING DINAH these stories, Aisha would give Dinah a goodnight peck on the cheek.

As Dinah lay in bed the morning after Beaux raped her, she thought about her grandmother's last days. On the board where Aisha lay dying, she'd motioned for Dinah, who had not left her side since she had become gravely ill, to come closer. Dinah had leaned forward, her tears falling on Aisha's brown wrinkled face, her brownish-black eyes cloudy.

"My seed, your mother's seed, and your seed came from my mother," Aisha rasped, "as will the daughters you will have." Aisha gripped Dinah's wrist until it hurt. "Protect them."

Then Aisha's heart finally gave out.

That was ten years ago. Aisha hadn't suffer in death, which was a blessing, since she'd suffered so much in life. She never found her husband or her children, never knew whether they'd lived or died. And she never returned to her beloved Benin. Celia told Dinah that Aisha had never forgiven herself for failing to protect her offspring. Although Master Solomon had treated her well, Aisha had despised him and all other white men for destroying her family. Her faith in her gods had never wavered, but nor had her hatred of white people.

Short in height, Aisha had been tall in stature. Although forced to take on her master's surname, she'd never answered to a first name other than the one with which she had been born.

CHAPTER TWENTY-THREE

SHA

JELANI SLEPT THROUGH most of the following day and did not leave her bedroom, except to go to the bathroom. Meanwhile, Sha holed herself up in her home office downstairs researching Erik Stevens' life. Her fingers flew across the well-worn computer keys. He and Jelani were "friends," "followers," or otherwise connected on all the social media sites. Sha discovered where Erik worked, what he liked to do on the weekends, his favorite craft beer, and what he'd had for breakfast that morning.

On the ABOUT US page on Trahon Investments' website, there was a picture of Erik's smiling, confident face next to his bio. He was a junior salesman at the firm, responsible for opening accounts, researching investment opportunities, and monitoring analyst calls. He'd graduated from Pepperdine University.

Sha was unsure what she would do with this information,

but gathering, distilling, analyzing, and reporting information was her profession. And it gave her something to do while Jelani slept.

Sha had never been an activist. She voted, cared for the environment—though she didn't do more than recycle, compost, and consider her ecological footprint without trying to reduce it—and was concerned about the condition her generation would leave the planet in for the next. She enjoyed life's small pleasures and had created a simple life for herself and her daughter. But sometimes external forces demanded deeper engagement with the world.

After checking on Jelani for the umpteenth time, Sha gamed for a while, then settled herself in the living room recliner with a beer and watched the evening news on TV. An older Black woman in a bright blue jacket and a white silk shirt, with long, straightened hair, reported from the National & World News Network's studio. The topic was a breaking story out of Southern California regarding the miraculous rescue of a teenage girl who'd been kidnapped off the street in front of her parents' home in Compton two years prior.

The camera cut to a reporter from the network's local affiliate interviewing the girl's mother from a room in the family's home.

"When I arrived home from work that day," the woman said, "I knew something was wrong."

The reporter's eyes narrowed, her face a mask of intense concentration. "Why is that?"

"My daughter was twelve. Old enough to know to come straight home from school. When I got home, though, the house was empty. I called my neighbors, everyone in my family, my friends, and my daughter's friends. No one had seen her."

"And that's when you called the police."

"That's right. They told me my daughter had probably run away." The woman squeezed her lips together. "I know my daughter; she didn't run away."

"What did you do?"

"I stood outside your news station and made a ruckus until a reporter and a cameraman came outside to interview me."

The reporter's eyebrow shot up. "Why did you do that?"

"The kidnapping of a Black girl wasn't news, so I made it news. And it was for a while. Until that beauty-pageant girl got kidnapped."

Sha sipped her beer, recalling that story. An eight-year-old white girl had been taken from her home in Dallas, Texas. The abduction had become national news and captivated the nation for months. Her mother and father had pleaded tearfully on television for her return, and it had been impossible to go anywhere without seeing the victim's cute, heavily made-up doll face smiling at the camera, her chin resting on her hands.

"If my girl had had blond hair and blue eyes," the woman told the reporter, "the police would have searched harder. After a few days passed, I knew that if I ever wanted to see her again, I'd have to find her myself. I searched everywhere: bus stations, warehouses, alleys…brothels."

"The search took two years, but it came at a personal cost, right?"

The woman nodded. "My no-good husband left me. My other kids felt neglected. I lost my job as a bank teller and lived off welfare. The only people who stood by me were my closest friends."

The reporter leaned forward. "How did you find your daughter?"

"I showed a photo of her to everyone. A homeless man on Rosecrans Avenue said he saw her get on a bus headed north, with an older white guy. I tracked down the driver. He remembered them and helped me trace their route."

"And several months ago, your investigation led you to a home in a small town in southern Oregon."

"My friends and I pretended to be housekeepers looking for work. A man answered the door, and we forced our way in. He threatened to shoot us, but he was no match for four Black women. We took his rifle away from him. While two of my friends held him, the other called the police. I headed downstairs to the basement."

"And what did you find?"

The woman swallowed. "He'd locked my daughter in a room. It was filthy and smelled like sh—. Bad. She was in there with two Black girls from California…and their children." She looked away. "Come here, baby."

The reporter's sympathetic expression turned businesslike as she faced the camera. "Yesterday, John Miller was indicted on three counts of kidnapping and hundreds of counts of rape." She paused. "He committed suicide in his Los Angeles jail cell this morning."

While the reporter said this, the girl joined her mother on the couch but sat a foot away from her. Despite the news that her captor and tormentor was dead, her face remained expressionless. Her eyes, vacant.

Sha exhaled to calm her nerves. Jelani could have been that girl.

The camera cut back to the female anchor in the network's studio. "Thank you, Madison, for that report. We hear so many horrifying stories of human trafficking and kidnapping that it's heartwarming to hear a story with a happy ending. But I must warn our viewers that it is dangerous to take the law into your own hands. It's still more prudent to rely on law enforcement than to seek justice on your own." Sha leaned forward. The anchorwoman's statement contradicted the glint in her eye, almost as if she were sending Sha a message.

After the broadcast, Sha called her mother and told her what had happened to Jelani. Nicole wept and asked if Sha needed her to go to Berkley. Sha replied it was unnecessary. She didn't add that the broadcast had confirmed for her that if something was going to be done about Erik, she would need to do it herself.

CHAPTER TWENTY-FOUR

OLIVIA

A CHANDELIER HUNG from the off-white ceiling. Tall arched windows separated by marble columns looked out onto South 10th Street. A mirror was centered on a champagne-colored wall. Underneath the ceiling, an intricately designed marble wainscoting surrounded the room. Customers spoke in muted tones, the sound of their cutlery low. Known for its old-world Italian cuisine and the best lasagna in the city, this deliciously smelling restaurant was a go-to for partners of the law firm courting high-end clients.

Olivia and her boss, Robert Penn, were dining with the CEO and CFO of a Japanese conglomerate, a potential ten-figure-a-year client—minimum. The conglomerate was looking for entertainment companies to acquire in the US. Discussing the legal aspects of these types of transactions was the part of these dinners Olivia most enjoyed. The small talk, not so much.

"Olivia?"

Robert stared at her. It wasn't the first time he'd called her name.

As the managing partner of Penn, Franklin, & Ross, Robert was responsible for the firm's operations. He had black hair and blue eyes and wore a black and white herringbone suit, a wide black tie, and a white shirt. He held his wine glass up, ready to take another sip. Olivia's husband was eating dinner alone again tonight—most likely trying out a new recipe to surprise her with on some future night—while the four of them drank their third bottle of red wine. What had Davis prepared? Was he eating in the kitchen or in the family room, on a TV tray, watching a 76ers game?

Olivia straightened her gray suit jacket. "I'm sorry. What did you say?"

Robert sipped his wine. "How's Nicole doing?"

"She's fine. Thank you for asking."

"Is she enjoying Atlanta?"

"What she sees of it. They're working her hard."

He shook his head and gave the potential clients a charming smile. "Brings back fond memories of my first job."

Olivia controlled her facial expression. Robert had started off in the mailroom of the law firm bearing his name, when his father had been the "Penn." *It's not the same.*

The veal with linguini was delicious. Olivia wished she could eat another serving.

"It's late," she said. "I should go."

"We haven't had dessert yet." Robert grinned at their clients. "And I believe there's more to discuss with our guests."

When his gaze returned to her, his smile did not quite reach his eyes.

Olivia turned to them and smiled. "Of course."

They paused their conversation as the waiter cleared their plates, tidied the white-linen tablecloth with a table crumber, took their dessert orders, and left. Olivia surreptitiously glanced at her own Cartier watch, wondering if she could get home before Davis went to bed. He might still be up because he'd been addicted to soap operas, lately. He taped The Young and the Restless, One Life to Live, and General Hospital on the VCR during the afternoon and watched them after dinner if there was no game on.

"Still want her to be a lawyer?" Robert asked.

Olivia adjusted the napkin on her lap. "Naturally."

"If she ever finishes law school, there'd be a place for her at our firm." To the clients, he said, "I've known her daughter, Nicole, since she was a child. She is going to be something."

The waiter returned with their desserts.

"What does she do in Atlanta?" asked the bespectacled CEO, his English precise.

Before Olivia could answer, Robert said, "She's in cable news. A producer. Mark my words, she'll be a superstar someday. Smart and pretty. Just like her mother. Did you know Olivia graduated Summa Cum Laude from LaSalle?"

The two other men glanced at each other, impressed.

While they dug into their desserts, Robert patted Olivia's hand and let it linger. After a moment, Olivia slid her hand out from underneath his, picked up her fork, and sliced through her chocolate cream cheese cannoli, the utensil clacking against her plate.

CHAPTER TWENTY-FIVE

JULIA

THE WEDDING TOOK place in September of 1925.

Since Julia couldn't afford to pay for any of it, Jean's parents, Dr. and Mrs. Wells, hosted the ceremony in the backyard of their lovely brownstone on Strivers' Row, one of Harlem's elite neighborhoods. Julia wondered why they didn't hold the wedding in a church.

Prior to the ceremony, she helped Augusta get ready in a guest bedroom on the first floor of the Wells's home. Her daughter sat on an upholstered stool facing the mirrored vanity, examining her makeup. Julia stood behind her in a simple peach-yellow dress and a matching slanted hat.

"Jean's parents have a beautiful home," she said.

Augusta's eyes lit up. "I know! Isn't it gorgeous?"

Julia frowned. "You've never been here?"

"Only once. To meet his parents."

"He's not close to them?"

"Jean's too busy to visit. They're busy, too. They entertain a lot and attend social events."

"Hmmm." How can you ever be too busy for your children? Julia opened her purse, extracted the necklace, and raised it over Augusta's head, fastening the clasp at the base of her neck. "Something old."

Augusta touched the antique twine-woven ring clipped to the gold chain and gazed at it in the oval mirror. "It's precious."

"Your grandmother gave that to me on my wedding day. It's yours." As Julia brushed her daughter's hair, she told her the origins of the ring and the story of how it was passed down in their family.

"I miss her," said Augusta.

"Me, too," Julia said quietly. "She'd have been proud of the woman you've become." She paused. "Is something else bothering you?"

"I wish Daddy were here."

Julia's eyes glistened. "He is."

"Sometimes, it's hard to remember him without looking at his picture. Is that bad?"

Julia shook her head. "He will always be a part of you. You don't need a photograph." She put her hands on Augusta's shoulders and bent so their heads were side by side. "You're beautiful."

"Thank you, Mama."

"I thank the Lord for giving me you." Julia debated with herself whether to ask Augusta the only question on her mind. But she had to know. "Are you sure?"

"About what?"

"About…getting married." She almost said, "marrying *him*."

Augusta patted her hand. "I'll be all right. Jean will take care of me. One day, the band will have a hit record, and he'll buy me a big house. Like this. You can come live with us."

"I have my own home. What if they don't make it? What will he do for a living?"

"They will."

"How can you be sure?"

"Because Jean rubbed the Tree of Hope."

Julia opened her mouth to say that was the stupidest thing she'd ever heard, but she pursed her lips instead. This was Augusta's day. She smoothed her daughter's hair. "You're so young."

Augusta cocked her head. "How old were you when you married Daddy?"

Julia smiled. "You're right." She embraced Augusta from behind, squeezing her tight. "I wish you every happiness."

Despite early morning clouds, the weather turned out to be perfect. The sun shone, but it was not hot. The affair was a small one…on Augusta's side of the aisle. Florence and Marian were her bridesmaids, Julia gave her away, and her brother, Hale, was the ring bearer. Her Aunt Aisha, Uncle Oliver, and their spouses had taken the train in from Boston, but none of her cousins could come. A scowling Ray Ray, dressed in his only suit, sat next to his parents in the second row. On the groom's side, the seats were filled with Jean's parents, his two older brothers, members of Jean's band, his friends, his friends' parents, his parents' friends, his father's classmates from high school and college and medical school, his father's hospital colleagues, and many leaders of the Negro community.

Jean sported a brown three-piece suit with a white shirt and a boutonniere pinned to the lapel of his jacket. Augusta wore a sleeveless white dress and a matching veil made by Julia.

After the guests were seated, the minister said, "Friends, family, loved ones, we have come together—"

Jean held up his hand. "Wait!"

If this nincompoop called off the wedding and embarrassed Augusta, Julia would slap him in the presence of all these people…Although part of her would be pleased. Augusta deserved better.

Augusta shifted on her feet. "What are you doing?" she whispered fiercely to him.

"Hale, come on up," he said.

Julia's son rose from beside her and walked stoically past the bride and groom to sit on a small wooden bench in front of the organ, the seat just vacated by a musician friend of Jean's who'd performed the processional.

"Hale!" Augusta whispered. "What are *you* doing?"

Julia stood. "Hale, get back here."

Augusta glared at Jean. "This isn't funny. He'll ruin our wedding day. Tell him to go back to his seat right—"

Hale began to play the chorus of "I'll See You in My Dreams." Augusta's mouth gaped. She glanced at Julia, whose mouth also hung open, and back at her brother. Julia's surprise turned to pride as she watched her boy play. After the last note, he turned to his sister, pointing his thumb at Jean. "He's been teaching me after school."

Augusta's eyes welled, and she hugged Jean around the neck. Julia wiped a tear from her cheek, wondering whether she'd been too hard on Jean and now needed to pay for piano lessons for Hale.

After being pronounced man and wife, they did not jump the broom. That was a tradition in Julia's family, not Jean's. Jean believed that Mrs. Jean Wells didn't need to adhere to antiquated traditions. Julia was disappointed at first, but she'd already had her own wedding.

After the reception, the couple returned to Jean's small apartment on West 142nd St. Jean believed its size would be fine until the birth of their first child. With the Palmer Parks Band being in high demand and Jean not allowing anyone to fill in for him, there'd be no honeymoon. The band was performing six to seven nights a week, and Jean insisted that Augusta come watch every performance. She was his muse, he said. Augusta had gotten used to going out nightly and found it hard to remember her life before Jean.

Once she got married, Augusta quit her job at the dress shop. Jean's salary was enough to support them and left Julia with one less mouth to feed. With her days free, Augusta visited Julia's apartment every evening, waiting for Julia to return home from work. Julia had quipped, "I see you more now than when you lived here." Augusta still had a key. When she'd tried to give it back after the wedding, Julia had said, "Keep it. It's your home, too. I want you to have a place to come back to."

Augusta had tried to force it into her hand. "I won't need it. I have my own place."

Julia's hand had enclosed hers. "You never know," she'd said in her end-of-discussion voice.

⤝

Augusta sat on the sofa in Julia's living room flipping through *The Messenger*, a Negro political and literary magazine, waiting for Julia to hang up her coat. She set the magazine down and skipped over to her mama.

"I know you're tired, Mama, but will you cut my hair, please? I want the style everyone's wearing. Jean says it'll look good."

"So, why doesn't Jean cut his hair that way?"

"Oh, Mama." Augusta squeezed Julia's arm and let go. "He said it would look good on *me!* Please?"

"I've been standing all day, child. With you gone, I not only make the dresses, I have to sell them, too. All I want to do is soak my feet in Epsom salts."

"Pretty please?"

Julia's smile was tired. "Go get the scissors. They're in the bathroom."

In Augusta's old bedroom, which had stayed the way she'd left it, Julia brushed out Augusta's hair. It was well past her shoulders.

"You have beautiful hair," Julia said, "just like your grandmother."

Gazing into a handheld mirror, Augusta turned her head from side to side. "It looks old-fashioned."

"Your hair is your crown. It's part of your spirit. Your identity. Are you sure you want to cut it?"

"Mama…"

"All right."

While her daughter carried on about Jean's band and how well they were doing and that someday they would be as famous as Cab Calloway, Louis Armstrong, and maybe even the Duke, Julia reluctantly sheared Augusta's hair.

"You've told me that before," Julia said. "When is this famous business supposed to start?"

"It takes time."

"What about you?"

"What about me?"

"While Jean is enjoying all this fame, what will you be doing?"

"Keeping my man happy."

"Is that enough for you?"

"And keeping a clean house."

"Your apartment's small." Julia tilted her head and looked at her firstborn's reflection in the mirror. "I thought you were planning to be a teacher."

"I wanted to be one when I was younger, but now I'm a modern woman."

"A lot of modern women work and get their education."

"Jean thinks I'm too smart to be a teacher."

"What does that mean?"

Augusta paused. "I'm not sure. Besides, I want to stay home with our children. Once they arrive, they'll take up all of my time."

"There's no rush. You'll have plenty of time for that."

"Not really." Augusta's eyes sparkled.

Julia stopped brushing. "Why do you say that?"

Her daughter grinned. "I'm pregnant!"

Despite the stone dropping to her stomach, Julia hugged Augusta. "I'm happy for you, dear." She straightened, squeezed the brush's handle, and resumed brushing her daughter's hair.

CHAPTER TWENTY-SIX

DINAH

CELIA SAT PERCHED on the edge of Dinah's bed. "Time to get up."

Dinah wanted to stay in her dreams with her grandmother. "I don't want to."

Her momma glanced at the old timepiece she'd borrowed from Master Sam's dresser. She never wanted to be late. Master Sam thought he'd lost it in town.

"I let you sleep an extra hour."

The previous night's betrayal slammed Dinah with the force of the winds that sometimes shook the limbs out of trees and the chairs off the house's balcony. Grief welled within her and she began to sob.

She'd known Beaux Devereaux her entire life. They had played together as children. She remembered the day she'd caught a monarch butterfly, opened her hands, and showed it to him. The light brown bangs on his forehead had fluttered in the wind. He'd grinned at her, agreed the butterfly was beautiful, then snatched it and run away. She could hear their laughter now, as she chased him around the elm tree trying to retrieve the insect and yelling for him not to kill it. He had never shown an interest in his studies, but he'd loved it when she'd read to him under that same tree, the leaves providing much-needed shade from the Carolinian summer sun. Master Solomon Devereaux's sister had taught Celia how to read when she was a child, and Celia had taught Dinah.

Back then, she believed she and Beaux were friends—equals—not knowing that the color of her skin made a difference—*all* the difference. Until the day Beaux turned nine years old and, goaded by his daddy, told Dinah to polish his boots.

"How did you find me?" Dinah asked her momma.

The whites of Celia's eyes were shot through with red. "I had a bad feeling, so I went looking for you. Nelson carried you here."

A pain seared Dinah's private parts. "It hurts, Momma."

Celia touched Dinah's face, avoiding the bruises, her fingertips calloused from sewing. "I know, baby."

"You have no idea what this feels like."

Her mother opened her mouth to respond but then closed it.

"Why did he do this to me?" asked Dinah.

"You think there always needs to be a reason for everything that happens. This is the way it is, and we can't change it."

"Why not?"

Her momma exhaled. "The law says he owns your body. But he doesn't own your soul."

Swallow Barn lay upside-down on the floor, open to the page where Dinah had left off reading the previous night. The story was about how wonderful it was to live on a plantation. She didn't know whether she could ever pick it up again. Why bother reading? To escape to somewhere else in her imagination? To better herself? She was never going to live anywhere but in this cabin, and she'd never be more than a slave.

"When he stopped playing with me when we were children, I thought something was wrong with me."

"There's nothing wrong with you."

Dinah hesitated. "Why do I feel like less than a person because I'm not white?"

"You shouldn't!" Her mother's voice was harsh. "And don't you ever say that again."

"I don't fit in anywhere. Like grandmother."

"I'm not sure where your brilliant mind came from, but it is nothing to be ashamed of or to hide. At least not from our kind."

"I was dreaming about her."

Celia brushed away Dinah's tears. "Like her, you've got to be strong, even when it's hard."

"What if I can't be?"

Celia withdrew her hand. "My momma didn't cross an ocean and lose everyone in her family but me just for you to give up."

A flood of sadness swept over Dinah. "I miss her."

Her momma kissed her cheek. "I miss her, too. But if she could survive what she went through, you can survive this. Now get up!"

The tree leaves were a vibrant red, orange, and yellow. The air was crisp. Birds squawked as they headed south for their winter respite. Celia and Dinah were met with the aroma of apples and freshly baked pie crust as they opened the house's back door. For once, Dinah was too miserable to be hungry.

When she entered the kitchen, Martha stared at the bruise on her face. "That son of a bitch!"

The cook gathered Dinah into her arms, her soft shoulder a welcome pillow. Dinah didn't cry. She'd spent all her tears that morning.

Martha released her and grabbed a jar off a shelf. "He'll get his."

That afternoon, standing against a white-painted wall in the ballroom with the rest of the house slaves, Dinah squeezed her legs together in case she was still bleeding. When she had risen that morning, she'd found blood stains on the board she slept on.

The first chords of a harp, played by a relative of the Devereauxs, permeated the crowded room. Celia clutched Dinah's hand for a moment, then let go. She had been working day and night, repeatedly going over all the details in her head to ensure nothing had been missed. The wedding had to be perfect.

The guests' murmuring ceased. Everyone, including Dinah, turned their heads to the ornate doors, where two slaves on either side, dressed in black suits and wearing white gloves, opened them for the bride's entrance. Anna Lawrence appeared, with one arm entwined through her father's, wearing a white silk dress with a lace collar and a ten-yard-long train. Her blond hair was parted down the middle and pinned up, except for loose tendrils spiraling down the sides of her face. Ms. Lawrence was petite, with blue eyes, an upturned nose, and skin never embraced by the sun. She carried herself like the princess her parents had raised her to be.

Beaux, his hair slicked back, stood at the front of the room, on time for once. He looked handsome in his high-collared white shirt, black morning coat, light-blue silk waistcoat, and gray trousers. His eyes lit up at the sight of his bride, and he broke into a broad grin. Ms. Lawrence passed Dinah as she proceeded toward Beaux. Beaux's gaze lingered on Dinah's face. Dinah didn't flinch, not wanting to disappoint her momma. Beaux noticed Martha standing beside Dinah and, his smile dimming, he returned his gaze to Anna.

Martha scowled. "I put the root on him."

"What do you mean?" Dinah asked.

The cook gave her a knowing look. "You'll see."

The groom took Anna's arm, and Anna's father retreated to sit next to his wife in the first row. The bride and groom faced the bishop, who presided over the Episcopalian church the Devereauxs—except for Beaux, who thought the services were boring—attended in Raleigh.

After dinner, the newly married couple danced in the ballroom in the company of their families and over a hundred guests. The slaves had pushed the tables and chairs against the walls. The tables were decorated with flowers and burning candles. Women's long gowns swooshed as couples spun around the glossy hardwood floor dancing the Virginia Reel. Perfumes and colognes collided in the air. Dinah glanced at the windows framed by thick, velvet drapes. It must have been a breathtaking sight if one were looking in from outside the house. Even Master Sam and Mistress Elizabeth took a spin. And, if Dinah wasn't mistaken, a joyous laugh escaped the mistress's lips.

Billy Devereaux flirted with a pretty girl from town. He signaled for Dinah to bring them champagne. She complied, bringing him two delicate champagne flutes imported for the occasion from France, wherever that was. Billy thanked her.

As she was returning to the kitchen for more champagne, a voice behind her said, "I can't stop thinking about you."

Dinah jumped, dropping the tray with a clatter.

Beaux was coatless, his hands jammed into his trouser pockets. "Good thing there weren't any glasses on it," he said.

Dinah picked up the tray and held it over her private parts.

"Nothing's changed between you and me," he said, "just because I've taken a wife."

Nearby, guests deep in conversation paid no attention to them. They couldn't hear him over the clinking glasses, the laughing guests, and the ongoing music. Across the room, Dinah's momma stopped serving guests and looked over at her.

"I'm sorry my passions got the best of me last night," he said.

Dinah faced him. His face was sweaty from dancing. She wouldn't let him get the best of her. "Would you care for something to drink, sir?"

He lowered his voice. "I didn't mean to hurt you, Dinah. I couldn't help myself. You're like one of those stars we were looking at."

Dinah fidgeted, wondering if he would take her again in front of all these people. She counted her breaths.

Beaux bent toward her, his lips grazing her earlobe. "I'll miss you every day that I'm gone, and I can't wait for my return." He straightened. "Get me another whiskey, will you? I'm parched."

"Yes, sir."

Suddenly, Beaux's face puckered as he grabbed his stomach. "What the hell?" He doubled over. A few of the guests looked their way. The stench of excrement filled the air. Beaux's grimacing face turned crimson. "Shit!" With legs pressed together, he galloped out of the room and into the foyer. A large brown stain spread across the back of his gray pants.

The guests whispered, eyeing each other with disapproving looks.

A giggled escaped from Dinah's mouth before she could cover it.

Martha came up beside her, pursing her lips. "Told you. Maybe next time he'll think twice before putting his thing where it don't belong."

"What happened?"

"I put buckthorn in his afternoon tea. You should use it whenever you're stopped up."

"I'll remember that."

Over the next few weeks, Dinah's nerves eventually settled as the bride and groom traveled to Virginia and South Carolina to visit relatives who had been unable to attend the wedding.

One night, she woke up with stomach cramps. She ran

outside and threw up in her momma's patch garden and continued vomiting every morning for the next week. Although Celia seemed concerned about her daughter's illness, she still forced Dinah to rise at her normal time and go to work in the house.

One morning, Dinah couldn't get out of bed. Her momma stared down at her, not with concern but with a look of resignation. Despite the frigid air that blew in through the spaces between the planks of their hut, Dinah's night shift clung to her body with sweat.

"Momma, it's hot."

"It is not hot, child."

"What's wrong with me, then?"

"I believe you're with child."

"A child! How do you know?"

"I can count."

CHAPTER TWENTY-SEVEN

SHA

A SCREAM PIERCED the quietness of the house. Sha jolted upright in bed and checked her smartwatch, which lay on the nightstand and displayed 1:13 a.m. She threw off the covers and rushed down the hall to Jelani's room. Her daughter was sitting up in bed, her T-shirt clinging to her chest and back with sweat.

Sha enveloped Jelani in her arms. "What's wrong, baby?"

Jelani's tears soaked through Sha's shirt and dampened her skin. "I had a nightmare. About…it."

"Are you ready to talk about it?"

Jelani shook her head vigorously.

Sha rested her chin on her daughter's wild hair. "I can't help you if I don't know what happened."

Jelani shivered. Sha pulled the comforter off the bed and wrapped it around the two of them, cocooning them inside.

"I don't know if I can," Jelani said. "It hurts to think about it, let alone talk about it. I don't want to relive it."

"Try. It's your first step to healing." Sha squeezed her. "I've got you."

Jelani buried her head into Sha's chest.

Sha wished she could turn back time. If she'd made her daughter stay home that night, they could have huddled together on the sofa and watched a movie, and the rape wouldn't have happened. But she'd been permissive with Jelani for most of her young life. Now, with her baby suffering, Sha realized woefully that their time together wouldn't last much longer. Jelani would be leaving for college in a year and a half and would probably never live at home again.

Unlike her mother, who'd worked all the time when Sha was growing up, Sha had never bought into the goal of having it all. She had resented her mother at times, but she'd come to understand as she got older that Nicole had done her best—after all, she'd possessed a gift that had to be shared with the world. But it hadn't been all work. They'd gone on wonderful vacations as a family: Amsterdam, Prague, Bangkok, Rome, Berlin, and Tokyo. Sha's parents liked to play tennis, so the family had traveled to watch the Grand Slam events in New York City, London, Paris, and Melbourne. Nicole had spent as much time with her as her schedule had allowed. And she'd never missed the important events like the coding tournaments and graduation.

When pregnant with Jelani, Sha vowed to be a good mother, which was why she'd chosen a flexible profession; she could work from anywhere. Jelani came first. Sha's work was not her life, but a part of it. It brought her fulfillment and joy but didn't define her.

"I met him at the club that night…," Jelani said, interrupting Sha's thoughts. "I've seen him there before. He's older. Handsome. White. Dresses nice. Money. He kept looking over at my friends and me, until he finally came over."

Sha recalled Erik's texts on Jelani's phone from before that night. Why was her daughter lying to her?

"He spoke to all of us but focused on me. He was nice, funny, and made me laugh. He'd noticed I was drinking red wine and guessed what kind I like. He got it right."

Sha bit her tongue to prevent herself from lecturing Jelani on being too young to drink. Her suspicions were confirmed, though. This wasn't the first time.

"After we finished our drinks," Jelani continued, "he asked me to dance. My friends were envious. I smiled at them as I followed him onto the dance floor, thinking I was the luckiest girl alive." Jelani's quiet voice reverberated against Sha's chest. "We danced for at least an hour straight. He smiled at me—he had a great smile—and asked if I wanted to go someplace quiet to talk. I didn't mind taking a break, especially to be alone with him, so I agreed. We left the dance floor, and he told me to wait for him. He left me for a minute. I waved to my friends across the room, and they waved back. They acted like they were excited for me. He returned with another glass of wine. I thought it was sweet that he'd bought it for me without my asking. He encouraged me to drink it before we went outside. I chugged it," she looked up at Sha apologetically and then lowered her head again, "then we left through one of the back doors."

"Where did you go?"

"To the parking lot. Next to a car."

"Was it his?"

"I don't know."

"What kind of car?"

"I can't remember, Mom."

Sha squeezed her. "Okay. Okay. What happened next?"

"We were having a good conversation. We joked with each other. All of a sudden, he pressed up against me and started grinding into me, telling me how beautiful I was. How he loved Black chicks."

Sha forced herself to hold still, despite the roil of anger pulsing through her.

"He was strong. I'd only had two drinks, but I felt drunk, really relaxed. And then he…tore my…" Jelani whimpered, her body heaving.

Sha rubbed her back. "It's okay, baby, let it out."

After a few minutes, Jelani's sobs subsided, and she sat up. "I don't know how I ended up on the bathroom floor. Maybe he brought me there, or someone else did, or I walked there myself. I've tried to remember, but I can't. I must have blacked out."

Sha had heard the stories. Date rape happened all the time on college campuses across the country. In high schools. Her daughter was a statistic among many.

"Did I bring this on myself, Mom? Why did he think he could do this to me?"

Sha lifted Jelani's chin. "This wasn't your fault. You did

nothing to deserve what happened to you. And it might not seem so now, but you'll survive this." She rose to allow her daughter to lie down, adjusted the comforter, and kissed Jelani's cheek. "Thank you for sharing that with me. Get some sleep."

She turned to leave.

Jelani clutched Sha's wrist. "Will you stay, Mom? Until I fall asleep?"

Sha smiled. "Of course." She wouldn't ever take these moments with her daughter for granted again. Each one was precious.

Jelani released her arm. "Tell me a story. The one about Aisha."

Sha nodded as if telling her teenage daughter a bedtime story was the most natural thing in the world. She settled again on the edge of the bed. Jelani closed her eyes.

"Once upon a time, there was a woman named Aisha who hailed from a village outside the Benin Empire. When she was a girl, she'd run around the village chasing her older brothers and sisters. She loved the feel of the African sun and wind on her face. The villagers would reward her for winning by giving her figs and melons. She grew up and married a handsome man named Oba from a nearby village. They had eight children, the youngest of whom they named Amare. Amare also loved to run around the village. ..."

CHAPTER TWENTY-EIGHT

OLIVIA

PENN, FRANKLIN, & Ross was located on Market Street in Penn Center, the heart of Philadelphia's Central Business District.

Olivia sat hunched over in her corner office on the twenty-second floor of the glass-and-granite skyscraper, marking up the latest draft of a merger agreement. Except for a photograph of her family and a desk lamp, the desk was clear of any objects so that Olivia could focus on one thing at a time.

She had taken the red-eye flight from LA, home to a subsidiary of the Japanese firm, and arrived in Philadelphia that morning. Most of that winter, she'd flown back and forth between the two cities. After changing into a fresh gray suit in an airport bathroom, she'd driven straight to the office. Regardless of how exhausted she was, she had to look sharp when she pushed through the building's glass carousel doors. She always had to be "on."

It was 10:00 p.m., only seven o'clock in California, and Olivia was still wearing her suit jacket. She had to fax the final documents to the client prior to midnight or risk having the acquisition called off.

She spun around in her chair to enter her changes into the computer on the credenza behind her. Next to the computer, a photograph of Mayor William J. Green III showed above the fold of the *Philadelphia Inquirer*. Above it blared another headline regarding his difficulties balancing the city's budget. She hadn't had time to read the article. She wondered what Davis thought of the fiscal situation.

She pressed the PRINT key and left her office. The cubicles and offices on the floor were empty and dark, except for hers and Robert's. His was the final review, and he had to sign off on the documents. The other attorneys, paralegals, and assistants had gone home.

In the copy room, Olivia stood in front of the laser printer as it spit out the one-hundred-page agreement. While she waited, she rolled her neck from side to side to relieve the stiffness. The constant traveling was taking its toll. What she wouldn't give for a warm bath. With bubbles. And champagne. She could have Davis prepare one for her before she arrived home. Maybe he could join her. The thought of what would come afterward made her feel more tired.

"How's it coming along?" Robert stood in the doorway in shirtsleeves holding a glass of gin and tonic from the bar in his office. Olivia never drank at the office until she finished her work, and even then, rarely. But most of the male partners did.

"Almost done," Olivia said. "I'll bring it to your office."

"No need." He entered the room. "I'll wait with you."

Olivia returned her attention to the output tray, the print job halfway completed. Besides the printer, the clinking of the ice against Robert's glass was the only sound in the room.

Robert stood next to Olivia for a moment, watching the agreement land on the tray, then moved behind her. His breath tickled the back of her neck as he began to massage her shoulders.

She shook him off. "What are you doing?"

"You look tense, and I saw you stretching. I know this engagement has been taxing. I want to help you relax."

"Thanks, Robert…but I don't need your help."

Robert returned his hands to her shoulders. His finger caressed her neck. "It's okay. I don't mind."

"I do," she said. "Stop it."

He stepped closer, the bulge in his pants pressed against her buttocks. "There's no one here."

She turned and slapped him. "What difference does that make? I'm married. For God's sake, Robert, you've met my husband!"

His cheek reddened from where she hit him. Anger flashed in his eyes. "I could make it easier for you, Olivia. You wouldn't have to work so hard."

"You gave me an opportunity, yes, but everything I achieved, I accomplished on my own. And that's the way I prefer it."

His eyes softened. "I'm sorry. I thought…over the years, you knew how I felt."

"What you're doing has nothing to do with feelings. It's about your positional power. You might pay my salary, but you do not own me. Who's your best litigator?"

"You know you are."

"Then you don't want to meet me in a courtroom."

Olivia's hand was shaking as she swiped the document off the printer and stormed out of the room.

⤎

She slept in the following morning.

When Davis's alarm clock clanged—Olivia had never heard it because she was usually long gone by this time—Davis pressed the button to turn it off and rolled over in bed, his afro matted against his scalp from where he'd slept on it. The center of the pillow was slick from his TCB hair product.

He sat up, his eyes widening in surprise. He closed them, rubbed his eyelids, and reopened them. "It is you."

Olivia lay with her head resting on the pillow next to him. "Silly."

Davis brought his warm palm to her forehead. "You don't feel sick."

Olivia chuckled. "I'm not."

"Why are you still here? Won't you be late?"

"I am taking the day off."

Davis sat up, the sheet falling to his waist. The top two buttons of his brown and teal checkered pajama top were unbuttoned, revealing his hairy chest. "Now, I'm worried."

"I'm fine. Really."

"If you say so." Davis yanked the covers off, his legs swinging to the side of the bed. "Well, I'm going to be late. I need to shower so I can catch the eight-fifteen."

"I don't know why you take the bus. We can afford a second car."

"The bus is fine. It gives me time to think or read or do nothing at all."

How terrifying. Olivia grabbed his wrist. "We could drive up to Atlantic City for the day."

Davis stared at her as if she were an alien.

"Yes, it's me," she said.

"I don't like to gamble," Davis replied.

"There are other things we can do. Like take a walk on the boardwalk. Eat corn dogs." She snuggled closer to him. "Take a stroll on the beach, hand-in-hand."

"It'll be cold. And most of the vendors will be closed."

"We'll wear coats and buy something to eat from whoever is open."

"I'll have to take the day off, too."

"Call in sick."

"I'm not sick."

Another thing Olivia loved about Davis was that he was unfailingly honest. He couldn't break a rule, no matter how small. He always drove the speed limit, regardless of whether or not there were police officers around. But this habit could be annoying, too, especially when Olivia was in a hurry to get somewhere.

"But if I have the opportunity to spend an entire day with you," Davis added, "it's worth telling my boss the truth. Let's do it!"

On the drive north on I95, Olivia told him about the previous night's incident with Robert and about all of her boss's advances over the years. Davis flexed his jaw as she spoke, his knuckles tensing as he gripped the steering wheel.

When Olivia finished, Davis touched her hand, keeping one hand on the wheel. "All this time. Why didn't you tell me?"

"I don't know." She removed the hair that had drifted into her eyes from the wind blowing through the half-open window. "I didn't want you to worry. Besides, I was handling it."

"One thing I don't worry about is whether you can take care of yourself."

Olivia sighed. "I'm not sure why I didn't tell you."

The turn indicator clicked as they bore right at the exit for Atlantic City. "I see how some men treat women in my office." He shook his head. "It's despicable."

Davis had been raised by his mother and older sisters. His father had abandoned the family when Davis was an infant; they'd never seen or heard from him again. From the love Davis had received as a child had grown an unwavering respect for women. His mother had supported four kids from wages she'd earned as a cleaner at the elementary school he'd attended. Other kids had made fun of her profession. Davis hadn't let it bother him. At least she'd had a job, unlike some of their parents. His family had never had enough money, though. Davis had worn his sisters' hand-me-down clothes, and the kids had made fun of him for that, too. Luckily, the sister closest to him in age had been a tomboy.

The dashboard showed that Davis was traveling at a steady clip, halfway between fifty and sixty miles per hour.

"All I want is to do a good job and not be hassled while doing so. I work my butt off, and I'm always the most prepared person in the room. A white man can dismiss my thoroughly researched argument based on little to no reasoning. It makes me feel unvalued, unappreciated."

"Maybe you should leave," Davis said quietly.

"I've thought about it. More than once. But where would I go? I've worked hard to get to where I am. To make partner. Besides, I love my job, my work. I just wish I didn't have to work with Robert. And he's not all bad. He taught me how to manage a law firm. How to present myself with clients. How to sell them, gain their trust. Being a success as a partner is more than knowing the law. It's about delivering great outcomes and making the client feel like a winner for trusting you with their business."

The crash of waves and the briny smell of the ocean signaled that they had arrived at the beach. The yoke of Penn, Franklin, & Ross fell from Olivia's neck. Olivia felt more relaxed than she had in a long time.

Davis parked the Buick in a lot near the boardwalk. He opened the driver's side door and looked over at her. "Are you okay?"

Olivia squeezed his hand. "I am now."

CHAPTER TWENTY-NINE

DINAH

"HOLD STILL."

Dinah tried to obey her momma, but then a giggle started in her belly. Her shoulders shook, and then the giggle escaped.

"I said, 'hold still.'"

Dinah calmed herself. Then she hiccupped, and hiccupped again.

Celia's hands dropped to Dinah's shoulders. "For the Lord's sake."

Dinah's hiccup transitioned into a giggle.

Celia's face softened, and she smiled. She grabbed a handful of Dinah's hair and plaited it tight to the scalp.

"Ouch! That hurts, Momma!"

"It must be done. Turn around and hold still. I won't tell you again."

Celia plaited the rest of Dinah's long hair. When she finished, she said, "Go look."

When he was a boy, Billy Devereaux had broken the great house's hallway mirror with an errant throw of a rubber ball while playing catch with Nicholas. Mistress Elizabeth had been beside herself, believing that the broken mirror portended bad luck for the family. She'd told Celia to dispose of it. Most of the mirror now hung on Celia and Dinah's cabin wall.

Gazing into it at her momma's handiwork, Dinah patted her hair. Her momma hadn't done a good job; the rows were uneven, the sections of hair were of different sizes. But that was the point.

Celia tied a headscarf tight to Dinah's head to prevent any of her hair from showing. "Beauty is a good thing for a white woman, but a curse for us. Maybe now he'll leave you alone."

Over the coming months, the swelling of Dinah's belly and breasts proved her momma right. Dinah also carried a secret she had never shared with her momma. She'd never wanted to have children. Any children. What kind of lives could slave children have, working until they died. What purpose?

When Beaux and Anna returned from their honeymoon three months later, the house slaves joined the Devereaux family on the balcony, which ran the full width of the house under a roof supported by immense white pillars, to welcome the newlyweds home. The front lawn was green again. The dogwood trees' white flowers bloomed. Butterflies flitted and bees buzzed on the blossoming pink flowers in the

Mayflower shrubs fronting the balcony. Dinah's face warmed from the sun, a welcome sensation after the cold winter.

The black carriage was drawn by four horses and driven by one of the stable slaves. The carriage door opened and Beaux jumped out, landing on the ground before a slave could set down the wooden step. He eagerly scanned the faces of the people on the balcony. He wore brown trousers, a white poplin shirt, and a black jacket, all dusty from the dirt roads. His hair had grown a couple of inches and now rested above his collar. When his gaze landed on Dinah, he smiled. Anna, in a taupe plaid traveling dress, held onto her bonnet as Nicholas helped her disembark from the carriage's interior. Master Sam Devereaux kissed her on both cheeks. "Welcome home, daughter." He looked at Beaux with uncharacteristic pride, the same way Celia looked at Dinah every day. "Son."

"Daddy."

The master slapped his eldest son on the back. "Come on in. I'll fix you a drink."

Dinah was standing behind a houseboy. When the boy ran to retrieve the couple's trunks from the back of the carriage, Beaux's loping gait faltered. He glanced at Dinah's swollen stomach, then at her face. His eyes sparkled. As he passed her, he whispered, "Now that's a welcome home." Dinah gritted her teeth as Beaux followed his daddy inside.

An hour later, as Dinah polished a brass candelabra on a mahogany table in the second-floor hall, she heard voices coming from Sam Devereaux's study, which was next to the master bedroom. She glanced up and down the hallway to ensure no one else was on the floor, then she tiptoed closer until she was just outside the open door. The whiskey bottle on the desk was half full. It'd been full when she polished it earlier that morning.

The interior room had a floor-to-ceiling bookshelf on one wall, filled with hardcover and leather-bound books that Dinah never saw anyone in the family reading. She'd gotten into the habit of borrowing a book—bunching the remaining books together so no one would realize there was one missing—reading it, then replacing it. Mounted high on the wall behind the desk, a stuffed deer head sentineled the room.

The master sat in a giant chair with an elaborately carved headrest. "This land has been in my family—"

His voice was raspy from decades of too much whiskey and cigar smoke.

"For generations, I know." Across the desk, Beaux lounged in the chair, his back to Dinah.

"—since my ancestors migrated from England a hundred years ago. Now that you're a married man, it's time for you to take on more responsibility around the plantation."

"Why? Nicholas does everything well. And he likes it. Let him do it."

"But you're my firstborn."

"I can't help an accident of fate."

"I didn't work hard my entire life so that you can enjoy yours. I was helping my daddy when I was six years old."

Beaux mumbled something inaudible.

Master Sam inhaled his cigar. Its aroma wafted out into the hallway. The mistress didn't like him smoking in the house, but she grudgingly allowed him to do so in this room. He held the cigar in the air. "Stop being an ungrateful son of a bitch." Smoke flowed out of his mouth, accompanying his words. "You need to grow up and stop acting without thinking of consequences. There's more to life than carousing with your friends and spending my money every night at the tavern."

"We just play cards and have a few drinks."

"It's more than a few, and I know that is not all you do. Yes, I'm talking about the women."

"That's over."

"It better be." The master rested the cigar in its holder on the desk. "The damn slave girl's with child."

"Her name is Dinah. And so what? That'll be more help around the house."

"That's not funny, boy, and get your feet off my desk. You're supposed to leave your muddy boots by the back door. It's what the mud area is for."

Beaux's riding boots dropped, one thud at a time, to the hardwood floor. "It's not my fault we came in through the front."

"I don't care about your…extracurricular activities," the master said, "but you've got to be discreet. You have the family's reputation to protect. And your wife's."

"Why would anyone care about me and Dinah? All the men copulate with slaves."

"What everybody else does is not my affair, but you are. You can't go around impregnating the house girls. We don't need daily reminders of your dalliances. If that's what you want to do, take your business outside. Or better yet go into town."

"Is that what you did?"

The master reached for his cigar. "Watch it, boy."

The two men smoked and sipped their drinks in silence.

At last, Beaux asked, "How was it…with you and mommy?"

Lines formed across Sam Devereaux's forehead. "What do you mean?"

"Did you love her when you met?"

Master Sam barked out a laugh. "What's love got to do with it? Your mother came from a respectable family, and she brought a substantial dowry."

"What about after you got married?"

"After we got married, what?"

"Did you love her? Do you love her?"

Master Sam scowled. "What the hell has gotten into you?"

"I thought—"

"That's your problem, son. Stop thinking. It's not your strong suit. Get your wife with child and produce heirs. Besides running this plantation someday, that is your sole purpose in life. Now leave me. I have work to do. And get rid of the mulatto girl. Send her back out to the fields, at least until she has the child."

"What if I want her to stay?"

"You needn't rub your wife's nose in it."

Beaux finished his drink and gently set the glass on the desk. "Like you?"

"You're on dangerous ground, son. You best leave."

Before Beaux could reply, Dinah scampered away. As she hurried down one side of the dual staircase to the foyer, she wondered what he'd meant by his last question.

∽

Dinah wiped her brow to no avail. The sweat trickling down her forehead stung her eyes and made it hard to see. Her dress was as wet as if she'd jumped into the river. Without cloud cover, the July sun cooked her skin. At least the headscarf kept her hair off her neck.

No matter how she moved, her belly was in the way. It felt like the child could pop out at any moment. Kneeling in the hard, unforgiving dirt, Dinah picked off the lower leaves of the tobacco plant and heaped them on the mule sled. Picked and piled. Picked and piled. People weren't needed for this job; a contraption could do it better and faster, and wouldn't have to be fed or clothed. Dinah shivered despite the heat, wondering what would happen to the slaves when the white men figured this out. She guessed they'd find other work for them or do away with them altogether. Maybe send them back to Africa. She wouldn't mind. She'd love to see Benin for herself. And she would be far away from Beaux and this place.

Dinah told others she didn't mind being a field hand again so as not to hurt their feelings, but she couldn't lie to herself. She hated the repetitiveness and the mindlessness of picking tobacco leaves. She not only missed the mild physical duties of being a house slave, but also the opportunity to think in comfort—the escape from the sun, the days when the open windows allowed in a cool breeze—and to solve the problems that presented themselves daily. The opportunity to use her mind. This wasn't something she could discuss with her best friend, Betty, who'd always worked in the fields.

Feeling lightheaded, Dinah dropped the leaf she was holding and sat on the ground.

Over in the next row, a slave called Martin looked around before eyeing her. "You all right there, Dinah?"

Dinah gave him a weary nod. "It sure is hot."

Martin glanced at her belly. "Hotter for you, I reckon."

The slight breeze that shimmied through the tobacco plants offered her no relief.

Martin scanned the field again, then stepped between the plants and into Dinah's row. Farther down the same row, Betty's eyes widened as she expertly extricated leaves without looking at the plants.

"What are you doing?" Dinah asked Martin.

"We've got time 'til Nelson comes back this way. Why don't you rest?"

A little older than Dinah, Martin was dark-skinned, with a strong forehead and a wide, proud nose. The only clothing the men wore were wheat-colored pants. The muscles on Martin's bare back, shoulders, and arms rippled as he worked Dinah's section, his movements rapid and efficient.

When he finished, he surveyed his handiwork. "Now you can go through the motions for a while."

He hustled back to his row and tried to catch up on his own work.

A horse's hooves clopped their way. When Nelson reached them, he said, "Whoa." His brown colt stopped. Although a slave, himself, Nelson enjoyed his authority as the overseer despite having to flog other Negro men, women, and children. He took no pleasure in it, but he had no choice. If he didn't, his replacement would flog him worse. He was better than the previous—white—overseer, who had relished in flogging slaves daily because he believed they continually needed to be broken in, ignorant of the fact that most slaves had already been broken in—or simply broken—by the time they arrived at the Devereaux plantation. That overseer had died a few years ago, in his house near the slave quarters, after drowning in his own vomit from too much drink. It was rumored he'd had help from some of his former victims.

"What's wrong with you, boy?" Nelson asked Martin.

"Nothing."

"Are you giving me eye service? Only working when I'm watching?"

"Nah, sir. Not moving as fast today is all."

Nelson cocked his head. "Are you sick?" He glanced over at Dinah. "Or something?"

Martin looked him in the eye. "I'm not sick."

Nelson gave Martin a hard look. "Make sure you catch up."

He clicked his heels and made a "tsk" sound. The horse took off.

"Thank you," Dinah said to Martin.

Martin reached for a plant. "You okay?"

Dinah nodded. Down the row, Betty was grinning.

The next morning, Celia bent over to shake Dinah, but Dinah was already awake. She'd lain awake most of the night because of the crashing waves of pain in her stomach. The board she slept on was slick with sweat.

"Momma, it's coming!"

Celia sent word to Nelson that neither she nor Dinah would be working that day. Celia's pleasant voice filled the cabin as she sang the same lullabies she'd sung to Dinah. But the songs did little to comfort Dinah, as the stabbing pains were incessant. She wished God would just take the baby out. She suffered in labor throughout the day, her momma and the midwife never straying too far from her bed.

After eight hours, Dinah's piercing screams interrupted the thick, humid afternoon air. Through her tearing, sweat-filled eyes, Dinah stared at the bundle of blood and white slime crying and squirming in her momma's arms.

Celia's chin dipped to her chest in resignation. "It's a girl. God's will be done."

CHAPTER THIRTY

DINAH

IN TIME, DINAH got used to working outside again. She found the work's mindless rhythm soothing; it gave her time to think about her daughter in peace.

At ten months old, the baby took Dinah's breath away. She still marveled that this miracle had come from within her body. Most days, she dropped Baby Sarah off early at a cabin where the older slave women took care of the slave children while their parents toiled in the fields. On pleasant days, after she'd fed Sarah, Dinah would bring her to the fields for part of the day in a sack on her back. Dinah couldn't stand to be away from her. Celia thought Sarah was too young to be in the sun all day and that she would have plenty of time to be outdoors. The rest of her life, in fact.

Dinah brought her daughter with her anyway.

Today, she'd left Sarah at the children's cabin. At noon, young slave boys dragged the cart out to the fields for the slaves' supper. Dinah picked up a slab of bread spread with hominy and returned to sit in her row on the moist earth. The springtime sun was warm.

"How ya doing, Dinah?"

Martin sat over in the next row, sipping from a cup of ditch water.

"I'm fine, Mr. Martin. And you?"

"Can't complain. Well, I reckon I can, but I won't."

That's what Dinah liked about Martin. After he'd helped her that day, they'd begun talking regularly. Usually, it wasn't more than a few words, in case Nelson was lurking nearby, but it was enough.

Five minutes later, the overseer trotted by on his horse. "Rise!"

Dinah shoved the rest of the bread into her mouth and glanced at Martin to see if he'd noticed. He was staring at Nelson, who continued to command the slaves to rise as he galloped through the endless rows of tobacco plants.

"You going dancing?" Martin whispered to her.

She chewed furiously. Martin's eyes twinkled as he waited for her answer.

Eventually, she swallowed. "I reckon I might," she whispered back, lowering her head so he couldn't see her smile.

After two more sunsets, Saturday night arrived. The slaves gathered in the clearing, the circle bordered by the slave cabins. The air was filled with the aroma of the food the women had been cooking all afternoon: roasted chicken, turkey, cornmeal, mashed potatoes, and greens. Men sat at one long table, women at another. Laughter filled the air, accompanied by music as two men played their homemade instruments: a violin and a harmonica. A third man kept the rhythm with his hands and feet. Solomon Devereaux had forbidden drums on the plantation, believing slaves used them to send secret messages to each other. He had passed that belief on to his son, Master Sam. Dinah didn't understand their concern. Who could hear the drums? The nearest plantation must be at least a mile away. And what messages would they send, anyway?

Dinah sat on the grass, wearing a beige calico dress and a red ribbon in her hair. Next to her, her momma held Baby Sarah, whose chubby little hand was wrapped around her grandmother's index finger. Despite her initial disappointment that Dinah had given birth to a girl, Celia had fallen in love with her grandchild.

The slaves paired off to dance. Betty and her beau, Ellis, were the first ones out there. Ellis had had a hard time adjusting to being a country slave; country slaves received less food, fewer clothes, and more whippings than city slaves. But he didn't miss Raleigh. He and Betty had been a steady pair since he arrived on the plantation.

The one musician clapped his hands, slapped them against his thighs, and stomped his feet. His intensity increased. Soon, the other two musicians ceased playing; the dancers' pace grew frenetic.

A shadow loomed over Dinah.

Martin, watching the dancers, held two metal cups. "Seems like work to me." He looked over at her momma. "Ms. Celia."

"Martin." Celia smiled as she rocked the baby.

Martin turned to face Dinah. "You feel like dancing?"

"No."

Martin's smile faded.

Dinah circled her arms around her bent legs. "Not to this one. Maybe to something slower."

Martin grinned and settled next to her. "It's too fast for me, too. Oh, this is for you." He handed her a cup of water. Dinah peered into his cup and exhaled in relief. He was drinking water, too. Other men drank spirits on nights like this. She knew firsthand what drink did to men.

Nelson and several men on horseback observed the revelry from outside the clearing, making sure it didn't get out of hand. The white men rested rifles across their laps in case it did. Nelson was unarmed.

The clapping slowed, and the other musicians resumed playing.

"Slow enough for you?" Martin asked.

"Yes."

He took her cup and set it next to his on the ground, then rose and held out his hand. Dinah placed her hand in his, and he led her toward the center of the dancing couples. They stood a foot apart, not touching. He moved. She watched his feet and mirrored his movements.

He lifted her chin gently. "Listen to the music and go with it. There's no right way to dance."

So she did. Instead of thinking, Dinah let the music fill her body and moved wherever it led her. She glanced over at her daughter and her momma, the latter's wide grin almost splitting her face in two.

Dinah gazed into Martin's heavy-lidded brown eyes and

then looked down. Martin raised her chin again. "Always keep your head up."

His fingers were rough but gentle, his full lips different from Beaux's. He made her feel warm inside.

She stepped closer to him.

CHAPTER THIRTY-ONE

SHA

JELANI REMAINED IN bed the entire next day, too. Sha called the Berkeley High School's attendance line to report that her daughter was unwell and would stay home. Unlike Sha, Jelani attended a public school; Sha had wanted her to have a less sheltered experience. Jelani liked school and performed well enough, but didn't apply herself much. She was more dedicated to her social media presence.

The only thing Jelani had eaten since the rape was chicken noodle soup. Even though it wasn't the most nutritious diet, it was better than nothing. She consumed water instead of energy drinks. While she slept, Sha read the texts streaming to Jelani's phone. Her friends had finally texted her, asking what had happened to her at the club and why she had ditched them for that guy. They wondered why she was skipping class without telling them where she was. Throughout the day, the tone of the texts became increasingly irritated.

They accused her of being rude when she didn't respond, and how dare she keep her whereabouts a secret from them. It was all Sha could do not to respond to them.

Erik Stevens hadn't texted.

There'd been a reason her daughter had felt relaxed with Erik that night. The drug tests had come back positive. He'd slipped Rohypnol into her glass of wine.

Sha worked out of her home office again, answering emails and reviewing IT project schedules between intermittent checks on Jelani. When she poked her head into Jelani's room at 10:30 p.m., silence pervaded: the TV, radio, computer, and phone were either off or locked. Jelani was sitting up in bed, staring at the wall. The image was disturbing, eerie, but Sha chose not to comment on it.

She was about to lie to Jelani.

"I have to go to the office. Something's come up."

"Okay."

"Will you be all right by yourself?"

Jelani nodded.

"Need anything?" Sha asked.

A shake of the head.

Sha was worried. She didn't feel right leaving Jelani alone. "Call if you need me. I'll come straight home." She turned to leave.

"Mom?"

Sha faced Jelani. She did not like the blank look on her face. "Yes, sweetie?"

"Don't forget to lock the door. And set the alarm."

Sha frowned, unused to receiving the same reminder she'd often given her daughter.

In the garage, Sha activated the security app on her phone and checked to make sure the exterior cameras in the front and the back of the house were working. As she was about to lock it, the tab for the interior cameras caught her eye. She clicked on it to check on Jelani one more time. Her daughter exited her bedroom and passed under the camera in the hall. Downstairs, Jelani checked every window and the front and back doors to ensure they were closed and locked. A tear splashed on Sha's phone, and she placed a hand over her heart. She was a bad mother for leaving, but her daughter would be safe at home alone for one night. Sha wiped her tears and backed the SUV out of the garage. She paused at the end of the driveway. Under the gabled roof, the house displayed many windows. Too many. For the first time, she felt her home was too exposed to the outside world.

She drove to Z21 under the speed limit and without the phone's navigation app.

Parked across the street this time, she sat in the Audi and scanned the faces of the patrons waiting in line. She didn't see Erik. She exited the vehicle and headed for the entrance. An Uber dropped two women at the curb in front of the red-velvet rope. The same bouncer, dressed in black pants and a black mock turtleneck, watched Sha approach, his eyes hooded and dark. His cologne smelled pleasant, not overpowering.

"You again?"

The patrons continued their conversations and didn't pay any attention to her. Sha pulled her cell out of the front pocket of her jeans and showed the bouncer the photo she had sent herself from her daughter's phone. "Have you seen this guy?"

The bouncer gave the photo a cursory glance. "Lady, do you know how many people come here every night?" A touch of an accent, maybe New York.

Softly, Sha said, "That is not what I asked you."

"Why do you need to know?"

She pointed at the picture. "He…hurt my child."

The bouncer's face softened. He took the phone and stared at it for a moment before handing it back. "Yeah, I've seen him. He comes in here a lot, but he hasn't been in tonight." He scanned the queue against the building's wall and looked back at her. "I've got to get back to work. Give me your number. If he shows up, I'll text you."

Sha hesitated. She didn't divulge her number readily, especially to strangers, but she told him. "Aren't you going to write it down?"

He tapped his temple. "No need."

Sha headed toward her car.

"Hey!" the bouncer said. Sha turned around. "My name is Dominic."

"Sha."

"S-h-a-w?"

"Without the 'w.'"

"I'll keep my eyes peeled, Sha."

Her expression must have been doubtful.

"Really," Dominic reassured her.

A prickle behind Sha's eyes threatened to form into tears. "Thank you." She looked again at the people in line but didn't see her quarry. Disappointed, she crossed the street, got in her car, and sat there for a long time, leaving the radio off. She hadn't brought anything to read. Her eyes did not stray from the front entrance except to check her phone in case Jelani had texted her. Other than that, she waited. And waited.

Erik did not show up that night, or the next two nights.

CHAPTER THIRTY-TWO

OLIVIA

"GOOD EVENING, MRS. BRADLEY!"

"Good evening, Mr. Brown." Olivia stopped at the top of the stairs in front of her brownstone to gaze into her neighbor's yard. "The phlox are beautiful."

Mr. Brown grinned at his work. "They're coming along." He inspected her landscaping. "Have you thought about planting some?"

Olivia followed his gaze. Her front yard was small and square, the grass bisected by the short walk. Against the stone foundation were bushes that had been there when she and Davis bought the place five years ago—once Davis had finally believed they could afford it, even though Olivia hadn't made partner yet.

"No, but maybe it's time I start.

"Let me know if I can help."

Olivia never asked for help with anything. "I will. Goodnight."

"You, too, Mrs. Bradley." Mr. Brown resumed watering his flowers.

After dinner with Davis, Olivia said, "That roasted chicken was delicious."

Davis grinned. "I have a surprise for you." From the counter, he returned with two plates. On each was a large slice of chocolate cake. "To go with your after-dinner coffee. I made it myself."

The cake smelled heavenly. Olivia grasped her dessert fork. "I can't eat all this!"

"Just eat as much as you can. Otherwise, it will go to waste."

They ate in silence. Olivia let an occasional groan of pleasure escape between bites.

"You've been quiet tonight," Davis said. "Something's bothering you. What is it?"

"I'm worried about Nicole. It's been too long since we've heard from her."

"How often did you call your parents when you first started working at the public defender's office?"

"Touché. Still, I'm worried about her."

Their daughter was normally expressive. She told them—especially Davis—almost everything. This total silence wasn't like her.

Olivia patted the remaining cake crumbs on her plate between the fork's tines and slipped the fork into her mouth. "At first, I thought she was just busy. Now I believe it's something more."

Davis stacked the empty dessert dishes, placed the uten-sils on top, and took them to the sink. After rinsing them and placing them in the dishwasher, he returned to the table.

"She'll be all right." He kissed Olivia. "She's having the time of her life."

Olivia studied the dark moles on her husband's face. He should have a doctor check them, she thought. She refrained from mentioning it. It was an effort to get him to visit the doctor's office.

"Do you want more coffee?"

Olivia touched his cheek. "Something's off. I can feel it." She pushed away from the table. "I'm going to call her."

"Olivia…"

"I'll drink another cup after I talk to my daughter."

She left the kitchen, walked down the hall to her home office, opened the French doors, and then closed them behind her. The walls were painted olive green, and the bookcases were filled with legal tomes, nonfiction books, and the novels and stories that Olivia's parents had written. A bay window faced the quiet street. Olivia sat in the leather execu-tive chair behind the leather-topped mahogany pedestal desk and clicked on the green-shaded banker's lamp. Picking up the cordless phone, she donned her reading glasses, which were secured around her neck with a chain, and punched in the number for Nicole's apartment.

The phone rang six times. Olivia was about to leave a message on the answering machine when Nicole answered.

"I'm glad I reached you." Olivia leaned back in her chair. "I'm worried. Why haven't you called?"

"Too busy. You know what that's like."

"I'm never too busy to call home."

"Well, I am."

This sullen voice did not sound like Nicole.

Through the French doors, Olivia saw Davis enter the family room across the hall carrying a large bowl of buttered popcorn he'd popped with a covered skillet on the stove.

"I'm still worried."

"Mother, I'm fine. Just swamped."

Davis left the family room without glancing in Olivia's direction.

"You sound tired," Olivia said into the phone.

"I am tired."

"How's the job going?"

"It's like that MJ song…They've got me working day and night."

"I'm being serious."

There was silence on the other end. "It could take some time to tell you. How much wine do you have?"

"A whole cellar's worth."

Davis came into her office with a steaming cup of decaf coffee and a coaster. He mimed for her to say "hi" to Nicole.

"Your father says 'hi.'"

"Tell him I said 'hello.'"

She did. After Davis left, she asked, "Where were we?"

"I'm not ready to discuss it, yet."

Olivia sat up. "What is it? Tell me."

"Mother…"

"Have you received a promotion?"

"No."

"But you work so hard. You should have received one by now."

"I think so, too," Nicole said under her breath.

"Are you sure you're putting the time in?"

"Yes, Mother. I'm working eighteen hours a day."

"Because when you're Black, you must work twice as hard and be twice as good—"

"To get half as far. I know. You've told me that my whole life. Trust me, it's not me. May I talk to Dad?"

Olivia almost laughed aloud at her daughter's attempt to change the subject. Olivia could press her—throughout her career, she'd deposed tougher witnesses than Nicole—but she let it go. "He's watching TV. I'll get him." She hesitated. "You take care. I love you."

"I love you, too."

Olivia placed the phone on the desk and opened her office door. "Your daughter wants to talk to you."

After a moment, Davis said, "Got it!"

Olivia circled behind her desk and picked up the phone. Nicole was already chatting with Davis, who listened to her from the extension in the family room. Her daughter was more animated with him than she'd been with Olivia. Olivia returned the telephone to its charging cradle, picked up the coffee cup, and slowly spun her chair around to gaze out the window, the blinds halfway drawn. She blew on the liquid to cool it. The street was quiet and dark, except for the circles of light emanating from the streetlamps. Her neighbors were in for the evening.

She sipped the coffee.

At times like this, she wished she had girlfriends to talk

to about her troubles, especially ones who had daughters. She was uncomfortable talking to her older sisters, and she kept her problems to herself. Dealt with them herself. It'd been difficult to let people in after what had happened with Ted. She had her husband, of course, and talked to him about everything, but it wasn't the same as talking to a woman. She couldn't discuss her private life with her colleagues; work and personal lives had to be kept separate. And she didn't want fake, meaningless friendships or have time for complicated, drama-filled ones. One of the reasons she loved Davis so much was that he was easy to get along with. He was calm, steady, and uncomplicated. At her age and with her profession, friendships were hard to come by, and she'd long been out of practice. It got lonely at the top. Besides Davis, she had her mother and Nicole, and that would have to be enough.

She set the cup down on the desk, took off her glasses, pinched the bridge of her nose, closed her eyes, and sat there for several minutes. What would her mother do? Her grandmother?

Olivia put her glasses back on and opened her personal organizer, thick with scraps of paper, business cards, and sticky notes. She flipped the pages to the address book section and found her travel agent's number. She lifted the phone again and listened for the dial tone to make sure Davis and Nicole had hung up. Olivia dialed and booked a seat for the next morning's first US Airways flight to Atlanta.

CHAPTER THIRTY-THREE

AUGUSTA

"I DON'T WANT to stay home," Augusta protested.

Jean straightened the lapels on his gray suit jacket, a pipe filled with Prince Albert tobacco clenched between his teeth. He removed the pipe and placed it in its holder on the oak dresser in their bedroom. "We've been over this several times, Auggie. The club isn't the best place for a child."

"But it hasn't been born yet," Augusta said.

"Still. I want my son to be born healthy and to have every advantage."

Augusta sat on their bed's blue and slate-colored bedspread and rubbed her belly. She hadn't yet started to show, and she felt nothing from the baby. "How do you know it's a boy?"

Jean inspected his hair in the mirror over the dresser. He had straightened it himself that afternoon with a mixture of lye, eggs, and potatoes. He glanced at Augusta's reflection. "I just do," he smiled, "and because I rubbed the tree yesterday."

The baby's name was a foregone conclusion: Jean Aaron Wells III.

"What am I going to do while you're gone?" Augusta whined.

Jean kissed her on the cheek. "You're smart. You'll think of something. I need to run. I can't be late."

The following morning, while Jean was still sleeping, Augusta went shopping along Lenox Avenue with Marian and Florence. Cars honked and a few men shouted catcalls at the three women. The afternoon was brisk. Augusta tightened the belt on her coat. She'd forgotten to wear gloves. After they passed a bookstore, Augusta stopped and retraced her steps.

On the cover of a book in the display window, a noose hung from a tree in front of a setting sun. Augusta felt an adrenaline rush. She called out to her friends, "Wait a minute. I'll be right back."

That night, after Jean left, Augusta removed the book she'd purchased that afternoon and hidden in a kitchen cabinet and retired early to their bedroom. She held the novel, its weight comforting, then ran her hand over the cover as she had done in the store: *A Southern Lynching* by Richmond St. Clair. A long-forgotten feeling infused her as she held it, as if she were coming home. For the first time in a long time, she wondered what it would be like to see Augusta Gibson Wells on a book cover.

She opened the book. He'd dedicated it to Margaret: To the woman I admire most. Was she Richmond's girlfriend?

Or wife? Augusta turned to chapter one but, after reading only a few pages, she closed the book, put it on the nightstand, and slid open the drawer. She pulled out a pad of paper and a pen and began to write.

⁓

"Come to Mama, Clara."

The toddler walked toward Augusta in fits and starts, her legs straightening at odd moments. Although Clara kept falling on the linoleum floor, she didn't cry. She got back up and kept walking, her short stubby arms reaching for her mother the entire journey, as if Augusta were the holy grail.

Clara screamed with delight as she tumbled into her mother's arms. Her smile was all gums. Her hazel eyes were alight. No one's eyes were that color in either Augusta's or Jean's family.

Augusta squeezed her precious daughter and kissed her on the crown of her head, where a few wisps of light-brown hair were beginning to show. "You did it!"

Jean sat on the opposite end of the kitchen floor with his legs spread out. "Come to Papa," he said.

Clara made the return journey in the same way. As she stumbled into Jean's outstretched arms, he hugged her, then held her with both hands, puffed out his cheeks and blew into her bare belly. Clara giggled. Augusta loved watching the two of them together. Jean set Clara down, and she headed back in Augusta's direction.

The last eighteen months had been good to them. The band was still in high demand, and Clara had been the missing piece to Jean and Augusta's family jigsaw puzzle.

Although Jean had been disappointed when he'd learned of the baby's sex, it hadn't taken their first child long to steal his heart. She was Daddy's little girl.

"I have an idea," Augusta said.

Jean looked at her with his smoldering eyes, a smile playing at his lips. "What's that, dear?"

"Let's go out tonight. Mama can come over and watch the baby."

Jean's smile faded. "This is my first night off in a long time. I want to relax and spend it with you and Clara."

"But you go out every night."

"I'm working."

Rain pattered against the window above the kitchen sink.

"It's not all work."

"What do you mean by that?"

"It's not like you work in a mine or on a farm or something. You're having fun. I'm getting stir crazy staying at home alone all the time."

"You have Clara."

Augusta kissed her daughter on the forehead and turned the child to face Jean. "Sometimes I need adult company." Augusta had considered asking for her old job back so that she could spend time with her mama and the other ladies, but she knew Jean would never allow it. And who would watch Clara? "Hey! I can wear the beaded dress you just bought me. We can go to the Savoy and swing dance. It has two bandstands!"

"I know that," Jean said tersely. The Palmer Parks Band had yet to receive an invitation to play there.

Augusta sighed and gave Clara a small push, sending her

on her way. "I can't remember the last time we went dancing. Can we go? Please?" She held her breath.

Jean leaned his head back against a white cabinet. "I don't want to, Auggie. I'm exhausted."

"But I never get to go out—"

"I said 'no!' Why do you always have to make my life so difficult?"

Augusta was stunned. "Your life...difficult?"

"Your man wants to stay home and be with you. Why can't that be enough? Is that why you're with me? Because I'm a musician?"

"I never cared about that. I love *you*, Jean."

"I'm tired." He stood. "I'm taking a nap."

He left the room, his footsteps padding down the hallway toward their bedroom. He didn't bother to look at his daughter, who careened across the floor reaching her arms out to him.

Clara almost made it.

CHAPTER THIRTY-FOUR

DINAH

"WHAT ARE YOU smiling about?"

"Nothing," Dinah said.

"You don't have to tell me, 'cause I know," Betty said. "It's 'cause you're startin' somethin' with Martin."

Dinah giggled at the rhyme.

They sat side-by-side on old wooden chairs on the front stoop of Celia's cabin, washing their dresses in a tin tub filled with creek water. It was Sunday, the day after the dance. What should have been a day of rest. More often, it was a chance for the slaves to catch up on their own chores, which they didn't have time to attend to during the week.

A thunderstorm had blown through earlier that afternoon, whipping the trees back and forth, the rain pelting the wood-shingled roof. Baby Sarah had flinched at every thunderclap but hadn't cried. Now, the air smelled fresh and clean. A light rain still fell on the porch's wooden overhang. Drops beaded near the porch's edge.

Dinah had known Betty her entire life. Her best friend was one of the few slaves on the plantation whose parents still lived together. Often, at least one slave parent was sold or killed or worn out to death. Given the transience of slave life, one learned at an early age not to become too attached to people. But Dinah cherished her friendship with Betty and couldn't imagine life without her.

"It was only one dance," Dinah said.

Betty lifted her dress out of the water to see whether the stain from the moonshine she'd spilled last night had come off. It hadn't. She dunked the dress back in the tub and scrubbed the stain with soap Dinah's momma had taken from the house. "I saw the way he was looking at you."

"When did you have time? You were too busy batting your eyes at Ellis."

"Martin sure is handsome," Betty continued, as if Dinah hadn't spoken. "With those big brown eyes, that smooth skin, and that broad back. We could wash our clothes on that stomach of his."

Dinah giggled again. "Hush now. I forgot to tell you what he said to me after we danced—"

Her friend stopped smiling and lowered her head, scrubbing the spot that no longer stained her dress.

Beaux Devereaux sat on his mare, watching them, a toothpick between his teeth. His dog, Jake, stood at attention next to him. Dinah's breath caught; she hoped he hadn't overheard their conversation. Beaux stared at her, tipped his hat to her, then, with his dog following, guided his mare toward the dirt trail that wended its way to the main road past the post-and-rail fence marking the front edge of the property.

Since her banishment to the fields, Dinah had only seen Beaux from a distance.

"He's a snake," Betty spat. "I guess you know that better than any of us."

Dinah's cheeks flushed. She resumed rubbing at the grass stain on the seat of her own dress.

"You have nothing to be ashamed of," Betty reassured her. "You did nothing wrong."

Dinah submerged the dress in the water. No one except her mother knew that Beaux had raped her, or that he was Sarah's father…Although Martha and the other slaves had probably guessed. There were no secrets in the slave quarters. Anyway, Baby Sarah's creamy skin was a dead giveaway; it was the same color as the parchment paper the mistress used to write her correspondences.

Betty dropped her hand in the water and squeezed Dinah's hand. "Forget him. Let's talk about pleasant things."

They resumed gossiping and giggling. After a while, Dinah's momma came out of the cabin with an armful of clothing. She pursed her lips. "Since y'all are having so much fun, you might as well wash my clothes, too." She dumped the clothes on the porch and went back inside.

The two friends exchanged glances and burst into laughter.

When they finished washing all the clothing, Dinah dumped the dirty water from the tub onto the grass. Some of it seeped under the crawlspace.

From afar, someone shouted, "Patrol!"

Then a familiar voice screamed.

Betty jumped off the porch. Dinah dropped the tub and followed her. The earth was still wet from the earlier storm.

Avoiding the puddles, they ran to the opposite end of the quarters, the end closest to the creek. A patrol was clutching the arm of Betty's little brother, Lukas, whose eyes were as wild as his hair, which he didn't cut often.

Dinah shook with helplessness and rage as the patrol tied the boy face-first to a wooden pole, leaving his toes scraping the ground. The man's two raggedy black dogs circled Lukas, barking and drooling and snapping their bared teeth at him.

The creek water rippled.

Another patrol stood several paces away, grasping a cowskin whip. "You want to see Jesus, boy?" Without waiting for an answer, he flicked his wrist. The lash whizzed through the air, ending with the sound of a loud crack as it slashed the boy's back. Lukas howled as his henna-toned skin welled.

Dinah flinched. She and Betty stood ten yards away from Lukas, out of reach of the blood-coated whip, in front of the slaves who had gathered there to watch. Betty sobbed throughout the whipping, her tears mixing with the light rain. Lukas's back bled. Ridges of skin rose, revealing open wounds.

The patrol, consisting of poor white men, apprehended and flogged any slave caught off the plantation without a pass. They also could enter cabins without notice in search of a missing slave. The whip-toting captain, reputed for "dancing with Negroes," whipped offending slaves until they screamed for mercy. He took it easy on Lukas by only meting out thirty-nine lashes. And letting him live.

When the whipping ceased, Betty stepped toward her brother.

"Get back, girl," the patrol said. He scanned the faces of the other slaves. "Nobody touch him! Ya hear?"

"Why did you whip him?" Betty screamed.

"We caught him praying again."

"If the Lord is our savior, you should want him to pray."

"The Lord is *our* savior." The patrol flicked his wrist, the whip's tail end coming within an inch of Betty's face. "Animals don't have souls."

When Dinah was a child, Aisha had whispered to her about their deities as Dinah drifted off to sleep each night, imploring her to turn to them when seeking answers to life's questions. Aisha had belonged to a coven of slaves who met in the woods in secret to commune with their gods and worship them through song and dance. If caught, the overseer would have flogged or killed them. Master Sam did not allow slaves to attend church or to pray, even in secret. The white man didn't want them to hope.

Betty screeched. "How long will you leave him there?"

The patrols mounted their horses.

"How long will you leave him there?" she screamed again.

The patrol leaned forward and raised his whip. He held the threatening position for a few seconds before turning his horse around.

They rode away, their dogs following close behind. The men's laughter reached back to Betty and Dinah like a slap across the face.

Betty stayed with Lukas throughout the night, talking to him in a low voice and providing him with food and water, while flies and mosquitoes feasted on his back. Lukas prayed through the pain.

Nelson cut him down just before dawn.

CHAPTER THIRTY-FIVE

SHA

FOUR DAYS AFTER she'd been sexually assaulted, Jelani entered the kitchen for the first time since the incident.

Sha sat at the white pine table, drinking coffee and reading the *Mercury News* on her tablet. Despite her daughter's ordeal, the world moved on. Politicians lied. People hurt each other. Stole from each other. Went on with their lives as if nothing had happened. As if the world Sha and Jelani knew hadn't just ended.

Jelani's hair was picked out into a 1970s afro. She was still wearing the long T-shirt she'd slept in.

"Morning, baby," Sha said. "Did you sleep all right? It's not noon yet."

"Funny." Jelani plopped down into the chair across from her. "Yeah."

"Yes." A correction that had yet to take. Sha would keep trying. "What do you want for breakfast?"

Jelani shrugged. "I don't care."

"Of course you don't. Sit tight. I'll make you pancakes."

Jelani's neck jerked. "You…cook? Do you want to order something to be delivered? I'll buy."

Sha laughed. Jelani didn't work and had no money.

Jelani gave Sha a tentative smile. She was going to be okay.

"They'll be good," Sha said. "Trust me. My Grandpa Davis taught me how to make them."

At the center island, Sha leaned between two stools and selected a skillet from the hanging rack of pots and pans.

"Mom?"

Sha placed the skillet on the burner. "Mm-hmm?"

"Where have you been going every night?"

Sha grabbed the unopened box of pancake mix off a cupboard shelf and quickly read the directions. "Why?"

"You haven't put in this many hours at work in a long time. Plus, you're acting weird. If I didn't know better, I'd think you're seeing someone."

"Why couldn't I be seeing someone?"

"You haven't for a while. Well…ever."

Sha poured the mix into a measuring cup and then into the skillet. "I told you. I've had several emergencies at work."

"Why so many?"

"I don't know. They've come up. Can you set the table?"

Jelani moved toward the cupboard. "Why aren't you looking at me?"

Sha turned briefly. "You're going to school today."

Jelani set two plates on the table. "And you're trying to change the subject."

Sha flipped a sizzling pancake with a spatula. The aroma of pancake batter filled the kitchen. "Hey, what do you say we go to a movie tonight? Get out of the house."

"What if you have another work emergency?"

"One of my directors can deal with it."

"Why haven't you let one of them take care of the emergencies that occurred over the past week?"

Sha slid a fluffy chocolate-chip pancake onto Jelani's plate, then her own. "When did you get so smart? You could be a debater like your grandmother." She replaced the skillet on the stove, opened the fridge to retrieve the orange juice carton, and sat across from Jelani. "Well?"

"Well, what?"

Sha filled each of their glasses. "How about we catch a movie?"

"That sounds good, Mom." Jelani rested her chin in her hand and slid a bite of maple syrup-drenched pancake into her mouth.

Jelani was growing up. She was placating Sha, instead of the other way around.

❧

Sha was frustrated.

Until she found Erik, she couldn't address Jelani's situation. Sha wasn't sure what she'd do when she found him, but she would worry about that when the time came. And she would find him. Like her mother and grandmother, she hadn't become successful by waiting for things to happen, even though she was a laid-back person. Her backup plan was to stake Erik out at his office, but she wanted to see him here, at the club. She didn't know why. Maybe it was to stop him from hurting someone else's child. Or because, with Dominic present, she wouldn't be confronting a rapist alone.

What had happened to her daughter wasn't fair. Sha wanted to kill the boy, but she didn't want to go to prison. Then where would Jelani be? She could live with Sha's mother. Regardless, Erik Stevens wasn't worth going to prison for. But he wouldn't get away with what he did, either. She could tell him off or try to physically attack him. But that wouldn't make a difference to him. She needed to hurt him where it would matter.

While she waited, Sha played Words with Friends on her phone against dozens of "friends" she would never meet in real life. She wasn't competing against them, but against herself, trying to top her highest score. She'd been hanging outside the club late every night, hoping for a glimpse of Erik. After work, she and Jelani ate dinner and talked about their respective days until Jelani went upstairs to do her homework. Sha watched the news or a Warriors game until it was time for her to leave. She told her daughter she was leading a major project at work, the details of which were confidential. The story sounded false even to her own ears.

One night in May, after the last patron had entered the club and there had been no sign of Erik, Sha left the Audi after having sat in it for several hours. The air was cool. She shook out her legs. Dominic was in front of the entrance, collecting the velvet rope and stanchion posts and putting them in a small room accessible from the outside. Sha crossed the street.

"Thank you," she said, "for helping me."

"I didn't do anything."

He lifted the valet podium with ease and deposited it in the storage room. He closed and locked the door and returned.

"Still," she said.

They stood for a moment. Small talk had never been Sha's strong suit. She waved at the club. "What do you do? Besides this?"

Dominic looked at her, puzzled. "Why can't this be my life's work?"

Sha's face flushed. "I thought…"

He laughed. "I'm kidding. I just completed my masters in cybersecurity at the University of Southern California."

Sha gaped. "That's a great program. What are you doing…here?"

"I'm taking a break before I work full time for the rest of my life."

"Have you chosen a company?"

"Not yet. I want to find the right fit. Besides, I enjoy working here. I don't have to think too much."

"Do you want to think?"

Dominic shrugged. "Eventually."

"How about now? If it's for a good cause?" Sha handed him her business card.

He glanced at it and nodded. "A Black woman in tech and a CIO. That's huge."

Sha couldn't wait for the day when her role as a Black leader in the tech field wasn't a surprise. "We need more of us."

CHAPTER THIRTY-SIX

OLIVIA

INSTEAD OF PREPARING for the trial that was scheduled at the end of the month, Olivia flew to Atlanta to visit her daughter.

She and Nicole sat on opposite ends of the white love seat in Nicole's living room, their shoes kicked off. Nicole sat cross-legged in her red, knee-length Hunt Club pajamas, and Olivia's legs were tucked underneath her. Olivia was still in the black slacks and lavender silk shirt she'd worn on the flight. An episode of *Dynasty* was showing on the white thirteen-inch television Nicole had brought from home. The TV was perched on a wooden board that rested on four red milk crates, two at each end.

"What a surprise, seeing you through the peephole."

A thunderstorm had started right after Olivia had entered the building.

"I should have come sooner."

"It's okay. I know how it is when you're prepping for a trial. Besides, you're here now."

Olivia shifted in discomfort at the fact that her daughter made excuses for her before she could make them for herself. Olivia always had an excuse ready. For Davis, for Nicole.

A white IKEA bookcase crammed with books leaned against a living-room wall. Adjacent to the living room, a dining area accommodated a small round table and two chairs. A Formica counter separated it from the cramped kitchen. When she'd arrived, Olivia had peeked into the bedroom, its only furniture a full-size bed. Most of Nicole's clothes and belongings spilled out of cardboard boxes and garbage bags, the tiny closet unable to house them all. Rain smeared the apartment's only window, blurring its view of the building next door.

Olivia glanced at the walls, bare except for the bookcase and a scotch-taped poster of the singing duo Hall & Oates. "When will you unpack? Decorate?"

Nicole laughed. "The minimalist décor isn't working for you?"

"I'll hire a service to unpack for you. Tomorrow, we can buy furniture, so it doesn't look…empty. Or I can contract with a designer—"

"I'm okay with the way it is, Mother. I'm going to take my time decorating it and making it perfect…for me. That's the joy of having my own place. Anyway, I don't want to spend a lot of money if I'll only live here for a year or two."

Olivia had never lived alone. She lived with her family until she'd turned eighteen. Her parents and Julia, Olivia's grandmother, had welcomed Nicole, the accidental child, with open arms. Other teenage mothers had not been as lucky.

"You're right," Olivia said. "At least the plant can keep you company."

They glanced at the artificial plant in the corner and laughed.

"A gift from a coworker I'd invited over. One look at my place, and she felt sorry for me. Given the hours we put in, she knew better than to buy me a real one."

"That was kind of her."

"It was. But guess what?"

"What?"

Nicole spread her arms. "At least you can sit in my living room," she teased.

Growing up, Nicole had never understood why they didn't use the living room unless they were entertaining guests. "Why do you call it a living room?" she used to argue. "If you don't want us to touch anything, why not call it a museum?"

This had never failed to make Olivia and Davis laugh, no matter how many times they'd heard it.

"I inherited that tradition from my mama," Olivia said. "She preferred we sit in the family room." She didn't mention that her sisters had told her their papa had owned a grand piano and used to play it all the time in the living room, which was the real reason they could never sit in there.

A newspaper, opened to a half-finished crossword puzzle, rested on the sofa between Olivia and Nicole. Next to it lay a blue-covered paperback book, face down in a V shape. "*Riverside Drive*. What's it about?" Olivia asked.

"A woman trying to make it in the news business!"

Olivia laughed. "You're obsessed."

Nicole gave her a knowing expression. "You taught me well. To be the best, I must be focused and stay ten steps ahead of everyone else."

"I taught you that? I don't remember saying those things."

Nicole shrugged. "You didn't have to."

A baby bawled in the apartment next door.

Olivia sipped her wine. "Have you made many friends here?"

"A few women at work."

"You sure you don't want a roommate? You could rent a bigger place. Share the burden."

"I've got this, Mother."

Nostalgia washed over Olivia. "Our first apartment as a family was smaller than this. Do you remember it?"

"A little."

"You were seven. We didn't have much money, much of anything, but the three of us were happy there."

"That's what I want, too. Those kinds of memories. I miss seeing you and Dad every day, but I like being on my own. I enjoy the solitude after the noise of the newsroom. It's how I recharge."

Olivia could learn something from her daughter. "You look thin."

"Sometimes I'm so tired when I get home from work, I only have the energy to eat a bowl of ice cream and watch TV before falling asleep."

"That doesn't sound healthy."

"Mother!"

"Okay, okay. How's work going?"

"Crazy busy. And I can't make any mistakes."

I still feel that way. "Thinking like that will sap your creative energy. Just try your best. That's all anyone could ask for." Olivia paused. "Even me. There's nothing wrong with asking for help when you need it. You're young in your career. You're not supposed to know everything."

"I don't want to look weak."

Did I teach her to think like this?

"But my boss told me," Nicole continued, excitement creeping into her voice, "that if I keep working hard, I'll earn a promotion in no time."

Olivia raised her glass. "You're on your way. Nothing can stop you now."

They clinked glasses. "One day, Mother," Nicole said, "I'll be just like you."

Olivia's smile faltered as her daughter drank. "I don't have all the answers. Sometimes, I had to fake it until I made it. I'm unsure if my way was the right way, but it worked for me. My career—my life—might have been easier if I hadn't been desperate to reach the top, but it wouldn't have been as fulfilling for me." She had never been this open with Nicole about her career aspirations. "I want you to be like you. You deserve it all." Quietly, she added, "To find that balance between career and family."

As she said those words, Olivia tried to hide her doubts. Could women really have it all? For her, work always seemed to win. She felt like a fraud.

"Tell me about your trip to AC." After Olivia finished telling her about eating hot corn dogs while walking against a biting wind on Atlantic City's boardwalk with Davis, Nicole said, "I can't believe you took a vacation. One day, I want to visit every state, different countries, all the wonders of the world. I've started keeping a journal."

"Oh?"

Nicole shrugged. "Who knows? I might write a book someday."

This pleased Olivia. "Like your grandmother."

As they sipped their drinks, Diahann Carroll strutted across a hotel lobby on the TV screen, several porters dragging her luggage and struggling to keep up with her.

"Have you met any interesting men?" Olivia asked.

"Ha! When would I have time to meet someone? The only guys I see are the ones I work with."

"And you can't mix business with pleasure."

"I *know*, Mother." Nicole had mastered that irritated-bored voice, usually accompanied by an eye roll, as a teenager. "You've told me that many times." She imitated Olivia. "'You'll have plenty of time to date when you've reached your destination.'"

Olivia laughed. Nicole had never imitated her, at least in her presence. "But you can be successful without sacrificing love. Or yourself." She peered into her empty glass. "Something I could have done better. But the reward of accomplishments is greater if you have someone to share them with."

Nicole picked up the wine bottle sitting on the floor and refilled both of their glasses. "Don't worry. Love is the last thing on my mind. Besides, I have you and Dad."

"Yes, you do. Always. But it's not the same."

As they continued to watch the nighttime soap opera, Olivia's face warmed from the wine. They mimicked the characters' dialogue and became giggly.

Despite its sparseness, the apartment was comfortable. Olivia was glad she had come. Her daughter was doing well and was on the right path. Olivia needn't worry so much about her. And the quick visit had taken her mind off work and Robert Penn.

"It's getting late," Olivia said. "You need to get some sleep. The early bird gets the worm."

"Mom, that's an old cliché!"

"Maybe, but it's true."

✍

After her impromptu visit with Nicole, Olivia became embroiled in a high-profile merger, her firm representing a national telecommunications company. She enjoyed the technical aspects of the case along with her involvement in the biggest merger in US history. Given the legal complications and regulatory implications, however, she spent a lot of time at the acquiring company's headquarters in Kansas City and in meetings with senior-level executives at the Federal Communications Commission in Washington, DC. The acquisition attracted significant media attention and consumed eighteen months of Olivia's life, so she had no spare time to travel to Atlanta.

Nicole had been too busy at the network to visit, except for a few days at Christmas. She even had to work Thanksgiving. "The news doesn't take holidays," she'd said.

She called her parents weekly and, every few months, she

sent them a letter or a postcard with the National & World News Network's logo embossed on it. When Olivia wasn't traveling, she and Davis would read and discuss their daughter's correspondences over dinner. When Olivia was away, Davis would read them to her over the phone while she lay in her hotel bed, still in her business suit, after a long day of meetings. She loved hearing not only her daughter's words, but also the pride in her husband's voice as he read them. The letters were only a paragraph or two long, but that was all they needed: to know that Nicole was all right.

Eventually, the cards and letters stopped coming. Soon after, the calls stopped coming, too.

CHAPTER THIRTY-SEVEN

JULIA

"CLARA, GIVE HER back the ball!"

Josie, almost two, sat in the grass in the shade of an elm tree and reached out her stubby arms. "Ba!"

"Mama, she can't throw!" Augusta's precocious three-year-old said.

"Your sister can play with it however she wants. Throw it to her."

"Okaaaaaaaaaaaaaaaaaaay…"

Clara threw the ball to Josie, who, of course, missed it, swiveling her neck to follow its arc as it sailed over her head. The ball rolled until it hit the bottom of the wooden fence.

Augusta pointed. "Go pick it up and hand it to her."

"All Riiiiiiiiight…"

Julia and Augusta sat on the porch swing on the back stoop. The dogwood tree was blossoming. Lush green plants manned either side of the steps, a butterfly flittering over the flowers. The grass was long; Jean hadn't had time to mow it lately. In the center of the backyard rested a six-foot plastic baby pool.

The Wells family had moved from their cramped apartment to a four-story brownstone on Seventh Avenue. Augusta's favorite part of the house was the small sitting room with rounded bay windows and a window seat that faced the avenue, where she could sit and people-watch. The house was close to restaurants and stores, some of them Negro-owned. Jean's favorite room was the living room, where he finally had enough space for a baby grand piano.

The family had just arrived home after attending services at the Abyssinian Baptist Church on West 138th Street. On the walk home, the pavement had been hot enough to burn through the soles of Julia's Mary Janes. Julia didn't care for the church or the congregation— especially the women, who cared more about other female worshipers' hats than about praising the Lord. One woman threw her hat up high in the air every time she got happy. Julia had never met so many gossipy God-fearing women in her life. She preferred her own church, Mount Zion, but Abyssinian was closer to Augusta's new home.

Despite his church upbringing, Jean had skipped the services again, exhausted after returning from a gig in the early hours of the morning.

Julia glanced at her granddaughters. They were both light-skinned, like their father, with thin wavy hair. She and Hale had moved in with the Wells family after Josie was born so that Julia could help Augusta with the children. Though she'd hesitated to leave the home she'd once shared with her husband, Clifford, she loved being a part of Clara's and Josie's everyday lives. In time, she realized that her former apartment was only a place. Clifford was with her, no matter where she lived.

Augusta had told her that Jean was trying hard for a third child. A son. Sometimes Julia heard them "trying" upstairs through her bedroom ceiling. On those nights, she turned up her radio receiver and, if they were still trying after the night's last program, she left the volume on high, preferring the sound of static, and buried her head underneath her pillow.

"What are you reading?" she asked Augusta.

Augusta lifted the magazine. "*The Crisis*. Isn't this cover amazing? An article about higher education."

"Oh?" The swing creaked. Julia enjoyed the light breeze on her face from the swing's rocking motion. "You're thinking about continuing your education?"

"Not really. I'm just enjoying the article."

"It's never too late."

"It is for me. I'm a wife and a mother. But…"

Her daughter glanced over her shoulder at the house.

"What are you doing?" Julia asked.

"Making sure Jean isn't nearby." She lowered her voice. "I haven't told him…yet."

"Told him what?"

"That I've been writing every day."

Julia welcomed the excitement in her daughter's voice, a tone she hadn't heard in a long time. "A letter?"

"No. I think it's going to be a novel."

"That's wonderful! What's it about?"

Augusta's eyes were alight. "I can't tell you."

"Okay. When will I get to read it?"

Augusta's forehead wrinkled. "I'm not sure yet."

"I always believed you'd be a wonderful storyteller. It runs in the family." After a few swings, she added, "I like your hair, by the way. It shows off your beautiful neck."

Augusta reached up and patted underneath the back of her bobbed hair, courtesy of a visit to the salon that afternoon. "Thank you."

"Does Jean like it?"

Clara was trying to teach Josie how to hold the ball, although the baby's hand was too small.

Augusta mumbled a response.

Julia thought she heard her say "I wouldn't know."

Julia headed along West 135th Street to a store that stocked a particular ingredient she needed for the dish she was warming in the oven.

Today was a special day.

A bell jingled as she entered the store.

A newspaper and magazine stand stood in the corner. Shelving lined one wall with cigarettes, tobacco, and pipes. The store smelled fresh, like pine cleaner.

The proprietor placed his hands on the counter next to the cash register. He was dark-skinned, wore round-framed glasses, and always had a hearty smile on his face. "Good afternoon, Mrs. Gibson. Been a while."

"Afternoon, Eddie."

"Casserole again?"

"It's my daughter's birthday."

"I'll get that brown sugar for you. Be right back."

As he came from behind the counter and shuffled across the tile floor, Julia slapped the leather gloves she was holding against her hand and approached the window.

She observed the passersby through the EDDIE'S stenciled in big orange letters on the window. Chryslers and Plymouths and DeSotos drove by. Coming from downtown, a streetcar packed with customers dinged for pedestrians to stay out of its way. A policeman pointed directions to a man. A beautiful woman—she might have been an actress or a singer—emerged from the Paradise Hotel across the street in the company of a man in a smart brown suit, whose arm was around her waist.

Julia sighed. Young love. When Clifford was courting her, he'd show up at her momma's house to ask her to go for a walk. They'd walk for hours with no destination. By the end of their courtship, she'd become familiar with every street in Boston's West End.

Julia stopped suddenly as she was turning back to face the counter. The man's suit appeared familiar. Jean owned a similar one, but it couldn't be him. She squinted. The slicked-back hair. The narrow face. The pencil-thin mustache. Yes, it could.

And the woman he was with wasn't Augusta.

Julia stepped away from the window and gasped, bringing her hand to her throat, although it was doubtful that Jean could see her from that distance. She needn't have worried. His eyes were focused on the woman. He kissed her on the lips and helped her into a taxi.

A crooked smile split his face, his hands in the pockets of his opened overcoat, as he watched the cab pull away.

"Here you go!" Eddie said, making his way back behind the counter.

Julia ignored him. Rage unfurled in the pit of her stomach as Jean turned and swaggered down Seventh Avenue toward home. He'd make it in time for Augusta's birthday party.

A tear rolled down Julia's cheek. Her daughter was so good. She didn't deserve this. Why hadn't Julia protected her better? She should have forbidden Augusta from dating Jean. Julia wanted to run after him now and tell him off, whup him, but what good would that do?

"Clifford, what should I do?"

"What did you say, ma'am?" asked Eddie.

"Uh…nothing."

"I have your brown sugar. The brand you like."

"Just a minute."

"Are you all right, Mrs. Gibson?"

Julia wiped her face, turned, and reached into her purse. "I'm fine, Eddie. How much do I owe you?"

She wouldn't let Jean take Augusta's favorite casserole away from her, too.

CHAPTER THIRTY-EIGHT

DINAH

A FEW WEEKS after Lukas's flogging, there was a knock on the cabin's front door after dinner time. Dinah answered.

"Is your momma home?" Martin asked with a serious expression.

Dinah jerked her head back. "My momma?"

Martin had been dropping by often to invite Dinah for a walk or to sit on the stoop and talk, but he'd never asked for her momma. Dinah opened the door wider to let him in.

Celia was sitting in a corner of the room next to the mud chimney where they slept on chilly nights, in a chair that had one leg shorter than the others. She loved to "rock" in it while she sewed. She was an excellent seamstress, a skill she'd learned from her mother, who used to sew patches of color- ful fabrics into her own dresses to remind herself of home. Of Benin. The mistress knew of Celia's talents and supplied her with material. Celia made extra money by charging other slaves for her services. This side vocation paid for necessities like coffee, tea, flour, and sugar, and luxuries such as utensils and a kettle.

Dinah escorted Martin across the dirt floor. The cabin didn't have much furniture aside from the two beds and the rocker, but everything was neat and always in its place. Celia set the needle and the dress on her lap and looked up at them.

Martin stared at Celia without speaking. What was he doing? One of Celia's curved eyebrows rose. Finally, he asked Dinah, "You mind if I talk to her alone?"

Dinah glanced at her momma, who had a gleam in her eye. There was only one reason Martin would want to speak to her in private.

"I reckon," Dinah said.

She left the cabin without a shawl and sat on the stoop. The slave children, dressed only in linen shirts, chased each other around the clearing. A slight breeze whispered in Dinah's ear as she studied the different colors of the oak and maple tree leaves.

She'd never believed she would fall in love. Never wanted to. But being with Martin made her mind and body react against her will. Instead of solving arithmetic problems while she worked, she stole glances at him working on the other side of the row. Her stomach fluttered every time he caught her looking.

She started counting the leaves and reached six hundred by the time Martin stepped outside and closed the door. "Let's walk," he said.

They strolled between the cabins to the land beyond the

quarters, the grass warm beneath their feet. The three white men on horseback shot them a glance then ignored them, accustomed to seeing them take this walk. Out of earshot, Martin stopped and faced Dinah, his smile bashful. The magnolia trees' shadows lengthened. Behind him, the setting sun streaked the sky with purple and red and gold.

"I bet you know what I talked to your momma about," he said.

Dinah's heart thudded in her chest. "I have an idea. What did she say?"

"That's between her and me."

"Well…what did you bring me out here to tell me?"

"Master Sam gave me permission to ask you a question." He took both of her slender hands in his gigantic, rough ones. "Dinah, I've loved you since I was three years old."

Dinah laughed nervously. "You don't remember that far back."

"Sure do. You were the only girl I wanted to be with. Now, the only woman. I want to share the rest of my days with you. Wherever you are, I will be."

"What about Baby Sarah?" She held her breath.

Martin's eyes widened. "You have to ask?" He grazed her lips with his for the first time and stepped behind her, encircling her in his arms, to face the descending sun. "I want to share the rest of my days with her, too. Since she's a part of you, she'll be a part of me, too. I'll raise her as my own."

⁓

A slave wedding was not legal, and the couple's owner(s) could annul the marriage at any time. It was a ritual that only

224

meant something to the couple, their friends and family, and the slave community. There wouldn't be a honeymoon. Nelson expected them in the tobacco field first thing Monday morning, but they didn't care. There would be music, a feast, and they'd be together from that moment on. Forever.

All week, the mood in the quarters was festive. The other slaves liked and respected Dinah and Martin. The women loved watching Martin play with Baby Sarah, carrying her around the clearing on his strong back playing Maya the Elephant, without a care about the dirt and mud coating his hands or the grass staining the knees of his trousers. Or sitting on Celia's porch, the baby scrambling onto his lap. He'd tell her a story that he made up as he went along while feeding her tiny pieces of biscuits sweetened with milk.

Martin was already Sarah's daddy in the ways that mattered.

The slaves remarked on how Martin treated Dinah, looked out for her, and loved her. He never raised his voice or his hand. Often, he'd do her share of the work while she talked to Baby Sarah in the fields. Nelson looked the other way as long as the work got done. When Martin wasn't working, he carved African icons for Dinah out of wood. Dinah kept them on an overturned box by her bed.

When Saturday arrived, Dinah woke up early, without her momma having to shake her awake, for once. She peeked out between two planks. Heavy gray clouds hovered overhead. She hoped the June rain would hold off until after the ceremony. She washed her hair and body with the well water Martin had brought in the previous night, behind a wall he'd erected to give her and Celia a modicum of privacy when they bathed indoors. Dinah enjoyed this rare time alone, before her momma and Baby Sarah woke.

Yesterday, she'd cleaned the cabin and swept the pine floor that Martin had laid over the dirt, in preparation for his moving in later that night. Dinah normally did this anyway, because Nelson inspected everyone's cabin on Sundays and jotted notes in a small black notebook he kept in his trouser pocket. He examined each occupant's personal hygiene, ensuring they didn't smell like—as the master called it—"Negro funk."

After bathing, Dinah lay on the board with Baby Sarah on their side of the curtain separating their sleeping area from Celia's. Dinah traced her baby's facial features with her index finger: the high forehead, the straight little nose, the thin lips. She loved watching Sarah sleep. Most nights, Dinah laid her head next to her baby to listen to her breathe.

Unlike those nights, time crawled this morning.

After sharing a breakfast of delicious cornbread that Martha had prepared and given to Celia the evening prior, Dinah left Sarah playing on the floor with a wooden doll Martin had made for her and moved to a chair.

Celia removed Dinah's headscarf and unraveled a braid. "You're crossing an important line when you become a man's wife. Your duty is to take care of him and be strong when he can't be."

"Aren't men stronger than women?"

"Not always, and not in all ways."

"I can't ever imagine Martin not being strong. He's invincible. But I will be if I have to."

Celia grabbed another braid. "You say that, but you don't

understand how strong you will need to be. You'll need to take care of your family and protect your future daughters on this land and from this place."

Dinah's hair fell halfway down her back when Celia finished unbraiding it. It had grown more quickly than normal. Celia brushed it out. Dinah held up a vanity mirror, recently acquired from the great house. She turned her head from side to side, then smiled at her reflection. Her hair was beautiful.

Since she and Martin had agreed that they wouldn't see each other until the ceremony, Dinah stayed inside all day, playing with Baby Sarah and talking to her momma, and daydreaming about jumping the broom with her man that afternoon. Two hours before the wedding was set to take place, her momma slipped the dress she'd made over Dinah's head, on top of which she then placed a crown of branches and twigs. Betty had given Dinah lilac petals to rub on her neck; Dinah loved their scent.

She was ready. As she paced the floor, Celia said, "Stop moving around and sit. You're worse than your daughter."

"I can't help it, Momma. I'm nervous."

After what seemed like an entire season had passed, someone knocked on the door. It was Betty, coming to get Dinah.

Dinah stopped pacing. Her momma clapped. "Finally! Thank the Lord!" They stood in the center of the cabin, face to face.

"I guess it's time," Dinah said.

"I guess it is." Her momma cradled her face and kissed her forehead. "I'm happy you found yourself a good man. I love you, baby girl."

"I love you, too."

Another knock.

"I want to give you something," Celia said.

"What?"

Celia slipped Aisha's ring off her finger and took Dinah's hand. "Your grandmother would have wanted you to have this."

Dinah's lips parted. *I'm not worthy. Not yet.* "You're giving this to me?"

"Yes."

Dinah touched the ring's smooth twigs. "For the ceremony?"

"For keeps. Protect this ring. It holds the power of our homeland. Don't let anyone take it from you. Sew it into your dress if you have to."

"Why would I have to—?"

The knocking was more insistent.

Dinah yelled toward the door. "I'm coming, Betty!"

Mother and daughter smiled at each other. Dinah held her momma's forearms for a beat and squeezed them before skipping to the door and opening it.

Betty stood on the front porch, tears streaming down her face.

Dinah seized her friend's wrist. A strange feeling crept into the pit of her stomach. "What's wrong, Betty? Are you all right?"

Betty's head bobbed several times, her mouth opening and closing.

"What is it?" Dinah asked. "Did they catch Lukas praying again?"

"Oh, Dinah, Dinah, Dinah!"

"What, Betty?"

Betty gasped for breath. "It's…it's…Martin."

The feeling curled upward to Dinah's chest. "What about Martin?"

"He's…he's…"

Dinah stepped out onto the stoop and scanned the quarters. Slaves stood on their porches, staring at her with pity.

"Why are they looking at me like that?" she asked. "Is Martin sick?"

Betty shook her head. "He's not sick."

"Tell me, Betty!"

Betty hesitated.

Dinah suddenly raised her hand to her mouth. "He's not dead, is he? Please, Lord, tell me my Martin's not dead. What happened? What happened to my Martin?"

A pained expression came over her friend's face. "No, Dinah, he's not dead." Betty swallowed and clasped Dinah's hands. "He's been…He's been sold."

Dinah felt as if a man had reached into her chest and seized her heart. She stumbled backward. Betty reached out and grabbed her arms to prevent her from falling off the porch.

"Sold!" Dinah said. "What do you mean 'sold?'"

"Lukas prayed in the woods last night. Around sunrise, he saw two men riding down the road on horseback, pulling a cart. He followed them, wondering what they were up to. They met Nelson at the edge of the clearing before going into Martin's cabin. They dragged him out, down his porch, and through the woods. He fought them the entire way. One of the white men whomped him so hard he fell, and you know how big Martin is. The three of 'em picked Martin up and swung him onto the cart like a sack of potatoes. The two white men rode off with him."

Dinah's mouth dropped open. She couldn't think. Couldn't find words. Couldn't breathe. "Why would the master sell Martin? He's one of his hardest workers." Betty wiped the tears from Dinah's cheeks while letting her own flow. "He's a good man, Betty. Who did Master Sam sell him to? Where did he go? Maybe he's close by! We must find him so we can still get married. I don't believe this! I don't understand. Help me understand, Betty."

"It wasn't Master," her friend said. "It was Beaux."

Dinah blinked. "What?"

"One of the house girls overheard him arguing with Master Sam. Beaux yelled at him for giving Martin permission to marry you. Master told him that slave marriages calmed us and made us less likely to rise up, but Beaux wouldn't calm down. He was so upset, Master Sam agreed to sell Martin to shut him up."

Dinah became lightheaded and collapsed on the stoop. She willed the gods to take her. Her wails racked her body and could be heard throughout the slave quarters; they may even have reached all the way to the stars.

She didn't stop screaming, even when her momma came outside to help Betty carry her to her bed.

CHAPTER THIRTY-NINE

DINAH

INCONSOLABLE, DINAH REMAINED in bed all day Sunday. Her momma brought her cornmeal, but the wooden bowl remained on the floor, untouched. Celia sat on the bed next to Dinah, holding her hand and smoothing her hair. Although her momma's touch felt pleasant, Dinah wanted to be left alone. She'd never dare tell Celia that, though. Instead, she rolled over to face the wall, hoping her momma would take the hint. Sarah climbed on top of Dinah, but her momma swept her up and took her outside. Dinah could hear them clapping as they played Miss Mary Mack on the porch.

Betty came by the cabin, but Dinah refused to see her. She didn't blame Betty for delivering the fateful message. She simply didn't want to be comforted.

Monday morning, Celia shook Dinah awake. Dinah opened an eye and peered through the planks. It was still dark outside.

"Wake up, Dinah."

"I don't want to."

"None of us do, child, but we've got no choice."

"I have a choice. I ain't getting up. I don't care what they do to me."

"I said get up, child."

"No."

Celia grabbed Dinah's arm and shoulder and yanked her out of bed.

Pain shot through Dinah's side as she landed on the pine floor. "Ow! What did you do that for, Momma?"

"To wake you up."

All Dinah's frustrations, all her disappointments, all her sadness welled up inside her. She stared at the low ceiling and wished she could sink through the floor, through the crawl-space, and into the ground. And stay there. She cried. When her tears petered out, she asked, "Why doesn't he kill me?"

"Stop talking foolishness and get up."

"What's the point? What's the point of being a slave? What kind of life is this?"

Celia pulled Dinah upright and joined her on the floor. She curled an arm around her and pulled her close. "This is foolishness talking. You can't let him do this to you."

"Why not? He can do whatever he wants. He owns me. That's what you said."

"In some ways, that's true. He can take you or any other slave woman."

"Then what can I do?"

"Have pride and respect for yourself. No one can take that from you."

Dinah couldn't endure this pain any longer. "How do you…"

"What?"

Dinah lifted her head. "Go on?"

Celia's eyes were damp. "I lean on our gods, my momma's words, and my love for you. When I look at you, I'm reminded of why I'm here. It should be the same for you with Sarah. Always remember who you are! You can bend, but you can't break."

That morning, Dinah assumed her place in the fields. The smell of tobacco leaves nauseated her. The heat suffocated her. As she worked, she thought of Martin. His kind face, his gentle hands, his smile. Any glimmer of happiness in this life had died for her on Saturday. She avoided looking at the next row, where Martin would never be again. Another slave had already taken his place.

By the afternoon, some of her resolve returned. She would mourn, but she wouldn't give Beaux the satisfaction of defeating her. She still had her daughter to think about. For Sarah's sake, she must carry on. By the time Nelson came by on his horse to inspect her progress, she was picking the leaves at her normal pace.

"Good girl," Nelson said. He hesitated, as if he wanted to say more, but he touched the brim of his hat and rode on.

A week later, Dinah was reassigned to the house. Martha was stirring grits in a big pot when Dinah and Celia entered through the back door. Dinah's stomach growled. She'd missed the aroma of good food. In the mudroom, her momma kissed her on the cheek and whispered in her ear, "Make Aisha proud." To the cook, she called, "Mornin', Ms. Martha."

"Mornin', Celia," Martha said.

Celia glanced at Dinah one more time before walking down the hallway toward the front of the house.

Dinah entered the kitchen. "Mornin', Ms. Martha."

"Sure glad you're back."

"Is that so?"

The cook stopped stirring. "You'd become a help to me." She grinned. "Besides, since they didn't replace you, I had to do all the work myself."

Dinah smiled faintly at the joke as she tied an apron around her waist. She grabbed plates to set the table for breakfast. "Is that why I'm here?"

"Nope." Martha turned back to the stove. "You know why you're here…but Mistress Elizabeth wanted you back, too."

"Why?"

"Says you're the hardest worker they've ever had. Smartest, too." Martha pointed at the dining room. "Now, show me she knows what she's talking about and go set that table."

Dinah hesitated. She didn't want to see Beaux this morning—or ever again—and was afraid she would tear him apart if she did. But she swallowed and pushed open the swinging door. The room was empty.

She resumed working in the house as if she'd never left.

✺

One September day, Dinah was dusting the top of the master's square desk in his upstairs study when she spotted a leather-bound book entitled *Bill of Lading*. She wondered what that meant. She hurried to the open door and poked her head out. The other doors were closed, the cavernous hallway empty except for the marble bust of the former president, Thomas Jefferson. She hurried back to the desk, circled behind it, looked at the open doorway once more, then opened the book.

The page was filled with columns and rows. It was a ledger. Dinah knew from her momma that it was a way of keeping track of things, like food supplies for the kitchen.

The first entry read "1827/6/25 Bght 3 neg., male, ages approx. 15–25, healthy, Virginia."

On the first page, each entry noted every slave bought and sold for the Devereaux plantation since June 25, 1827. Dinah scanned the bookcases, wondering where the book for 1807 was, but she didn't have time to search for the purchase of her grandmother. After another glance at the door, she flipped through the pages with hands trembling from the fear of a whipping—and of what she might find. She reached a blank page. She scoured the entries listed on the opposite page, her finger trailing down the page until it stopped at the last transaction, one in different handwriting from the rest. The entry, in Beaux's scrawl, read "1847/06/11 Sold 1 neg. to spec. for $900, male, age approx. 28, healthy, New Orleans, Louisiana." Under the far-right column, titled REMARKS, he had written "hardworking boy. Good with wood. Good riddance!"

Martin had been sold to a speculator. The Devereauxs had reduced the man, Dinah's future husband and the father to her children, to an inventory item unworthy of a name.

Dinah closed the book and allowed her tears to fall. She couldn't have cared less if the master were to have entered the room at that moment.

At least one of her questions was answered. Martin wasn't living on a nearby plantation, which ruled out any chance of receiving a pass to go see him. As if Beaux would ever permit that, anyway.

Dinah didn't know where Louisiana was, but she knew it was far away. She had heard of New Orleans, and of the houses that were rumored to sell Negro slaves like thoroughbreds in a section of the city. They would inspect Martin for his strength, durability, and speed. The highest bidder would change Martin's given name and give him his surname, making him almost impossible to locate.

A slave owned nothing. Not even his name.

CHAPTER FORTY

SHA

SHA'S PATIENCE WAS finally rewarded.

Across the street from the club, she laid her head against the Audi's headrest and yawned. A small to-go cup of Blue Bottle coffee, black and cold, rested in the beverage holder next to her. Sha stretched her neck back and forth, then stared at the long, ever-present line. Erik, wearing dressy jeans, a collared black shirt, and a jacket, stood with three other guys chatting up the two women behind them. Sha sat up immediately, awake. Taking several deep breaths, she gripped the leather steering wheel to prevent herself from flying out of the car and beating the man to death in front of so many witnesses.

The line shuffled toward the entrance. Erik handed his ID to Sha's favorite bouncer. Dominic glanced at him, then at the ID, examining it for an unusual length of time. Erik shot him a questioning look and said something. Dominic responded before returning the card to him and waving them in. After Erik had passed, Dominic held up his hand to the customers next in line. He fished out his cell phone and his fingers flew across the display, which Sha found odd. During the time she'd been watching him, the bouncer had been the epitome of professionalism.

Dominic pocketed his phone and allowed customers to enter again.

A chirp. Sha looked down at her phone. It was a text from a number she didn't recognize. *Dominic.* He'd texted her Erik's name, home address, date of birth, and driver's license number. There was a second text, which read "Good hunting, Sha."

Sha looked over at Dominic, who lifted his chin to her. She texted back, "Appreciate you."

Sha waited in her car while Erik was in the club, her eyes never leaving the entrance. Two hours after he'd entered, he came out with the same friends, their hair and faces slick with sweat. Sha swallowed the bile in her throat at the sight of him. The men zigzagged down the sidewalk, talking and laughing. They piled into a black car parked down the street. The driver navigated out of the tight space, pinging off the cars in front of and behind him like a bumper car at an amusement park. When he finally extricated the car and took off, Sha thought that she should follow him to look at the license plate and call 911 to report a drunk driver.

Instead, she went home.

✍

The next day, Sha got up, got dressed, and left the house before Jelani woke up. Rather than heading to her office in

Oakland, she took the on-ramp for the I-80 West freeway to San Francisco. When she found a parking spot down the street from Erik's gentrified brick apartment building, she was unsure of how long she'd have to wait. Not long, it turned out. Erik came out the front door in a dark business suit, white dress shirt, and sunglasses—despite the sun's absence, probably to hide eyes bloodshot from partying late into the previous night. Sha waited until he crossed the intersection, then started the car to follow him.

The early morning fog cloaked the city and sometimes obscured Erik's movements. Sha sped up so she wouldn't lose him. He continued for six blocks before entering a high-rise glass office building on California Street, in the financial district.

Sha cruised by the building. She didn't plan to confront him today.

When she arrived at her company, she greeted her staff in the cubicles on either side of the aisle. Instead of veering to the kitchen for a cup of coffee, she headed straight to her office. After closing the door, another rarity, she sat behind her glass desk and booted up her laptop. The dual monitors came to life. Although the door was closed, her employees could see her through the glass walls. Behind her, white bookcases bracketed the large window. The shelves displayed her IT manuals, business and leadership books, and various technological and humanitarian accolades. The only color in the room came from the two beanbag chairs—one bright yellow and one blue—where Sha conducted her one-on-one staff meetings and sometimes ate lunch.

For several hours, Sha went through the motions of her

work. Around 11:00 a.m., she locked her computer, exited her office, and murmured to nearby staff that she'd scheduled an early lunch commitment. But food was the last thing on Sha's mind. She headed back to San Francisco. The fog had lifted, and the sky was sunny and clear. Now that she had seen where Erik lived and worked, she wanted a sense of his routine. The parking gods were still with her. She found a space with a clear view of the front entrance to the building Erik worked in. He came out at noon with two male office workers. Sha exited her SUV and checked the time left on the meter she'd fed earlier. Another hour and forty minutes. On the packed sidewalks, pedestrians veered around a sleeping homeless man.

Sha weaved in and out, following Erik and his coworkers past food trucks and vendors parked on one side of the busy street. Her stomach growled as she inhaled the aromas of gyros, tacos, and curry. She had eaten little since Erik Stevens had come into her life.

The trio entered a deli a few blocks away. The door chimed as Sha allowed two women to enter the restaurant before her. Inside, a rectangular, glass-enclosed display counter showed an array of meats and cheeses. The aroma of freshly baked bread filled the air. Tables were crammed together in the tiny space to accommodate as many customers as possible. The room hummed. People lined up to place their orders or sat at tables eating and chatting. Sha lingered near the door, pretending to examine the menu on the wall behind the counter but eyeing Erik. When it was her turn, she ordered an Italian sandwich with prosciutto, salami, and provolone cheese, and a sparkling water, and then dropped a dollar in the large plastic tip jar.

When her order was called, she took her sandwich to a table in the corner.

"May I join you?"

Sha looked up as she chewed a bite of her sandwich. She hadn't noticed the young Asian woman approaching. The woman was wearing a plain black dress and holding a red tray. "It's packed. Do you mind?"

Still chewing, Sha shook her head and moved her tray closer to give the woman room on the table.

They ate in silence, for which Sha was grateful. The woman shielded her from Erik so she could observe him unnoticed.

The woman ate quickly and picked up her tray. "Thanks."

Sha nodded.

No sooner than she had left, a Black woman around Sha's age, with dark brown twists and wearing an expensive double-breasted dark blue suit, asked, "Is this seat taken?"

What is this…Grand Central Station?

The woman shrugged in apology. "There's nowhere else to sit."

"It's fine," Sha responded.

The woman had an oval face and a piercing in her right eyebrow. "This place is always crowded." Sha's tablemate held out her hand. "My name's Mikala."

"Uh…Sha." Damn! Should she have given her real name? What if this woman knew Erik?

Oil and vinegar dripped from Sha's fingers. She wiped her hand, and they shook.

"Nice to meet you, Sha. Do you come here often?"

Sha took back her hand, smiling uncertainly. "Is that a line?"

Mikala touched her palm to her forehead. "Sorry. It came out that way, but no."

They ate in silence.

"I'd still like to know the answer," Mikala said.

Erik and his buddies were laughing and talking with their mouths full. They stressed emphatic points by punching each other's upper arms or bumping fists. They didn't care how loud they were. Sha took another bite of her sandwich. She couldn't eat any slower. Maybe she should talk to this woman so she'd have a reason to sit there longer.

"No," Sha said.

"I presume you work around here? Wait, that's prying. I'm sorry. I tend to do that."

"That's okay."

"What do you like to do?" the nosy woman asked.

"Not 'what do I do?'"

"Who wants to talk about work on their break?"

Sha hesitated. "I watch the Warriors."

"Do you go to the games?"

"No. I stay home and watch them on TV."

Why was she telling this woman her business?

Sha glanced over at Erik's table. Nothing had changed there. Why was she following this boy? Why hadn't she forced Jelani to stay home that night?

Mikala followed Sha's gaze, then looked at her. "You don't look like the type that's attracted to younger men."

Sha jolted. "I'm not. I was thinking."

Mikala's eyes narrowed. "Hmmm."

Sha rarely explained herself to anyone. She wondered

how she could spy on Erik with this snoopy woman sitting across from her.

Mikala observed Sha's hand on the table, her fingers moving as if she were typing. "You need to calm your energy. You should meditate."

Sha almost rolled her eyes. *I do.*

Mikala finished her sandwich and picked up her tray. "Maybe we can go to a game sometime."

Sha looked at her quizzically, forgetting about Erik. Mikala navigated through the tables and left the deli. Erik and his coworkers had left without clearing their tables. How had they slipped by her? Sha wouldn't have made a great detective.

A business card lay on Sha's table. Sha hadn't seen one in a long time. She picked it up. It was of heavy stock, white with gold trim. Embossed in black was:

Mikala Belin, Esquire
Environmental Lawyer
Spalding, Holland, and Andrews
555 California Street
San Francisco, CA 94104
415.555.5555

The same building as Erik's. On the back was a phone number written in blue ink with large numbers, a slash through the zeroes in the German style. Sha glanced at the door—Mikala was long gone—and back at the card. She didn't know what to make of what had just happened.

⤸

Over the next week, Sha tailed Erik as he carried out his daily routine. She learned his habits: where he ate lunch, where he ate dinner, and what bars he frequented after work. He hadn't gone back to the club. Maybe he hadn't appreciated Dominic's scrutiny of his identification the last time he'd been there. The following Saturday, at a park near his apartment building, Erik played Ultimate Frisbee with the same group of guys he hung out with every weekend, according to his Instagram stories. Scanning the sidelines, Sha didn't think any of the spectators were there to watch him.

She studied how he interacted with people in person and online. He did not appear to have a girlfriend, since he tried to pick up every attractive woman he met. He hit on them indiscriminately, regardless of their race, age, socioeconomic status, and whether they were with another man—or woman. Every woman was his for the taking. His birthright. Sha's mother had told her stories about what their ancestors had put up with. Nothing much had changed.

White men took whatever they wanted.

CHAPTER FORTY-ONE

OLIVIA

NICOLE LOOKED UP, wide-eyed, at Olivia, who stood next to Nicole's desk holding her purse in front of her. "I'll call you back," she said into the phone. She removed the headset from where it was lodged between her ear and her shoulder and hung up. She rose. "What is it? Is something wrong with Dad?"

"No. He's fine."

Nicole plopped back into her seat. The chair rolled on its wheels. "Whew! You scared me! What are you doing here?"

There were at least seventy employees sitting at metal desks in long rows on the rectangular floor. Windowed offices surrounded them. Florescent lights blanketed the ceiling. Employees pecked away at their desktop computer keyboards using WordPerfect, the latest state-of-the-art word processing software; some still used typewriters. Their shouted conversations, among themselves and over the phone, made for a noisy workplace. The room reeked of cigarettes, stale coffee, and take-out food.

"I'm here on business and thought I'd take you to lunch."

Nicole looked skeptical. "Since when do you have business in Atlanta?"

"Since now. Let your mother take you out to eat."

"Sounds better than the break room." Nicole glanced over her shoulder at an office. "I need to finish this article first."

"I'll wait. What's it about?"

"Ronald McNair, the astronaut killed in the Challenger disaster. He was one of the first Black astronauts to go to space."

"Too bad he wasn't a teacher."

Of the seven crew members who had died, the white high school teacher, Christa McAuliffe, had received the most attention. Nicole furrowed her brow as she stared at her word processor. "I might use that."

"Be my guest," Olivia said. "No attribution required."

"It's unfair. Why is a white life more important?"

"It isn't."

"Hmmm. I might use that, too." Nicole clicked at her keyboard without looking up from her computer. "Sorry, there's nowhere to sit, unless you want to park on the edge of my desk."

"I'll stand."

Nicole scrutinized her. "Nice suit. What size is it?"

Olivia glanced down at her black Anne Klein suit, which matched her purse. "Mine."

Nicole laughed.

Olivia had watched Nicole work prior to approaching her desk. Her daughter looked professional; she was wearing a black skirt, a white dress shirt, and a black and brown checkered jacket with padded shoulders that made her look like the wide receiver on a football team. She'd straightened her naturally curly medium-length hair and dyed it auburn.

Nicole finished typing and reviewed her work. "I'll be right back."

She hurried to a chest-high, institutional-green filing cabinet on top of which a dot matrix printer chugged out her document. After ripping it off at the perforations, she rushed over to the office she'd glanced at earlier, knocked, then entered, shutting the door behind her.

Olivia placed her purse on the desk, sat in Nicole's chair, and swiveled back and forth. The employees sitting at the desks on either side ignored her. Scotch-taped to Nicole's computer were studio photographs of Barbara Walters, Diane Sawyer, and Carole Simpson. A dictionary, a thesaurus, the Associated Press style book, and a World Atlas lined the edge of the desk. Pads of lined paper and news scripts were stacked next to a framed photograph of their family. Olivia picked up the photo. It was taken at a football game at Nicole's high school. In it, Olivia was wearing a maroon leather blazer and Davis a battered brown aviator jacket. Nicole was standing between them, grinning, in her green and silver cheerleading uniform. They looked so young. Where had the time gone? A warmth spread through Olivia as she gazed at her precious family. She touched her husband's smiling face through the glass frame. His chin was raised, his pride in his daughter evident. Olivia imagined him in his office in Philadelphia, analyzing the municipal government's capital expenditures, his fingers a blur over the adding machine keys.

She returned the photo to its place.

Five minutes later, her daughter came out of the office and hastened back to her desk, her face pinched. Did her boss not like the story? Olivia rose, refraining from asking her what was wrong in front of her coworkers. She pasted on a smile. "Ready?"

On the way out, they passed a white water cooler with paper cups. A man in an expensive gray three-piece, single-breasted suit stepped out of the office that Nicole had entered earlier. Tall and blond, his big head was disproportionate to the rest of his body. His face and hands were tanned, except for a circle on his left ring finger. He looked at Nicole, and then at Olivia. He grinned, his green eyes roaming the length of Olivia's body before lingering on her breasts.

Nicole bit her nail, something Olivia had never seen her do. A flash of anger tore through Olivia—she wanted to hit him, yell, make a scene—but a deep sadness quickly replaced the feeling.

She pointed to her own face. "Up here." The man's gaze met hers, and she extended her hand. "I'm Olivia Bradley. Nicole's mother."

He shook it. "I'm—"

"I know who you are."

Everyone did.

His smile dimmed, but then rekindled. He placed his hand on her daughter's shoulder. Nicole flinched.

"You should be proud. Nicole is one of our hardest work-ers. I'm glad she's on the team. I have great plans for her."

"I'm sure you do, but she has her own plans." Olivia took her daughter's arm. "Let's go, Nicole."

CHAPTER FORTY-TWO

JULIA

AUGUSTA MET JULIA in the brownstone's foyer. "Where have you been, Mama?"

"None of your business."

Pointing at the paper bag, Augusta asked, "What did you buy?"

"You shouldn't ask so many questions on your birthday." Julia removed her black leather purse from the crook of her arm and placed it and the bag on a small mahogany console table. She never set her purse on the floor; her momma had told her it was bad luck. Shrugging out of her coat, she smiled at her precious daughter. "But I will tell you it's a surprise."

"Does the surprise go into whatever smells good in the oven?" Augusta's eyes twinkled as she grabbed Julia's hand and the bag. "Come on." She led Julia into the dining room.

In a corner, a cherrywood cabinet with two glass doors

housed a complete china set. A matching sideboard stretched along one wall. A tablecloth covered the rectangular table, which was set for dinner. Jean sat at the table with his shirtsleeves rolled up and his burgundy tie loosened. His suit jacket was thrown over the top of the chair next to him. He struck a match and bent over to light the candles on the cake, grinning at Julia.

"Mama! Glad you made it back in time!" Jean said.

I wasn't sure you would.

Jean hugged Julia. The unfamiliar perfume wafting off him made Julia want to gag. She glanced at her daughter, who must have smelled it, too. Augusta wasn't paying attention to them. She was smoothing Josie's hair.

Julia extricated herself and stared at Jean's face. His facial expression gave nothing away. She wanted to slap him.

"What's wrong with you, Mama?" he asked. "You look like you've seen a ghost!"

"I experienced a fright crossing the street."

Jean let her go. "You better be careful. We wouldn't want to lose you."

Julia couldn't say the same of him.

Josie broke free from her mother and took Julia's hand. "Granny, don't be frightened. Come sit with me."

Julia looked into her granddaughter's big, chocolate eyes and took in her long eyelashes and dimpled cheeks. This girl stopped her heart. Josie patted the seat of the oak chair between herself and thirteen-year-old Hale, who'd just come in from playing outdoors. Now, taller than Julia, he reeked of teenage boy. She pecked him on the cheek before sitting beside him.

"Yuck," he said.

"Someday, you'll think differently."

Hale wiped his cheek. "Not today."

Julia grabbed him around the neck. "Boy, you'd better not wipe off my kisses." She kissed his face several times until he laughed.

Jean finished lighting the candles.

"Mama, can I help you blow them out?" Clara asked.

"No, baby, it's Mama's birthday," Jean replied.

Clara's face fell as if he had stolen her favorite ball.

"I think she was talking to me," Augusta said, sliding into her husband's seat at the head of the table. She reached for her daughter. "You can help me."

Jean's jaw flexed.

Clara scrambled onto Augusta's lap.

"Ready?" Augusta asked. "One, two, three, blow!" Their cheeks expanded with air, and they blew.

After "Happy Birthday" had been sung, Augusta unwrapped her presents. A new dress and perfume from Jean. Julia wondered if it was the same fragrance of which he reeked. Julia had given Augusta a copy of *Quicksand*, Nella Larsen's first novel. The remaining two gifts were wrapped carelessly—Augusta had saved her daughters' presents for last. Clara had drawn a picture of their family at the park. Julia couldn't remember the last time Jean had come with them, but there he was in the picture, the only stick figure with a mustache, standing at the bottom of a slide, ready to catch Clara. Josie gave her mother a gray rock she had found in the real park.

After their casserole dinner, and as everyone dug into

their chocolate cake and ice cream, Julia said to Jean, "Got the night off?"

Jean, sitting in a chair next to Augusta with his arm around her shoulders, squeezed his wife to him. "Yes. I wanted to be with Auggie tonight."

"It's nice when you have nights off. Do you ever get days off anymore?"

"Not really. Since I have my own band now, I'm the one who meets with the club and restaurant owners to set up gigs. A lot of logistics to deal with."

Jean and Palmer had had a falling out over a year ago. Jean believed the Palmer Parks Band should have featured more piano solos, and the band's name had always grated on his nerves—he complained it demeaned the rest of the band's members. Since Palmer had founded the band and managed it, he wouldn't consider changing it. He had also told Jean his piano playing was too frenetic and should be more nuanced. So, Jean had quit and struck out on his own. Only Francis had joined him.

Julia scooped up a dollop of ice cream but didn't eat it. "Oh? Is that what you did today? Met with club and restaurant owners?"

"Sure was." He stuffed cake into his mouth, chewed, and swallowed. "Why are you so curious?"

She shrugged. "I'm fascinated with the music business."

"Since when?"

"Since you married my daughter."

Jean leaned back in his chair. "I'd be happy to talk to you about it any other time, Mama, but tonight belongs to Auggie."

"I'm also curious because I thought I saw you today."

He rubbed the back of his neck as if he'd endured a sudden crick in it and glanced worriedly at Augusta. "Oh?"

"I yelled your name, but you didn't look my way."

"That's strange. It couldn't have been me. I was in a meeting." He turned to his wife. "Would you like coffee, dear, to go with your cake?"

As the kids chatted away and Jean flirted with Augusta, Julia found it difficult to stop staring at her son-in-law.

She'd had no idea he was such a skilled actor. And liar.

CHAPTER FORTY-THREE

DINAH

WHENEVER BEAUX ENTERED a room in the house, Dinah would suddenly remember a task she had to complete elsewhere. When he demanded something from her, she'd send another slave to serve him. To avoid him altogether, though, was impossible. Whenever he saw her, a sly grin would spread across his face, as if they shared a secret, and he'd tell her—only her—to fetch water or food for him. Any excuse to touch her hand.

One evening, after turning down the master and mistress's brass bed and refilling the water pitcher on their dresser, she surveyed the bedroom once more to make sure everything was perfect before stepping into the hallway and closing the door. When she turned around, she landed in Beaux's arms.

Beaux grinned, his hair plastered against his forehead with sweat. "Looky what I found."

Dinah turned her head. His breath stank of the familiar combination of whiskey and tobacco.

If she screamed or called for help, he'd hit her, or worse. Now she lived with a fear greater than that of pain, and she had much more to lose. She would not let him hurt Sarah or separate the two of them.

"Guess what? My wife and mother traveled to Richmond to shop and visit relatives."

Dinah glanced over at Jefferson's bust, as if it could save her. "I know."

"That means I'm all alone."

"Your daddy's here, and your brothers and sister."

Beaux wagged a finger at her. "That's not the kind of company I'm looking for."

Dinah squirmed and tried to move away from him. "I best be getting home."

Beaux squeezed her tighter and forced her to look at him. "I just told you I'm by my lonesome tonight."

"You could read a good book…sir." It was a joke. Beaux didn't read books or newspapers.

"And I have a surprise for you. A present."

"I don't need your presents."

"That's why it's called a present, because you don't need it. I want to give it to you." Beaux pulled her closer. "And I don't want to be lonesome."

He swept her up in his arms. Dinah dropped the rag she'd been using to dust the master's bedroom furniture. Beaux carried her in strides to his room at the end of the hall. After they entered, he kicked the door shut with his heel, threw Dinah on the bed, and leaped on top of her. Slaves' voices drifted through the open window as they tended to the horses in the barn. The leaves of nearby trees rustled in the light breeze.

Like the last time he raped her, Beaux did not bother to remove either of their clothes. He popped open his trouser buttons to free his member. Dinah squeezed her eyes shut as he entered her, but she didn't scream or cry. It didn't hurt as much this time. She forced her mind to go blank. She did not even count.

After Beaux finished, he remained still, his full body weight upon her. "That was good." When his breathing returned to normal, he rubbed his moist penis against her leg. "You intoxicate me," he said, then ripped Dinah's clothes off. And his, too. His chest was smooth with fine hair. His long legs were fit from riding. After the second time, still naked, Beaux moved to the dresser. He removed something from the bottom drawer.

Emotionally spent, Dinah wanted to think about Sarah to help her get through this. But she didn't want to bring her daughter into this bedroom.

Beaux poured himself a glass of water from the pitcher resting on the washstand, came back to the bed, and lay next to her. He propped himself up on one elbow. He took a sip and offered her some. She shook her head. He scrunched his mouth as if to say, "Suit yourself."

Beaux set the glass on the nightstand and handed Dinah a piece of material. "Here."

It was a red silk scarf, her favorite color; he'd remembered from when they were children. Dinah ran her hand over the embroidery and rubbed the fringe around its perimeter between her fingers. Although it was hard to see with only the light from the oil lamp illuminating the room, she could tell it was beautiful and expensive. Nicer than anything she owned.

She recalled the red ribbon she'd worn to the dance for Martin.

Beaux pouted. "What's wrong? Don't you think it's pretty?"

She continued to stare at it. "I do, sir."

"You don't have to call me 'sir' in here." He smiled and snuggled next to her. "Isn't this better? Wouldn't you rather lie with me in this soft bed than somewhere on the ground out there with him?"

Dinah stiffened. Beaux had never spoken to her of Martin.

Beaux pulled her tighter to him. "I know you still think about him, but you've got to forget that boy. He's gone for good."

Despite herself, she cried. Beaux used his smooth thumb to wipe the tears from one cheek, then the other.

"Don't cry," he said. "You don't need him. Everything you need is right here."

"Everything I needed left with Martin."

Beaux's expression turned pensive. He reached out and gripped her face, applying increasing pressure to her jaws until she couldn't move her head.

"Not everything. You like having Sarah here, no?"

Dinah gasped. Her heart thumped. After losing Martin, she couldn't lose her baby, too. She nodded. Beaux released her, and her head dropped to the pillow. She slipped the scarf under the pillow as Beaux pulled the sheets aside and climbed on top of her again.

❧

"'A' is for apple," Sarah said, "'B' is for biscuit, 'C' is for corn."

Dinah clapped. "That's right!"

While her momma rocked in the defective chair, grinding corn in a mortar with a pestle, Dinah relaxed in a real cherrywood rocking chair—another present from Beaux—in a corner of their cabin. Sarah, wearing a gunny-sack dress, sat on her lap.

Dinah, treasuring the moment, watched her daughter's thin lips move as she recited the alphabet. Soon, Nelson would put her to work: running errands, tending vegetables, fetching water from the well, bringing wood into the house for the stoves, and cleaning the Devereaux family's boots and shoes.

After knocking on the door frame, Betty entered the cabin without invitation. Celia had left the door open to let in the spring air.

Sarah wiggled off Dinah's lap. "Aunt Betty!" She dropped to the floor and ran to Dinah's friend, who scooped her up in her arms, rubbing her nose against the child's. Sarah squealed with delight.

Dinah rested her head against the chair's headrest. "Was that Lukas I heard screaming earlier?"

Betty nodded. "Patrol caught him praying again."

"Why doesn't he stop?"

Betty shrugged. "He can't."

What would it be like to believe in something so fervently? At her momma's suggestion, Dinah had begun reading the Bible for solace. But she still found more comfort in counting. Unlike her grandmother, she and her momma did not gather with the few slaves who prayed in the woods in secret. Lukas prayed with them sometimes, but mostly he said his devotions alone. He didn't want to pray only when the slaves gathered, but whenever the spirit moved him. No one else on the plantation prayed as much.

The rhythm of Dinah's life became routine. She served in the house by day and bedded Beaux on those nights his wife was away. Sometimes, he took her when his wife was home, catching Dinah unaware as she stored items in the cellar or cleaned a room rarely in use.

Anna Devereaux traveled often. This time, she was in Tennessee, visiting her relatives. She seemed to have a lot of them.

One day, Dinah was in Beaux's room, scrubbing the oak floor with soap and water. The previous night, he hadn't been able to wait until they reached the bed, and he'd taken her there. The more Dinah inhaled the evidence of their deed, the harder she scrubbed. She was safe from him for now; he was outside overseeing the overseers.

Dinah winced as the hinges of the bedroom door squeaked open. She looked up from where she was sitting on the floor. It wasn't Beaux. It was Anna, who was not expected to return until the following morning. She entered the room, white gloves in hand, wearing a burgundy traveling dress and a black shawl. Dinah didn't move. She didn't interact with Beaux's wife often. Anna had never spoken to her or acknowledged her existence. Now, her pointy chin was raised, and her icy blue eyes burned with hatred. She *knew*.

Anna laid her gloves on the dresser, removed the pin to free her blonde hair, and placed it next to the gloves. She opened the dresser's top drawer and rummaged through it until she found the red scarf Beaux had bought for Dinah. She walked toward Dinah, dropped the scarf on her head, and left the room.

CHAPTER FORTY-FOUR

SHA

ON A WEEKEND afternoon in May, Sha and Jelani strolled through a farmer's market a few blocks from their home. On both sides of the street, the tables and booths were loaded with produce brought in from farmers who lived outside Berkeley, and with flowers and handmade items—dolls, belts, soaps—sold by local and outside vendors.

Sha spotted a Rubik's cube. Her mother had kept one in her home office when Sha was growing up. Whenever Sha had snuck into Nicole's office, she'd always found the Rubik's cube solved, each side a uniform color, no matter how many times she'd mixed it up. She'd never tried to solve it herself; it belonged to her mother. Nicole had never said anything about Sha messing up her cube. Sha had never fessed up to doing it, although Nicole had known it wasn't her husband who'd done so.

Sha fished a warm roasted almond out of a paper bag and

popped it into her mouth. When she finished chewing, she asked Jelani, "How are you doing?"

"Better."

Sha searched her daughter's face; Jelani was telling the truth.

"Almost like myself," Jelani added.

Jelani's hair was pulled straight back and held together by a tie. Jelani no longer spent an inordinate amount of time on her hair. When she did, Sha would know she'd healed completely.

"Have you talked to your friends lately?"

"No."

"Why not?"

"I have nothing to say to them anymore. They don't care about me—not really—and they weren't there for me when I needed them. When I see them in the halls at school, I avoid them or pretend I'm late for class. I can't even look at them."

"I notice you don't have your phone."

Jelani shrugged. "Now that I'm no longer on social media, I don't need it."

"Still. You should carry it with you." *To be safe. In case I need to find you.*

They stopped at a stall filled with baskets of fruit and bought apples and grapes.

After they walked away, Jelani said, "I had a dream last night."

"A nightmare?"

"No, definitely a dream. I was standing on a beach looking at the sunset, and at the bluest water I've ever seen. Black women dressed in white dashiki dresses stood around me, chanting, 'We are here. We are beautiful. We are proud. We are home.'" Jelani's face flushed. "Is that weird?"

"No."

"Am I losing my mind?"

"No."

A man walked by them, his cologne heavy. Jelani stopped walking and shivered. Sha clutched her daughter's arm. "What is it?"

"He smelled like…him."

Sha tugged her daughter to keep walking. "It's not him."

Jelani gave her the evil eye. "How do you know?"

They passed the last stall. Sha hesitated. "Let's sit for a moment," she said.

They headed toward an iron bench that stood on the sidewalk in front of a closed boutique clothing store.

Sha placed their purchases on the side of her opposite Jelani. A neighbor walked by, and Sha raised her hand in a silent greeting. "You won't like what I'm about to tell you," she said to Jelani.

"Okayyyyyyyyyyyyy."

"At the hospital, the nurse gave me a list of support services to help women—"

"Mom, I'm not going."

"I'm not suggesting you are. I found someone else, not on the list, who specializes in talking to young Black women."

"Is it because I told you about the dream?"

"No. I've been thinking about this for a while."

"I don't need anyone else. I have you."

Sha took Jelani's hands in hers. "I'm not a professional. I want you to have every opportunity to heal, and it'll be good to talk to someone who is unbiased, who doesn't know you. So you can speak freely."

Not all men were like the one who had hurt her daughter. Hurt *her*. Sha wanted Jelani to heal—not to go back to being who she was before, but to become her best self.

"I don't want to talk to a stranger."

"It might be easier."

"I don't know."

"You can't heal what you don't reveal."

Jelani tilted her head. "Are you trying to rap, Mom?"

Sha released Jelani's hands and chuckled. "Uh…no."

"I thought Black women were supposed to be strong and handle everything themselves. Isn't that what you always told me? What Grandma told me? You never asked for help."

"But I should have. Being strong doesn't mean you don't ask for help when you need it. Asking for help is being strong *and* smart. We Black women have borne the weight of every tragedy, every situation, but we no longer need to bear the pain alone. Therapy isn't only for white people."

"I'll think about it. I have so much school work. I'm not sure I'd have the time."

"I'm the parent." Sha touched Jelani's chin. "Some things aren't up to you."

"What's going on with you? Why all the late-night visits? Where did you disappear to early this morning?" Jelani searched her face. "If you're not seeing someone, is it something I should be concerned about? Are you sick?"

"I've just had a lot happening at work," Sha lied for the umpteenth time. "Are you ever going to tell me the truth about Erik Stevens?"

Jelani looked away. "How did you know?"

"A mother knows."

Jelani turned to her, a flash of anger crossing her face. "You went through my phone."

"Yes. I—"

As quickly as the anger had ignited, it dissipated. "I get it. You were worried about me." Jelani sighed. "I met him at the club a few months ago. We exchanged numbers. We never…We just texted before that night."

"Why didn't you tell me?"

"I don't know…then once I didn't say anything, it was hard to admit it. I was afraid if I told you, you might accuse me of bringing this on myself somehow."

Sha started. "I'd never do that! No woman brings rape upon herself."

"I said 'no' multiple times. I couldn't fight him off. I'm sorry for keeping that from you. No more secrets, okay? I promise."

Sha hugged her daughter. A woman around her age helped an older woman navigate through the passersby. Sha needed to visit her mother soon. She often felt a pull to see her parents, spend more time with them, especially as they aged. Before it was too late.

She couldn't reciprocate Jelani's promise. "It's getting late. We should get back to the house to cook dinner."

CHAPTER FORTY-FIVE

OLIVIA

MOTHER AND DAUGHTER walked several blocks away from the network's headquarters to a Poplar Street bistro, a favorite with office workers on their lunch breaks and tourists taking a break from sightseeing. The sun was bright, but still weeks away from when its heat would beat down on the skin. To Olivia, it felt like old times, like when she and Nicole would stroll down Philadelphia's 20th Street to Sammy's for a Philly cheesesteak sandwich.

Inside the restaurant, the smell of bread, grease, and fried food filled the air. Customers occupied almost all the tables, which were packed close together. At the hostess station, Olivia asked for a booth in the back corner.

Once seated, Nicole peered at Olivia over the top of her menu. "Why are you really in Atlanta, Mother?"

Before Olivia could answer, the waitress came up to the table pulling a pen and pad out of her apron pocket.

Nicole ordered a BLT sandwich, potato chips, and a New Coke. Olivia ordered the same, still unsure what was wrong with the old Coke. They were silent until after the waitress returned with their sodas and left.

Olivia was worried about Nicole, but she tried not to let it show. Calmly, she said, "Tell me about your boss. What has he done to you? Has he hurt you?"

Nicole leaned back against the booth's faux leather, as if to avoid the inevitable onslaught of questions.

Olivia wanted to kick herself. She'd immediately gone into lawyer mode.

"You noticed, huh? He's a creep."

"I could tell."

"No matter how hard I work, he compliments me on my outfits or my hair."

"That's not acceptable."

Nicole slurped her soda and fiddled with her knife. "It's…weird."

A rage started in Olivia's stomach and crept upward. "It's more than weird. Has he touched you?"

Nicole lowered her gaze. "How did you know?"

"I work in corporate America. And I'm a mother."

Nicole's lips quivered and her shoulders shook. She bit the nail of her index finger. Her vulnerability pained Olivia.

She clasped Nicole's hand. "No matter what has happened, I won't let you suffer anymore."

This was a lie. She couldn't protect Nicole from the business world and promise that this wouldn't happen again. She wished they weren't having this conversation here, that she could whisk Nicole away from the network and take her back on a plane to Philadelphia, where she could watch over her. She wouldn't even swing by Nicole's apartment to pick up her things, although Nicole wouldn't want to leave her Rubik's cube behind. Olivia would buy her another one.

Nicole's fingernails were bitten to the quick. She withdrew her hand and balled it into a fist.

Olivia reached across the table and gently unfurled Nicole's fingers. "You shouldn't bite your nails." She hurried on before Nicole could tell her to stop lecturing. "Not because I said so, but because one day you'll be on television. Your nails need to be nice. I'll find a salon and make an appointment."

Nicole stared at her nails with a doubtful expression. "Can we go together?"

"Of course."

A middle-aged Caucasian couple wearing Atlanta Braves hats, t-shirts, and blue jean shorts over the whitest legs Olivia had ever seen stared at them from the next table. Sometimes, white people got on her nerves. They believed everything was their business. Olivia scowled at them. "Can I help you?"

They looked away.

To her daughter, she said, "What you're dealing with is called sexual harassment. There's no need to be ashamed."

The waitress returned with their sandwiches. She glanced at Nicole with a concerned expression. "Do you want these to go, ladies?"

"No," Olivia said. "We're staying right here."

✍

Olivia handed Nicole her mobile phone. Nicole called the network and asked the receptionist to inform her boss that she'd gone home sick. Mother and daughter now sat on a bench under a maple tree in a park near the restaurant, eating their sandwiches. Since it was a beautiful day, they'd decided to eat the second halves outside. Their suit jackets lay folded on top of the bench, and their shirt sleeves were rolled up their forearms. They were both wearing Ray-Ban Wayfarer sunglasses, which Olivia hoped would make it easier for her daughter to confide in her.

On a swing set, kids shrieked with laughter as they pushed each other higher and higher. Couples and singles lay across blankets talking or reading, or just allowing the sun to warm their faces. The city sounds—sirens and honking cars—seemed far away. A group of ten women wearing pink or green or purple tights, headbands, long, fluffy white socks, and high-top white aerobic shoes mimicked their instructor's movements. "Physical" was playing on a boombox next to the instructor's feet.

Olivia bit into her sandwich as she watched the exercisers. "Should we feel guilty?"

Nicole took a big bite of hers, too. "I don't."

They finished their sandwiches in silence. "That sandwich was good."

"Yes, it was, Mother. Thank you."

Olivia balled up her sandwich wrapper and placed it on the bench, next to her. She turned to her daughter. "Tell me what's happening at work."

Nicole gathered their trash and threw it in a nearby trash can. She returned, leaned back, and exhaled. "My boss is horrible."

Olivia pressed her. "What does he do? Specifically."

"He makes lewd comments. Touches me."

"Give me an example."

Nicole hesitated. "This is embarrassing."

Olivia tipped up her daughter's chin. "You shouldn't be the one who's embarrassed."

She released Nicole and waited.

"He likes to walk behind me to watch my butt. He told me he loves women with big butts and wishes his wife had one."

Olivia held her rising anger in check. "Lucky woman. What else does he do?"

"Touches me on the sly when I walk by him on the set or in the control room, or gropes me when we're walking down the hall together and no one is around."

Olivia's stomach clenched. "Is it just you, or does he harass the other women?"

"He hires pretty ones with no plans to promote them. We complain to each other, but that's as far as it goes. One woman already quit, and she was our best producer." Nicole stared at the kids on the swings. "A female coworker told me that unless I sleep with him, I'll never receive a bonus or move up in the organization. If he finds out I confided in anyone, he'll fire me."

"What if you file a complaint with Human Resources?"

Nicole shook her head. "The employee relations manager would investigate my claim, but it's my word against his. After she found no evidence of harassment, my boss would make my life a living hell until I quit, or he'd make up a fireable offense. I've seen it happen to others." She faced Olivia. "I'm sorry I didn't tell you sooner. I thought I could handle it. I'm the first one to arrive in the morning and the last one to leave every night. I take on the toughest assignments without complaint. I've busted my butt for the organization, and I thought that'd be enough. It's not fair!"

"Life isn't fair, but it's how you react to your circumstances that matters."

"What goes on behind the scenes has always fascinated me. Despite what's happened, I love my job and the network. We're on the cutting edge of news. If I'm going to do this for a living, I have to be here. I don't want to leave."

"Who said anything about leaving?"

Nicole sat up, looking puzzled. "But how can I stay?"

A couple holding hands walked by on the paved path that wove through the park and disappeared past the hornbeam and redbud trees. A plane roared overhead, having just left William B. Hartsfield Atlanta International Airport.

"We're not letting him drive you out of your chosen career."

"But what can I do?"

"I'm not sure yet, but I know what you're going through."

Olivia told Nicole about how she'd warded off Robert Penn's advances for years—the touching, the innuendoes, the double-entendres—and the recent late-night incident.

Nicole sighed. "I thought he was a good guy."

"In some ways, he is. He's been supportive of my career and nominated me for partner, an opportunity I wouldn't have received at most white-shoe law firms. I'm grateful to him for what he's done for me, but his generosity doesn't entitle him to sleep with me. I have earned everything I've accomplished."

"Does dad know?"

Olivia nodded. "But he's letting me handle it."

Nicole slumped against the bench. "I wish I could slap my boss. Or punch him in the face. Kick him in the balls. Oops, sorry, Mother."

"Whoa…," Olivia said, although she'd had those same thoughts when she'd met him earlier.

The aerobics class ended. Women gathered in small groups to talk. Some toweled themselves off, drinking Gatorade. A yellow-billed cuckoo cooed from the limb of a nearby tree.

"Remember when you first learned to ride a bike?" asked Olivia.

"Not really. I remember watching the eight-millimeter film Dad took of it."

"After your father removed the training wheels, you took off. And then you fell and scraped your knees on the side-walk. You know what you did next?"

"No."

"You righted the bike, blood flowing down both your legs, and tried again, and you didn't give up until you reached the end of our block without falling. You turned and flashed us the peace sign. I was proud of you." She held Nicole's hand. "I'm proud of you now."

Nicole's eyes glistened. "Thank you, Mother."

"Do you know why I work so hard?"

"Because you're a workaholic?"

Olivia chuckled. "No. It's because I remember hearing stories about how some men—Black and white—treated the women in our family going generations back."

"Maybe I shouldn't get married."

"That's not the lesson of this story. There have been good men, too. Like my father. Like Davis. It's just that the bad ones seem to find us first."

"What is the lesson?" Nicole asked.

Olivia had always been strong for Nicole. Maybe it was time for her to be vulnerable, too. She told Nicole about Ted. "After what happened with him, I never wanted to rely on any man or let one be disrespectful to me. Like you, I wanted to support myself. Being a single mother was hard, but it was important for me to get my education. And my mother insisted on it. She'd put off her education and regretted it. I wasn't going to make the same mistake. And I could have done it on my own, but Davis was a godsend."

"I love how he loves us. He's been a great dad, especially when he didn't have to be."

"Oh, yes, he did, if he wanted to be with me!"

Nicole laughed. "Still. You met a good man." The participants in the aerobics class left the park alone or in groups of two or three. "Do you remember my first dance recital?"

Olivia racked her brain. "No."

"Because you weren't there. I was in the sixth grade." Olivia had recently started her first job. "I was backstage. Looking through the gap in the curtains for you. Dad was sitting in the first row. He saw me, smiled, and waved. The seat next to him was empty. I thought you were going to be late. During the recital, I made a few mistakes, got out of step. I kept glancing at the chair, glad you weren't there to see my mistakes, but at the same time wishing you were there. You never showed. Dad knew I was disappointed and took me out for ice cream afterward. He's always been there for me."

Tears fell down Olivia's cheeks.

"Most of my friends' mothers didn't work. They were home for them. I don't hold that against you, Mother. And I'm not trying to make you feel bad. I looked up to you. And wanted to be like you. Be successful. I still do. But I never aspired to be an attorney. I wanted to change the world. This isn't about proving anything to you. It's about proving I can do it to myself."

Olivia wiped her tears away. "I ensure my clients receive everything they deserve."

"It's not the same. We report on the stories that aren't told. Bring the world to Americans' living rooms. So our citizens won't be myopic."

Olivia felt an emptiness she'd never experienced, even after Ted had deserted her. "I'm sorry. For not being there."

"It hurt then, but I understand better now."

A yellow kite flew overhead. A Caucasian boy with a bowl haircut ran around as if the kite were pulling him.

Olivia liked to win at everything. Even when Nicole was young and they played Monopoly or raced, Olivia had never let her win. She'd wanted her daughter to know how it felt to lose and survive, and when Nicole finally beat her, she'd know it was for real.

But this situation—dealing with a lecherous boss in her first grown-up job, her dream job—was worse, much worse. Nicole had led a sheltered home life. Olivia and Davis had protected her. In some ways, when something shattered a perfect world, the negative impact was much greater. That world was gone forever for Nicole.

"Many people at the public defender's office and at the

law firm counted me out because I was a young mother. I worked hard. Harder than all of them. But it wasn't to prove my worth to them. It was important to me to make it—for you—so you could know what a resilient Black woman looked like. So you could show your own daughters. Everything I've done—and do—is for you."

Nicole smiled. "I'm proud of you, too. I couldn't wish for a better mother. You've given me a great life."

Olivia started crying again. "I love you."

"I love you, too."

Olivia wrapped her arms around her daughter and held her tight, their heads touching. She struggled with being unable to think of a solution that could instantly solve her daughter's problem.

When they released each other, Olivia said, "But you're strong, too."

"I don't feel strong."

"You haven't quit your job, and you've tried to handle your problems on your own."

"Not successfully."

"Sometimes, we all need help." Olivia didn't pause to think about the hypocrisy of her statement. *Do as I say, not as I do.* "One day, women won't have to put up with workplace harassment, but that day is not today. Your boss and those other men don't know our bloodline. I've told you the stories of what the women in our family have endured. A hell of a lot more than what these horny white men can do to us."

Nicole cocked her head. "How is that going to help me now?"

"They have no idea what we're capable of."

CHAPTER FORTY-SIX

JULIA

LATER THAT NIGHT, after the birthday party, Julia tossed and turned in bed, debating whether to tell Augusta about Jean and the woman leaving the hotel together.

The next morning, after breakfast, she and Augusta sat drinking coffee at the kitchen table. Hale had left for school. Augusta was holding the *New York Age.* As Julia studied her daughter over the brim of her cup, she wondered—not for the first time—if Augusta's eyes would fall out of her head from reading so much.

Jean was still asleep upstairs.

Augusta's face was gaunt, and there were dark circles under her eyes. She was looking at the newspaper but didn't appear to be reading.

"Let's go to the park today," Julia said.

Augusta blew on her coffee and took a sip. "That's a good idea, Mama. The kids would love that."

After washing the dishes, cleaning the kitchen, and helping the girls get dressed and bundled into their coats, Julia and Augusta walked the short distance to St. Nicholas Park with the children. Clara and Josie skipped ahead of them on the sidewalk. When they arrived, the girls sprinted across the expanse of grass and dirt to join some neighborhood kids. Josie tripped and fell. She yelped. Her sister helped her up and brushed the dirt off her knee, and they resumed running.

Green ash, locusts, and hackberry trees lined the paths. Red, yellow, and orange leaves crunched beneath Julia's and Augusta's shoes as they strolled toward an iron bench. A flock of birds flew south.

Once seated, Julia said, "How are you and Jean doing?"

Augusta exhaled. "Is that why we're out here?"

"Answer the question."

"Fine, I guess."

"That doesn't sound good."

"We have our difficulties, like other couples."

"Your daddy and I didn't have many difficulties."

Softly, Augusta said, "Jean isn't Daddy."

Ain't that the truth, Julia thought.

"How come you never remarried?" Augusta continued. "Hale and I would have understood."

Julia had started shaking her head at "remarried." "There will never be a man like your father."

"Do you miss him?"

"Every day." Julia glanced up at the cloudless sky. "But I'll see him again."

"Don't you get lonely?"

"I'm never alone. God is with me. And I have my work

and you children." Julia clasped her hands in her lap. "I don't mean to get in your business—"

"But you're about to get into my business."

"I'm your mother. Your happiness is my responsibility."

"I am happy."

"You don't look happy. Being a wife doesn't mean giving up being a woman, having your own life."

"I have the girls."

Julia hesitated, as if she'd just thought of her next question. "What does Jean do during the day?"

"Are you losing your memory, Mama? Didn't you ask him that yesterday?"

"I'm asking you now."

Augusta watched her daughters play tag with the other kids. "He meets with club owners. Books gigs. He says they're doing so well that someday we might move to Strivers' Row."

"Is that what you want? To live on Strivers' Row?"

Augusta shrugged. "I guess. The girls wouldn't have to share a room, and it'd be great for them to be closer to Jean's parents. Have all of their grandparents on the same block." She paused. "Why all the questions? What do you really want to ask me?"

"I saw him."

"You said you thought you saw him."

"No. I definitely saw him. He was with a woman, coming out of the Paradise Hotel."

"Maybe it was a business meeting."

"The only business he was conducting was funny business."

"Why are you telling me this?"

"Because you should know." Julia's eyes narrowed as she studied the worry lines on her daughter's brow. "Or do you already? He stunk like he worked in a perfume factory."

Augusta did not respond. Then, "I didn't suspect him at first. After we were married, he was still as kind, attentive, handsome, and charming as he'd been when we first met. I thought I was the most special woman in the world for him to want to be with me."

"You are special."

Augusta's smile was rueful. "Then a lot of other women are special, too." Clara tagged a boy too hard. He fell face first on the ground. "Help him up, Clara!"

Clara complied. A squirrel chased another up a nearby tree.

"When did it start?"

"Before we were married, I think. I'd heard rumors he'd slept with Jessie's former girlfriend."

"I'm sure that went over well with the band."

"Jean never fit in with them. Not really. Now, I know the reason." She studied her hands. "I remember passing a pregnant woman on the street. He smiled at her, and she ignored him as if she were avoiding him. I saw her at a club later, and she turned away when I looked at her. When washing his shirts, I'd see lipstick on the collar." Augusta rubbed the sleeves of her thick wool sweater. "He'd laugh and say it was a friendly kiss from a woman friend or an acquaintance. His fans' perfume got absorbed into his clothing. His band was working hard to make it, late into the night and early morning. Always an explanation. An excuse. Why he wouldn't come home to me. If only he'd told me what I was doing wrong, I could have changed it."

"Why would you have to change?"

"Then the calls started. The phone would ring in the middle of the night. If Jean wasn't home, the person on the other end of the line hung up when I answered. He'd lied to me about high school. He never finished. He had trouble reading, said the words he read on the page differed from the words that formed in his mind. His teachers used to get exasperated with him. Believed he was dumb or trying to be funny. He hid his performance from his parents. His papa wanted him to be a doctor, like him and Jean's older brother. Jean resented him for it… " Augusta's eyes watered as she looked at Julia. "You were right about him all along. All those dresses. He doesn't have any sisters."

"Hmph," said Julia. "And his family never belonged to a church."

"He lied about that, too. Thinking back, I don't know of a time when he wasn't lying to me and cheating on me, Mama."

A sob escaped from deep within Augusta. Julia scooted closer to her daughter and put an arm around her. Augusta laid her head on Julia's shoulder.

They sat in that position for a long time, watching Clara and Josie play with their friends. The shrill of their laughter, their shrieks of joy, made Julia and Augusta smile despite their pain. Besides his music, these two girls were the only good Jean had brought into this world.

"You know what the worst part is?"

"What's that, dear?"

"I still love him. No matter what he's done. What he does. I can't stop loving him."

Julia lifted her daughter's chin and looked into her brown eyes. "What about loving yourself?"

CHAPTER FORTY-SEVEN

DINAH

OVER THE YEARS, Dinah bore more children by Beaux Devereaux: Jacob, Gracie, Moses, and Harriet. She'd given up the notion of finding love and companionship with a man of her own kind. No one could replace Martin, and Beaux would never allow it. She stopped resisting intercourse with him; it was another task she had to perform of many.

Most important, she couldn't risk being separated from her children. Beaux could decide to sell them—or sell her—or a new master could force her to have his offspring.

It was better to stay with the devil she knew.

He never hit her again, but she also never forgot her place. She was his property.

Occasionally, Beaux wanted her to shave him. He'd sit in a wooden chair near the washbasin in his bedroom, a fluffy towel protecting his blousy white shirt, never flinching as the straight razor slowed at his Adam's Apple. He'd stare at her with his hazel eyes via the handheld mirror, a smirk on his face, almost daring her to cut him. She'd think about it but smile at him and restrain herself instead.

Beaux had asked Dinah many times to move into the house to be more available to him. Though warmer inside, the accommodations wouldn't have been that much better than her bed in the cabin. He wanted her to sleep in the hallway outside his and Anna's room. Or, he offered to make room for her in the attic. She'd have declined anyway, but she wouldn't consider a proposition that kept her apart from her children.

Eventually, Beaux had given up asking.

Meanwhile, Anna had given him three children, despite constantly threatening to divorce him because of Dinah. In a recent North Carolina Supreme Court decision, the judge had ruled in favor of a husband who'd beaten his wife and insisted his slave mistress share their bed. Anna knew that any case she'd bring would be hopeless.

"At least I didn't ask you to share our bed," Beaux had said to Dinah one night as he told her about Anna's latest divorce threat. Dinah had pretended to be asleep.

Dinah accepted her life. Over time, her "relationship" with Beaux evolved past copulation. There was no foreplay or touching or genuine affection, but they talked a lot; or, rather, he did. Sometimes, on pleasant days, whether or not Anna was away, Beaux would make Dinah sit on the edge of the balcony in front of the house with him. He would sip whiskey in between puffs of a cigar and swing his legs back and forth while they looked up at the stars. At first, he discussed inane things like the weather. Then, he moved on to social matters. Beaux loved to entertain her with gossip about the townspeople, the families living on other plantations, and the lengths to which women went to snare a man.

"You think all women are that way?" she'd asked once.

"I do."

"What about the ones who write books? Or run businesses?"

"They still need a man."

"I don't need one."

"That's right. You've got me."

Dinah had bitten her tongue.

They discussed their children. Beaux didn't hide his slave children from his friends. He bragged to them about his strong Negro boys and his pretty girls, and how they'd pay off for him someday. He was prouder of them than he was of his children with Anna.

For Beaux, his connection with Dinah was stronger than the one he had with his wife. He even opened up to Dinah about his relationship with Nicholas. She remembered the long-ago conversation that Beaux had had with Master Sam in his study, prior to her banishment to the fields because of her pregnancy. Nicholas was smart and a great hunter. Everything came easily to him. Beaux liked hunting, too, but never joined his father and brothers because he did not want to hear what a great shot Nicholas was. He didn't begrudge Nicholas's gifts. He just wished his father was not so quick to point out Beaux's lack thereof.

Beaux shared his hopes and dreams and fears with Dinah. Dinah never shared hers, which revolved around her children. She wanted a better life for them than the one she'd lived, and she hoped that they would be free one day.

She had not forgotten about Martin. On a small table next to her bed was a wood carving of an African princess he had made for her. The intricate detail spoke to the many months it took him to make it. He had given it to her the evening before they were to be wed and said, "I can't wait to marry you tomorrow." Every night, after her prayers, Dinah picked up the carving and held it against her heart. "Good night, Martin, wherever you are." Sometimes, she clutched it while she slept and wondered whether he still thought of her, too.

One day, as a light snow fell outside, Dinah was dusting around the square desk in Master Sam's study while Beaux pored over the financial ledgers. He wore a checkered linsey-woolsey shirt, the top few buttons unclasped to reveal a white undershirt. His dog, Jake, lay at his feet. With Master Sam getting older and his eyesight going bad, Beaux had taken over more responsibility for the plantation. He raked his hair with his hands.

"God dang, I can't figure this out."

Dinah gazed at the numbers over his shoulder for a moment and pointed. "The total is wrong. It should be three hundred and sixty-nine."

Beaux's mouth parted. "How do you know that, girl?" He didn't seem displeased.

Although Beaux knew Dinah could read, he didn't remember that Celia had taught her figures, too, just as Dinah was now teaching her own children late at night by candlelight, along with their mother tongue, Edo.

"Just a guess. Was I right?"

He shot her a strange look. "Good guess." He crossed out the incorrect number and wrote in the correct one.

Pleased with herself, Dinah resumed dusting, humming a hymn she liked.

CHAPTER FORTY-EIGHT

SHA

AFTER A PEACEFUL weekend with Jelani, Monday morning, Sha was ready. She wore a light gray J. Crew suit and, in case she needed to make a run for it, white Jordan sneakers. She'd used product on her hair to relax the curls.

Jelani came out of her bedroom zipping up her stuffed backpack. She slung it over her shoulder and gave Sha a double take.

"Big meeting?" she asked.

Sha didn't dress up for work unless she was giving a presentation to potential investors, clients, or board members. Her work wardrobe usually comprised jeans or joggers, a white T-shirt, and an untucked, un-ironed, long-sleeved button-down shirt with the sleeves rolled up regardless of the weather.

"Yes," Sha said.

"You look like money. Is that a new suit?"

"You act as if you've never seen me in a suit."

"It's been a while."

"I'm running late. You need a ride?"

"Do you mind?"

Jelani no longer wanted to drive herself to school or ride with her friends. Sometimes, she even walked the mile, something she hadn't done since her freshman year.

After dropping Jelani off and watching her until she entered the building, Sha took Interstate 80 West and headed over the Bay Bridge. The sun shimmered through gaps in the clouds, the rays of light reaching the rippling water. A helicopter hovered overhead as she entered the skyscraper's parking garage. Sha parked in a visitor spot and followed the signs to the elevator. In the lobby, she found a seat on a low leather couch next to a young man in an off-the-rack suit who muttered to himself as he prepared for a job interview. Sha pulled her laptop out of her briefcase and pretended to work, periodically checking the front entrance to see whether Erik was entering the building. She stared at the screen saver as she typed indiscriminately.

"Hi there."

Sha's gaze panned upward. There stood Mikala in a blue double-breasted suit, with a black briefcase hanging from a strap on her shoulder.

"Do you work in this building?" asked Mikala.

Sha straightened. "No. What are you doing here?"

"I work here. Didn't you get my card?"

Sha had forgotten. "I did." She leaned a little so she could see around Mikala and watch for Erik. She didn't want to miss him.

"But you never called."

"Well…um…I was busy."

Mikala exhaled. "I get it." She turned to walk away.

"Wait!" *What am I doing?* "I really have been busy."

"Would you be interested in going to a game?" Mikala asked.

That would keep Sha away from Jelani for too long. "How about dinner instead?"

Mikala smiled. "I'd like that. I need to go. My first meeting's at nine."

"I'll call you."

"We'll see."

Fifteen minutes later, Erik entered the building.

Sha pressed a key on her keyboard, pretending to fire off an email, then stowed her laptop in her briefcase. She swung the strap over her shoulder, hurried to the marble counter manned by a security guard, and scrawled an indecipherable name on the sign-in sheet. Under the COMPANY column, she wrote the name of a company listed on the building owner's website.

While workers streamed past her, Sha lost sight of Erik. She rushed to the bank of elevators. The ones on the left went to floors two through twenty-four. The right elevators shot up to floors twenty-five to forty-eight. Erik was in a car on the right. He caught her eye and shot his arm out to prevent the doors from closing. Sha forced herself to walk toward him and stepped inside the crowded car. Erik grinned and sized her up with a discreet appraisal. His hair was cut short on the sides, longer on top, with gel keeping it in place. His mustache and beard were trimmed close to his face. His green eyes seemed to see through her facade. Sha understood why her daughter had been attracted to him. She squeezed in front of him and faced the shiny metal doors. As she did, his hand grazed hers. She couldn't tell if it was accidental or intentional. She forced a smile and nodded her thanks, not trusting herself to speak, her mouth dry. As the elevator ascended, she silently counted off the floor numbers so she wouldn't turn around and punch him.

Maybe mindful meditation worked.

Sha inhaled the woodsy, spicy scent of Erik's cologne and could have sworn she felt his breath on the back of her neck. At every stop, he pressed against her as he moved aside to allow the passengers behind him to exit. At the thirty-third floor, he brushed her as he exited the elevator. He grinned, a gleam in his eye.

"Have a good one."

Before the doors shut and the car rose, Sha glimpsed Trahon Investments' large black and blue logo on the wall. Shaking, she rode to the top, then down to the lobby.

On the drive back to Oakland, she kept rubbing her arm, trying to erase Erik's touch and expel his energy from her body.

CHAPTER FORTY-NINE

JULIA

SIX WEEKS AFTER Julia had confronted Augusta with the news of Jean's infidelity, life somehow moved on. Julia and Augusta often glanced at each other as they went about their day, and Augusta took comfort in the fact that someone else shared a burden that she had carried alone for so long. They never discussed Jean's infidelity again.

A surprise snowstorm had brought Harlem to a standstill, and a light snow continued to fall.

Julia awakened to a noise, coming from somewhere within the house. It sounded like a scream. Julia felt around on the bedside table for Clifford's pocket watch. It was 2:00 a.m. She heard the sound again—this time, she was sure it was a scream—and hopped out of bed, grabbing her night robe off the bed's foot end and draping it over her nightdress. She ran out into the hallway.

Her two sleepy grandchildren stood, in pajamas, in

front of the door to their bedroom. Hale was there, too. Julia glanced heavenward, thankful they were okay.

"What's going on?" Hale asked.

Josie rubbed her eyelid with her little fist. "What's that noise, Grandma?"

"It came from upstairs," Clara said. "Sounds like someone's hurt."

"Go back to bed," Julia said to Hale, who gave her a look. "Go on."

Hale reentered his room and shut the door.

Julia took each girl by the hand, one by one, and tucked them both into their separate beds on opposite sides of the room. Their dolls, stuffed animals, and balls were organized on the shelves above them. On Clara's side was Hale's old erector set. On her way out, Julia turned in the doorway. Josie's breath had already deepened into sleep. Clara was staring at Julia.

"Go to sleep, now," Julia said.

The doorknob was cold. After shutting the door, Julia climbed the stairs to the third floor on the carpet runner. Her bones ached in a way they didn't use to, especially the ones in her hands as she grasped the banister. At the end of the hall, she approached the bedroom that Augusta shared with Jean.

Julia hesitated, then knocked.

No response. Then whispers and a shuffling of feet across the oak floor. Finally, the door cracked open, and she saw half of Jean's face.

"Is everything all right?" she asked.

"Everything's fine, Mama. Go back to bed."

She stared at him. "You're sure?"

His jaw stiffened. "I'm sure."

"Augusta?" she called.

Silence. Then, "I'm fine, Mama."

Julia eyed Jean. Despite the chill in the house, his forehead glistened with sweat.

Jean shifted his gaze away from her. "Goodnight, Mama." He closed the door and left her standing there.

Julia went back down to her room and crawled into bed sluggishly.

Augusta was not fine. Not fine at all.

Julia whipped off the quilt and knelt on the area rug that covered the hardwood floor. Clasping her hands together for the second time that night, she prayed to God for guidance on how to help her daughter.

When Julia entered the kitchen the next day, Augusta, still in her silk pajamas, was stirring something in the pot on the stove. Her shoulders were drooping.

"Aren't you freezing in those pajamas?"

Augusta shook her head.

Julia sniffed. "Oatmeal?"

Hand on her hip, Augusta nodded.

Julia sat at the table and poured herself a cup of coffee from the sterling silver pot Jean had bought his wife for their last wedding anniversary. The snow had stopped, although inches of it still covered the lampposts and the cars parked along the street.

Julia sipped the strong black coffee. "The children aren't up yet?"

Augusta shook her head.

"That's unusual. Clara's normally running around the house before dawn. What about Hale?"

Another head shake.

Julia took another sip. "You're not speaking this morning?"

No response.

A coldness spread through Julia. "Look at me."

Augusta grabbed a ceramic bowl from the counter and scooped oatmeal into it. She opened the silverware drawer, extracted a spoon, and walked toward the round kitchen table, setting the bowl on the place mat in front of Julia. Before she could turn back to the stove, Julia slammed her cup down, sloshing coffee over the rim. She reached up to touch the side of her daughter's face. Augusta's left eye was purplish and swollen.

"My Lord! What happened?"

Augusta flinched and turned away. "It's nothing."

Bile rose in Julia's throat. Through clenched teeth, she said, "He did this." She started for the stairs.

Augusta grabbed her wrist and laughed. "It was me. I was careless. I ran into that door"—she pointed—"last night. That's what I get for trying to fetch a glass of water in the dark. No wonder he thinks I'm clumsy."

"You're not that clumsy. I'm going to—"

"Keep your voice down, Mama. You'll wake the children. He didn't do this. I fell all on my own."

"I thought you ran into a door." Julia calmed herself. That son-in-law of hers could wait; her daughter needed her now. "Come here, child." She stood, wrapped Augusta in an embrace, and rubbed her back. Augusta's thin body shook with tears.

"I love you, sweet baby girl," Julia said, easing Augusta into a chair and then sitting next to her. She took her daughter's hands in hers. "This is not okay. You shouldn't be defending him."

"Don't you believe in forgiveness?"

"Some people don't deserve it. No man is worth this."

"He's all I've got."

Julia squeezed Augusta's hands. "You should want more."

Over the following week, Julia avoided Jean as best she could. After everyone went to bed, she walked the halls at night. She tiptoed upstairs and placed her ear against the door of his and Augusta's bedroom, listening to make sure her daughter was all right. Thank God, Jean's snores were the only sounds to come from their room. Maybe there wouldn't be a third baby.

To get out of the house, Julia offered to go to the grocery store for Augusta and lingered there longer than necessary. She offered to run other errands. The snow had melted, so she didn't have to be as careful with her steps.

On a chilly December day, the sun radiating light but not heat, Julia was walking down 140th Street, her tote bag half full of groceries. Honking cars jammed the street after nights of hibernation. A woman entered the post office. Julia stopped. She didn't know the woman, but she looked famil-iar. She was medium-complexioned, curvy, and dressed in a dark blue dress and matching hat. She looked like Jean's type. Julia guessed she was in her early twenties. She didn't follow the woman in. Instead, she stood on the sidewalk, an idea forming. Her momma had always told her, "if God gives you a sign, follow it. Wherever it takes you." She turned around and nearly knocked over a dapper gentleman. Without stopping to apologize, she hurried home.

She needed to write a letter.

CHAPTER FIFTY

DINAH

THE EXPANSIVE ELM'S turned leaves rippled in the wind. Squirrels chased each other, oblivious to the sacredness of the ceremony taking place. A red-winged blackbird chirped as the midmorning sun warmed the faces of the Devereaux family's slaves gathered at the burying ground in the woods, two hundred yards from the quarters.

Dinah stared at the unadorned pine box, twirling Aisha's ring on her finger.

Joining the other slaves, she raised her voice in song. Martha's warm hands took one of hers, Betty held the other. Dinah's children stood in front of her, except for Moses, the youngest boy, who lay on the ground. She didn't have the heart—or the energy—to tell him to stand. She never realized that Sarah, her eldest, possessed such a beautiful voice.

Standing off to the side, Master Samuel Devereaux, Beaux, and his younger brothers, Billy and Nicholas, were present to pay their respects. Mistress Elizabeth, Beaux's sister, Mary, and his wife, Anna, were absent. Yesterday, Dinah overheard Master Sam imploring his wife to bury Celia in the family plot closer to the house, but she refused.

"I put up with that woman my entire adult life," Elizabeth had said. "I shall not lie beside her throughout eternity."

Dinah was grateful the mistress had refused. Her momma would have wanted to be buried next to her mother, Aisha, and the rest of their people.

A few years ago, Master Sam finally relaxed his rule against slaves congregating to pray. Once, after the patrol beat Lukas, the boy had shouted to Samuel Devereaux, who'd witnessed the beating, "Why don't you want us to find the Lord?" Master Sam responded, "He's our Lord, not yours." Lukas said, "The Lord is big enough for everyone." The master stared thoughtfully at him before walking away. The following Sunday, he'd allowed the slaves to have church in the old barn used for curing tobacco. In time, he discovered that religion, instead of agitating them, calmed them in this life and gave them hope for the next one. It also made it less likely that they'd kill him in his sleep.

He forced them to convert to Christianity, the white man's religion. Many of them did. The older slaves continued to pray to their African deities in secret.

Reverend Jones, a slave, walked five miles from another plantation to preach to them every Sunday. As one of the few slaves who could read, Dinah read a passage from the Bible every week. Earlier today, they'd had the funeral service in the barn. After the burial, a prayer meeting would take place there.

Now, numb with grief, she caressed the old, worn copy of the Bible her momma had found in a dresser drawer in the master's bedroom over two decades ago.

"We aren't supposed to steal," ten-year-old Dinah had said to her.

"It's not really stealing, it's borrowing. Since it belongs to the master, and we belong to him, it also belongs to us."

Young Dinah had scrunched up her face at her momma's logic. "We can steal anything we want from Master Sam?"

"No." Her momma snuggled her close and patted her hair. "But borrowing this is OK. Read it. The Lord won't mind."

Dinah smiled now through her tears as she recalled all the things her mother had "borrowed" from the house, including the books she'd given Dinah to read. Nelson never found them hidden underneath her bed during his weekly inspections.

The hymn finished, and the last singing voice faded. A white butterfly landed on Sarah's shoulder. Her daughter looked at it, then at Dinah. Sarah did not brush it away.

The Reverend Jones began the eulogy. He had a long face and a gray beard and mustache. While he spoke warmly of the woman he barely knew, Dinah found it hard to think about her momma without breaking down. She thought of her daddy instead. She didn't remember him, but her momma used to talk about him. Big Moses was handsome, with an intelligent mind. Intelligence was a negative attribute for a male slave on a plantation, and the master sold him. Her momma told her she'd inherited her smarts from her daddy. When Dinah looked in the mirror, she couldn't see any trace of Moses, as her momma had described him, in her features. As she got older, her momma stopped talking about him. It must have hurt too much.

Dinah tasted her tears.

"Let us pray," Reverend Jones said, bringing her out of her reverie.

After the prayer, the two slaves who'd dug the grave lowered the box containing her momma—her best friend, her confidant, her inspiration—into the ground. Some slaves sniffled and wept. An older woman, the same age as Celia, wailed to her African gods. Dinah stepped between her children. The gravedigger handed her a shovel. Leaves crunched underfoot as she scooped up the soil and flung it onto the pine box.

She gasped at the sound, the finality of it, and released the shovel. Her knees buckled and dropped to the soft dark-brown earth. The slaves quieted as she whimpered and whispered prayers. Her son, Moses, crawled to her and laid his head on her lap. She gathered him in her arms, holding him close to her chest as she rocked back and forth, staring at the small wooden board that marked the grave.

Dinah read the words she'd etched into the wood with a sharp rock, almost using up the entire board:

Celia Devereaux

Loving daughter, mother, grandmother,

friend, and a strong Negro woman

1807 - 1858

CHAPTER FIFTY-ONE

SHA

SHA AND MIKALA were seated outside in front of Cafe Z, a bistro on Hearst Avenue. She'd chosen a place in Berkeley so she wouldn't be too far from her daughter, in case Jelani needed her.

"You came," Mikala said. She wore a white sleeveless dress that showed firm shoulders and biceps. Sha wore her standard uniform: jeans, a button-down blue Brooks Brothers shirt with rolled up sleeves, and a white T-shirt underneath. On her feet were brand new white Nikes. She felt warm; whether from the extra clothing or the company, she didn't know.

Sha frowned. "You didn't think I would?"

"I gave it fifty-fifty."

"Then you don't know me," Sha said, her tone light.

"Which is why we're here."

After they ordered, Mikala said, "You never told me what

you did for a living. Is it a secret job? Like the CIA? Or NSA?"

Sha chuckled. "No, it's not that mysterious. I'm in IT."

Mikala's mouth parted. "I still shouldn't be surprised."

"No, you shouldn't."

The server brought white wine for Mikala and a pilsner for Sha.

Mikala held up her glass. "To no surprises."

Sha hesitated, then clinked her glass to Mikala's. She told Mikala about GirlsCode Ventures.

"That's amazing. Being good by doing good. I love it! It's not my area of expertise, but if your firm ever needs legal help, I'd be glad to provide pro bono services."

A lawyer might come in handy, Sha thought. For personal rather than professional reasons.

"That's generous of you." Sha sipped her beer. "My father was a lawyer, as was my grandmother."

The waiter brought their food. They ordered another round of drinks.

"You never wanted to be one?"

"Never. Too much debating at home."

Sha never told people who her mother was. If she did, the conversation would be about Nicole. Sha loved her mother, but didn't want to talk about her all the time.

Mikala nibbled on her salad. "What else do you do when you're not working? Besides watching the Warriors?"

Sha glanced at the small, circular, dark brown birthmark on her forearm. The same one her mother and daughter shared. "I have a daughter. Jelani. She...takes up a lot of my time."

"How old is she?"

"Almost seventeen. She's a junior in high school."

A breeze riffled through Mikala's twists. "That's a tough age. Is she going to college?"

"She is, but hasn't decided which one yet."

"Decisions, decisions. Do you have a preference?"

"Wherever she'll be happy."

"That's a good answer."

The server returned and asked how they were enjoying their meal. When they assured him they were, he retreated.

"What does she want to major in?" Mikala continued.

Sha shook her head. "I don't think she knows what she wants to do when she grows up."

"If she goes away to school, what will you do? How will you fill your time?"

Sha twirled her sesame seed pasta. "Good question."

She hadn't contemplated what she'd do when Jelani left home. Or being alone. Sha hadn't been alone since…she'd gone off to college herself. She sipped the third beer that had miraculously arrived at their table.

"You have a southern accent," Mikala remarked.

"Only when I've drunk past my quota." Sha glanced at the bottle. "I guess this is my last beer."

"Where are you from?"

"Atlanta."

"How did you end up out here?"

Sha told her.

"Do you miss the South?"

"I miss my parents sometimes, and my grandmother."

The server cleared away their plates. They declined

dessert. After he left, Mikala asked, "Besides Jelani, what else do you like to do?"

"Reading. Gaming. And I do puzzles." Sha paused. "I have this patch of land in my backyard that I'm thinking about turning into a garden."

"I know a bit about gardening. If you could use some help."

"I'd like that," Sha said, surprising herself.

CHAPTER FIFTY-TWO

OLIVIA

OLIVIA TRAVELED SO much now that Davis rarely picked her up from the airport like he used to, at the beginning of her career.

On the flight from Atlanta to Philadelphia and the taxi ride home, she ruminated on Nicole's predicament. She held no illusion that Nicole could solve her problems as Olivia had. Nicole's harasser was the cable network's star employee; Nicole was a low-level assistant producer.

As she passed the Johnson House, where two out of five generations of Johnsons had been active participants in the Underground Railroad, Olivia's thoughts expanded beyond her daughter. If she, Olivia, was experiencing sexual harassment, weren't other women in her firm most likely encountering it, too? All these misbehaving men wouldn't stop on their own. What did it say about her—a woman and a partner—if she allowed the behavior to continue?

Mr. Brown wasn't outside watering his flowers. Olivia had been looking forward to chatting with him. She entered the brownstone and left her red Samsonite suitcase near the front door. She shrugged out of her coat and hung it up. In the family room, a 76ers game was in progress on the wood-paneled television. Davis sat reclined in one of the Barcaloungers enjoying a Dr Pepper, his feet on the footrest, his kicked-off slippers on the white shag carpet. He was wearing a blue polyester track suit with red and white stripes.

He smiled at Olivia. "It's the playoffs."

Maurice Cheeks delivered a no-look pass to Charles Barkley for the dunk.

"Nice pass," Olivia said.

Davis returned his attention to the TV. "Man, I missed it!"

"They'll show it again." Olivia crossed the room, gave her husband a peck in the center of his forehead, removed her suit jacket, and threw it on the sofa. She sat in the other recliner and laid her head back against the headrest. She and Davis watched the game together in silence. During the commercial break, Davis reached out to the table between them for a walnut and the aluminum nutcracker. "How's our baby girl?"

"She'll be all right."

Davis cracked the shell and popped the nut into his mouth. "That doesn't sound good."

"She'll be all right," Olivia repeated.

Davis held her gaze before sipping his soda. "She's her mother's daughter." He offered Olivia the can. She took it. "Not sure what's going on with her, but the person at the other end of your wrath has no clue what's coming."

Olivia sipped from Davis's drink. "You've got that right."

∽

Over the next few weeks, Olivia went through a slow period at the office. The telecommunications merger had closed. The acquirer's bank had sent the law firm its proceeds from the transaction. She was managing other cases, but none of them consumed her day or her mind. She thought mainly about her daughter's situation and what—if anything—she could do to help Nicole.

One morning, after dressing for work, she examined herself in front of the full-length mirror on the bedroom closet door. Her skirt was snug at the waist. To deal with Nicole's situation, Olivia needed to be in shape.

Later that day, instead of heading to the partners' cafeteria for lunch, Olivia went to Blockbuster and bought Jane Fonda's aerobics VHS tape. She decided she'd try to keep up with the actress-turned-instructor three times a week.

After a couple of weeks, feeling energized, she flew to Atlanta and took a taxi to her daughter's apartment. Nicole answered the door, her hair uncombed, her face wan. She'd called in sick, which was unusual for a girl who was full of life and who rarely became ill. After letting Olivia in, Nicole headed to her bedroom and crawled underneath the sheet. The cover was sprawled across the gray carpet. Nicole's clothes hung in the closet or were stacked against the wall. She hadn't had time to buy a dresser.

Olivia was alarmed by Nicole's condition, but she remained outwardly calm. She sat on the edge of the bed. "You look thin."

"I'm all right."

"You need to eat. He should be the one suffering, not you."

Nicole groaned. "What am I going to do? I can't call in sick every day. When I go in, he doesn't leave me alone. I might as well quit."

"You'll go back to work tomorrow and avoid him if you can."

"That will be hard to do."

"It won't be for long. I have a plan."

Nicole's eyes narrowed. "To do what?"

"You'll see. But I need a few days."

Although it was July, Nicole hadn't turned on the window's air conditioning unit. Olivia took a handkerchief out of her purse and wiped her daughter's sweaty face, then kissed her forehead and tucked her in. When Nicole was almost asleep, she said, "I have to go."

"Where?"

"To a hotel."

"You can stay here. Sleep on the couch."

"I know, but I've got things to do."

Olivia turned on the AC and left.

CHAPTER FIFTY-THREE

Julia

"MRS. GIBSON! THIS IS a surprise."

Julia stepped into the studio. The room smelled of paint. "I hope you don't mind," she said, gesturing toward the house. "Your wife said it was okay."

Ray Ray grinned. "Then it's okay. Please come in." He wrapped Julia in a warm embrace. "Let me take your coat." He hung Julia's coat on a peg behind the door and motioned to two stools below a window that allowed in the weak winter sunlight. "And clean up." He washed and wiped a paintbrush with a rag and placed it in a jar filled with different size brushes on a table splashed with various colors. "How are you? How's Augusta?"

Julia had seen little of Ray Ray after she'd moved from West 147th Street. She had attended his wedding to a girl from the old neighborhood. The couple lived in a small house two blocks away from where Julia had raised her two children.

Ray Ray had built a studio in the backyard. His appearance had changed. He sported a mustache, and his body was more muscular, the last vestiges of his baby fat having disappeared. He wore brown knickers held up by suspenders and a beige shirt with three buttons, its sleeves rolled up to the elbows.

Julia didn't answer, so Ray Ray asked, "What brings you back to the old neighborhood? Visiting friends?"

Julia shook her head. "I came to see you, Ray Ray."

"It's just Ray now."

"Ray, I need your help."

Ray Ray looked at her quizzically. "With what?"

Next to the table stood an easel displaying a painting of an African man in tribal regalia, with one foot on a slave ship and the other in the jungle as a lion, an elephant, and a gorilla looked on. The man's muscles were flexed, resisting the shackles that pulled him toward the ship. There was a United States flag on the ship's bow.

"You've done well for yourself," Julia said.

Ray Ray studied his work. "Can't complain. Every morning, I get to wake up and do what I love." He looked back at Julia with a concerned expression. "What can I do for you, Mrs. Gibson?"

Julia was hoping Ray Ray's and Augusta's history would be enough for him to help Julia.

"It's Augusta."

Ray Ray straightened. "What about her?"

Julia explained to him what was happening between Jean and Augusta. The veins in Ray Ray's forearms bulged as he clenched and unclenched his fists, pacing in front of the easel. "He hit Augusta? I always knew he was bad news. You could tell that by looking at him. I'll teach that mother—sorry, Mrs. Gibson. Where is he?"

"Sit down, Ray Ray. Ray."

"I'm going to give him what's coming to him."

"Please, sit down. I've got something better in store for him."

Ray sank back onto the stool. As Julia described her plan, his breathing slowed and his body relaxed.

"Will you help me?" Julia implored.

Ray placed his rainbow-painted hand on hers. "Do you have to ask?"

⸻

Ruth opened the door. "Aunt Julia."

Julia stepped into the hotel room. The two women hugged.

Julia leaned back. "It's been a while. My, you've grown."

"You should see me with makeup." Ruth gestured. "There's only one chair."

"The bed is fine."

They sat side-by-side at the foot of the bed. Julia didn't bother to remove her coat. She gazed at her youngest niece, daughter of her older sister, Aisha. Aisha had been named after her own and Julia's great-great-grandmother. Ruth wore a gray knit sweater and black tapered trousers. Her hair was short and straightened, framing her round face. She was as striking as her mother.

"How's my sister?"

"Bossy as ever."

Julia laughed. "Tell her I'll visit soon. Thank you for coming."

"You said you needed my help, so I'm here. Tell me about Augusta's husband."

After relaying Augusta's situation to her niece, Julia also divulged the plan she'd set in motion when she'd written to Ruth ten days ago, after having seen the woman who resembled her entering the post office.

"What a cad," Ruth said.

"Do you think you can do it?"

"I've always wanted to be an actress." Ruth stood and ran a hand down her curvaceous hip. "I'll make him drop to his knees," she purred.

CHAPTER FIFTY-FOUR

DINAH

"WAKE UP," DINAH said. "We can't be late."

Sarah groaned and rolled over on Dinah's former bed. Dinah remembered the feeling. She wished she could let her daughter sleep, but duty called. She shook her again until she turned back around. Sarah's long, light-brown hair was mussed. Her hazel eyes were half-lidded. Dinah no longer saw Beaux when she gazed upon Sarah's face. Only her precious daughter.

"We *can't* be late," Dinah repeated.

Dinah had already been up for an hour; she'd bathed and fed her other children breakfast. After Sarah bathed and got dressed, mother and daughter left the cabin and walked through the quarters to the house. Red and orange leaves swirled across their path. Dinah recalled the first time she'd taken this walk with her momma.

"Mornin', Ms. Martha," she said as they hung up their shawls.

"Mornin', Ms. Dinah."

Dinah hugged the cook. "Thank you for what you did for Momma. The food was delicious. She would have been pleased."

"You don't have to thank me. Celia was family." Martha patted Dinah's shoulder. "Don't you go upsetting yourself. Your momma wouldn't like that. Besides, she's free now."

"You're right." Dinah pulled away, brushed away her tears, and straightened her dress. "I brought help."

"I see." Martha's eyes twinkled. "Hope she's better than the help Celia brought me."

"Hush!" Dinah smiled. The cook was well past sixty. Sarah would be helpful to her. "Don't forget, the mistress is having ladies from town over for afternoon tea."

Martha's jowls jiggled as she shook her head. She'd gained weight over the years from "tasting" all the food she cooked. "I haven't lost my memory." She made a shooing motion with her hands. "Now, get out of my kitchen so we can work."

Dinah glanced at her daughter before touching her hand. "You'll do fine. Listen to Ms. Martha." She left the room as Martha began explaining that afternoon's menu to Sarah.

Upon her momma's death, Dinah assumed Celia's responsibilities in the great house: overseeing the household—including the house slaves—managing the events, and attending to and traveling with the mistress. Beaux hated Dinah's absences and was extra arduous with her in bed on her return. Dinah had overheard him telling his mother that she traveled too much. Mistress Elizabeth had told him it was none of his concern, and that he should be more concerned with his wife's travels. By now, Dinah could run the household in her sleep; Celia had been an excellent teacher. Dinah's life was better than most slaves', and she felt blessed.

Eventually, Sarah fell into the same routine Dinah once had and became so efficient that the mistress said to Dinah, "She's a hard worker, like her momma." Responsible for bathing Beaux's younger children, Sarah often "borrowed" an extra bar of soap and brought it back to the cabin. "Your Granny Celia would be proud," Dinah had told her.

Word of the unrest occurring across the fledgling country couldn't help reaching them on the plantation. Master Sam, Nicholas, Billy, and other menfolk gathered in the parlor over whiskey and cigars to discuss the rumors that the southern states were threatening to secede from the Union. The men hoped North Carolina would be one of them and yearned for war. In another room, Elizabeth Devereaux told her daughter, her daughter-in-law, and the men's wives that she didn't want her sons going off to war. Beaux did not participate in discussions regarding national events. He would slip out of the house and go for long horse rides. He'd confided to Dinah once, after fornicating, that he had no desire to fight.

Dinah wondered what would happen if the North won the war. It was rumored that the owners would be forced to free the slaves. She couldn't imagine what that would be like. Aisha used to tell her how good freedom felt. Dinah had never considered running away. At first, it was her ties to her momma and her grandmother that had kept her feet planted.

Now, unless Master Sam freed her children, she was as tethered to this plantation as the Devereaux family itself was.

⁊

In the ornate ballroom, the reception was in full swing. To his parents' delight, Billy Devereaux married a woman he'd been courting for the past year. Billy had grown long sideburns. His big-toothed smile was on full display as he danced with his bride, who wore a simple white muslin dress. That afternoon, Dinah had tried to tame his cowlick with grease, but now it stuck up from his head for all the guests to see.

Dinah liked Billy. Unlike the rest of his family, he had always been uncomfortable with the master-slave relationship, never referring to them as "slaves" or "Negroes"…or worse. He preferred the term "servants." As far as Dinah knew, he was a gentleman and hadn't taken slave girls for his personal use.

Earlier that day, Dinah had stood at the center of the room directing the slaves as they organized and set the tables in preparation for the ceremony. They'd polished the silverware and the centerpieces that held the flower arrangements until their sheen was visible from across the room. The scent of irises, cardinals, and roses filled the ballroom. The floor-to-ceiling windows had been cleaned to the appearance of invisibility, as if one could reach through them to the outdoors and touch the fall foliage.

Couples twirled around the dance floor. The bride and groom finally took a break. As Dinah collected empty flute glasses from guests, she glanced over at Beaux, who stood alone just inside the door to the hallway surveying the guests and sipping champagne. When Beaux spotted Dinah, he raised his glass to her. Billy joined his older brother, clapped him on the back, and said something to him. Dinah was too far away to overhear their conversation. While his brother talked, Beaux's smile faded and he stared across the room with admiration. Dinah looked over her shoulder, following his gaze.

The young woman who garnered his attention wore a plain, neat dress. Her hair, normally in a headscarf when she worked in the house, was worn loose and framed her pretty face. She was holding a tray of champagne glasses, and her eyes shone as she watched the dancers.

Dinah dropped the glass she'd just picked up, something she hadn't done since her first month working in the house. She knelt quickly to sweep up the shards with a napkin. Though muted by the music, the sound of the glass shattering against the floor drew Beaux's shameless attention back to her and away from their fourteen-year-old daughter.

The day after Billy's wedding reception, Dinah oversaw the cleanup of the ballroom and then entered the kitchen, rubbing her neck and fanning her face. She greeted Martha. The cook stood in a corner hacking away at a pig, separating the meat from the offal and scraping the latter into a bucket on the floor. Blood spattered her white apron and sprayed across the floor as Martha pointed the cooking hatchet at a pitcher on the table. "Grab some lemonade." She motioned toward the sitting room, where the mistress was entertaining Billy's new in-laws. "She won't notice."

"You sure?" Dinah checked the entrance to make sure she wouldn't be overheard. "She might come back tonight to measure how much is left."

The two women laughed.

"Go ahead," Martha said, "and cool yourself off."

"Don't mind if I do." Dinah poured the lemonade into a glass, leaned against the waist-high side table, and took a sip. "Yum. That's sweet." She held her forearm against her damp forehead. "Where's Sarah?"

"The mistress told her to sweep the balcony. It was filthy with footprints after last night's comings and goings."

"She has to help you get supper ready." Dinah took another sip and set the glass on the table. "I'll go check on her." She pointed at her glass of lemonade. "Don't let anyone take that, you hear?"

Martha lifted the hatchet from her shoulder and grinned at her gravely. "Don't worry."

As Dinah walked along the hallway's wide pine planks, the grandfather clock chimed the noon hour. Dinah stopped at the ballroom to check whether all the furniture was back in its rightful place. It was. There was no sign that a wedding reception had occurred there the previous night.

Humming a hymn from last Sunday's service, Dinah crossed the grand foyer and opened the front door to the balcony. Her daughter stood at the south end holding a broom handle with both hands. Dinah opened her mouth to call her inside, then closed it. Sarah wasn't alone. The person speaking to her was leaning against the other side of a pillar with his legs crossed at the ankles, blocked from Dinah's view…

except for the bottom of one boot. Dinah recognized it; she'd cleaned Beaux's boots many times. She tried to remain calm.

"Sarah!" she said. "Go to the kitchen and help Ms. Martha."

Her daughter jumped. "I'm not finished sweeping yet. I was resting for a bit."

"Rest inside. I'll finish this out here."

Sarah hesitated, then walked toward Dinah. She glanced back at Beaux, who'd swung to leaning against the opposite side of the pillar, facing them. He grinned and waved. Sarah handed Dinah the broom without looking at her. After the door closed behind Sarah, Dinah pointed the broom handle at him. "Leave her alone. I mean it."

CHAPTER FIFTY-FIVE

SHA

A WEEK AFTER encountering Erik in the elevator, Sha arrived for an appointment at Trahon Investments wearing the same gray suit, this time with a light blue shirt. She waited on the couch next to the receptionist's desk, beneath the massive logo. When Erik entered the reception area, a flicker of recognition crossed his face, but he couldn't place Sha. They shook hands. His hands were soft and his nails were manicured.

"Erik Stevens," he said.

"Ms. Bradley."

Sha had kept her mother's maiden name. A legacy of sorts.

Erik stuffed his hands in his pockets while he surveyed her body once more. "Pleased to meet you."

"Thank you for seeing me."

"No problem. Follow me."

When he turned, Sha wiped her hand on her pants.

Many of the doors along the hallway opened to identical-size offices. Employees within were talking on the phone via headsets or typing on their computers. Erik led Sha to a windowless interior office. He motioned with his hand at the guest chair, then sat behind his sleek, uncluttered desk.

He leaned back in his ergonomic chair. "Coffee? Tea?"

There was no furniture in the room aside from the desk and chairs. No shelves or tables filled with tombstones commemorating investment deals. No photos of Erik with famous clients or politicians.

"No," Sha said. "I do not like to waste time. If you don't mind, let's get started."

"I don't like small talk either." Erik grinned. Sha masked her rage at the thought of him assaulting her daughter. "You told our receptionist over the phone you're looking to switch investment advisors."

"I am," Sha said. "My current broker isn't aggressive enough."

Erik's forehead creased with faux concern. "How so?"

"I want the highest return possible." Sha gave him a pointed look. "I'm not interested in how it's achieved."

A light flickered in Erik's eyes. He leaned forward and clasped his hands on the desk. "How much are we talking about? I mean…how much are you looking to invest?"

"I recently exercised some options, so a million to start." She paused. "Depending on your results, there could be more."

Erik blinked several times and tried to suppress another grin. He didn't ask himself why, of all the brokers in the city, she'd come to him.

Sha coughed a deep-throated cough into her elbow. Erik hustled around his desk and bent over her, touching her upper back. His touch was gentle; Sha used all of her self-control not to recoil.

"Are you okay, Ms. Bradley?"

Through more coughing, she said, "A glass of water."

"Of course. Right away." Erik rushed out of the room, the overpowering scent of his cologne lingering behind.

Sha peeked at the door, then, moving quickly, pulled a thumb drive out of her jacket pocket and inserted it into Erik's computer. She could have hacked the computer remotely, but she wanted her revenge to be up close and personal. She clicked the Windows button and the letter "R" and typed in the program's name: REVENGE. While the computer was processing, she briefly considered the possible unintended consequences. According to Newton's third law, for every action, there was an equal and opposite reaction. She might be setting in motion consequences she would know nothing about. But she was doing the right thing, she kept telling herself.

Her index finger hovered over the mouse only for a second before she clicked on "OK." She glanced at the office door, then at the spinning hourglass on the screen, and then back at the door. The program finished uploading, and Sha snatched the drive out of the USB port and put it in her pocket just as Erik reentered the room. Erik's eyes widened when he saw her standing behind his desk.

"I was looking for a Kleenex," Sha said, searching the surface of the desk with a helpless expression on her face.

"I'm sorry. I don't have any. I can get some."

Sha approached Erik and took the glass he held, brushing his hand with her fingers. His jaw clenched as he gazed into her eyes with a hunger she hadn't seen directed at her in a long time. She coughed again to break the spell. Erik stepped back.

Sha took a sip of water. "I think I'll be all right."

"Are you sure?"

"Yes."

"Shall we continue?"

They returned to their seats to discuss her investment goals, asset allocation models, and details of the account transfer. While Erik did the talking, Sha's breathing slowed, and her mind regained its peace. She'd done the right thing. Not only for her daughter, but for the other daughters who would encounter Erik.

When they finished, Erik said, "Ms. Bradley, thanks for entrusting me with your valuable assets. It will be a pleasure working with you."

Sha smiled for the first time since she'd been in his presence. "The pleasure will be mine."

On the way back to her Oakland office, Sha picked up a latte at Café Exquis, an independent coffee shop around the block from her building. She loved its vibe and its Afrobeat background music. When she needed a change of environment, she sometimes brought her laptop to the shop to work.

On the eleventh floor of her office building, she alighted from the secure elevator that opened to a large room. Her staff were working hard in their cubicles, most of them listening to music on headphones or earbuds. Only Sha and a few others were privy to the symphony of their furious collective keyboard-tapping. Sha, holding her large, warm to-go cup, breezed by her employees without a word. She imagined the thoughts swirling in their heads, given the way she was dressed—still in the suit she'd worn to visit Erik—and the hours she'd been putting in lately, which didn't involve them. From the macro—is the company going public? Is it in trouble? Will it be bought out? Will there be layoffs? Will I lose my job?—to the micro—What project is she working on? Why is she working so closely with the new guy?

Sha was friendly with her staff but had not let any of them get close to her. She made excuses as to why she could never go out to happy hours with them. She never joined them for lunch, preferring to eat alone in her office. Never told them of her vacation plans. Wasn't connected with them on social media. In fact, she wasn't on social media at all. She was the boss, and she wanted to keep some distance. But she was the type of leader who wanted everyone's voice to be heard, especially the historically marginalized voices, similar to the Black girls she was trying to help bring into the tech field. Sha wasn't afraid of making tough calls or calling someone out when needed. She was not sure whether her employees liked her—and she didn't care—but she hoped they respected her. She cared about them as people and did not enjoy keeping secrets from them. But she wouldn't be allaying their concerns today.

At her glass desk, she set down the coffee cup and removed her suit jacket, hanging it on the back of the chair. She booted up the program that she and Dominic had developed. A mirror image of Erik's desktop was replicated on one of her monitors; she now had remote access to his computer. She marveled at the program's beauty. She typed furiously, though she was careful about the position of her wrists after having suffered a bout of Carpal Tunnel Syndrome from all-night coding sessions earlier in her career.

She sent Dominic a message via Teams. "Can you come to my office?"

"Be right there," Dominic typed back.

The former bouncer had started working at GirlsCode Ventures a week earlier, on Monday. On his first day, Sha had realized that he not only had a photographic memory, but was a coding genius. The project she had assigned to him—officially—was to develop a game for teaching preschool girls coding skills. He was further along than a more senior team member would have been. Earlier that week, Sha had asked him to work surreptitiously with her on a program to access the software used by Erik's investment firm. Together, they had hacked out the code in forty-eight hours.

A minute after Sha had contacted him, Dominic's bulk filled her doorway. Sha preferred working with him here; she wouldn't miss her late-night visits to the club.

"Come in," she said, "and close the door."

Dominic did as instructed, removing his headphones, from which the tinny sounds of classic R&B emanated—much different from his former employer's music. Sha gestured to the only other upright chair in the office. With his bulk, she didn't think he'd be comfortable in a beanbag chair.

"What's up, Ms. B.?"

"It worked."

"Good to hear."

"Thank you…for everything."

"You don't have to thank me. I was happy to do it. He deserved it for what he did."

"Still. I appreciate your helping my daughter. Helping me."

They sat for a moment in uncomfortable silence.

At last, Dominic said, "Sha?"

"Yes?"

"My girlfriend's Black, as is our daughter. Not all men are bad. Just the lost ones."

Dominic reminded Sha of her grandfather. When she was a child, Grandpa Davis had been a gentle giant. She gave Dominic a faint smile. "I'll keep that in mind."

"Glad everything worked out. Do you need anything else?"

Sha shook her head.

Dominic rose, slipped the headphones back on, and lumbered out of her office.

Sha spent the rest of the afternoon and evening teaching herself how to use Trahon's investment program and finalizing her plan. She couldn't afford any mistakes.

Although the end justified the means, she was not proud of herself. Ever since Erik Stevens had come into her daughter's life, Sha had become a consummate liar, lying to her daughter, her colleagues, and her staff. She'd been distracted from her work. But she'd retained some ethics. She did not open the file on Erik's computer marked PERSONAL.

CHAPTER FIFTY-SIX

OLIVIA

A FEW DAYS after arriving in Atlanta, Olivia called Nicole from her suite. She had checked in on her daughter every day. "How about dinner tonight? Here at the hotel."

"It'll be late. I have to put the six o'clock news to bed."

"7:30?"

"I'll be there."

That evening, they were seated in the five-star restaurant off the lobby of the Ritz-Carlton. The room had a classical feel, with its baroque architectural detailing.

After they ordered, Nicole asked, "Are you going to tell me what you've been doing since you got here?"

"Let's eat first."

"I guess you want to talk about what's happening at work."

The waiter returned with their glasses of red wine and retreated.

"Actually," Olivia said, "I want to talk about anything but work."

Nicole's eyes bulged. "Really?"

"Really. I want to enjoy this time with you."

"Okayyyyyy…"

They shared a laugh. Olivia enjoyed hearing the melodic sound of her daughter's laughter.

"I have something to tell you." Nicole hesitated. "I think I've met someone."

Having attended a predominantly white high school, Nicole had a lot of white male friends, but none of them had asked her out. She'd never spoken of dating anyone in college.

The waiter brought their food. Olivia waited for him to leave, then leaned in. "Tell me more!"

"You'll like him," her daughter said.

Olivia cut into her chicken breast, which was smothered in brown gravy. "Why is that?"

"He graduated from Morehouse, and he's a lawyer."

Olivia finished chewing. "You're right. I like him already."

"And he just made partner."

"Even better. How did you meet?"

"I was doing research on an Atlanta law firm that is representing Black men who've been wrongfully incarcerated. He was the attorney I interviewed."

"You could have interviewed me."

"I could have." Nicole smiled. "But he's cuter."

Olivia pursed her lips. "I imagine so. Where's he from?"

"Here. Anyway, he asked me out afterward. I wondered about the ethics—of going out with an interview subject—but it was only one date. What could it hurt? And I'm so low on the ladder, who'd care?"

"How did the date go?"

"We've been dating for a few weeks."

Olivia glanced at her wedding ring, the upgraded one Davis had given her after he'd been at his job for five years. It had a 1.25-carat diamond. The engagement ring he had given her, with the tiny diamond, rested against her chest on a gold chain. "So. Pretty well."

"This was a treat, Mother," Nicole said after they'd finished their desserts. "The food was delicious, and I enjoyed our conversation, but I must get back to the office."

"Tonight?"

"Like New York City, the news never sleeps." Nicole drained the rest of her wine, her tennis bracelet sparkling from the lighting overhead. "Besides, you know what it's like. How many times did you leave us during dinner to go back to the office?"

"Ouch."

Nicole grabbed her hand. "I shouldn't have said that. I'm sorry."

In the lobby, hotel guests sat on overstuffed chairs and sofas, their drinks resting atop red oak coffee tables. The walls were painted bronze and hunter green.

Olivia faced her daughter in front of the revolving doors that led outside to Peachtree Street, which were manned on either side by uniformed doormen in black suits with red ties.

Nicole reached out her arms to give Olivia a hug. "Thanks for dinner."

Olivia grabbed her daughter's hands instead. "I need ten more minutes. I want you to come upstairs with me to my room."

Nicole's eyes narrowed. "What for?"

"I have something to show you."

⁕

Olivia led Nicole into her suite. Nicole scanned the sitting room, including its peach-painted walls and the three windows that provided a magnificent view of downtown Atlanta.

"Even though I've finally unpacked, I can see why you'd rather stay here than in my apartment."

"It wasn't that. I've had a lot to do, and I didn't want to bother you."

"Aren't you missing something?"

"What?"

"Milk crates!"

Olivia laughed. She loved the Ritz and refused to stay anywhere else when she traveled alone. "I think I've earned this. Don't you?"

Nicole beamed. "Yes, you have, Mother."

Tears pressed against Olivia's eyes. For once, she didn't know what to say.

"I hope I can afford something like this too, one day," said Nicole. "Now, I hate to rush you, but I need to get back to work. Why am I here?"

Olivia crossed the room to her briefcase, which rested on the Queen Anne desk, and pointed to the plush white sofa. "Take a seat."

With her back to Nicole, she pulled the items she'd

purchased from different stores around the city over the last few days out of the case and brought them over to the couch. She hadn't wanted to attract attention by buying all the items from one establishment. She sat next to her daughter and set the purchases on the low-lying brown coffee table in front of them.

Nicole surveyed the equipment. "What's all this?"

For a moment, Olivia worried her plan wouldn't work. That she might put her daughter's safety at risk, or that she might get her fired. She shook off these feelings. There were other jobs. Her daughter's self-esteem was paramount. It was time for Nicole to don her imaginary battle suit and go to war.

"Take off your shirt." Olivia unraveled the long cord attached to a microphone. "I'll show you how this works."

CHAPTER FIFTY-SEVEN

RUTH

RUTH SAT AT a table for two near the stage of a club on West 125th Street, wearing a tight black dress. Her makeup was applied lightly, except for her sultry, ruby-red lipstick. Men kept approaching her table asking to join her, but she told them she was waiting for someone.

A whiskey sat on the table in front of her. Although she wasn't much of a drinker, she sipped it for appearances as the band played. They were talented—the piano player, most of all. Customers crowded the dance floor as the Jean Wells Band began to play. In February of 1929, the people of Harlem, like most of the country, were happy and gay. The economy continued booming, and the stock market kept climbing. The good times would never end.

Ruth spurned the many offers to dance by smiling and shaking her head and telling the men she preferred to watch the band. But she was there to watch its leader. He was movie-star handsome, with an angular face, a trim mustache, and a slender body. Too slender for Ruth's taste. He played the piano like no one she'd ever seen, the instrument an extension of himself. His elegant hands flew across the keyboard. There was a faint stripe on the third finger of his left hand, where his wedding ring should have been.

The warmth inside the club was a welcome relief from the numbing cold outside. People had shed their coats, hats, and gloves. Ruth's fur-collared coat was draped over the back of her chair. Cigarette smoke fogged the air.

Jean made eye contact with Ruth, as he'd been doing throughout the night, his straightened hair damp on his forehead. He flipped the hair out of his eyes. During a slow song, while couples danced, he leaned into the piano as he stared at her, as if he were making love to it. To her. He seemed to be trying to hypnotize her. Ruth stared right back. She and Jean had never met. She had just begun her senior year at Smith College, and because she couldn't afford to miss any classes, she hadn't attended his and Augusta's wedding. She hadn't seen her cousin much since they were children.

After pounding out the last note of the set, Jean hurried off the stage without a word to his bandmates and headed straight to Ruth's table. "Is this seat taken?" he said.

"I don't know." Ruth gave him a doe-eye look. "You tell me."

Jean licked his lips, sat on the chair across from her, and signaled to the waiter. "I'll have what she's having."

The dancers returned to their tables, and the volume of conversation increased.

"I haven't seen you here before," said Jean.

"You haven't been looking in the right place."

Jean shook his head. "I'd have noticed you. That dress becomes you."

Those bedroom eyes, Ruth thought. No wonder her cousin had fallen for him.

"Are you alone?" Jean asked, smoothing his mustache.

Ruth glanced slowly over each of her shoulders. "Looks that way." With her elbow on the table, she brought a cigarette to her shapely lips. She took a sensual puff, then held the holder with a casualness that had taken hours to master. She'd practiced in front of her bedroom mirror after studying the mannerisms of Josephine Baker, Fredi Washington, and Nina Mae McKinney. Jean watched her every move. "But I don't mind being alone," she said.

The waiter placed a glass in front of Jean, breaking the spell. Not bothering to thank him, Jean swiped the drink off the table and took a gulp. The waiter departed. Jean set the glass down and gazed at Ruth with an exploratory look that would have made Ferdinand Magellan proud. "A woman like you should never be alone. It's against God's will."

"Are you a religious man?"

"Hardly. Did you enjoy the music?"

"You're good." Ruth sipped her drink. "I'll give you that." He was better than good, but she didn't want to stroke his ego with compliments.

Jean leaned back and rested his forearm on his chair. He glanced at the stage, where the other band members were picking up their instruments. "I need to get ready for the second set. What are you doing later? A few of us are meeting at the Braddock Hotel bar for a drink after the show. Care to join?"

Ruth pretended to think about it. "Not tonight." She stood and offered him a limp hand, like the movie actresses did. "It was a pleasure meeting you. I'd wish you good luck with the next set, but I don't think you'll need it."

Jean rose, too, still holding his glass. He didn't take her hand. "Was it something I said?"

"Why would it have anything to do with you?"

Jean gave her a bewildered look. "Huh?"

"I have somewhere to be."

Jean looked crestfallen. "A suitor?"

Ruth smiled but didn't answer.

Jean brought her hand to his moist lips. "Can I see you again?"

"If the fates allow."

"What if I don't believe in fate?"

Ruth withdrew her hand. "Then it will be your loss." She turned and walked away.

From behind her, Jean said, "You haven't told me your name!"

Pretending not to hear him, Ruth weaved her way through the tables toward the club's entrance, knowing his eyes were tracking every swing of her hips. She added an extra swing as she sashayed out the door.

"You came back."

"Don't go getting a swelled head," Ruth said. "I like the music."

Jean beamed. The first set had just ended, and he'd hopped off the stage before the final note and, without asking, joined Ruth at the same table she'd sat at the previous night. He ordered a whiskey. Tonight, Ruth wore a fire-engine red, slip-style dress with a matching hat, high heels with tiger-stripe straps, and bright red lipstick. Jean leaned forward. "The music, huh?"

"The music." Ruth's smile was demure. "All right, the scenery isn't bad either."

Jean laughed, glancing at her half-filled glass. "Another drink?"

"I'm fine. A lady must keep her head."

"I like a woman who's not afraid to lose her head. Come on, one more."

"After I finish this one."

In the dimness of the club, it felt as if a spotlight was shining on just the two of them.

Jean rapped his knuckles on the table. "I want to get to know you better." He waved his hand. "Away from here."

"How do you propose to do that?" Ruth brought the glass to her lips, her tongue touching the rim.

Jean stared at her tongue and licked his lips. "Why don't you come back to my hotel room after the show?"

Ruth set down her glass without drinking. "Aren't you impatient?"

Jean's eyes sparkled. "I'm a busy man. I don't have time to waste."

"Why are you staying at a hotel? Don't you live in Harlem?"

"I do. But I like to crash right after a gig and not have to find my way home."

"To your wife?"

"Who said I'm married?"

Ruth refrained from looking at his left ring finger. "Surely, some beautiful woman has snatched you up by now."

"Maybe I haven't met the right one yet."

Poor Augusta. Ruth's heart hurt for her cousin. "That's… hard to believe."

"Jean!" a band member yelled. He didn't look happy.

Jean glanced at the stage. "My hotel room? What do you say?"

"I shouldn't. I'm taking the train back to Boston tomorrow."

"Boston!"

"That's where I live."

Jean's smile evaporated.

"I'm visiting relatives," Ruth explained.

Jean pouted.

"But I visit them often." Jean brightened and sat up. "Tell you what. Why don't you come to *my* hotel room? That would save me some time. I still need to pack for my trip home. It will allow us to…get to know each other better."

Jean's grin could have lit up New York City. "I love the way you think." He raised his glass to her. "'Til then." He drained the rest of the drink and rushed back to the stage. He'd forgotten to order another cocktail for Ruth.

Jean played the second set with unbridled fervor. He didn't bother to disguise his lust for Ruth, glancing at her so often one would have thought she was the only person in the room. To him, she may have been. Ruth pretended to adore the singular adulation while ignoring the stares of the patrons sitting at nearby tables. She wondered if any of them knew Augusta or were friends with her.

After the final set, Ruth waited for Jean near the entrance

to the dressing room. When the band members came out, a few perused her body with down-and-up glances as they passed her. "Jean is a lucky man," one of them said. Ruth smiled at him but said nothing.

The band member, who yelled at Jean earlier, said to another, "This ain't right, man. Augusta is a good woman." He strode past Ruth without looking at her.

Jean emerged from the dressing room, still wearing the burnt orange suit and black shirt, opened at the collar, that he'd worn for the performance. The sweat glistened on his slender, hairless chest. He held his leopard-skin coat over one arm. He'd splashed on cologne to conceal the stench of sweat and liquor, but he still reeked of both.

"Ready?" he said, a slight slur to his words, his eyes glassy. He'd already had plenty to drink.

Outside, Ruth tugged at the soft fur collar on her coat and wished she'd brought a scarf. The wind was biting. Other revelers were emptying from other clubs, heading off in twos and threes, either for another club or for home. Jean took up a brisk pace once Ruth told him of her hotel's location. They passed closed stores and four-story brick buildings with fire escapes. For two blocks, Ruth struggled to keep up with him, her high heels clacking against the sidewalk.

The nondescript hotel did not have a doorman. The night manager, his lips curled, looked up from his magazine and eyed Ruth as she crossed the lobby.

"Fourth floor, please," Ruth said to the elevator operator. The operator closed the metal gate.

The paint on one wall was peeling.

The car shuddered and ascended.

CHAPTER FIFTY-EIGHT

DINAH

AFTER A FEW weeks, the excitement from Billy's wedding wore off. The newlyweds were in Tennessee on their honeymoon.

Prior to the couple's return, Dinah and Sarah prepared Billy's room, which was across the hall from Beaux's and Anna's. At the sound of horses' hooves, Dinah didn't bother looking out the second-story window; instead, she hustled down the staircase and out the front door, with her daughter trailing behind her. Harnessed to the horse was a wagon piled high with goods. Dinah and Sarah watched from the balcony as houseboys unloaded it. The air was crisp.

Beaux sat on his horse, grinning. He cocked his head back and let loose an arc of tobacco juice, almost hitting a boy. He lifted his hat and smiled at Dinah. "I think I got everything you wanted."

After negotiating with a tobacco buyer in town, he'd

picked up household items that were on the list Dinah had given him that morning.

Dinah shielded her eyes from the setting sun. "Looks like it."

Sarah darted around her.

Dinah reached out a hand to stop her and missed. "Sarah, what are you—"

"Helping," she said.

"They don't need help."

"Let her be, Dinah," Beaux said.

Sarah joined the two boys. Carrying the goods into the house took many trips. Dinah issued instructions on where to place the items.

"I know, Momma," Sarah kept saying.

After they finished, Beaux rode out past the pigpen and the cattle corral to the stables. While the rest of the family was drinking tea and talking in the sitting room, Dinah went upstairs to make sure all the bedrooms were ready for the evening. Master Sam retired to bed earlier these days. After inspecting the master and mistress's bedroom, she entered Beaux's. She made sure the water pitcher was full and the bed was turned down. Prior to leaving the room, she glanced out the window. On the front lawn, Beaux was talking to Sarah. He towered over her in his riding boots. He handed her a package wrapped in shiny paper, then kissed her on the cheek.

Sarah giggled.

&

"Look what Master Beaux bought me, Momma." In their cabin, Sarah twirled in an off-the-shoulder dress with lace across the bosom and hemline. She had seen Mary do the same thing when she'd received a new dress.

Dinah slapped her. "Take that off! Now, child."

Sarah rubbed her reddened cheek, her eyes filling with tears. "Why did you do that? It's lovely." She lifted the hem. "Touch it."

"I'm not touching that thing. Take it off, I said."

Sarah stamped her foot. "Why?"

"Because you're not keeping it."

"Why not?"

"Because you can't."

"That ain't no reason."

"It's my reason. Take. It. Off."

Sarah hesitated. "I want to wear it!"

"What did you say, girl?"

"I want to keep it, Mama."

"Gifts from white men come at a price."

"But he's my daddy! He wants me to look pretty."

"That's not all he wants, and you will not pay that price!" The rage that had been simmering within her since Martin was sold exploded. "I told you to take it off!" She lunged for Sarah with both hands and snatched the dress right above Sarah's breasts.

Sarah yelped and tried to jump back, but Dinah wouldn't let go. She held on as the dress ripped down the middle, split into a V, and fell to the floor.

Sarah cried, not bothering to cover herself. "That was the nicest thing I owned!"

"You don't own it! He owns it! Nothing in life is given to us for free. Understand? He wants you to be obliged to him."

"So?"

Dinah's chest felt aflame. "A girl isn't supposed to be obliged to her daddy. That's not right. It's the devil's work. You must stay far away from him. You hear me?"

Dinah dropped to her knees and ripped the fabric into smaller and smaller pieces. Her hands shook with rage. She was having trouble breathing.

Sarah's eyes grew enormous. "What's wrong with you, Momma?"

Jacob, Gracie, Moses, and Harriet gathered around Dinah and began screaming, too.

"Momma!"

"Momma, what's happening!"

Dinah ignored her children as she picked up the dress pieces, grabbed the box of matches next to the lamp on her bedside table, and stomped out to her garden. It was night, and no one was in the clearing. She set the pile of fabric down and dug into the sweet, cool earth, which had been softened by the afternoon rain, until she formed a large enough hole. Sarah stood on the porch in a shift, watching her. Dinah placed the scraps in the hole, struck a match against the small box, and threw the lighted match on top of the pile. She waited for the material to catch and then covered it up with the soil. She stood and clapped her hands, shaking off the dirt.

As she passed Sarah on the porch, she said, "Never accept anything from him again."

∻

Over the next few days, Dinah didn't let her daughter out of her sight. She accompanied Sarah to the house in the morning and walked her to the cabin in the evening, even on the nights when she returned to the house to lie with Beaux.

One night, as they walked back to the cabin accompanied by a crescendo of crickets, Sarah said, "Momma, you've been like my shadow. I can't breathe. I promise I won't go near him."

"It's not you I'm worried about." Dinah stopped walking. "I'd do anything to protect you. Any of you children."

"I know that."

Dinah's heart melted as she gazed at Sarah's angular face. She touched her daughter's cheek. "About the dress…You know why I did that, don't you?"

"I think so."

"Once you make that choice, you can't unmake it."

"But he already owns me."

"It's not the same. You didn't get to choose how you came into this world, but you do get to choose how you live in it." More quietly, Dinah said, "I don't want you to end up like me. I want you to have a different life. And over my dead body will I let anyone take that from you. One day, you will have a daughter, and you'll understand."

The next day, when Dinah arrived at the house, Mistress Devereaux summoned her to the parlor. The lady of the house, in a white day dress with purple and pink flowers, sat with her legs crossed on a white swan fainting couch. "I need the house to be perfect, Dinah. My sister is coming for a visit."

"Yes, ma'am."

"She'll inspect everything. I don't want her to find a speck of dirt."

"Yes, ma'am."

Dinah remembered the mistress's sister. Catherine had married a Whittier from South Carolina. The last time Catherine had visited, ten years ago now, she'd kept her white gloves on the entire visit and slid her index finger over every interior surface, raising it periodically to keep everyone apprised of how well the slaves dusted.

Over the next several days, the house slaves scrubbed and polished the house from top to bottom. When they finished, Dinah asked to borrow one of Elizabeth's white gloves.

"Whatever for?" the mistress asked.

"You'll see."

Elizabeth Devereaux stared at her before sashaying upstairs. She returned and handed the glove to Dinah. She winced as Dinah slipped her hand into the glove and pulled it up to her elbow. Dinah refrained from assuring her that her Negro skin wouldn't rub off on it.

Dinah pointed toward the ceiling with her index finger, then slowly slid it down the smooth banister. She held the finger up again. The glove was still white. The mistress smiled and nodded crisply. "Perfect. You run this house better than your momma did."

Dinah hesitated, unsure if that was a compliment or a dig at her momma. "Thank you, ma'am." She pulled off the glove.

"You may keep the glove."

What am I going to do with one glove?

Before she left for the evening, Dinah scrutinized each room again. She hadn't seen Sarah in the last hour and wondered if her daughter had gone back to the cabin without her. She was supposed to have waited. Dinah headed down the hallway toward the back door when she heard a noise in the cellar.

She groaned. Rats…of all days.

The slave boys set traps outside, but sometimes the rodents got in anyway. Dinah imagined what Mistress Catherine would do if one of them scampered through the house or, worse, over her shoes. One thing Dinah knew, those darn rats wouldn't leave their droppings in her spotless house. Although the situation could have waited until morning, when a boy could take care of it, she wanted to inspect it herself. She grabbed a few traps from the pantry and opened the cellar door. It was usually pitch black down there at night, but the moonlight coming in from a high window provided illumination.

Dinah heard another noise. It didn't sound like a rat. Puzzled, she took the lamp off a hook on the wall at the top of the stairs and lit it with the matches she kept in a nook there. The Devereauxs rarely ventured down to the cellar, unless it was to retrieve a bottle of wine. Slaves would occasionally go down to store or retrieve the family's keepsakes, clothing, and other goods, but no one should have been there at that time of night. Dinah held the lamp in front of her, brushed away a cobweb, gathered her dress in the other hand, and crept down the cement stairs. The odor of mold and mildew became stronger as she neared the bottom. Someone was whispering. Dinah inched forward into the room.

Beaux stood facing an old dresser, his back to her. Sarah, her face partially hidden, stopped struggling when she saw Dinah.

"That's better," Beaux said. "Don't move." He'd shoved Sarah against the dresser. The top of her dress was ripped, exposing her breasts. But that wasn't the worst part. Sarah's face was bruised, and her lip was cut.

A fire roared through Dinah. "Stop it!"

Beaux turned, the ties of his beige cotton shirt unfastened, revealing his smooth upper chest. His tan riding breeches were unbuttoned. He looked at Dinah but didn't move away from their daughter. Sarah's fingernails had left three gashes on his left cheek.

Dinah experienced a small sense of satisfaction as she glanced at her daughter. *Good for you.* "Beaux, let her go!"

She never called him by his given name, even when they were alone.

"Dinah, keep your voice down, for Christ's sake."

"No, I won't! She's a child!"

Beaux scrutinized Sarah. "She doesn't look like a child to me. Besides, we're just having a little fun here…right, Sarah?"

Sarah whimpered, her gaze resting on Dinah, beseeching her help.

Dinah's face shook with anger. "You're the only one who is having fun."

"Go on. This ain't your business."

"She is my business. I said let her go."

He chuckled. "At least I'm keeping it in the family."

"This isn't funny! If I'm not enough for you, you can choose from plenty of other slave women, if that's your predilection."

"I don't want other women. Besides you, she is the only one."

"She's your daughter."

"And my slave. I can do with her whatever I please." There was a hardness to his voice. "As I can with our other daughters. Gracie will come of age soon, no?"

Sarah gasped. "She's only seven!"

Dinah flew at Beaux. "Leave your daughters alone! Sarah, run!"

While Dinah beat Beaux's face and chest, Sarah squeezed out from under his arm.

As she ran up the cellar stairs, Beaux grabbed Dinah's wrists. His straight nose flared. "You shouldn't have done that, Dinah." He let out a heavy sigh and punched her in the temple. A flash of pain exploded on the side of Dinah's head. Her limbs went limp, and she dropped to the cement floor. The father of her children stepped over her and followed their daughter up the stairs.

CHAPTER FIFTY-NINE

Sha

ONE SATURDAY, SITTING in chairs warmed by the July sun, Sha, Jelani, and Mikala gathered around a teak table on the patio in the backyard of Sha's house. While Sha bore down on the coffee press for the second time that morning, she gazed at the pinks, reds, and yellows of sunrise that still lingered in the sky. Decorative lanterns and tiki torches surrounded the patio. A gas firepit rested, unlit, on one end. A birdbath hung from a stand at the other. Sha's rhododendrons and azaleas were in bloom near the shrubs. Next to it there was a vegetable patch where, the weekend before, Mikala had shown Sha and Jelani how to plant tomatoes, broccoli, spinach, and cauliflower. Mikala and Sha had remained kneeling side-by-side in the dirt when Jelani had left to take a shower. Mikala had wiped a streak of dirt off of Sha's cheek, then leaned in and kissed her chastely on the lips. Their first kiss.

Mikala had taken a shower in the guest bathroom. The

three of them had eaten pasta for dinner, prepared by Mikala. She'd cooked two versions, one for Sha and Jelani and a vegan version for herself. Jelani had tried the vegan dish and liked it, announcing afterward that she was now vegan and then went to her room. Sha had poured a big bag of sea-salt popcorn in a bowl, and she and Mikala had watched the Warriors play the Kings on the living room TV, Sha settled in her recliner, Mikala on the sofa. The attorney knew the game; she did not spend the night.

Their breakfast plates were empty. The three of them had cooked together, and they'd devoured their oatmeal, turkey bacon (for Sha), and avocado. Sha refilled Mikala's cup with coffee, then her own. Jelani was reading Angela Davis's *Women, Race and Class*. She'd left her cell phone inside the house. Mikala closed her eyes and turned her face to the sun. The book she had been reading on spirituality lay open on the table, its pages rustling in the light wind. Sha clicked the newspaper app on her tablet and navigated to the business section. A large photograph of Erik Stevens greeted her.

Mikala's eyes were still closed. Jelani was engrossed in the book.

Erik didn't look so good. Wearing one of his dress shirts, the top button unfastened, and tieless, he held a sign. On it was his name, a series of numbers, and SAN FRANCISCO POLICE DEPARTMENT. He was not grinning.

Jelani's chair scraped against the stone patio as she stood. "I'm getting more juice. Does either of you want anything?"

"No, I'm fine," Sha said.

"Ohm," hummed Mikala, in deep meditation.

Jelani raised her eyebrows and shot a questioning glance

at Sha. Sha shrugged; she didn't always get Mikala either. Although it'd only been a few weeks, Mikala had fit right into their small family, as if she'd always been a part of it. Sha's irritation at Mikala's nonstop questions had turned into curiosity about the woman with the inquisitive mind. Jelani was okay with their burgeoning relationship. When Sha had gathered the courage to ask her about it, her daughter had cut her off. "I just want you to be happy, Mom."

The wind chimes by the French door tinkled as Jelani entered the house. Sha returned to reading the article. The police had arrested Erik at his office the previous day for embezzling from his clients' accounts. The paper reported that he hadn't covered his tracks well. In fact, he hadn't covered them at all. The investigators had recovered all the money and returned it to his victims across the Bay Area.

The program Dominic and Sha had developed had worked to perfection: When Erik's customers transferred their funds to the investment bank, instead of being deposited into the proper escrow accounts, the funds were diverted to the personal account Erik received his payroll deposits in; Dominic had obtained Erik's account information by hacking into the firm's HR system. The best part of the program was that it had self-deleted after all of Erik's clients' funds were stolen; it couldn't be traced back to Sha's or Dominic's computer.

Sha read the article one more time before exiting the app.

On a walk through the neighborhood two nights prior, Sha had confided in Mikala about Jelani's rape. Mikala had been heartbroken and asked whether there was anything she could do. She knew many therapists and had offered to call them. Sha had thanked her but told her she had it under control. She didn't want to start their relationship with a secret, and she wanted Mikala to understand what her daughter was going through. She hadn't been entirely forthcoming; she hadn't told Mikala that she'd meted her own form of justice for Erik Stevens, and she never would.

Ironically, if the sexual assault hadn't happened, Sha might never have met Mikala.

"She's not the only one who needs therapy," Mikala had said.

Sha had stopped walking. "What do you mean?"

"You need it, too. Someone to talk it out with. It will make a difference. Change your life. So you won't be on guard all the time, and you'll learn to trust again."

"I'm not the one who was hurt."

"Yes, you were."

"That's in the past. I don't need therapy now."

Mikala had taken her hand. "Yes, you do."

Mikala's beautiful oval face was still tilted toward the sun, the sunlight glinting off her eyebrow piercing.

The grass was cut to perfection, thanks to the lawn maintenance company that mowed once a week and the recent lifting of California's restrictions on water usage. From the patio, steps led down to an in-ground pool with a jacuzzi. Sha vowed to spend more time with her daughter out here over the next year, before Jelani left for college. She had tried to shield Jelani from reminders of the night that had changed both their lives. The rape was something that could never be erased. Neither of them would ever be the same, but Sha wouldn't let the incident define the rest of her daughter's life.

She and Jelani could finally move on. But Sha needed to do one more thing first.

❧

One month later, Sha sat in the rear of a courtroom in the Civic Center Courthouse in San Francisco. Also in attendance were a reporter, several courtroom groupies, younger people taking notes—presumably, law school students—and a couple who looked older than Sha. The woman cried throughout the proceedings, her male companion's arm around her shoulders. Erik's parents, Sha surmised. The court reporter's gentle typing calmed Sha, but it also reminded her she should be at work. She'd been lying to her daughter and coworkers again for the past week, telling them she'd been summoned for jury duty. Instead, she was a spectator at a trial. She had to see this through, though.

Erik sat at the defense table, biting his nails as he waited for the verdict to be read.

The judge peered over her owl glasses. "Will the defendant please rise?"

Erik obeyed.

The jury found him guilty of grand theft embezzlement. When the forewoman finished reading the verdict, Erik's shoulders sagged, and his mother wailed. Stripped of his Series 7 license, he was banned from working in the securities industry for life. And although he wasn't convicted of rape, the judge sentenced him to five years in prison. Like many Black men, he would experience what it was like to serve time for a crime he hadn't committed.

Sha wanted to yell that the sentence wasn't long enough.

After the judge pounded the gavel and exited through the door to her chambers with her black robes billowing around her, Sha weaved through the spectators exiting toward the front of the courtroom. Before Erik's mother reached him and a police officer whisked him away, Sha called his name from behind the lacquered wooden bar separating the audience from the prosecution and defense tables and the judge's bench.

Erik's normally gelled hair was dry, lank, and unwashed. His skin was sallow. He'd lost weight. He cowered close to the table.

Sha waved him over.

He cast his eyes downward, this time at his feet rather than at her body. "Ms. Bradley, I didn't take your money. I swear it."

"But you took my daughter's innocence, you bastard."

His lips parted, uncomprehending.

"Jelani," she said. "The girl you raped in the Z21 parking lot."

His expression was still blank. "I have no idea who you're talking about."

Sha was overcome with vertigo. She fought hard to remain standing until the feeling passed. She inhaled and exhaled deeply several times to find her center, grateful to Mikala for having helped her improve her mindfulness meditation. Without it, Sha might have killed him with her bare hands in this courtroom. With one last look at him, she shook her head and walked away. She doubted Erik Stevens would do well in prison.

CHAPTER SIXTY

OLIVIA

OLIVIA'S HOTEL SUITE in Atlanta now resembled an office. Olivia had rented a facsimile machine, a word processor, and a copier/printer. They had been delivered to her and were now arranged on the desk and an adjacent table. She had informed Robert Penn, the managing partner, that she needed to stay in Atlanta indefinitely because of a family matter. When she had finished speaking, he'd remained quiet. Eventually, he'd said, "Very well." Olivia had been unsure whether he was unhappy for personal or professional reasons, but she didn't care. There wasn't much Robert could do about it. Olivia was a valuable member of the firm, and she'd brought in several high net-worth clients over the years, some of whom were Black. If she left the firm, they would leave with her. Robert also had the specter of a sexual harassment case looming. When Olivia had convinced Robert that she could take calls, type correspondence, and review and mark up contracts and briefs just as well from Atlanta, he'd relented.

Outside the window, the day was gray. Midmorning, the park two blocks away was nearly deserted. Still wearing the plush white robe with the Ritz Carlton logo over her left breast, Olivia slipped a cassette tape she'd brought with her into her Walkman, put on the headphones, and shut out the sound of the first raindrops as they pinged against the windowpane. She selected a document from the top of the stack on her desk, hunched over the papers, and began to read, red marker in hand.

That afternoon, she went for a walk to enjoy the fresh air after the rain had stopped. She wouldn't be gone long, in case Nicole called. Her high heels clacked on the sidewalk. A city bus whooshed by. Six blocks away from the hotel, a raindrop fell on her forehead. She hadn't brought an umbrella or a raincoat, believing the day's precipitation had ended. Another drop fell, then another. Cars' windshield wipers moved back and forth. Olivia couldn't run in heels. Besides, she still wasn't in good enough shape to run back to the hotel without stopping. So, she didn't try. The skies opened, and the rain poured down. Within minutes, her hair was plastered to her head and her suit was soaked, sticking to her body. Rain slid beneath her collar. There wasn't any use getting angry as she normally would. She couldn't do anything about it. If Robert Penn could see her now. She laughed and could not stop. A mother steered her young daughter out of Olivia's way. A teenage boy wearing headphones smiled at her. When she reached the hotel's entrance, the doormen hesitated, then opened the doors for her. She walked through them, her shoes squishing with every step across the lobby floor.

Her hair was a mess, and her suit and shoes were ruined. And the world hadn't ended.

❦

That evening, Olivia's hotel room phone rang.

Olivia removed her headphones and placed them, along with the document she'd been reading, on the desk. Her hair was still damp and curly from that afternoon's excursion.

"Nicole?" she asked.

"No. It's your husband."

"Oh. Hi."

"Why did it take you so long to answer?" The baritone of Davis's voice felt like a long-distance embrace.

"I was listening to Whitney. I guess the volume was too high." Olivia sang the chorus to "Saving All My Love for You." She couldn't dance, but she'd been told from a young age she could sing.

Davis cleared his throat. "You'd better. How's Nicole?"

"She's fine. Still dealing with a situation at work."

"Want to tell me about it?"

Olivia didn't believe it was her place to tell Davis; it was Nicole's story to share. She also wanted to protect him from being charged as an accessory once she'd carried out her plan to resolve Nicole's situation. No need for both parents to end up in jail.

"No."

"Shouldn't we let her fight her own battles? Like we did?"

"A woman's battles are different."

"She's strong, like her mother. Let her handle it."

"She needs her mother. I won't argue about this, Davis. Not today. Not ever."

Davis exhaled. "I learned early in our relationship that arguing with you is futile."

Pain, sadness, and anger clashed within Olivia. She choked out, "This is my baby we're talking about."

"I get it," Davis said, his voice soothing. "When are you coming home?"

"It shouldn't be much longer."

"I miss you."

"I miss you, too, but I must keep the line free in case Nicole calls. She needs me."

Davis was silent for a long moment. "I need you, too."

"What are you doing tonight?" Olivia asked into the phone.

"Nothing," Nicole said.

"Wear your best summer dress and be in front of your apartment in an hour. I'll be by in a taxi to pick you up."

"Mom, I can't just leave work—"

"Fifty-nine minutes." Olivia hung up.

That evening, she took Nicole to the Rialto Center for the Arts, where the Georgia State University dance team put on a tap-dance performance. As they watched the students dance on stage from cushioned seats, the shine in Nicole's eyes and her enthusiastic clapping were worth the price of admission.

When the taxi arrived back in front of Nicole's apartment, Olivia said, "I'm coming up for a minute."

Nicole shot her a puzzled look, one she had been giving her a lot lately. "You sure it's not too late?"

"It is, but not for the reason you think."

Seated on the living room sofa, Olivia reached into her Louis Vuitton purse and pulled out a small box. She handed it to Nicole. "This is yours."

"Mine? What is it?"

"Open it."

Nicole looked inside the box.

"Be careful," Olivia said. Nicole gently lifted the twine-woven ring. "You might have been expecting another tennis bracelet, but this ring is much more valuable. I'm going to tell you the story behind it." When Olivia finished relaying the story of their ancestors, she said, "This ring reminds us of our courage and power. Our inner strength comes from Aisha, Celia, Dinah, Sarah, Julia, and Augusta. They guide us." She smiled ruefully. "Sometimes I forget and believe it is all my doing, my will alone. But that isn't true. Besides our blood, it's the only thing we possess from our homeland. My mother gave it to me on my eighteenth birthday. Rightfully, it should have gone to my sister, Clara, but she was always playing ball, and my mother feared she would damage it or throw it. And Josie had a habit of dropping everything. Frankly, I think your grandma forgot about the ring until she and my father had me. I was the surprise baby. They hadn't planned on having children, thinking they were too old." Olivia sighed. "I should have given this to you a long time ago."

Nicole gazed at the ring. "The women in our family are so resilient," she said.

"We come from Aisha. We have to be."

A week later, after a leisurely solo lunch at the hotel's restaurant, Olivia returned to her suite to review a corporate acquisition contract. The hours flew by as she lost herself in the details. At a knock on the door, she set the document down on the desk, removed her reading glasses, and rubbed the bridge of her nose where the glasses had been resting. She padded to the door to peer through the peephole and frowned.

Nicole must have come straight from work, as she was still in her suit. Her shirt was damp with sweat, either from exertion or the heat outside. Or both. She usually called before stopping by.

Olivia let her in. "Are you all right?"

Her daughter strode past her and spun around.

Face flushed and eyes wide, she unbuttoned her shirt and, oblivious to the impending pain, yanked off the tape that held the recording device to her chest. Its outline remained on her skin.

Olivia flinched and touched her daughter's shoulder. "What are you doing?"

"I'm better than all right," Nicole said. "I got him!"

CHAPTER SIXTY-ONE

JULIA

JULIA CAME DOWNSTAIRS to find Augusta sitting on the window seat in her pajamas and with her hair still wrapped, staring out onto Seventh Avenue. The curtain-framed window allowed in an abundance of natural morning light.

Julia sat beside her. "What's wrong, baby girl?"

"It's Jean," said Augusta without turning.

"What about him?"

"He didn't come home last night. He's never stayed out the entire night. He's with another woman. I just know it."

Rain splashed against the window.

"I wouldn't jump to conclusions."

"What if he leaves me? What will I do? I don't have a job."

Whose fault is that? Julia bit back the retort. Her daughter needed comforting now, not criticism. "You'll live. That's what. Whatever happens, you'll be fine."

Augusta held her elbows with her hands across her chest. "How do you know that?"

"Because I know. Things always work out the way they should."

"Where else could he be? The clubs are closed."

A neighbor on his way to work in a wool overcoat and a Hamburg hat opened his umbrella. Cars drove by, sending up small waves of water.

"Maybe he got drunk and bunked with one of his friends, or someone in the band."

Augusta shook her head. "I've called around. No one saw him after he left the club, though I can't get a hold of Francis. I called Jean's friends too. His brother. No one has heard from him. I even called members of Palmer's band. They haven't heard from him since the breakup and didn't sound like they cared to ever again." Augusta paused. "His bandmates knew something and were afraid to tell me. They sounded as if they felt sorry for me. They know about him." Her shoulders sagged. "Everybody knows."

Julia wished she could absorb Augusta's hurts into her own body and free her daughter from pain. "Where are the children?" she asked.

"I told them to stay in their rooms. I needed quiet. I have a headache."

Julia rose and headed toward the hallway.

"Where are you going? They're fine, Mama."

"I'm not checking on them. I'm ringing the police."

An hour later, a Negro police officer in a black uniform with a black tie clipped to his shirt stood in Augusta's living room. Julia had seen him around the neighborhood. She took his raincoat and policeman's cap, and he sat down next to Augusta on the sofa, removing his white gloves. Julia settled on Jean's piano bench.

"Ma'am, I need to ask you some questions to help us locate your husband."

Augusta clasped a handkerchief in her lap. "All right."

"What did you do last night?"

"I was here with Mama, playing rummy."

"What time was that?"

"Eight."

"'Til when?"

"Eleven, and then we both retired."

The policeman looked over at Julia to corroborate Augusta's story. Julia nodded.

The officer leaned forward, elbows on his thighs. "When did you realize your husband wasn't at home?"

"Around three. I got up to use the toilet." She glanced down at her hands. "His side of the bed was still made."

"Was that unusual? For him to be out that late?"

"Yes."

"What time did he usually come home?"

"Two."

"Would he ring you if he was going to be later than expected?"

"No. He wouldn't want to wake the children."

"When did you start to worry?"

"I tossed and turned until six, then got up and started calling around. I was waking everybody up this morning."

"What was he wearing when you last saw him?"

Augusta told him.

The policeman hesitated. "You two getting along?"

Augusta shrugged. "We're getting along okay."

"If you were having, say, marital problems, where would he stay?"

"With someone I've already called."

"I'll need a list of names." The officer shifted in his chair. "Were there…um…other women?"

"That's none of your business."

"It is now, I'm afraid. Any chance…he could have taken off?"

Augusta looked him square in the face. "My husband wasn't perfect, officer, but he was a good daddy. He'd never run off and leave his children."

A few days passed. Julia was braiding Clara's hair in the second-floor bathroom when there was a knock at the front door. Julia looked in the mirror at her granddaughter, who met her gaze with her hazel eyes. Clara was standing on a step stool in front of Julia. Her light-brown hair had thickened since she was a baby, but not by much. Julia set the brush down next to the sink and hustled down the stairs, lifting her dress so she wouldn't trip.

She opened the door to the same policeman standing on the stoop. The rain had finally stopped.

"Any word?" she asked.

Before he could answer, Clara caught up to Julia and clung to her dress. With one side of her hair half-braided and the other side an abundance of long curls, she stared up at the officer. "Did you find my Daddy?"

The policeman glanced at her, then at Julia. "I need to talk to his wife."

"Tell your Mama the policeman's here," Julia said. Augusta was upstairs, lying down, felled by another headache. "Go on, child." Julia stepped back. "Please come in, officer."

The officer removed his hat, held it under his arm, and did as he was told. Clara ran up the two flights of stairs to her parents' bedroom, her bare feet slapping against the wood floor on one side of the carpet runner; it was the only sound in the house. Josie was playing alone quietly in the children's bedroom. Hale was outside playing with his friends. Julia and the police officer remained in the foyer, neither looking at each other nor speaking.

Augusta shuffled down the stairs. She had not bathed, fixed her hair, or eaten much since Jean went missing. "Have you found my husband?"

"Ma'am, we've talked to his bandmates, his friends, his girl…uh…friends. No one has seen him. But—"

Augusta exhaled. "Spit it out. If it involves another woman, you can tell me."

"All right, then. A band member came forward."

"Francis," she said tiredly.

"How did you know?"

"He's the only one that would. What did he say?"

"After the performance, Jean left with a woman."

Augusta cinched the top of her house robe with one hand. "Go on."

"She wasn't a regular…acquaintance…of your husband's. He accompanied her to her hotel room. We found the hotel. Her room was empty. The night clerk had seen them enter but hadn't seen either of them leave. The day clerk didn't recall seeing anyone fitting their description coming or going. None of the other guests saw them—or, if they did, they're keeping mum. The woman didn't bother to check out."

Augusta swayed and laid her hand on the mahogany console table to steady herself.

Gently, the policeman continued, "We think he took off with this woman, Mrs. Wells. Leaving the band, you, and your children behind. I'm sorry."

CHAPTER SIXTY-TWO

OLIVIA

NICOLE ADJUSTED THE cuff of her blue dress shirt before picking up a magazine. "I'm going to get fired for sure," she whispered.

"No, you're not."

Unlike her daughter, Olivia wasn't nervous. Instead, she felt light, ready, her mind and body at ease, as calm as soft music playing on the stereo. Given the number of high-stakes boardroom negotiations she'd taken part in over her career, she had played on this field many times. Even though it was an away game, this was her turf. She'd pinned up her hair to stay cool.

Nicole scanned Olivia's three-piece power suit, then looked down at her own simple black suit. "Do I look okay?"

"Extremely professional."

Nicole gave her mother a faint smile and flipped through the pages of the magazine.

From behind the reception desk, a young white woman with feathered blond hair said, in a southern accent, "Mrs. Bradley, Ms. Bradley, they're ready for you."

No, they are not.

Olivia picked up her briefcase, rose from the couch, and followed the receptionist. Nicole dropped the *Newsweek* on the table. "Here we go," she said under her breath.

The room was a typical corporate boardroom, with wood-paneled walls and a familiar smell: a mixture of cologne and sweat, not too different from the odor entrenched in the boardroom at Olivia's law firm in Philly. Nicole's eyes widened, and not only because she'd never been in this room.

Around the dark, rectangular walnut-wood table sat ten white men in their fifties and sixties wearing white shirts and wide ties without suit jackets. They looked at each other in surprise, not realizing that their adversary—and the reason this meeting had been convened—was a Black woman. Most of them were leaning back in their dark brown leather chairs. In front of them were notepads and pens embossed with the company's logo. Pitchers of ice water rested at either end of the table; the men's glasses had already been filled. No one offered Olivia—or Nicole, their employee—anything to drink. No one sat in the chairs lining the walls. Except for the receptionist holding her stenographic notebook, they had not invited their support staff to observe the meeting.

Olivia sat at the vacant seat at the head of the table, facing a floor-to-ceiling window that afforded an amazing view of downtown Atlanta and the suburbs. The morning sun glared into Olivia's eyes. She did not shade them. She nodded at the man at the opposite end of the long table.

Well played. It was a strategic move she'd have made if their roles had been reversed. Nicole, in the chair to Olivia's right, stared at him. She had never met the top boss.

"I appreciate your giving us this audience," Olivia said.

Chairman, CEO, and President Reed Elliott dipped his head and glanced at his watch.

"This better be good," said the overweight man to his left. "We're busy men. What do you want?"

"That's cutting to the chase," she said. "And you are?"

Olivia knew who he was. She'd done her homework on all of them; she suspected they hadn't conducted any research on her. They would regret that mistake.

"Henry Montgomery Benning, National & World News Network's general counsel."

"I would say 'nice to meet you,' but it isn't under these circumstances."

"Likewise." Henry waved his hand. His flabby jowls shook. "Get on with it."

"Henry, I want you to listen to a story."

Henry scowled. "We don't have time for stories."

Olivia shot him a look of faux surprise. "Your network tells stories twenty-four hours a day. Believe me, you have time to listen to this one."

She pulled a Montblanc pen and a legal pad out of her black leather briefcase, which rested on the floor. The men around the table watched her every move. She reached in again, emerging with a tape recorder.

The wheels at the bottom of several chairs creaked as the men shifted in their seats.

"What is that?" Benning said.

"A tape recorder."

"I know that, woman," he spat. "What are you doing with it? Here?"

"You're about to find out." She scanned the men's faces. "Are we ready to begin?"

A few of them glanced at their boss.

"All right, then." She pressed Play.

"Did you finish the story on the Pripyat evacuation?" said a distant male voice.

"Yes." Nicole's voice was closer. "Here you go."

Silence. "Why was the city evacuated?"

"The Soviets aren't saying. There's a nuclear power plant near the city called Chernobyl. I think there was an accident or explosion there, and the Soviets are trying to cover it up."

"Come on! You read too many spy novels. There's no way they could cover up something that big."

"Well, something bad happened if they had to evacuate an entire city."

A pause. A rustling of papers.

"This looks good," the voice said.

"The story?" Her daughter's voice was filled with hope.

"That, too, but I was talking about your ass. We can discuss the story later."

"Take your hands off me."

"You're pretty. Come on, Sug, give me some."

"Please. Stop."

Clothes rustled. There were sounds of a struggle. A zipper opened.

Olivia's jaw set. Although she'd listened to the recording

many times after Nicole had given her the tape recorder, it was still difficult to hear this man assaulting her daughter.

"You've been holding out on me for too long." The voice was husky and close now. "Every night, when I lie in bed next to my wife, all I can think about is my brown sugar at the office."

During this exchange, the men in the boardroom shot nervous looks at each other and at their boss. Reed Elliott's face remained impassive. Nicole brought her hand to her mouth to bite a fingernail then looked at her newly polished nails and lowered it.

"I'm not yours," Olivia's daughter said on the recording.

"You could make your life easier if you were," the man said. "I'll promote you to producer tomorrow. Hell, you're so smart and attractive, I'll groom you to be an anchorwoman someday. Wouldn't that be hot? Anchoring the desk together during the day, making hot jungle love at night?"

"What about your wife?"

"She's used to me working late. You and I can get to know each other, inside and out, if you know what I mean."

"Let me go!"

More struggling sounds.

"I need to get back to work," Nicole said.

"You are working…for me. You can record this as overtime."

"Stop it!"

His voice hardened. "My patience is wearing thin, Missy. You need to get with the program, or I'll fire you like the others. Your playing hard to get was cute at first, but it's getting old. As you will be by the time you're promoted here."

The zipper closed.

The best evidence was the kind that spoke for itself.

After ten seconds of dead air, the tape finished spooling. Silence enveloped the boardroom. Olivia made no move to press STOP. She glanced at her wedding ring and wondered what Davis was doing. She imagined him sitting at his desk at work, eating the ham and cheese sandwich he'd prepared that morning.

Finally, the general counsel said, "That recording proves nothing. We can't be certain whose voice that is."

Olivia stared at him incredulously. "He has one of the most recognizable voices in the world. Don't you watch your own broadcasts?"

"It's still not proof."

Nicole followed the conversation like she was observing a ping-pong match. She appeared less nervous, more defiant.

"Ah. Proof." Olivia retrieved a stack of documents from her briefcase. "I also have recordings of him talking to my daughter on the phone." She divided the documents in half and passed one stack to the man next to her and the rest to Nicole. "Please take one and pass it down. These, gentlemen, are the reports of three certified voice analysis experts who will testify under oath to the anchorman's identity."

"We'll hire our own experts," Benning said.

Olivia ignored him and pulled out another set of documents, divided them, and handed them out. "Take the one with your name on it," she said.

Benning's eyes tracked the papers exchanging hands on their way to him. "What's this?"

"You'll see."

Olivia had hired private detectives to prepare background information on every man in the room: affairs, business shenanigans, sexual harassment allegations. Unsure whether evidence of the anchorman's wrongdoing would be enough, she had to make it personal.

The men read their reports. She heard, "Jesus!" "Shit!" "Oh, my God!" "I'm screwed!" "My wife is going to kill me."

Nicole beamed.

Henry Montgomery Benning ignored the man next to him trying to hand him the report of Henry's misdeeds, of which there were many. He pounded his fist on the table, his wattle flapping like a boat's sail on a blustery day. "This is blackmail! And illegal…recording conversations without the other party's consent. We'll fight this. We'll take you to court, you goddamn ni—"

The head of the network held up his hand. The general counsel closed his mouth.

Married to a popular singer, Reed Elliott was charismatic and photogenic and enjoyed rock-star-like fame himself, his private life covered by the media in equal measure to his business dealings. He stared down the long table at Olivia. She hadn't provided a dossier of his own transgressions. An olive branch. She hoped he'd appreciate the gesture.

Quietly, he asked, "What are you proposing?"

"I could sue you and win," she said, "but I have two other options for you."

"Which are?"

"The first is that I can make copies of these documents and this tape and send them to every major news organization in the country. Your competitors will welcome them with glee. Your firm's reputation will take a considerable hit. You might recover…someday. Who knows if you'll stay in business long enough to find out?" Although there would be significant reputational and financial ramifications for the organization, the personal consequences for Reed Elliot, as NWNN's majority shareholder, would be just as great.

Reed's face was expressionless. "And the other option—"

"—is a three-parter. First, you'll implement a comprehensive anti-harassment policy and training program. Second, you will fire the man in question."

He exhaled. "And the last part?"

Benning sat back in his chair and crossed his arms over his sizable stomach. "She wants money, I bet."

Olivia ignored him again. "Neither Nicole nor any other woman who works for this organization and has come forward alleging harassment will face retaliation. Henceforth, supervisors will evaluate their work performance and eligibility for promotion based on their merits, not on who they've slept with. If I hear of any harassment or retaliation, believe me, gentlemen, I'll be back…And it won't be a pleasant reunion."

The chairman stared at her for a long moment. "Give me a week."

"You have twenty-four hours."

Nicole turned to Olivia as they left the boardroom and said, "Mother, you're a badass."

CHAPTER SIXTY-THREE

AUGUSTA

WEEKS WENT BY with no word from or of Jean.

And then, one day, Augusta stopped feeling sorry for herself. She bathed, styled her hair, straightened up the house, and helped the girls prepare for school instead of letting her mama do it. She went to the store and bought food for her family. She began taking long daily midday walks. As she passed by the stores, restaurants, and bars—all of her and Jean's old haunts—it was almost as if she were reacquainting herself with Harlem. She missed it. The girls adjusted, too, and stopped asking about their father every minute. Her mama never mentioned his name.

One positive outcome of his disappearance was that he hadn't left them empty-handed, as other women's husbands had done. Augusta had found a significant amount of money stashed in coffee cans in the basement's icebox—Jean didn't trust banks.

During one of her walks, two months after her husband had gone missing, Augusta stopped in front of the window of a bookstore. The birds and tree leaves had returned to Harlem, and Augusta had left the house without a jacket. A streetcar clanged, warning pedestrians to get out of its way. Different books were displayed from the last time Augusta had been there, but the sign in the corner still said NEGRO-OWNED. Why not, she thought, and entered.

The only customer, a girl of twelve or thirteen, sat cross-legged on the floor against a bookcase, reading. The book's pages ruffled as she turned them. Augusta smiled. It was as if she were looking in the mirror at her younger self.

The store's owner greeted her. "I haven't seen you in a long time."

"You remember me? I've only been here once."

A tall man with short, curly hair, the owner wore a brown cardigan over his white shirt and black tie, paired with black trousers. He pushed his glasses higher on his nose. "I never forget a face. Have you been away?"

"Something like that."

"Well, welcome back. My name's Charles."

"Augusta."

"Let me show you around, Augusta."

As they walked down the aisles between the bookcases, Charles pointed to the different sections: philosophy, history, Negro history, and fiction. There was an entire section for Negro literature. She tipped down a book from the top shelf: *Plum Bun,* by Jessie Redmon Fauset. She ran her fingers over the smooth front cover, then opened it to the title page and gasped.

"Yep, she signed it," Charles said.

Augusta ran her hand over the famous author's signature. "She's one of my favorites."

"Why?"

"She doesn't portray us as stereotypes. And she can write!"

"Do you read a lot?"

"Every chance I get."

"Who else do you like?"

"Why, Zora and Nella, of course!" She pointed at their books on the shelves as she spoke.

"You seem well read and knowledgeable about books. Are you looking for a job?" Charles asked.

Augusta blinked.

"I could use the help."

Augusta didn't point out that he only had one customer.

"Do you want to work here?"

"Would I!"

Charles pointed at the book Augusta was holding in her hands. "You're holding your first week's wages."

"Really?" Augusta cradled the book against her chest. "I accept."

She earned little working part-time at the bookstore, but she enjoyed having a purpose outside her home and her children, and she loved her job as a matchmaker; customers came in not knowing what they were looking for, and she found the perfect book for them. Plus, she was surrounded by books all day. It was how she imagined heaven to be.

One late October day, as Augusta was shelving a stack of books, a woman around her age came into the store with a young boy. The woman wore a brown fur-trimmed coat over a green day dress and had a matching hat and purse. The boy was dressed like a little grownup, with a brown coat over a white shirt and tan suspenders holding up his brown trousers. The day was colder than normal for that time of year.

The woman scanned the room, searching for assistance. Charles was next door at the shoe shop, drinking a cup of joe with the owner; he'd left Augusta in charge of the bookstore.

"Can I help you?" Augusta asked.

The woman squeezed her son's hand—too tightly, judging by the boy's grimace. "Do you have any children's books?" she inquired.

"Certainly. This way." They followed Augusta to a section at the back of the store bright with colorful book covers. "How old are you?" Augusta asked the boy, looking at his face for the first time. Although she was sure she'd never seen him, he looked familiar. He didn't look like one of the girls' friends. He had a medium complexion and his cheeks were sprinkled with freckles. He looked like Jean.

"Three and a half," the boy replied.

Augusta looked at the woman. It was the same one who'd ignored Jean on Lenox Avenue and averted her eyes when Augusta had spotted her at Bill's Place four years ago. She wondered if Jean, wherever he was, knew he had a son. She smiled at the boy. It wasn't his fault who his father was. She selected a book with a rabbit on the cover. "I think this is just the book for you."

The boy grabbed it. "Wow!" He hugged it to his chest.

The woman rubbed the top of his head. "Thank you for being kind to him." She hesitated. "I heard about Jean. You're better off."

Augusta nodded but did not trust herself to respond. She knew it, too, but it didn't make her feelings for him just disappear, as he had.

After the woman and the boy left, Augusta resumed shelving books. It was partly cloudy outside, and the street was unusually crowded; most people should have been working. She returned Wallace Thurman's *Blacker the Berry* to the stack on the table and approached the window. Some people walked by in shock. Men in business suits were crying, as if someone important had died, or staggering around as if drunk. She peered closer. Maybe they were drunk. She opened the door and shouted to a sober one, "What's happened?"

The man's eyes were vacant, his mouth slack. "The world has ended."

After October 29, 1929, life in Harlem—like the rest of America—changed. Many people lost their jobs. Ordinary folks who'd invested in the stock market for the first time with borrowed money were wiped out. Some committed suicide by jumping off apartment or hotel balconies. Others, who had lost their homes, slept on the streets or in store entryways. The air hung heavy with despair. For many months, however, the neighborhood's vibrant nightlife remained unchanged. Although people didn't have enough money to buy food, they could scrounge enough to buy liquor and drown out their sorrows. But then clubs started closing one by one, Bill's Place among them. Smalls Paradise was one of the few that stayed in business.

The bookstore remained open. Instead of selling books, Charles loaned them out for two pennies a day, which allowed him to stay in business and provided his customers with an affordable way to continue reading, entertaining themselves, and keeping their minds off their misfortunes.

One evening, Augusta and Julia were sitting in matching rocking chairs on the brownstone's back stoop. The girls were playing catch with a ball, though Josie was distracted by the doll Jean had bought her shortly before he left.

"What are you making?" Augusta asked Julia.

"A dress for Ray's wife."

Julia still worked at Rose's; their customers brought in dresses to mend rather than buying new ones. Since Jean's disappearance, Ray often stopped by the house to check on Augusta. They'd rekindled their friendship.

"Why?"

"I can't imagine Ray's selling many paintings these days."

"Oh. That's nice."

"What are you writing?" her mama asked.

Augusta scanned the words on the paper. They still weren't flowing. "A short story about a girl who grows up to play professional baseball."

"Clara?"

"If anyone can do it, she can."

"With that arm…You've got that right." Julia stitched in silence for a moment. "You write as much as you read now."

"I can't stop. It's like breathing."

"You're so absorbed in your writing these days, you forget to wash clothes and clean dishes and bathe your children."

Augusta chuckled. "I lose myself. And I can write without fear now."

"What would you fear?"

"Jean used to read my journal. I didn't know until the day he hit me. I'd written that his band would never be as successful as he hoped." The dogwood tree in their backyard had flowered. "You think that's why he left?"

Julia stopped sewing and examined her handiwork. "Only he knows." She resumed sewing. "You should take a class."

"What for?"

"You always wanted to be a teacher. Teach!"

"It's too late for that, Mama."

"It's never too late to pursue your dreams."

"What about the girls?"

"That, right there, is the best reason to do it. Wouldn't they be proud of their mama? You need to bury your former life and plant new seeds so they'll grow. So you can thrive and pass that legacy on to your daughters. I can help with the girls."

Augusta stopped rocking. "I haven't studied in so long. It'll be difficult."

"Not difficult, just unfamiliar." Julia looked at her pointedly. "And when did our people ever fail to tackle something just because it was hard?"

Augusta's heart quickened. "You think I can do it?"

"You're a descendant of Aisha." Julia held up the pretty cotton blue-plaid house dress. "Of course you can."

The following September, Augusta enrolled in a creative writing class at Hunter College. After she finished that course, she became a full-time student. Three years later, she received a bachelor's degree in education and became an English teacher at the local high school.

Augusta entered the teachers' lounge. Filled with mismatched chairs and a sagging couch, the furniture was not much more comfortable than what the students sat on. A burner for instant coffee sat atop a wooden table by the yellow cinderblock wall. Augusta waited behind an unfamiliar male teacher as he poured coffee into his cup. After he'd moved away, she filled her cup, then sat in a chair and placed the cup on a table. She leaned back and closed her eyes. She didn't mean to ignore her colleague, but she needed a moment to herself. The kids in her English Lit class had been unruly.

"Hello," the man said.

I should be friendly, Augusta thought, remembering how it had been for her when she'd begun working at the school a few years ago and didn't know anyone. The teachers had been kind and made her feel welcome. She sat up, opened her eyes, and extended her hand. "Hi, I'm…" She examined the familiar face. He was wearing a blue cardigan sweater over his white shirt and black tie. His brown hair was sprinkled with gray. His round glasses were now gold-framed.

The man lowered his cup. "Fancy seeing you here."

Augusta's lips parted and her hand fell to her lap. "What are you doing here?"

Richmond St. Clair raised his hand in greeting. He boasted ten pounds more than when she'd met him at that literary party a lifetime ago.

"I work here." He smiled. "Read any good books lately?"

"It wasn't lately, but I read your novel."

"What did you think?"

"I remember wishing I'd met your grandmother."

"What about you? Did you ever write a story about yours?"

"As a matter of fact…"

CHAPTER SIXTY-FOUR

DINAH

DINAH DIDN'T KNOW how long she had been lying on the cellar's cement floor.

After she came to, she shuffled up the stairs and gingerly made her way to the cabin, holding her pounding head. White breath escaped with every exhale. She passed Nelson, who was leading his horse to the stables. The overseer stopped but didn't speak to her or make a move to help her. When she entered the cabin, Dinah's four other children were asleep, two to a bed, but Sarah was not in her bed. Dinah tamped down her panic and turned to go outside to look for her. Had Beaux caught up to her? What was he doing to her? Before she could leave, Sarah entered the hut.

"Where were you?" Dinah asked, her voice rising.

"I hid in the woods. I wasn't sure if he was coming after me."

"Thank the Lord!" Dinah grabbed her daughter in a fierce hug.

Sarah's girlish body shook with tears. Dinah's cheeks were wet, too.

After helping her daughter to bed, Dinah checked on the other children before changing into her night shift and falling onto the board her mother used to sleep on, now padded with floral cushions the mistress had thrown out. She lay on the side of her face opposite to where Beaux had hit her.

The next morning, she and Sarah were standing outside the cabin, preparing to go to the house. Her daughter shivered from the cold. The bruise on Sarah's face had turned purple. Dinah hadn't looked in the mirror to see what her own bruise looked like.

"Come straight home after you're done working," said Dinah. "Don't talk to him. Avoid him. If he comes to you, make an excuse to leave the room. We'll talk more later."

Sarah stared at the bruise on Dinah's face. "I'm sorry, Momma. I tried to avoid him, but he grabbed me and took me down there. When I screamed for you, he hit me and told me to be quiet."

"I didn't hear you. Otherwise, I'd have come running."

"I scratched him," said Sarah, crying, "but he was so strong."

Dinah kissed her cheek. "I know, baby, but he's not stronger than me."

Across the clearing, Nelson sat astride his horse, staring at them. Dinah held his gaze for several moments until he galloped off.

After Dinah had served the Devereaux family breakfast—she'd instructed Sarah to make the beds and straighten the bedrooms to avoid encountering Beaux—she left the house through the back door. Given her stature, she no longer reported her whereabouts to anyone.

She walked the hundred yards to the edge of the fields. Still on his horse, Nelson looked over at her. She inclined her head toward the quarters. Nelson nodded and returned his attention to surveying the Devereaux's property, both their land and their people.

Dinah went to her cabin and waited. It was unusual for her to be there during the day. Harriet was in the children's cabin. The rest of her children were old enough to work in the stables, the yard, or the house.

Half an hour later, Nelson joined her.

If anyone spotted them together, they wouldn't think it unusual. Dinah often coordinated with him on managing the slaves: she, the house slaves, and he, the field labor. They sat across from each other at the small table where Dinah and her children ate their meals.

"I saw Sarah's face," he said. "Master Beaux?"

Dinah nodded.

"Damn!" Nelson rarely swore. "I'm not surprised. I've seen the way he looks at her."

"Everyone has. I need to get Sarah out of here." She waited. "I know, Nelson. I know you help free people from this evil place."

Every once in a while, a slave would disappear. The only way a slave could run away was with Nelson's help. Dinah had always wondered how he did it, and who else was working with him, but she'd never asked him. She didn't care, as long as he kept doing it.

"I'm sorry I couldn't help Martin. There was nothing I

could do. It happened fast. Master Beaux was hellbent on selling him before your wedding."

Dinah reached across the table and placed her hand on his. "I don't blame you."

Nelson glanced at their joined hands. "I'll help your daughter."

They talked for another half hour, developing a plan. Before Nelson left, Dinah handed him the Bible her mother had given to her long ago. "Make sure she takes this."

"I will."

Afterward, Nelson returned to the fields, and Dinah to the house. At day's end, instead of returning to the cabin, Dinah said to Sarah, "Let's walk." The two women were silent as they walked alongside the creek, the same route Dinah used to take with Martin, passing the white men in frock coats on horseback. Dinah's stomach was hollow, and her mouth was dry. In Edo, she said, "It's time for you to go." Although the men were not close enough to hear, she did not want her words carrying on the wind.

"What do you mean, Momma?" Sarah responded in the same language.

"If you stay, he'll hurt you and take away one of a woman's most precious gifts. If he does, you'll never be free of him. And you'll never be free."

"I don't want to be free. I want to be with you."

"I've made up my mind. You have no choice."

Sarah cocked her head. "That doesn't sound like freedom to me."

Dinah smiled through her tears. "Don't be smart, child. I'm your momma. I'm with you wherever you go. Like my momma, and her momma, and her momma before that. They are always with us, guiding and protecting us."

"I can't leave you."

"Don't cry. They're watching." Dinah wiped her own tears and waited for Sarah to compose herself. "Living without freedom isn't living. You should live a good life. A happy one. Free from this place. I want you to find joy."

"What if I stay and work in the fields?"

"That man will never leave you alone. And then after you, it'll be Gracie, and then Harriett. I can't let what happened to me happen to all of you."

"You were right, Momma, about him. I won't lie. I loved his attention. He made me feel special. I thought it was because he wanted to be a good daddy to me. I know you said Martin was like a daddy to me, but…I don't remember him. Don't be angry."

Dinah touched the unbruised side of her daughter's face. "I'm not."

Sarah's eyes glistened. "Where shall I go?"

Dinah told her.

Sarah cried. "That's so far!"

"I'm hoping it's far enough." Dinah embraced her. "We've got to be strong."

"I don't know if I can be."

"Yes, you can. It's in your blood. Be proud you're Aisha's great-granddaughter, but find your own way in this world." She released Sarah and glanced at the twine-woven ring Celia had given her on what was to be her wedding day. She slipped it off her finger and slid it onto Sarah's. "Take this. It's yours now. Cherish it. It will give you strength. Promise me you'll protect yourself and keep your daughters safe. Tell them the stories I've told you about who we are and where we came from."

Sarah glanced at the ring. Tears streaked her lovely face. "I promise."

"I told you not to cry."

Sarah smiled. "Why are you crying?"

"Because I love you, baby girl. With all my heart."

"I love you, too, Momma."

Dinah wiped Sarah's cheeks. "No more tears." One of the men on horseback was looking at them. "We need to get back, or they'll think we're up to something."

In front of the cabin, Sarah watched as Dinah pulled weeds from her garden, fenced in by wooden planks, and threw them on the yellowed grass.

After dusk, a horse galloped toward them. Dinah's stomach clenched. She was having trouble breathing. He'd come too soon; Nelson stopped on the opposite side of the garden. From their squatted positions, mother and daughter looked up at the overseer. The sun was setting behind him, and his hat rested on his back, cinched by a string tied around the front. His broad chest filled out his work shirt.

"Sarah," he said, "you need to come with me."

Outside their cabins, slaves stopped what they were doing and pretended not to stare. The ones inside made their way outdoors to see what was going on. The pained expressions on their faces were mixed with relief that Nelson had not come for them.

"I did nothing wrong!" Sarah yelled.

"That bruise didn't get there by itself. I won't tolerate

fighting." He beckoned to her. "Get up. Don't make me drag you."

Dinah rushed over to him. "Don't hurt my baby, Nelson! Please don't hurt my baby! I hit her for being too proud."

"You'd never lay a hand on that child. Get on back." To the folks standing on their porches, he said, "All y'all. Get on indoors. This ain't no business of yours."

Dinah knelt by her garden again. "This isn't right."

Sarah glanced at her mother, rose, and squared her shoulders. Nelson remained on his horse while Sarah walked beside him, staring straight ahead, as they headed to the small, unpainted wooden shack where Nelson performed his private whippings.

As her eldest daughter walked away, despite the pain, Dinah's chest filled with joy at the thought of the woman she'd made. Soon after Nelson and Sarah entered the shack, a whip cracked. Her daughter's blood-curdling screams filled the night air.

Dinah brushed the dirt from her hands, wiped her tears with a sleeve, and hurried into the cabin. Her four other children stared at her with huge eyes. They knew by her expression, though, that it was best they didn't speak. Dinah picked up a doll she'd made of straw, buttons, and yarn when Sarah was a child. She sat in the rocking chair and set it in motion, cradling the doll as she used to cradle Sarah.

The screams from the shack were fainter inside the cabin. Fat tears rolled down Dinah's face. The woman in the shack with Nelson continued to scream, and Dinah was fine with that. She wanted her to scream forever. While Nelson struck the floor with the whip, alternating with Betty's screams,

Sarah would be running across the shallow part of the creek, with a sack of food and Celia's Bible. She would meet Reverend Jones, traveling on horseback, a mile down the road, where the creek joined the river. She would scramble onto the horse cart and hide underneath a blanket before the preacher covered it with Bibles. The patrol left Reverend Jones alone, as they were accustomed to seeing the old man walking or riding North Carolina's back roads. He'd stop in Raleigh, where he'd usher Sarah through the back door of the bank manager's home. The bank manager was another member of the Underground Railroad. His wife would help change Sarah's hairstyle and give her some of their daughter's clothes. The following morning, Sarah would accompany the banker to a meeting in the port town of New Bern. From a distance, she could pass as the white banker's daughter. In the basement of a New Bern home, they'd encase her in the false bottom of a wooden box punched with holes and load her onto a cargo ship bound for Boston, Massachusetts. Dinah would never see her daughter again, but she was at peace, preferring that to the destiny that would have awaited Sarah on the Devereaux plantation.

While overseeing the household, Dinah occasionally snuck into the master's study and pored over the ledgers that detailed the slave transactions. There wasn't enough time to read them all in one sitting. With a fountain pen, she'd place a tick mark where she had left off. She didn't worry that her markings would be discovered. No one else read the books; Beaux opened the current ledger only to enter new transactions.

It took her years to read every book. She always skipped the book that held Martin's entry, but she found her grandmother's transaction. She never could find a record of her daddy, Moses, being bought or sold, much less of the date he'd married her momma. She was puzzled, as the Devereauxs kept a thorough inventory of the arrival, departure, births, deaths, and marriages of their slaves. Over time, Dinah finally realized that Big Moses had never existed. Celia had made him up.

Her momma had never told her the truth, but Dinah should have known. Over the years, Celia had talked less and less about Moses, afraid of giving her secret away. Dinah would have been smart enough to suss out inconsistencies in her story. Celia had always been afraid that another slave or someone in the family would tell Dinah the truth—even Master Sam, himself. This was why Celia had become the perfect slave. Dinah remembered all those nights her momma had tucked her into bed and then returned to the house to "finish her work." While Dinah was reading the books her momma had borrowed from the house, Master Sam had been raping her momma.

Although Dinah resembled her momma, she could tell by looking at her nose, her cheekbones, and her light brown eyes that her daddy had been with her all along. As had her half-brother, Beauxregard Solomon Devereaux.

CHAPTER SIXTY-FIVE

SHA

SHA SETTLED ON the couch in front of the living room TV to watch the season's first game. She'd lit a few candles, which Mikala had given her, over the fireplace and on the coffee table. She inhaled their calming mahogany scent.

Though victorious in avenging her daughter, Sha felt, in part, diminished—as if she'd sunk to Erik's level somehow, even though she knew she hadn't; in any case, Sha no longer blamed herself for what had happened to Jelani. Maybe therapy was working.

But her vigilante days were over. She wanted to get back to her simple, tranquil life. She had a peaceful home and a partner who brought her a sense of calm. The two of them attended a yoga class twice a week, and Jelani, who had also continued with her therapy sessions often joined them. The yoga, therapy, and meditation allowed Sha —and Jelani—to sleep through the night.

She and Mikala gardened and took long walks in the morning to battle the slight pouch Sha had developed from drinking beer. They shopped. The difference between them was that Mikala shopped without a list. At Trader Joe's, she bought whatever items "spoke" to her. Sha still brought the paper from the side of the refrigerator in case any of the necessities didn't speak up. The couple had recently taken up tennis.

Miles down the road of recovery, Jelani joked that Sha and Mikala should go out on a date so that she could spend the evening alone. She wasn't afraid anymore. Right before Sha and Mikala headed out to the movies, Mikala had exchanged a knowing glance with Jelani, probably regarding Sha's fashion sense.

Sha planned to take Mikala and Jelani to visit Atlanta. With trepidation, she'd called and told both her mother and her grandmother about her relationship with Mikala. Afterward, she'd paused, unsure of how they'd react.

"I always knew you were gay," her mother had said.

"What?"

"I've known since you were three."

Sha had scoffed. "I didn't even know."

"A mother knows."

"I'm glad you found love," Olivia had said.

At work, Sha had taken on additional responsibilities; she'd begun teaching coding classes, herself. Girls from all over the US signed up for her online class. Her favorite students were those whose questions stumped her. She hadn't needed to worry about the trajectory of the world; it would be safe in these kids' hands. Or at least it had a chance.

◈

Golden State's hot shooting guard drained his fifth three in a row.

Sha punched the air. "Yes!"

A few minutes later, Jelani appeared in the hallway in her pajama, a long black T-shirt with BLACK FEMINIST emblazoned in white across the chest. Follow-up exams had confirmed that she was free of STIs and should not have a problem conceiving children. She no longer suffered from nightmares, and she had gotten straight As on her most recent report card.

Sha tore her eyes away from the TV. "Nice shirt. Too loud?"

Jelani shook her head. Her ringlets looked like Mikala's.

Sha frowned. "It's Saturday night. You're not going out with your friends?"

A shadow crossed her daughter's face as she walked toward the sofa. "All they want to do is go to clubs and pick up guys. I'm past that. Besides, I'd rather stay home with you."

"Am I the consolation prize?"

Jelani gave her a sheepish smile. "No."

"Come sit."

On the television, the point guard made a beautiful, behind-the-back pass to the deadly shooter on the wing. Three-pointer. Good. In excellent form already, the team could enjoy another championship season.

Sha placed her glass on the end table and picked up the remote. "We don't have to watch this. The Warriors are going to win."

"Does it even matter? Aren't there like three hundred games?"

Sha smiled. "Not that many."

"I don't mind, Mom. Really."

Sha could watch the highlights online later. "Let's watch something else."

She flipped through the stations and stopped when she came to their favorite movie, the old classic, *The Color Purple*. Jelani selected one of the colorful sofa pillows Mikala had bought—to lighten up the gray, she'd said—placed it on Sha's shoulder, and laid her head against it.

Sha put her arm around her daughter. "You okay?"

Jelani nodded.

Sha lowered the volume on the TV. After having watched the movie so many times, they'd both memorized the dialogue.

"How's therapy going?" Sha asked.

"It's good. She's helping me. You were right, Mom. To make me go."

"I'm always right."

Jelani lifted her head and shot her a look before resettling it against the pillow. "She and I talk about self-love, understanding who I am, and forgiving myself, knowing that the rape wasn't my fault."

"I told you it wasn't."

"I needed to hear it from me," Jelani said softly.

Sha stroked her daughter's hair. "He can't hurt you ever again. You're safe. You shouldn't be afraid to go out."

"I'm not anymore. It has nothing to do with him. I *choose*

not to. Everything that seemed important then seems lame now."

Silent for a while, they watched Shug Avery walk toward her daddy in his church, singing about God trying to tell you something. Jelani sang the lyrics under her breath until the scene ended.

"To understand who I am," Jelani said, "I need to know my history. Mom, tell me more about my father."

Sha's hand stilled on the top of her daughter's head. Jelani hadn't asked about him in a long time. "You're right." She took a deep breath. "I met this white guy at Berkeley my freshman year. Good-looking. Wavy, brown hair. He was kind. A good listener. Never hit on me. We did everything together: studying, listening to music, watching TV, bar hopping, throwing the frisbee on the quad. I could be myself with him. Awkward. Quirky. One night, sophomore year, after too many beers at a bar near campus, we stayed up late talking, sitting on my bed in my dorm room. We were laughing at something I'd said, then the air changed. He looked at me, his eyes strange, and divulged his true feelings for me. I told him I loved him, too, but not in that way." Softly, she said, "He didn't believe me."

"What happened?"

"He left my room angry and then showed up again—wasted—well after midnight. I let him in to sleep it off on the floor, and I went back to sleep. I woke up because he was on top of me, holding me down with his full weight. He wasn't that big, but he was physically stronger than me. His mouth covered mine, so I couldn't scream. Couldn't breathe. Before, he'd asked nothing of me. Then he took everything."

"Did you report him?"

Sha shook her head. "I didn't know what to do. I loved him. He was my best friend. I was in shock that he could do something like that to me. I became depressed. Stopped calling home. Stopped bathing. My schoolwork suffered. I almost dropped out. My mother took a leave of absence from her job and willed me out of my funk. Nine months later, you arrived."

Sha braced herself for Jelani's reaction.

Jelani sat up. "Wait! What? My *father* raped you? I've lived my entire life thinking he was a good man. That he was dead. That's what you told me."

"He is dead…to me. Besides, I didn't want you growing up knowing all that." She squeezed her daughter. "I wanted you to know only love."

"What happened to him?"

"Shortly thereafter, he quit school and vanished. I never told him about you or heard from him again. I rented an apartment for the last two years of school. Grandma Olivia came to live with me to help take care of you so I could finish my degree."

"She did?"

Sha nodded. "So I understand your pain. That experience strengthened me, made me more determined. I took my power back. And it gave me my greatest blessing. It gave me you. Sometimes things don't happen to you, they happen for you. Use it for good."

Jelani pointed at the TV. "Like Shug. God is trying to tell me something."

"Something like that."

They watched the movie in silence for a while longer.

"Do you think Mikala is the one?" Jelani asked.

Sha had asked herself the same question. She couldn't think when Mikala was near. "I can't tell the future, but it feels good between us."

"I like her. You think I'll ever find love like that?"

Sha squeezed her tighter. "You will. Just don't go looking for it. It'll find you." Sha thought about the first time she met Mikala, in the sandwich shop. "It found me."

Her daughter laid her head back on the pillow and said nothing for a long time, then, "You know you've been enough, right?"

"What do you mean?"

"You raised me. You're my mommy and my daddy. I couldn't ask for a better life. I know how lucky I am."

"Do you forgive me?"

"For what?"

"For allowing you to get hurt."

"There's nothing to forgive. I think it's more important that you forgive yourself."

Sha's eyes watered. *It was time.*

She disengaged from Jelani. "I'll be right back."

Sha crossed the living room, passed the dining room and kitchen, and walked down the hall to her home office. Next to the portrait of her famous mother, she pressed her thumb against the pad built into the wall, releasing the picture frame. She unlocked the safe behind it and reached past her will, birth certificates and passports, a list of passwords, other important documents, and stacks of American and Euro paper currency, to pull out a small glass case and an old book. She closed and relocked the safe, replaced the painting, and returned to the living room. She handed both items to Jelani, who set the Good Book on the end table and peered into the glass case, which fit into her palm.

"I was going to wait until next year," Sha said, "when you turn eighteen, but I want you to have it now."

Jelani opened the case and stared inside. "What is it?"

"It's a ring. It belonged to your great-great-great-great-great-great-great grandmother, Aisha."

"This belonged to Aisha?" Eyes wide, Jelani looked at Sha, who nodded. "Holding something that belonged to her…It's unreal…But at the same time it makes the stories you told me real."

"Since you were little, I've only told you part of the story. The part in Africa. When our people were free. It's time I told you the rest."

Sha recounted the stories of Aisha, Celia, Dinah, Sarah, Julia, Augusta, Olivia, and Nicole, and of how the ring had been passed down to each of the women in their family line.

"Did you know your grandmother was a cheerleader, too?"

Jelani's mouth gaped. "Nana Nicole?"

Sha laughed. "We were all young once."

Jelani's gaze returned to the ring.

"That ring has power," Sha continued, "and it comes with a responsibility: You are not only responsible for yourself and your future daughters, but for other Black women as well."

"And someday I'll pass it down to my daughter." This was the first time since the rape that she'd mentioned having children. Jelani set down the case and picked up the Bible, her hand trailing down the cover. "This is old."

"It belonged to Dinah. Open it."

Jelani stared, wide-eyed, at the list of names on the first page.

"You wanted to know your history," Sha said. "There it is."

CHAPTER SIXTY-SIX

OLIVIA

OLIVIA WAS DAYDREAMING about walking along the beach hand-in-hand with Davis. With her heels kicked off under her mahogany executive desk, she grabbed the piled carpet with her toes as if it were sand. Perhaps it was time for her to retire.

She turned her gaze from Philly's morning sun, its light streaming through her office window, and reared back a gray metal ball in the Newton's cradle on her desk, then released it. The ball at the opposite end shot up then returned to its original position. The three balls in the middle remained stationary, illustrating the laws of conservation of momentum and energy. Mesmerized, she repeated the motion, as she often did lately, knowing it was demonstrating a lesson for her.

The Philadelphia Tribune lay spread out before her. She perused the front-page article regarding the Challenger's successful maiden voyage to space before turning to the business section. The article above the fold was about the huge shake-up at National & World News Network. Executives had been dismissed for conduct unbecoming of the network's employees. During her weekly chat with Nicole the night before, her daughter had told her that many of the men in the boardroom were no longer with the organization. The most shocking announcement was that NWNN's award-winning anchorman had left the network for personal reasons.

In the article, Chairman, CEO, and President Reed Elliott stated: "It's a new day. NWNN is the best news network in the world, and we expect all its employees to exemplify its core values and abide by our code of conduct."

The code of conduct had only recently been created. Better late than never.

Olivia should have been basking in her victory, but she mostly felt tired; she knew no other way of getting through life than by fighting.

"Mrs. Bradley," came her assistant's voice over the speakerphone.

"Yes?"

"Your daughter's on the line."

Olivia tensed. She picked up the handset. "Nicole?"

"Mother!"

"Is everything all right?"

"Why wouldn't it be?"

Olivia exhaled. She was afraid the network had found some excuse for firing Nicole. "Because we just talked last night, and a call from you during the day is rare."

"It's better than all right! Guess what!"

Olivia smiled, envisioning her daughter bouncing up and down as she had when she was a young girl eager to explain something new that she'd learned. "What?"

"I got a promotion! Tune in to NWNN tonight. I broke a story!"

"That's wonderful! Did you let your father know?"

"No. I wanted to tell you first."

A flush of pleasure surged through Olivia. She couldn't remember being this happy.

"And the executive producer apologized on behalf of the network and said I was right about the Chernobyl story."

"Of course you were."

"Are you proud of me, Mother?"

Olivia understood the weight of her answer. "Baby, I would be proud of you no matter what you did. I love you because you're you."

Nicole was silent for a moment. "I abhorred what he did, but I still admire his work… His ability to get to the essence of a story. Is that weird?" She could never say the anchorman's name.

Olivia thought of Robert and her own conflicting emotions. "Not at all."

After she hung up, Olivia folded the newspaper and slipped it into the trashcan, then gathered the documents she'd been working on. She was about to put them in her briefcase to bring home, but she put them in a desk drawer instead. They could wait until tomorrow.

The phone buzzed.

"Is it Nicole again?" Olivia asked her assistant.

"No. A Mrs. Ainsworth to see you."

"Who?"

"She doesn't have an appointment, but she said it's important."

This was highly unusual. Olivia didn't represent individuals or normally receive drop-in appointments. But she was curious. "Send her in."

Some partners kept their office doors open so they could hear what was going on in the hallway. Olivia's door was closed so she could shut out distractions.

Her assistant opened the door and held it as a woman around Olivia's age with a Lady Di haircut entered the room. She wore a light green dress, sheer pantyhose, and a diamond necklace. She scanned Olivia's office tentatively, as if to ensure they were alone.

Olivia nodded at her assistant, who then left and closed the door behind her. She gave the woman a perfunctory smile and gestured toward a guest chair. The woman sat, crossed her legs, and placed an accordion file on Olivia's desk. "You don't know me, but you know my husband. Of him, anyway."

Puzzled, Olivia flipped through her mental Rolodex of clients, suspects, attorneys, and—

"Ainsworth is my maiden name," the woman continued in her Southern drawl. "The former NWNN anchorman is my husband." She nodded at the file. Her green eyes were dry. "In there is proof of everything he did to me."

"I'm sorry about whatever has happened between you and your husband," Olivia said in a soothing voice, "but I don't understand why you're here."

"I want a divorce."

"I'm a corporate lawyer, but I would be happy to recommend someone." Olivia didn't know any attorneys in Atlanta, but she could leverage her firm's referral network.

The woman shook her head. "The receptionist told everyone what happened in that boardroom. None of the wives can stop talking about it. I want the best." Her eyes blazed. "And I want you to bury him."

"I'm glad you brought me here."

"Me, too."

The days were growing longer. Six months after the shake-up at National & World News Network, Olivia and Nicole strolled down Seventh Avenue in Harlem. Nicole wore an oversize shirt with blue parachute pants. Olivia was in a black and gray sweatsuit, one of a matching pair she had purchased for herself and Davis at Christmas. Her daughter's head swiveled, taking in the sights. There was The Corner, where musicians used to play for free. The Tree of Hope was no longer there. It had been cut down in 1934 to widen the street. A piece of it now lay in the Apollo Theater, and amateur musicians still rubbed it for good luck. Rose's clothing store, where Olivia's mother and grandmother had once worked, was now a liquor store. The neighborhood wasn't as nice as it had been when Olivia was growing up. Discarded Styrofoam cups, newspapers, and cigarette butts littered the street. The air was filled with exhaust and the smell of cooking oil from fast-food restaurants. But there were flashes of its old charm; in addition to the Apollo, the Cotton Club was still there. Olivia told Nicole the stories her mother used to tell her, of the remarkable people Augusta had met, artists and writers who had migrated from all over the United States to call Harlem home; of the rent parties; of the music and literature.

They stopped at a bookstore. Customers were reading or speaking quietly. At the front of the store, Nicole picked up a novel by Langston Hughes: *Not Without Laughter.* "We only studied Hemingway, Faulkner, and Fitzgerald in high school. I read Fitzgerald's take on the 1920s"—she waved her arm at the rest of the works in the Black Literature section—"but didn't learn anything about the Harlem Renaissance."

Olivia pursed her lips. "There's a reason for that."

After they made their purchases and left the store, Nicole stopped abruptly in the middle of the sidewalk. Pedestrians veered around them. An old man grumbled, "folks just stop when they want to" but continued walking.

"I have an idea!" Nicole said.

Olivia smiled at the familiar light in her daughter's eyes. "What?"

"I'm going to write a story about it. The Harlem Renaissance."

Olivia's heart swelled with pleasure. She took Nicole's arm. "Mama would love that. Let's go back to her house and tell her."

CHAPTER SIXTY-SEVEN

DINAH

WORD REACHED THE mistress that her sister's carriage had been delayed in Fayetteville.

The day after Sarah left, Dinah had helped Martha in the kitchen because, as Dinah told everyone, Nelson had whipped Sarah so severely that she'd spent the night in the whipping shack and was still there, unable to stand. Nelson had ordered everyone to leave her alone; no one was permitted to visit her, including her momma. Dinah went about her work, affecting worry about her daughter's condition but donning the blank, efficient mask she wore every day.

When Beaux took over running the plantation, he let Dinah manage the household ledgers. "You're better at numbers than I'll ever be," he'd said. Dinah had caught on quickly. She worked at the wooden table in the small room off the kitchen, where she now sat reconciling the monthly figures. The house gradually grew quiet. Most of the family had retired to bed. Martha and the rest of the slaves had left for the day. And although Jake normally slept in the mud room these days, Dinah had shooed the dog outside earlier. In the stillness, the sound of her steel-nib pen scratching the lined paper provided a rhythmic calm.

She felt Beaux's presence at the door. Drink in hand, he cocked his head toward the second floor and walked away. Reluctantly, Dinah closed the ledger, not bothering to leave a tick mark to indicate where she'd left off, and followed him upstairs. She paused at the entrance to his room. In his trousers and undershirt, Beaux was staring out the window at the expansive front lawn, a cigarette in his hand. He'd long ago stopped obeying his mother's orders not to smoke in his room. At thirty-four, he was still handsome. The laugh lines etched into the skin near his eyes and on his forehead enhanced his good looks. Riding horses every day kept his stomach trim. He turned to Dinah and snuffed out the cigarette as she approached him, then swooped her up in his arms as he'd done when they were younger. He dropped her on the bed and tore at her clothes with a long-absent fervor. While he thrust into her, he asked, "Where was Sarah today? Nelson told Billy she's sick."

"That's right."

"That's too bad," he said, "I better see her tomorrow."

Dinah said nothing.

"What is it? You jealous? Because you caught us in the cellar?"

Caught you. "Why would I be jealous of my daughter?"

"Because Baby Sarah's all grown up."

"She's not that grown."

Beaux licked her ear. "I remember you at that age."

Polish my boots, he'd said. "I remember you, too."

As if Dinah hadn't spoken, Beaux said, "I always noticed you. Even when we were children playing together. 'Til I wasn't allowed to anymore. You were the prettiest girl, even prettier than the white ones. I wanted you before I understood what that meant. Who knows? If you'd been white, maybe we would've gotten married."

Dinah bit back the retort that if they'd been married, she would have been visiting her momma like Anna was doing now, and some other slave woman would have lain here instead.

"You need to stop being so rigid with her, Dinah. If it's not me, it'll be someone else. Someone who might not treat her nice. At least I'll take care of her. And of all our daughters."

Dinah tensed at the thought, but then relaxed. She'd done the right thing by sending Sarah away.

Beaux's jabs became more frenzied, his breathing heavy. He was close. He raised his head, his groans guttural. The veins in his neck bulged.

"You mean rape them like you've been raping me all these years?" she said.

He scowled. "Rape?"

Dinah took the knife from under the pillow, where she'd hidden it earlier that day after making Beaux's bed. As Beaux climaxed, she plunged the knife into his throat and twisted it. Beaux's eyes popped open. He froze, his Adam's apple stopping midswallow, and then his body slumped on top of her, his penis still inside.

Dinah pushed her heavy, dead owner off her and rolled her dress back down. She got out of the bed and looked down at him. "You'll never touch any of my daughters again."

CHAPTER SIXTY-EIGHT

SHA

SHA AND JELANI tried a new sport—pickleball—and sometimes convinced Mikala to play with them. The three of them went to black theater productions, the opera, museums, and lectures, activities Jelani would have found boring in the past. She learned a lot from these outings, but Sha did, too. Sha understood her own privileges better and vowed to continue to eliminate barriers for others whenever she could.

Sha had also started dabbling in making computer games and gaming apps for phones, rather than just playing them. She loved the challenge of creating a world, characters, and the obstacles they faced. Her target audience was girls. She wasn't sure the games would ever be good enough to sell, but the experience of creating them gave her joy.

A week after Sha gave Jelani the ring and the Bible, she took her daughter to Shattuck Avenue for brunch. They sat at a table for two outside a vegan restaurant and waited for their server. Traffic on the avenue was light. Passersby stopped at the chalkboard on the sidewalk to look at the daily specials, written in pink cursive. After she and Jelani ordered, Sha pointed at the Bible. "You can't carry that everywhere if we want it to last."

Her daughter held it up. "Have you read this, Mom?"

Sha sipped her sparkling water. "It's been a while."

Jelani opened it, flipped through the pages, and pointed. "Sarah wrote this! Although the English is different, that's her handwriting!" She held it up so Sha could see it. She turned to another page. "And Dinah!" She turned to another page. The curls on her head danced as she moved. "Julia under-lined many lines of scripture and wrote in the margins: about her life, her feelings, her thoughts about certain passages. I don't think she liked Augusta's husband very much. She underlined in John 9:16, 'This man is not of God, because he keepeth not the Sabbath day.' Augusta wrote in it, too, but it wasn't until later in her life. Gran Olivia and Nana Nicole and you"—Jelani cleared her throat—"wrote nothing."

Sha shifted in her chair, feeling like she used to when her mother would catch her coding after she was supposed to have been asleep. "Well…it's an antique. I didn't want to damage it."

The server brought their dishes. Jelani placed the book in her purse. "I've been thinking," she said.

Sha chewed a bite of her crunchy broccoli salad. "What about?"

Jelani picked up her fork but didn't eat. "I want to use my voice. I feel a responsibility to speak out about what hap-pened to me."

Sha frowned. "Are you sure?"

Jelani nodded.

"Yes, you'll inspire others, but your words might also bring out the crazies. With great responsibility come other things. Will you be ready for that? It could get rough."

"If I don't speak, he wins. Men like him win."

Sha didn't love the idea, but she would not let Jelani know that. Although Jelani was on the cusp of womanhood, Sha still wanted to protect her. "You're right. You must stand up for yourself. No one else will."

Jelani took a bite of her chickpea shawarma salad. "I've also made another decision."

Sha pointed her fork at her. "You're going to college."

"I know; it's not that. I'm going to speak about our ancestors, their resilience, where I get my strength from. And to do that, I need to know more than what's in this Bible."

"What are you planning to do?"

Jelani's eyes shone. "Talk to them."

CHAPTER SIXTY-NINE

OLIVIA

OLIVIA WOULD NEVER forget the day her granddaughter called to tell her she'd been accepted to the University of California at Berkeley. It was a Sunday afternoon. The weather was lovely, and Olivia was in her home office reading Zadie Smith's *On Beauty*. She leaned back in her chair, resting her bare feet on the desk. The open window let in sounds from the street: children playing, couples strolling by, music blaring from cars.

"Congratulations, my dear! I'll let you tell your Grandpa!"

She covered the cordless phone's mouthpiece with her hand. "Davis!" She waited. No answer. "Davis, Sha is on the phone! She has something to tell you!" Davis still didn't respond. He was probably engrossed in the game. The Sixers were playing the Celtics on the big, black projection TV he'd insisted they buy over seven years ago.

Olivia said into the phone, "Hold on. I'll get him," then

placed the phone on the desk and crossed the hall to the family room. Her husband was slumped over in the recliner. Having retired from his job at the city, he fell asleep in that chair more often, but it was odd for him to do so during a game against the Sixers' top rival. Olivia shook him. He toppled over, his body thudding onto the carpet.

Olivia screamed.

She knelt beside him and rolled him onto his back. Her lips locked over his, and she breathed into him. She paused, turned her head, and listened. Nothing. She placed one hand on top of the other and pumped his generous heart. She lost count of how many times she pressed down. Davis didn't respond. He had been complaining about indigestion more often lately, now Olivia knew it had been something more. She should have insisted that he go to the doctor for a checkup.

Olivia staggered over to the wall phone and picked up the extension.

"Are you still there, Sha?"

"Yes, Grandma."

"Tell your mom to come home. I need her."

Olivia finished eating the chicken and broccoli dinner she'd prepared. She washed her dishes and placed them beside the pot and skillet in the dish rack next to the sink. Ambling over to the back door, she looked outside. Frost covered the wrought-iron furniture on the patio. No wonder her bones ached. She needed to make a trip south.

Turning off the kitchen light, she made her way gingerly

down the hallway and entered the family room. She sat in her recliner, placing a glass of cherry juice on the small table between it and the other recliner, which was empty and always would be.

It had been five years since Davis's heart attack. Olivia often regretted the amount of time she'd focused on her work instead of on him. He'd always been there for her; she couldn't say she'd reciprocated. As the breadwinner, Olivia had thought she was the family's rock, but Davis was the one who'd dedicated his life to her and her daughter. Perhaps being the perfect husband and father was its own type of stress. In their later years together, Olivia had tried to be a better wife. Not perfect, but better.

She looked up at the ceiling, knowing Davis was admonishing her for having these thoughts. Her work had made her happy. And that was all he'd ever wanted her to be. Olivia missed him every day. His clothes still hung on his side of the closet in their bedroom. The various ball caps he'd collected from the cities they had visited over the last two decades sat atop his dresser. They'd taken yearly trips to places like London, Paris, Rome, Lisbon, Amsterdam, and Bangkok, and weekend road trips in the red Caddy to the Poconos, the Hamptons, or Cape May. Olivia had learned that taking time off made her not only a better wife but also a better attorney. She'd returned to her work refreshed and with the experience of being with and understanding other people, like the ones she and Davis had met on their travels.

Nicole had given the eulogy at Davis's funeral and spoken of how he exemplified unconditional love. Olivia, who had spoken eloquently for a living, had not been able to trust herself not to break down speaking about the only man she'd ever loved besides her father.

She sipped her juice, then picked up the remote control.

Olivia had been wrong to believe that attaining partner status was the pinnacle of her career. Soon after Nicole's first promotion, Robert Penn had retired, saying it was time for someone else to run the firm and prepare it for the next century. Olivia had always wondered if he'd retired because he was uncomfortable working with her after she'd rejected his sexual overtures. Regardless, the other partners had voted her managing partner of Penn, Franklin, Ross, & Bradley. She should have wanted that job all along. But her legacy would not only be her name on the firm's letterhead; it would also be the anti-harassment policy she'd created and implemented during her tenure overseeing the firm. She envisioned a day when women could work without harassment and didn't have to endure it to succeed. The policy became the model not only for legal firms, but also for many organizations across the United States. Olivia had set up internship programs for students from many HBCUs and increased the number of Black women attorneys hired by the firm. She had been so busy focusing on her own career that she hadn't realized she should have been bringing more Black women along with her. Later in her career, she'd kept her office door open and encouraged the firm's attorneys to drop by at any time.

Even though he'd been in his eighties, Mr. Brown had helped her plant phlox in the front yard and taught her how to care for them. They would talk for a long time every day after Olivia returned home from work, until the day Mr. Brown became infirm and then died.

Now retired, herself, Olivia had taken up bridge and spent most of her time traveling around Maryland, Virginia, and Tennessee in her Caddy to play in tournaments and spend time with the friends she had made at them. Her bridge buddies. She and Davis had purchased a second home in Atlanta to be near Nicole and her family, and Olivia now spent the winters there. She didn't have the heart to sell the home she'd shared with Davis in Philadelphia.

Scanning the room, her gaze landed on the mantle over the fireplace. None of the awards or accolades she'd garnered over her career sat atop it. Instead, next to photos of her ancestors rested framed photographs of her husband, their daughter, their son-in-law—Nicole had married the Atlanta lawyer—their granddaughter, Sha, and their great-granddaughter, Jelani. Olivia clicked on the TV. After several commercials, the logo for the cable news network, which had stayed the same since the network's founding over two decades ago, swept over the screen. As it faded, it was replaced by a regal woman wearing a white jacket and a black top, her straightened, auburn-highlighted hair falling to her shoulders. Her makeup was expertly applied, and her fingernails were flawless.

Nicole's stoic face stared into the camera. "Good evening. I'm Nicole Bradley. In our top story tonight, President Barack Obama officially repealed the 'Don't Ask, Don't Tell' military policy." Olivia began to cry. She glanced at the coffee table in front of the sofa. On it sat a book Nicole had written regarding the origins of NWNN and her journey to becoming one of the first Black anchorwomen for a global news organization. Olivia looked up to the ceiling, raising both of her arms. "Mama! Davis! She did it!"

CHAPTER SEVENTY

JULIA

THE GREEN LEAVES and flowers had returned to the magnolia tree in Augusta's backyard. Julia closed her eyes and tipped her face to the warmth of the early afternoon sun before opening them again. She sipped her lemonade. Her heart swelled with pride as she looked at Hale, who sat next to her, his wife, Faye, sitting on the other side of him. After graduating from high school, Hale had secured a job in construction. When the war came, Julia had begged him to flee to Canada to avoid serving. Even if she were never to have seen him again, she'd been afraid that the past would repeat itself and loath to lose another loved one for this country. But Hale had gone to war, served with distinction, and, afterward, rejoined the same construction company. He was a foreman now. Faye wasn't perfect—there seemed to be little depth to her—but Hale loved her, and she treated him well. So, Julia loved her, too.

Across the table from Hale and Faye sat Clara and Josie, who were both attending Hunter College—their mother's alma mater. Clara played on the softball team. The sunlight bathed their hair, revealing shimmers of red highlights.

Julia reached for Clara's and Hale's hands. Everyone held the hands of the person sitting on either side of them, and Hale said grace.

Josie picked up the plastic fork she'd dropped, rubbing it on her dress sleeve. "What a great idea to eat outside, Grandma!"

"I agree," said Clara.

"It's lovely, Mama," Augusta said.

The Second World War had just ended. An excitement that hadn't been seen since the twenties pulsated throughout the city, the country. As the girls chatted about school and the good-looking military men who'd returned home from the war, they passed around the dishes Julia had prepared from recipes she'd learned from her mother: fried chicken, baked beans, mustard greens, potato salad, and sweet potato pie.

Augusta and Richmond, who had married, sat across from each other, with Richmond sitting next to Faye, and Augusta sitting beside Josie. After Jean had been missing for three years, the state of New York had granted Augusta a divorce on grounds of abandonment. Richmond had been spared from fighting in the war because of his poor eyesight. After publishing a novel about his grandmother and her journey to Harlem—a sequel to his book about his grandfa-ther—he had continued to teach and authored more books. Although they'd been critically acclaimed for their realism, his novels hadn't done so well commercially. Richmond was comfortable with that.

Richmond's mother, Margaret, sat at the opposite end of the table from Julia.

Augusta had not only finished several short stories but, ten years after she'd taken up writing, her first novel: the story of a girl who overcame many obstacles, based on the life of her Granny Sarah. Augusta had spent many late nights pecking away at the keys of her secondhand Remington typewriter while Richmond typed at the desk beside her. Hale's old bedroom had become their shared writing space. Richmond had called his publisher, who'd purchased the rights to Augusta's book. Augusta had since completed three others. Julia no longer worried about Augusta's health.

Once the arthritis had made it too painful for her to sew any longer, Julia had quit the dress shop and stopped making her own clothes. She volunteered to cook and sell cakes, pies, and pastries at the church's bake sales. She also taught Sunday school classes once a month. Although she would never forgive Jean for cheating on and hitting her daughter, she finally forgave Clifford for dying and herself for wishing she hadn't let him. And she'd been wrong. Clifford had died for a purpose: so Julia could be surrounded by her family on a glorious day like this. Free.

The family had flourished since Jean's disappearance.

Richmond pushed his half-frame glasses up the bridge of his nose. As he knifed through a watermelon, Julia recalled the last night she and her niece, Ruth, had both seen Julia's former son-in-law.

CHAPTER SEVENTY-ONE

RUTH

JEAN AND RUTH exited the hotel's elevator on the fourth floor, his arm around her shoulders. As they walked along the stained corridor carpet, Jean's hand dropped to Ruth's waist. By the time they were in front of her room, it was on her buttocks. A jazz song played loudly inside the room.

"I must have left the radio on," Ruth said.

Jean licked and nibbled at her ear as she inserted the key into the lock.

"You can at least let me get inside," she said, "and turn on the lights."

"We won't need lights," Jean said, his voice thick.

When they entered, Jean kicked the door shut and scooted Ruth farther into the room, his erect penis pushing against her backside. He spun her around and kissed her.

She pulled away. "I thought you wanted to get to know me better."

"This is getting to know you." Jean resumed kissing her. Ruth remained motionless, unresponsive to his kisses. Jean didn't notice. The stench of stale cigarettes and spilled beer filled the room. Neither Jean nor Ruth bothered to remove their coats. A bed squeaked in the room next door, its headboard slamming against the adjoining wall.

"I still don't know your name," Jean murmured, his tongue jabbing Ruth's lips apart. As he explored her mouth, his hand sunk lower on her breast.

A stain discolored a tile in the low ceiling. Ruth wondered what Augusta was doing while her husband groaned and caressed her panties through her dress.

Click. The lights came on.

"Her name is Ruth…You can call her 'cousin.'"

Jean's head shot up to look over Ruth's shoulder, like the jack-in-the-box toy Ruth used to play with. He released her as if he'd touched a hot stove. "Cousin!"

Julia sat in a faded green upholstered chair in a corner of the room near the window, still holding the table lamp's pullchain. The radio continued to blare beside it. There was an expression of rage mixed with sadness on her face. She swept a Winchester 20-gauge shotgun off her lap and pointed it at Jean. "Thanks, niece. You can go."

Jean stared at Ruth, his mouth gaping. "Niece?"

Ruth wiped her lips with the back of her hand and rearranged her dress. "Will you be all right, Aunt Julia?"

Julia patted the stock of the gun. "I'll be fine. Give my sister my love."

Ruth blew her a kiss and left.

CHAPTER SEVENTY-TWO

JULIA

JEAN HELD UP his hands. "Let me explain, Mama."

"Don't you think it's a little late for that…*son*?"

"Wait! That woman—your niece—meant nothing. I mean…She means something, but not to me."

"What about the other women?"

Jean swallowed. "How do you know about them?"

"A mother knows. In your case, everyone knows."

"I won't lie to you. There have been others, but none of them meant anything to me. You know me, Mama."

Julia's blood had been boiling since she'd witnessed Jean's infidelity firsthand. Now it simmered. "That I do."

The hotel room's radiator rattled.

"I love Auggie. She's the only woman I want to share my life with."

"You have a funny way of showing it. And her name is not Auggie."

"What?"

"Her name is Augusta. You couldn't even let her have that."

Julia pulled the trigger.

Ray had bought the gun and the Maxim Silencer through one of his artist friends, who'd also shown Julia how to shoot it. Following Julia's instructions from two days earlier, Ruth left the hotel room, crossed the hall to a door that led to the stairs, and hurried down the four flights. At ground level, she held the door open for Ray, who came up those same stairs wearing a black leather coat and carrying a large industrial blanket. When he arrived on the fourth floor, he eased open the door to ensure the corridor was empty prior to entering the room.

"You okay, Mrs. Gibson?"

Still sitting in the green chair, Julia glanced at Jean, who lay on the floor with blood seeping from his open chest wound onto the threadbare carpet. "Better now."

They watched Augusta's cheating husband take his last breath before Ray wrapped him in the blanket and hoisted him onto his shoulder as if he were carrying him out of a fire…An appropriate image, since Jean's soul was on its way to hell.

Ray nodded at Julia and left the room.

Julia stayed behind to clean up the mess.

She turned the radio off.

As Julia scanned the faces of her family seated around the picnic table, she thought back to the day a few months after Jean's "disappearance" that she'd convinced Augusta to accept the table that Ray had built for her. It had been a gift, to take her mind off her troubles. Ray had said it was a shame that Augusta was letting a beautiful backyard go to waste. From the window seat in the sitting room, Augusta had waved and said "fine," then gone back to staring out the window waiting for Jean to come home. Ray had poured the concrete slab where the kiddie pool used to be and spent hours smoothing the slab to perfection.

Julia glanced under the picnic table at the slab and then back at Augusta, who was laughing at something Richmond said. Julia had never told her daughter the truth about what happened to Jean. Unlike Augusta, she knew exactly where he was.

CHAPTER SEVENTY-THREE

DINAH

THE MORNING AFTER Beaux was murdered, the slaves did not rise early to head to the fields or the house. Not because of the snowflakes drifting down from the sky; precipitation wouldn't keep them from working on a normal day. Instead, they gathered in a half-circle in the clearing, whispering among themselves about the sudden tragedies that had befallen the Devereaux plantation. First, Sarah— "Such a good girl. Never caused her momma any fret"— had died yesterday afternoon from the wounds inflicted on her by the previous night's whipping. Dinah, distraught over losing her firstborn a few hours before, had killed the master's son. Everyone remarked that the extreme reaction—"She done lost her head from grief"—was unlike her. She'd always been quiet and slow to anger. She was the smartest slave—the smartest person—on the plantation, serving the family well for over three decades. The slaves scratched or shook their heads. The whispering ceased as Nelson led Dinah by the arm to one side of the clearing. He held his horse's reins in the other hand.

Dinah had killed the eldest Devereaux son, her half-brother and the father of her children. There would be no arrest, no trial, no jail for her, and no opportunity to defend herself. The law rested in the slaveholder's hands. Master Samuel Devereaux would decide her fate.

The front door of the great house opened. The master crossed the balcony, shuffled down the steps, and ambled toward the slaves, leaving large footprints in the accumulating snow. An eternity later, he faced Dinah. A black beaver hat rested on his bald pate. The remaining puffs of hair on the side were white; his eyebrows were white and bushy; and his skin was pasty from having spent the latter years of his life indoors.

He'd aged a decade since yesterday.

"We let you into our home," he spat, his eyes slits. "We treated you well. Like family. Hell, you were family. And this is how you repay us? Repay me, who was good to your momma? Repay my father, who was good to Aisha?" He glanced at his family, who'd come out onto the balcony. Mary, a woman now, held the mistress's arm. Mistress Elizabeth was wrapped in a thick shawl, with a woolen bonnet on her head. Billy's arms encircled his wife and their newborn baby. Nicholas—still a bachelor—stood next to his brother. Anna, who'd arrived home from Raleigh that morning, stood apart from them. They were too far away to hear Master Sam, but the slaves could.

"That boy cared about you," Master Sam continued.

"He didn't run around on you. There were no other women, except Anna. A fifteen-year assignation is more than lust, girl. Even a Negro should be able to figure that out, especially a smart one like you." The old man's jaundiced eyes were wet, his chest and shoulders heaving.

Dinah's gaze never left her father's. "He was coming after Sarah. Our other girls."

Master Sam waved this detail away. "That's the way it is, girl. My daddy bedded your granny. Celia and I had you. I should have sold you when I sold Martin." The mention of Martin's name brought unwelcome tears to Dinah's eyes. "If I had, Beaux would still be alive. He'd have gotten over you. Eventually." He puffed out white air. "One thing you should know before you're sent to hell, or wherever you Negroes go…Beaux would have never let you go—but he planned to free the children you had together one day."

Dinah's mouth parted.

"Now," he said, "they'll never be free, and they'll end up like your oldest. I'll make sure of it."

A yelp escaped from Dinah. "They had no part in what I did."

Master Sam spat at her. The spittle hit her cheek, mixed with snowflakes, and slid down her face. With her wrists being bound by rope, she was unable to wipe it off. Master Devereaux shot her one last look and trudged away, slowly retracing his steps. He passed his family, still standing on the balcony, and entered the house, banging the front door closed behind him.

Dinah glanced around at the snow-covered roofs of the cabins, then at the other slaves, the top of their heads covered with snow, like treetops. Her own head was heavy with snow. Betty bawled, the tears rolling down her sweet, heart-shaped face. Two nights before, Dinah had shared her plan to kill Beaux with Betty. The two old friends had talked, laughed, hugged, and cried through the night and into the morning. Dinah now gave Betty a sad smile. She gazed at her children next. Nine-year-old Jacob, seven-year-old Gracie, five-year-old Moses, and two-year-old Harriet. Dinah's time with them on this earth had been too short. Her only solace had been that Betty and her husband, Ellis, would take care of them like they were their own children, and that Harriet and Gracie would be safe from their deceased father.

Dinah stared at her children for another moment, then looked away and did not look back at them again.

Nelson told the horse to stay and gently boosted Dinah onto the saddle. Once she settled, he arranged the noose around her neck, pulling the rope taut. His eyes were dull.

"You're a good woman," he said softly, so that only she could hear. "A woman of substance, faith. Your Martin was a good man. You'll meet your love in the next world, Dinah, where the two of you will never be parted. And I'll keep an eye on your children. I promise."

Dinah's eyes glistened. "Thank you, Nelson. For everything." She inhaled the fresh, crisp air. She straightened and lifted her head to study the clouds, white and low in the sky, like a bed of cotton. She wished it were nighttime so she could gaze at the stars one more time. A hush filled the space of the snowy clearing, except for the shifting of the horse's hooves beneath her. Even the slave children were quiet.

Dinah's chest lightened. She had no regrets about what she'd done and welcomed what was to come.

"I'm coming, Momma, grandmother. I'll see you soon, Martin."

She nodded at Nelson before looking back up at the sky.

Nelson hesitated, then said, "Git!"

The horse whinnied and took off.

CHAPTER SEVENTY-FOUR

SARAH

AT CERTAIN POINTS along the eighteen-day journey to Boston, Sarah didn't think she'd make it. She had a close call at the dock in New Bern as they were loading her onto the ship. A deckhand took an unusual interest in the box she was hidden in. The banker told the hand that it contained important documents, and that he would hold the deckhand personally responsible if anything happened to its contents.

The young man straightened. "No problem, sir. I'll make sure they get there undisturbed."

The man Sarah had met in Raleigh, whom she'd known for the duration of a night spent at his house and a horse ride, had saved her life. She would never forget his and his wife's kindness.

The boat sailed through storms off the coasts of Delaware and New Jersey. The banker's wife had packed Sarah sufficient food and a water pouch for the trip. Although there were holes bored into the box, Sarah found it hard to breathe and thought she would suffocate. She lay in her own urine and feces, and would do so until the box was opened at the journey's end. She counted, like her momma, to keep her mind off the stench and the boredom. Most of the time, she stared at the twine-woven ring her mother had given her. And held on to the hope that she would survive.

Through other members of the Underground Railroad, Sarah was placed in the home of a Negro family in the West End, a predominately middle- and working-class neighborhood of free Negroes. She became the Garrisons' live-in maid, and they became her family. Mr. Nathaniel Garrison was an attorney with his own practice. He specialized in defending abolitionists, protecting civil and property rights, and handling estate cases for a Negro clientele in Boston. His wife, Frances, became like a second mother to Sarah. Frances nurtured and healed her, and she continued Sarah's education where Dinah's teachings had left off. Frances had been educated at Mount Holyoke Female Seminary, and she soon filled Sarah's head with a variety of subjects: arithmetic, grammar, philosophy, literature, mathematics, and history—African and American.

Despite the increasing normalcy of her freedom, Sarah's life was still stressful. The Fugitive Slave Act allowed slaveholders to reclaim and retrieve their property, even if the person ran away to a free state. In a recurring nightmare she had, Sarah would turn a corner and end up in the arms of a grinning Beaux Devereaux. She'd wake up bathed in sweat.

Sarah sent word to Nelson through the railroad that she'd

made it to her destination. When his reply letter brought news of her mother's death, she wanted to die, herself.

Over the years, Sarah tried to convince her brothers and sisters to come North, but even after the war ended, they didn't want to risk the journey or leave North Carolina.

Mr. Garrison's law practice flourished. Eleven years after Sarah had moved in with his family, he hired his first employee. One evening, Sarah answered a knock on the townhouse's front door. A dark-skinned man in a black broadcloth suit and a red tie stood on the front porch.

"May I help you?" Sarah said.

The man stared at her, open-mouthed.

Sarah pointed at his hands. "Are those for Mr. Garrison?"

The man bobbed his head several times. "They're…uh… papers. Important papers. He asked for them."

"Well, then, you'd better come in. It's nippy out. I'm sure he'd rather read them inside."

Before Sarah could call Mr. Garrison to the door, he came down the stairs, holding his spectacles. He put them on. He glanced from Sarah to his new associate, Louis Webster Cabot, and asked the latter to stay for dinner.

By the end of the evening, Sarah and Louis were smitten.

Fourteen years later, Sarah and Louis were blessed with three children of their own. Contrary to when they'd first met, Louis was articulate. He was also handsome, smart, and hardworking, and he rose to the position of partner in Mr. Garrison's growing law firm. Sarah, in addition to raising their children and taking care of their home, sold ready-to-eat meals she made in her kitchen using the recipes she'd learned from Ol' Ms. Martha.

Notwithstanding the Emancipation Proclamation and the Union's war victory, Boston was still segregated. The Cabot children could not go to a public school with white students. And their family couldn't attend the white church. But Sarah didn't care about any of that as she helped Aisha, Oliver, and Baby Julia get dressed for church, where she sang in the choir.

She and her children and her children's children would forever be free.

EPILOGUE

"I AM A descendant of kings and queens."

Jelani wore jeans, ankle-cut black boots, and a red, black, and green T-shirt with a print of Audre Lorde's face on it. A lavalier microphone was clipped to the collar. Jelani had recently had her right eyebrow pierced, and she wore her hair in long braids. She stood alone on stage in front of a packed auditorium, and darkness obscured her audience. The room's lights were directed at her. The air conditioning offset their heat.

"My name is Jelani Bradley." In Edo, she said, "*Jelani* means 'strength.'" She repeated the last sentence in English, then continued in English. "When I was growing up, my Iya used to tell me bedtime stories about my great-great-great-great-great-great-great grandmother, Aisha Iden." Jelani spread her arms. "I am standing on hallowed ground. On this spot, over two hundred years ago, Aisha, her husband, and their eight daughters were sold to different owners. Although Aisha never saw any of her family again, she never forgot them."

Jelani spoke to the audience about her female ancestors. As she did so, a photograph of each woman was projected on the screen behind her.

"My ancestors were exporters, household managers, seamstresses, teachers, authors, law firm partners, and technologists. And everyone knows my broadcasting legend grandmother, Nicole Bradley." Jelani gestured to her nana, who sat in a cushioned seat in the front row. "To me, she's just Nana Nicole." Jelani smiled at her nana, who was flanked by Sha on one side and a seventy-seven-year-old Olivia on the other. Olivia's hair was dyed black, and she was still as sophisticated as when she'd dazzled clients and opponents in boardrooms. She waved at Jelani. Jelani waved back.

Jelani took the glass case containing the twine-woven ring off a small modern table that also held a bottle of water. She held it up. "My mother, Aisha Dinah Bradley, recently gave this ring to me. Everyone but me calls her Sha." She winked at her mother. The audience laughed. "This ring has been passed down from the first Aisha to many generations of women who endured pain. Pain that could have broken them—*but did not.*"

In addition to the notes Jelani had found in the Bible, there were photographs and several sheets of paper, weathered by age, that provided a brief history of their family written by Augusta. Jelani had called her Gran Olivia and Nana Nicole to learn more about their ancestors. She'd traveled to Harlem to talk to her great aunts, Josie, aged ninety-three, and Clara, ninety-four. She'd walked the streets of Harlem with Sha, visiting Julia's and Augusta's haunts, whether or not the buildings still existed. Josie and Clara were in the audience today. Jelani had learned that Clara had been one of the first women to play in the Negro Baseball League.

For several months following her visit to Harlem, Jelani

had spoken to genealogists, librarians, and city clerks and traveled to Portsmouth, Raleigh, Boston, New York City, Philadelphia, and Atlanta to pore through archives and census records. Sha had funded her research and taken time off from work to travel with her. After receiving the results of an online DNA test, Jelani connected with other descendants of Aisha, many of whom were present in the auditorium. Jelani spoke about her rape and its impact on her life, how it had made her feel, and how her friends had deserted her. She held nothing back.

"I can stand on this stage today with the courage to speak my truth because of the long line of strong women who came before me. Throughout centuries, Black women have been taking care of Black men, Black children, white men, white women, and white children. Now, we must take care of ourselves. Show up for and protect each other. Like Aisha did for her daughter, Celia, like Celia did for her daughter, Dinah, all the way down the line to me." Her eyes brimmed with tears as she thought of all the sacrifices these women had made for her. "As I will do for my daughters. We can't be afraid to take on systems of oppression. Our oppressors are no match for us. We must become leaders in the boardroom, at all levels of government, and in conversations about our future. It's time. As Aisha used to tell Celia, 'remember who you are.' Thank you."

Following thunderous applause, Jelani remained on the stage while many people waited in a makeshift line to talk to her. The last person was a young woman around Jelani's age. She was dark-skinned, pointy-chinned, and wore a white dashiki blouse over white tights. She was severely knock-kneed.

"My name is Adanna," she said.

Jelani held out her hand. "Nice to meet you—"

Adanna ignored it and hugged Jelani instead. "My great-great-great-great-great-great grandmother was Aisha's daughter. Her name was Amare, and she ran like the wind. Aisha had told her not to run away from her owner. Amare didn't listen."

The video of Jelani's speech went viral on the internet. Jelani became a much sought-after public speaker and changed the conversation on how girls and women should be treated. She advocated for speaking up about abuse. Her childhood friends reached out to her and apologized for having abandoned her the night she was raped. They vowed to stick together and support each other.

Other women contacted Jelani to share their experiences of sexual assault. Victims came forward to reveal that Erik Stevens had raped them. Since there was no statute of limitations on rape in California, Jelani and the other women pressed charges. Later, he was charged with another thirty-six counts of rape, sentenced to two-hundred and eighty-eight years in prison to be served consecutively, and ordered to pay nine hundred thousand dollars in damages.

Other descendants of Aisha Iden found Jelani through social media and ancestry sites. A year after Jelani's speech, many of the female descendants joined her and Adanna on a trip to the village outside the former Benin Empire where

Aisha had been born. A descendant from each of Aisha's nine daughters was present. In a field, they gathered in a large circle and joined hands. They said, "We are here. We are beautiful. We are proud. We are home."

"I'm glad you're here, Mama M," Jelani said to Mikala, who stood beside her. After her mom had married Mikala, Jelani had never referred to Mikala as her "stepmom."

Mikala squeezed her hand. "Me too."

Mikala had a yin-yang symbol tattooed on the inside of her wrist, as did Sha. Mikala had helped Jelani find her spiritual center. They were soulmates in a different way from how Sha and Mikala were soulmates. Sha was gazing at Mikala's face, a contented smile on her own. People said relationships were hard, but for Jelani's mothers, it seemed easy. They disagreed every once in a while, but they were best friends. Jelani hoped to find love like that one day.

Jelani turned to her mom. "I feel like I'm home."

"You are," said Sha.

Jelani attended Spelman College. After graduating, she received her master's and PhD in African and African-American Studies from Harvard University and became an activist and a Harvard professor. She wanted to change the system from within. She also hosted a popular podcast and wrote many nonfiction books empowering Black women.

Bend, Don't Break was her first novel.

The End

ACKNOWLEDGMENTS

In 2012, I wrote Sha and Jelani's story in a short story entitled "Justice for One." After my wife, Audi, read it, she said, "This could be a novel." I didn't believe her. But then what is wont to happen when she gives me good advice, like Stephen King's "boys in the basement," my "girls in the basement" started working, and an idea formed. In addition to Sha and Jelani's story, I wrote a collection of short stories about five remarkable Black women, who ended up being related. With the help of some of the people below, that collection became the novel, *Bend, Don't Break*.

I would like to thank:

My editor, R., for their invaluable feedback and significant contributions in making this a better novel.

Readers of early drafts: Kimberly Pollock, Abby L. Vandiver, Cathy Pegau, and Sharon Pelletier.

Catherine Palmer, Aimee Kaiser, and Paulla Estes for their feedback on Augusta's first scene.

Robert Levy for his words of wisdom.

My cats, Lorde Morrison and August Baldwin. Your constant companionship while I am writing is comforting, even when you are sleeping most of the time.

My family and friends who have supported my writing career from the beginning.

My readers who have taken the time to read my work; told me how much my work meant to them; and/or left a review on their favorite bookstore platform. I am grateful and honored by your support.

For their love and support and showing up, my sons, Travis and Brandon.

My daughter, Jasmine, whose strength and perseverance is an inspiration to me and everyone that knows her.

My grandmothers, Lillie and Helen, both of whom were resilient women but showed their strengths in different ways. They have been gone from this world for many years, but they are always with me. I still miss them.

My mother, Julia, who continues to epitomize resilience. Her strength and perseverance shaped who I am. Thank you for your love and for encouraging and supporting me.

Finally, to Audi, one of the most resilient women I know, who faces every obstacle and tragedy with a magnanimity I can only admire and hope to emulate one day. Audi was the impetus for me to become a writer and has been a constant source of support for my writing. She is my muse, my first reader, and my last reader. Without her, this is another novel that would not exist.

ABOUT THE AUTHOR

Julie L. Brown is the author of the historical fiction, *Bend, Don't Break,* the alternative-history novel, *No One Will Save Us,* and the creator, under the pen name J. L. Brown, of the Jade Harrington series, political thrillers which include the novels, *Don't Speak, Rule of Law,* and *The Divide,* and the short story, "Few Are Chosen."

Julie earned an MFA in Creative Writing from the Stonecoast program at the University of Southern Maine. She resides with her family in the Pacific Northwest, where she is working on her next novel.

You can find her on:

Website: julielbrown.com

Instagram: @julielbrownwrites

If you would like to receive an email when I release my next book and other exclusive offers and updates, you may sign up for my newsletter via my website. Your privacy is important. Your address will never be shared, and you can unsubscribe at any time.

Thank you for reading *Bend, Don't Break* and don't forget to leave a short review on Goodreads and your favorite bookstore's website.

www.ingramcontent.com/pod-product-compliance
Lightning Source LLC
Chambersburg PA
CBHW050848210726
48290CB00004B/1128